the

PRINCESS

Also by Wendy Holden

The Governess
The Duchess

the

PRINCESS

a love story

WENDY
HOLDEN

WELBECK

First published in 2023 by Welbeck Fiction Limited,
an imprint of Welbeck Publishing Group
Offices in: London – 20 Mortimer Street, London W1T 3JW &
Sydney – Level 17, 207 Kent St, Sydney NSW 2000 Australia
www.welbeckpublishing.com

A CIP catalogue record for this book is available from the British Library

Hardback ISBN: 978-1-78739-756-9
Trade paperback ISBN: 978-1-78739-757-6
Ebook ISBN: 978-1-78739-758-3

Printed and bound by CPI Group (UK) Ltd., Croydon, CR0 4YY

MIX
Paper | Supporting
responsible forestry
FSC
www.fsc.org   FSC® C171272

10 9 8 7 6 5 4 3 2 1

To Vanda

Chapter One

Beneath a hot blue summer sky, the bells of the great cathedral pealed joyfully over the city. The crowds roared their delight. The glass coach moved through the streets, pulled by proud white horses and attended by gold-braided footmen.

From behind the polished crystal windows, the teenage princess-to-be peered excitedly out. She could scarcely believe the number of people who had come to see her, all jostling on the pavements, madly waving flags and shouting her name. Never had she felt so loved.

Or so beautiful. Her professionally done make-up was perfect; a light touch because of her youth but enough to enhance her loveliness for the TV cameras, the audience watching across the world. Her thick blonde hair gleamed, held in place by a diamond tiara. Her cream silk dress was so huge, it almost filled the carriage; her father, sitting beside her, was nearly hidden behind its folds.

'Bigger!' she had laughingly told the designer, when he had asked how large and long the train should be. 'Let's make it the biggest one anyone's ever seen!'

She had said the same to the florist. More roses! More lilies! More orange blossom! Why hold back, on this glorious day? She felt extravagantly, deliriously happy, and she wanted everything, from the pearls in her ears to the lace rosettes on her shoes, to express it.

'Darling, I'm so proud of you!' Her father, eyes brimming with tears, reached for her hand, on which the great engagement ring glittered. The

wedding band itself, made from a special nugget of gold, was with her soon-to-be-husband, the prince. Who, even now, was ascending the red carpet up the cathedral steps, passing in under the pillared portico, handsome in his uniform, his decorations glinting in the sunshine, his sword hanging by his side.

The thought made her almost weak with joy. All her dreams had come true. She was a beautiful princess who was marrying a handsome prince. But far more importantly she was in love, and beloved herself. She had given her heart to her husband and he had given his to her. Their marriage would last forever, they would have lots of children and be happy ever after. He would never leave her, never let her down. She had suffered much, but from now on, everything was going to be perfect.

'Well?' Diana was staring at me from the opposite seat in the train carriage, her thirteen-year-old face bright with expectation. 'Sandy, don't you think that's the most romantic ending *ever?*'

I looked up from the paperback she had passed me. It was called *Bride to the King* and was evidently much-read. The picture on the cover was of a blonde woman in a big white dress embracing a dark-haired man in uniform. He wore a blue sash and a sword by his side. 'Definitely,' I nodded.

'Absolutely the best!'

I knew I could take her word for it. I was quite new to the romantic fiction genre, but Diana had read literally hundreds. Her favourite writer was Barbara Cartland, whose novels featured dashing heroes with jutting jaws and beautiful heroines with heaving bosoms.

Love was their constant theme. Head-spinning, heart-racing, eternal Love. It was the most important thing of all, and Diana and I were obsessed by the idea of it. You fell in Love, it overwhelmed you and once you were in it, everything was perfect. It sounded like a particularly delicious bath, deep and warm with lots of bubbles.

'Shall I tell you something amazing, Sandy?' Diana asked.

I nodded eagerly.

'My daddy's got a new friend. She's called Lady Raine Dartmouth.'

That was, I concurred, an extraordinary name.

'That's not the amazing thing!' Diana leant towards me, her blue eyes huge and excited. 'Her mother is actually *Barbara Cartland*!'

Astonished as I was, I was also aware that this sort of thing seemed typical of Diana's family. From what I had heard from other people, and Diana herself, the Spencers were unbelievably dramatic and exotic. And I was now going home with her for the holidays, I would meet them all.

I had met Diana at school, although we had not been friends initially. We came from very different backgrounds. I was an orphan, my parents had died in a car crash when I was a baby. Aunt Mary had brought me up. She was my father's older sister; an austere spinster of modest means. She was undemonstrative, but believed in the proper education of girls. Undaunted by the fact that she lacked the money for good schools, she had scoured the *Daily Telegraph* for scholarship opportunities.

Of these, my current school was the latest. And, I hoped, the last, although Aunt Mary's quest to find the best school for the least outlay was something of a mania with her. But I was fed up of moving and wanted somewhere I could settle down, sit exams and go on to university. After which, Aunt Mary assured me, the world and all its opportunities would open up.

The school occupied a large pale house at the end of a long, tree-lined drive. Sweeping green parkland stretched to either side. With its imposing portico and castellated stable-yard, it looked glamorous and impressive.

On the day I was dropped off, the families saying farewell on the drive looked glamorous and impressive too. Beside each was a shiny new trunk painted with at least four initials. New hats, bags, tuck boxes and sports equipment were piled round it. Not far away was the shiny family car.

Aunt Mary did not have a car; we had come on the train. Transporting my own battered second-hand trunk, sporting just the two initials, had required help that was not always willingly given. My blazer, too, was second-hand, while my skirt, hand-made by Aunt Mary to save money, was not of the regulation cut. My shoes, meanwhile, looked like barges, bought two sizes too large so I could 'grow into them' and forcing a clumping, graceless walk.

I looked around me, wondering who I would be friends with, if anyone. Socially, I did not aspire to much. To pass muster and blend in would be enough.

My new peers looked much the usual mixture. There were the confident and beautiful ones, the bouncy and sporty ones and the plain ones, among whom I – small, plump and heavily bespectacled – would be one of the plainest. Also conspicuous were the girls who had never been to boarding school before but who had read Enid Blyton and begged their parents to send them. They were easy to identify: wide-eyed, looking excitedly about as they tried to spot real-life equivalents of the heroines of St Clare's and Malory Towers.

I felt rather sorry for them. They would be shattered to discover that the world of midnight feasts and classroom pranks did not exist. Nothing about a real boarding school was anything like Enid Blyton novels. In Enid Blyton, girls were celebrated for their individuality. In real life, conformity was everything. In Enid Blyton, rich girls with titles were taken down a peg or two.

In real life, they were worshipped. As a poor girl in a succession of wealthy schools, I had more reason to know that than most.

I felt a brief, hopeless stir of loneliness, anticipating the games lessons where I would be the last picked for teams, the dancing lessons where I wouldn't have a partner. Then I took a deep, sinew-stiffening breath. I was lucky to be here and it was a means to what would ultimately be a glorious end. Aunt Mary had done her best for me and it was my duty to get on with it.

My aunt said a final hurried goodbye, shut the door and the taxi set off. Amid the lavish hugs and kisses of everyone else, I walked towards the school and the future.

The dormitory was as usual: long rows of beds facing each other. One unexpected touch was the portrait of Prince Charles at the entrance. He wore a crown of futuristic design, which looked comical with his big ears and hangdog expression. A small plaque beneath explained the photograph had been presented to the school by one of the governors.

There was the usual panicked scramble to bag beds next to hastily made friends. Over the years, I had learnt that the best way to hide not being in demand myself was to bag one of the beds by the wall. I made my way towards it, passing on my way a bed covered in small furry animals. There must, I reckoned, be about twenty, of differing sizes, colours and species, all carefully arranged and staring up with expectant glassy eyes.

I met their gaze with concern. As I literally couldn't afford to put a foot wrong, Aunt Mary had obtained the school's catalogue of regulations. She had taken me carefully through strictures ranging from not running in corridors to the number of toys allowed on one's bed. Two, as it happened. Whoever this menagerie belonged to was going to be in trouble when, as we had been warned would happen any minute, Matron came to inspect the dormitory.

I looked over at the gaggle of girls chattering and shrieking as they unpacked night cases, shook out pyjamas, flung slippers about and spanked each other with hairbrushes. While I didn't feel like one of them, nor did I want to see any of them publicly humiliated. Matrons, in my experience, were invariably sadists. That it might be someone's first night away from home would not move them to pity in the least.

I started to gather up the animals and hastily shove them under the bed.

'What are you doing?' demanded someone behind me.

I turned and found myself looking at a tall and beautiful girl. She had very red lips, thick golden hair and big glassy blue eyes. Her skin had a pale glow, with a rich rose tint high on her cheeks. There was something glossy and luxuriant about her. I thought of a dewdrop in the centre of a flower, or thick cream in a glass jug.

'Hiding your toys,' I said. 'You're only supposed to have two and you'll catch it if Matron comes in.'

She said nothing, but I glanced around as I walked away and saw her hurriedly concealing the remainder of her collection.

The bed nearest the wall was, as usual, the last to be picked. I put my trunk down next to it and began to unpack. The girl in the adjacent bed, who introduced herself as Catherine, had evidently been watching the cuddly-toy exchange.

'You know her father's a viscount, don't you?' she whispered. 'Lord Althorp. She's the Honourable Diana Spencer.'

I wasn't surprised. Both her cut-glass voice and her glossy looks had suggested one of the elect. I was less sure about the honourable: she hadn't even said thank you.

Matron appeared in the dormitory doorway. 'Stand by your beds!' she bellowed.

There was a collective gasp, some suppressed squeals and a general scattering of girls. She marched along, black brogues crunching heavily on the lino, inspecting the beds with the zeal of a field marshal. Her small eyes with their metallic glint switched meanly about. We stood ramrod straight, hardly daring to breathe.

Stopping by one bed, Matron swooped triumphantly on some framed photographs lovingly arranged on the cabinet. 'You're allowed *two*. No more,' she snarled at the evidently dismayed owner. 'These are confiscated.'

'But . . . they're my family.' The girl's lip trembled.

But the black brogues were already crunching pitilessly away. I slid a glance at the Honourable Diana Spencer. That could have been you, I thought. You and your toys. But she was looking somewhere else entirely.

Scarcely had the door slammed behind Matron than another of the elect, whom I had heard the others call Celia, sauntered from her bed in the room's starry centre to my humble spot by the wall.

'Name?' she barked at me.

I felt a familiar sinking feeling. Surely it couldn't be starting already? Usually I had a couple of days' grace before I was picked on. Fear had dried my throat. I swallowed hard. 'Alexandra. But my friends call me Sandy.'

'I'll call you Alex*an*dra then,' Celia said, to snorts all round. 'From up North, are we?'

Over the years, I had tried to disguise my accent. But it never entirely disappeared. The English language, anyway, conspired against northerners. It was dotted with traps; words that we pronounced with a short 'a' and everyone else with a long one. My own name was a case in point. Alex*arn*dra was the aspirational way to say it, but I had never had the confidence.

'So where are you from, Alex*an*dra?'

I hesitated. Our town was almost a byword for jokes about the north. And much as I dreaded naming it, I hated myself more for being ashamed. 'Huddersfield,' I said, more loudly than I had intended.

Celia's face went blank, as if unable to believe her luck. Then she burst into incredulous laughter. "Uddersfield! Eeh, everyone. Come an' meet Alex*an*dra from 'Uddersfield.'

I kept my head high and forced my lips not to tremble. I clenched my hands to stop them shaking but could do nothing about the watery feeling in my knees.

'I've never been to 'Uddersfield,' Celia snorted. She was stalking around me, like a ringmaster might circle a strange animal. The rest of the dormitory was gathering and the sniggering had increased in volume. 'What's it like? Can you get your udders feeled?'

'Very funny,' I said in an attempt at sarcasm. 'I haven't heard that one before.'

But I could feel tears pricking behind my eyes. I bent my head so that my hair would fall over my red, humiliated face. Don't cry, I told myself. Don't let them win. But they had won already. I knew Celia's type all too well. She was the worst sort of bully and my life from now on would be a living hell.

I felt a tug on my blazer sleeve. Celia had homed in on my uniform. 'This blazer is *ancient*. The badge is *completely* the wrong colour. And why are you wearing that skirt? It shouldn't have pleats.'

I said nothing. Holding back the sobs with all my might, I prayed for Matron to return. Anything to distract my tormentors. And, as if in answer to my prayer, a stir now went through the group. I felt the energy change.

'Stop bullying her,' said a light, clear voice.

I raised my head slightly and peered through the strands of hair. It was her. The viscount's daughter. The blonde girl with the toys. The Honourable Diana.

'We're just having a joke.' Celia's smile was one of angry unease. 'Where's your sense of humour?'

'I just don't think this is very funny,' Diana said. 'How would you like it if it was you, Celia? How would any of you like it?' She looked round with her wide blue eyes.

It was not a dramatic intervention, there was no shouting or gesturing. Diana spoke quite normally, even mildly. But to me it was like a bomb going off. No one had ever stood up for me before, let alone put themselves in my oversized shoes and invited everyone else to do the same.

As Celia stalked off, nose in the air, followed at a distance by the others, I felt a gratitude so violent I could only mutter my thanks. But Diana was already walking to her bed.

Chapter Two

As at all my other schools, girls without family to take them out spent Sunday afternoons in the dining hall. Amid the scent of boiled cabbage from the just-finished lunch, we sat at the long tables and made desultory conversation as we waited for our more fortunate peers to come back.

I had learnt to take a book with me, usually a story about someone so miserable they made me feel positively fortunate. *Jane Eyre* had kept me going for a while. Now I was hunched over *The Wolves of Willoughby Chase*. I had just got to the part where orphaned Bonnie is forced to exist on two raw onions when I heard a light voice say hello.

I looked up in surprise. Standing before me, blonde hair lit by the sun streaming in through the dining-room windows, was the tall figure of my dormitory saviour.

Since the Celia incident, I had seen little of Diana. As expected, she had been taken up by the school elite; the beautiful and the grand. She also seemed to be in the lower forms for most subjects, while I was in the top ones. What view of her I had was from a distance and she was always with a group of laughing girls. That someone like her had intervened to help someone like me seemed increasingly like something I had imagined.

I thought she must have come to the dining hall to fetch something. But she sat down on the bench next to me, her back against the table, and started swinging her long legs.

'What are you doing here?' I asked. I did not mean to sound blunt, but awkwardness made me shy.

'Same as you.'

'The hall's for people whose parents can't come.'

She swung her legs out. 'Well, that's me. My parents can't come.'

'Why not?'

'Because they're divorced.'

'What does that mean?'

'It means that my mother doesn't live with my father.'

'Why not?'

'Oh,' she said dismissively. 'It's not very interesting. Where are your parents, anyway?'

I hated explaining that I was an orphan. People were always either embarrassed for themselves or sorry for me. I found both excruciating. I took a deep breath. 'Actually, I don't have parents.'

The blue eyes widened. 'Not at all? Not a single one?'

I shook my head.

'Oh, so you're an orphan?' Her tone was interested, rather than awkward.

I nodded.

'What happened?'

Her directness surprised me. Most people shied away from asking.

'They died in a car crash. But I don't remember. I was only a baby.'

Her blue eyes remained on me, curious, thoughtful. 'What's it like?'

'What's what like?'

'Being an orphan.'

I shrugged. 'It's what I'm used to.'

'But can you remember them? Your father's tall figure in the doorway? The scented rustle of your mother's dress as she bent to kiss you good night?'

I stared at her in surprise. Scented rustle? Tall figure? Where on earth had she got that from? 'Er, no.'

'Don't you miss them horribly?'

I hadn't been asked this before, not even by Aunt Mary. Especially not by Aunt Mary; feelings were never discussed at home. It was hard to know how to answer. 'You just try not to think about it and get on with things,' I replied eventually.

She nodded but said nothing.

I worried I had sounded cold and uncaring. 'I never really knew them,' I elaborated. 'So it's hard to miss them.'

She was looking at me very intently. 'But how do you *really* feel about it?' she asked. '*Inside*, I mean?'

I don't really feel anything, I was about to insist, when something swept through me that might have knocked me off my feet if I had not been sitting down. It was like a hurtling black ball that burst into my heart, followed by the most aching sense of loss that I had ever known.

Overwhelmed, I hung my head and felt the painful sting of tears. At some distant level, I realised that I was crying in front of this girl again. But, as before, there was nothing I could do about it.

Something pressed the far side of my arm. She was hugging me. I slumped into her, fighting for control. My nose was running. She passed me a tissue, which I took gratefully. 'Sorry,' I sniffed, awkwardly detaching myself.

'It's all right,' she said, letting go easily, as if it was nothing to be embarrassed about at all.

After that, we sat in companionable silence and read. She, too, had brought a book, a somewhat tatty paperback called *The Queen of Hearts* by an author I had never heard of, Barbara

Cartland. The cover was a sort of bad painting in which a blonde girl in a white dress looked adoringly up at a dashing man in uniform.

She seemed gripped by it, turning over the pages with a breathless anticipation. But I found it hard to return to Bonnie and her raw onions. I felt different after our conversation; lighter, as if a burden had been laid down.

Eventually, the sound of car doors slamming and cheerful farewells from outside the windows announced that the others were back from their fun family afternoons.

After that, Diana returned to her usual group. Perhaps their families took her out with them. At any rate, she was not in the dining hall the following Sunday, or the one after that.

I was disappointed, but not surprised. Expecting us to become friends would, I knew, have been unrealistic. Nonetheless, I felt grateful to her. She had released me from the effort of pretending not to mind. Being allowed to feel sad, to miss the parents I had never known, was a liberation.

Term progressed. I worked hard, as I was supposed to, and did well, as I was supposed to. Diana, meanwhile, seemed to plough a rather less steady course. She developed a reputation for daring, for never turning down a challenge. On one occasion, I watched as, egged on by the others, she ate eight slices of bread and butter and two kippers at a sitting; a new record for gluttony.

As stories circulated of her climbing high trees and running down the drive at midnight, I grew concerned for her. Encouraged by the ever-admiring crowd, she seemed to be taking more and more risks. I watched, worried, from the back of a gaggle of girls on the edge of the school outdoor swimming pool as Diana, arms outstretched, soared high into the air from the topmost board. My heart was in my mouth, and for some time after that, whenever I closed my eyes, I saw her long body in its black school swimming costume against the boundless blue of the sky, plunging down like a bullet and slicing into the water like a knife.

Then rumours began about her dancing in the dining hall at night, against school rules. When, finally, they filtered down to our end of the dormitory, I looked at Catherine in dismay. 'She'll get into trouble,' I said.

Catherine gave me a wise look. 'Well, she wouldn't be the first Spencer to do that. Her sister got expelled, you know.'

Sheer horror flashed through me. I didn't enjoy school much, but being expelled from it was the worst thing I could imagine. As well as the shame and disgrace, it would mean the derailment of all my future hopes. I had never heard of it actually happening though; Miss Rudge, the headmistress, did not seem like the expelling type. 'What for?' I asked.

Catherine was clearly enjoying my obvious amazement. 'Drinking.'

'Drinking what?' It didn't seem like a crime to me.

'Alcohol, of course. Vodka.'

I felt naïve and unsophisticated. I hardly knew what vodka was, let alone why a schoolgirl would drink it.

'Lights out!' yelled the dormitory monitor, a bossy girl called Rose.

Darkness flooded the room and we huddled under our blankets. I could not settle, however. I was agitated and my mind tumbled with questions.

I edged myself towards Catherine. 'Why did she drink vodka?'

Catherine was almost asleep, and came back to consciousness with a snort. 'What?'

I repeated my question in a whisper.

'It doesn't make your breath smell, so no one's able to tell,' hissed back Catherine.

But someone had obviously been able to tell in the end.

'I don't mean that,' I whispered. 'I mean, why drink it at all?'

'Who knows? Those old aristocratic families do crazy things. For the fun of it, I suppose.'

It sounded like a waste to me, but the idea that Diana, who had helped me, would end up sharing her sister's fate was an awful one. I decided to keep an eye on her.

From my bed at the end of the dormitory, it was difficult to monitor the rest of the long room, but I would do my best.

I dozed, half-awake, straining my ears for any noise that might be someone creeping out.

Once the initial whispering and giggling had died down, there was nothing for some hours. It seemed that the Diana dancing rumours were unsubstantiated talk, after all.

I must have dozed off, because something suddenly woke me up. I sat up in bed. All was silent. The moonlight blooming behind the thin curtains showed a row of prone and slumbering girls. And then, at the far end by the door, a movement. Someone was slipping out.

I lifted my covers and climbed reluctantly from beneath them. Winter was approaching and the nights were already cold. The chill air seized me as I groped for my dressing gown. I fumbled for my slippers and hurried down the lino between the beds. Reaching Diana's, I saw with dismay that it was empty.

Outside the dormitory, my heart began to thump. I realised that my actions potentially also had consequences for me. Roaming about the school at night was strictly forbidden. If I was caught, there would be trouble. Quite how much, I didn't want to dwell on.

As I sped through the gallery towards the staircase, I glanced at the portraits hanging on the panelled walls. Their stern gazes seemed to warn me to turn back before it was too late.

I carried on, however, down the slippery polished stairs. Above me hung the huge and heavy brass chandelier, which, as always, I imagined pulling away and plunging to the ground with a mighty crash.

The passage at the bottom was dark and deserted. I had never been around the school at night; it was entirely different from the daytime, when it was full of the chatter and clatter of girls. It seemed so different, more like the private house it once had been. I started to wonder who had lived here and whether their spirits now walked the corridors.

So terrifying was this thought that I almost scurried back up the stairs. Then I paused. Above the boom of my heart, my ear had caught something: a faint snatch of music. It was coming from the direction of the dining room.

I hurried along the passage, in which, as always, the smell of cabbage lingered. The music got louder as I reached the double doors. I recognised it now, some swelling Tchaikovsky from *The Nutcracker*.

I opened the door a crack and peered in. Slabs of moonlight fell through the windows onto long tables set for morning breakfast with rows of white plates. An orange sat on each, all glowing eerily away like orange lamps. Dancing between them, white flannel school nightdress billowing, was Diana.

Her eyes were wide open, but I could see that she was somewhere very far away. Propelled by the music, she sped over the parquet in her bare feet. I had no idea where she had got the record player from; some nearby office, perhaps. I felt awed at her daring, but far more at her dancing. I had never known she was as good as this.

It was transporting to watch as first she spun, then lengthened out into a graceful arabesque. Where she had learnt this sequence of rippling steps which seemed to grow naturally out of her feet, one leading to the other, I could not imagine.

In Madame Vacani's lessons, we rarely got beyond the basic positions.

Her movements made a romantic dreamworld out of the mundane dining room with its cabbage smells. There was a mysterious radiance about her, a quiet strength and an absolute authority, as if she knew exactly what she was doing and why.

Then something pulled me back from the dreamworld and into the here and now. A sound, coming from behind. Footsteps in the passage, firm and adult, approaching rapidly. Someone was coming.

Chapter Three

My stomach surged into my throat. Without thinking, I dashed into the dining room and wrenched the needle off the record. The triumphant crescendo of the 'Grand Pas de Deux' stopped abruptly and Diana dropped the arms that had stretched yearningly into the chilly air.

She whirled to face me, her tranquil expression now indignation. 'What are you—?'

But before she could finish her sentence, I clapped my hand over her mouth.

When last she had asked this, I had been trying to save her from Matron, but the stakes now were far higher. There was no time to talk. With one foot, I pushed the record player under the nearest table, whilst grabbing her and pulling her down with me. I had managed to shove her between the chairs just as the dining-room door swung open.

From where we crouched, not breathing, I could see the bottom third of the doorway. And, backlit by the lights in the passage, the bottom third of the dressing-gowned, slipper-shod figure that stood there.

The slippers got closer. They were tartan, with a pom-pom on the top. That they could be part of such a terrifying scenario seemed absurd. Nonetheless, our faintest noise could condemn us.

There was a sound of a yawn, then rustling. As the slippers moved off, there was a faint squeak of rubber sole on parquet. We heard them make a tour of the room, then return to the entrance. The light in the passage faded; the dining-room door had closed.

Under the table, Diana and I grinned at each other. But there was no time for exultation. 'Come on,' I said. 'If they see our empty beds, we'll be for it.'

We crept back silently in the dark. Only once we were safely under the covers did I remember that the record player was still under the table. So, the following day, when I was called out of Maths and told that Miss Rudge wished to see me, I feared the absolute worst.

After my broken night, I was tired and out of sorts. The bravery and decisiveness with which I had dealt with Diana had deserted me. I trudged the polished corridor towards the Head's office, trying not to think of Aunt Mary and how badly I had let her down. Never in my life had I felt quite so wretched.

A bright autumn sun shone cheerfully through the clean windows of the corridor. Silver wall lights gleamed on the panelling and the air was sweet with the scent of furniture polish. All was orderly and elegant. I would be leaving all this behind, I thought, looking at the framed row of previous headmistresses in their university gowns. And I would never be a graduate now.

As Miss Rudge's door approached, I felt my knees start to shake. I thought of Diana, and the stupid risk I had run for her sake. Even if she had been expelled, she was from a grand family. She would be fine. Yet even now, at this ghastly moment, I could not entirely regret my actions. I had owed her, after all.

'Enter,' came the grave voice of Miss Rudge in answer to my knock.

I cast a last look around the sunny corridor and, feeling like one condemned, obeyed her instruction.

I had previously encountered the headmistress only at school assembly and had never been in her office before. It was unexpectedly domestic: big and comfortable with large windows. There were framed pictures on the walls and a warm fire flickering away in the hearth. Before it was a pink sofa and two pink chairs.

Miss Rudge, middle-aged with short curly hair and glasses, sat at a large desk in the middle of the room, writing briskly with a black fountain pen. She looked up as I came in. 'Ah, Sandy,' she said in a neutral tone that told me nothing. 'Thank you for coming to see me. Take a seat, will you?'

I perched, puzzled, on the edge of one of the fireside armchairs. Someone in the amount of trouble I was might have expected to be told to stand. The fire felt warm and luxurious and made me think about the cold, bleak future stretching before me.

Miss Rudge blotted her notepaper, clicked the top back on her pen, stood up and came over to join me. 'I'm afraid I've got some rather bad news for you, Sandy,' she said as she sat down on the sofa. 'It's about your aunt.'

I swallowed. She was right, this was all about Aunt Mary. Of the two of us, she would feel this most. She had been single-minded in her determination that, despite our lack of money, I should have every opportunity. And this was how I had rewarded her.

Miss Rudge leant forward. 'She's not very well,' she said gently. 'In fact, she's really quite ill. She's in hospital.'

My posture until now had been drooping and defeated. Now, galvanised with shock, I sat bolt upright. 'Because of me, Miss Rudge?' I was certain it was my fault; news of my crimes the previous night had caused my aunt's collapse.

The headmistress looked surprised. 'Why ever would that be the case? You are a credit to the school and I'm sure your aunt is very proud of you.' She paused. 'However, she is suffering from pneumonia. We received a telephone call from the hospital this morning.'

'Pneumonia?' I gasped. Aunt Mary was never ill. That she had something this serious was unimaginable. 'Will she be all right?'

That she wouldn't seemed all too imaginable. It had happened to me before, after all. I searched the headmistress's face anxiously.

Miss Rudge wasn't entirely reassuring. 'Her recovery will take some time and this means, unfortunately, that you will not be able to go home for the half-term holidays.'

I stared at her, trying to process all this dramatic information as it came. Relief on one account was followed by fear on another and then incomprehension. 'So where will I go?' I asked.

'Is there a friend you can stay with?'

My insides shrank with shame. I thought of the groups on whose edges I hovered, the girls who occasionally suffered me to tag along. I shook my head, hot blood rushing to my face. 'Not really,' I mumbled.

'Well, that's a pity.' Miss Rudge spoke as if I wasn't already aware of the fact, or that the news of Aunt Mary's illness wasn't traumatic enough without the additional misery of exposing my social shortcomings. 'You'll just have to stay at school in that case, won't you?'

Later, lessons over, I went into the gardens. The day was ending with a blazing sunset. Ribbons of purple and pink rippled across the sky, underlit by fiery red and backed by burning gold. There was something volcanic about it which matched my mood of violent despair.

I had been battling against this despair ever since leaving Miss Rudge's office. But now, alone in the darkening grounds, I gave way to my overwhelming misery. Sitting on a bench overlooking a small pond, I sobbed as if my heart would break. I wept for the devoted aunt who lay ill in hospital and for the cheerless holiday I would spend at school. But most of all I wept for myself and the loneliness that was, ironically, my only constant companion. Having no parents was bad enough, but having to admit my lack of friends to the headmistress had been agonising. What was wrong with me? Was it really all my fault?

The sunset raged above me as I sobbed out my storm of tears. Eventually, it passed and I just felt heavy and sad. The sunset was fading and night gathering rapidly. I was by now completely lost in self-pity and also freezing, but had remembered that staying outside in the winter could mean dying of cold. If you were lucky, you fell asleep and just slipped away without knowing anything about it.

I found a grim satisfaction in the idea of being discovered in the morning as a lifeless corpse. No one would be sad, but they might be sorry. Standing over my stiff, frost-sprinkled body, Miss Rudge might regret her careless cruelty on the subject of my social life. The girls might regret only tolerating me, and never actually being my friend. 'We left her alone,' they might say to each other, 'and look what's happened.'

But it was now that I realised, to my horror, that I was actually not alone. Someone was sitting on the bench beside me, silent in the freezing darkness. I could see a vague outline, but nothing more. When they had come, and for how long they had been there, I had no idea.

'Who is it?' I asked, my voice sharp with fear.

'Me. Diana.'

Once, I knew, my heart would have leapt. But I felt as if I no longer cared. In fact, something like rage swept through me.

I thought about all the stupid things she had done, and that her sister had done. *Her father's a viscount. Those old aristocratic families.* I thought about how they wasted their opportunities, these girls who had everything. Remembering how I had almost wasted mine on her account, I felt even angrier.

As my handkerchief was sodden, I scraped my sleeve across my nose and sniffed hard. I didn't care what she thought. 'What are you doing here?' I demanded.

'I've been looking for you.'

Again, this had none of the impact it once would. The world was stacked against people like me and entirely weighted to people like her. She had no real interest in me, I was sure. 'Why?' I growled.

'I wanted to say thank you.'

'What for?'

She laughed. 'For what you did last night. Obviously.'

I shrugged in the darkness. 'You're welcome.'

'Doesn't sound as if I'm welcome. You sound quite cross, actually.'

I did not reply.

'What's the matter?' she asked.

I clamped my mouth shut. I wasn't going to tell her anything about how I felt. I had done that before. She hadn't cared, not really.

'Well, thanks, as I say,' she went on, conversationally. 'If you hadn't come in, I would probably have been caught.'

I turned my head. If I really looked, her straight, lovely profile was just about visible. Her perfect pale skin and her thick golden hair seemed to seize and reflect the little light that was left. 'Yes,' I said harshly, 'you probably would. But what difference would that have made? '

'Well, they might have thrown me out.'

This breezy admission only enraged me more. 'People like you,' I said, almost too angry to get the words out properly, 'you have no idea what it's like for people like me. You can throw away your opportunities because it doesn't matter. Your life is so easy. Whereas I have had to watch every step, memorise every rule, come top of every exam, just to have a tiny bit of what you take for granted.'

My words, hot and furious, seemed to echo round the frozen garden.

She said nothing for a while. Then I heard her take in breath, as if about to speak. 'I agree with you,' she said. 'Except for one thing.'

'Which is?'

'That life is so easy for people like me.'

I leapt on this immediately. 'Well, of course it is,' I thundered. 'You've got millions of friends, your father has a title and you not only have a family, you have an incredibly old and grand family. Whereas, if you remember, I don't even have parents.'

I probably should have stopped there, but my anger demanded an outlet, so I went on.

'My one living relative is ill in hospital, so I've got to stay at school all holiday. If she dies.' I was now getting completely carried away, 'I'll have no one. As it is,' I added with bitter triumph, 'there isn't a single person on this planet who actually loves me. What do you think *that's* like?'

There was a brief silence. Then Diana said, in a low, flat voice, 'I know exactly what that's like.'

I wasn't convinced. How could someone like her know anything of what I had suffered?

'When my mother left,' she began, still in the flat voice, 'I thought it was because she didn't love me any more. I thought it was all my fault.'

'Your mother left your father?' I was hazy about divorce, but thought it meant the other way round.

The blonde head nodded. 'Drove off in her car. I can still hear the noise of the tyres on the gravel. I ran down the drive after her, but she didn't stop. I couldn't run fast; I was only six.'

I wasn't especially imaginative, but could picture in my mind's eye the desperate, crying child. The deep gravel swallowing her small feet. The sound of the car growing fainter, then fading altogether.

'The housekeeper told us that she'd gone on holiday, so we expected her to come back,' Diana went on. 'But she never did.'

I'd come across housekeepers in *Jane Eyre*. But I hadn't realised people had them in real life. I wondered who 'we' were. 'You and your sister?' I asked.

'My *two* sisters, my brother and me.'

I was shocked at their mother. To leave two children seemed bad enough, but four? 'How awful.'

'It *was* awful,' she agreed. 'I used to sit on the steps and cry. I cried so much, I cried all the colour out of my eyes.'

'They're still quite blue though,' I said.

'You should have seen them before. And then Mummy got married again without telling us. Didn't even ask us to the wedding.'

What a terrible woman, I thought. 'You must have been heartbroken.' It wasn't a word I had used in conversation before. But I had never before had a conversation like this.

'I was,' she agreed. 'I could have been a bridesmaid. I love weddings.'

I hadn't really meant that. 'Heartbroken about her leaving,' I corrected. 'All of you.'

'Oh yes,' she conceded. 'Very. We still are, actually, but we show it in different ways. Sarah's horrid to everyone, Jane's polite to everyone and Daddy just hides.'

I didn't know what to make of this statement. That there were different ways to express misery had never occurred to me. But she sounded utterly matter-of-fact about it. 'Hides?' I asked. 'Where?'

'In his study. He says he's writing letters, but he never puts any out for the post.'

'What about your brother?' He was the only one not yet accounted for.

'Charles? He cries. I can hear him, down the passage. *"Mummy, Mummy!"'* She imitated an infant wailing. 'I long to go and comfort him. But I'm too scared to get out of bed in the dark, so I have to stay there. I lie there, just hating myself.'

I was dismayed, but also fascinated. It was all so dramatic and emotional, as unlike my peaceful existence with Aunt Mary as it was possible to imagine. I thought of her in her hospital bed and crossed my fingers.

We were silent for a while. The cold was bone-chilling and the darkness profound, but neither of us suggested going inside. Perhaps we both recognised how bleakly appropriate the climate was to the conversation.

Diana stirred. 'Well, as I say, I know how it feels to think that no one loves you, that it's all your fault and that you're worthless.'

I could see now that she was right. Being from a grand family was no protection against heartbreak.

'I never meant to tell you any of that, by the way,' she said. 'I've never told anyone else about it.'

This surprised me. 'You've got hundreds of friends, though.'

'Not real ones. They don't really care. They just egg me on to do more and more stupid things. *"One more slice, Spencer! One more kipper!"'* She caught the patrician braying of the dining hall exactly. She was a surprisingly good mimic. 'But you egg me on to do less.'

We both laughed. I thought about her dancing between the tables and suddenly remembered the record player. Had it sat there all night, after all? Who had found it?

'No one,' Diana said. 'I got up early and put it back.' As she spoke, she huddled closer. I felt warm, happy. 'I'm sorry about your holiday,' she said.

The warm feeling instantly disappeared. I imagined the dormitory, empty apart from myself.

'So,' the light voice next to me went on, 'why don't you come and stay for half-term with us?'

Chapter Four

The train from school would take us to King's Lynn in Norfolk, the nearest station to where Diana lived. Her old nanny was picking us up. But that was some time away yet. She rummaged in her bag and produced two more paperback romances. 'You choose,' she said generously.

I took the books and looked at them. One thing I had learnt from the novels of Barbara Cartland was that you could judge a book by its cover. That of *The Loveless Marriage* had a bride in virginal white gazing at a groom in red tartan. *Dreams Do Come True* had a woman in a long frilly blue dress and a dashing man in a cape. 'A shy English Rose blossoms into an exotic Bird of Paradise in this thrillingly romantic twist on the tale of Cinderella,' I read on the back.

Diana, of course, had read it already, several times. 'One of my absolute *favourites*,' she enthused. 'I love Cinderella ones, where the heroine's all plain and hopeless but then becomes beautiful and adored.'

'*The Loveless Marriage* for you then,' I said, passing it over.

'Not on your life.'

Her tone was unexpectedly vehement.

'OK,' I said, passing her *Dreams Do Come True.*

She didn't take it. She was staring at me. 'I'm not talking about books. I mean *actual* marriage.'

I frowned. 'I don't understand.'

'The Loveless Marriage. I'm not going to have one of those.' Her brows were knitted; she looked almost fierce. 'I'll only marry when I'm madly and passionately and *wildly* in love.'

I nodded. 'Of course.' She hardly needed to tell me that. We were both in love with Love, and nothing else would do.

She took *The Loveless Marriage* anyway.

I was deep in *Dreams Do Come True* when I heard Diana shouting. The train had halted. The sign outside the window said, KING'S LYNN. Doors were slamming: it must be about to leave. Absorbed in our books, we hadn't noticed. Coursing with panic, we jumped up, snatched our cases from the overhead rack and leapt out. I looked about for someone who looked like an old nanny.

'There she is,' gasped Diana. 'Merry!' she shouted.

Standing on the platform was not the well-upholstered elderly matron I had expected, but an elfin young woman with a mane of long blonde hair. She wore faded jeans whose skin-tightness around the hips gave way to wide flares at the bottom. Despite the cold weather, her tight cheesecloth shirt was tied above a narrow waist, exposing inches of toned midriff. Was Merry really her name? I wondered. I had thought it something that went before 'Christmas'.

'This is my friend Sandy, she's an orphan,' Diana announced excitedly. 'Isn't that tragic?'

'Very,' said Merry. As I cringed and reddened, she winked at me, which made me feel slightly better.

She led us into the car park and raised the boot of an ancient blue Simca, her silver bracelets jangling. Instantly, we were surrounded.

'Let me!'

'Do you need some help?'

Merry lounged back against the car's battered blue flank, watching amusedly as several middle-aged men practically fought over our two little bags.

Finally, we were on our way. Diana was in the back, having insisted I take the passenger seat. Now I was closer to Merry, I could see that she wore a tiny Coca-Cola can round her neck on a chain. Her eyeliner was smudged and her long blonde hair needed brushing, but that didn't detract from her beauty. In a funny way, it seemed to increase it. Her pungent scent, which I later discovered was called patchouli, filled the inside of the car.

We drove through an autumn landscape lit up by a low mellow sun. Norfolk was huge, I thought. I had never seen countryside like this, stretching endlessly into the distance under a seemingly infinite sky.

Merry's silver bracelets rattled as she twisted the steering wheel, and her rings knocked against the gearstick. She spoke with a rural accent I didn't recognise. 'So, girls, what have you learnt at school this term?'

'Fork only for pudding. Never use spoon without a fork,' Diana recited. 'Tip soup plate away from you.'

I had by now discovered that, while I had sat scholarship exams, the only entrance requirement for the others was neat handwriting. Deportment, elocution and how to manage a large house and servants seemed the real focus of the school curriculum. I hadn't told Aunt Mary though. She would instantly move me to somewhere more academic and I would never see Diana again.

I decided to join in. 'Never use salt cellars! Spoon salt in a heap at the side of your plate!'

'I always use a salt cellar,' said Merry, laughing. 'I obviously went to the wrong school!'

'Put your napkin on your lap immediately!' Diana chanted.

'Never use the word "nice"!' I riposted.

'Or write Bucks. on an envelope. Always Buckinghamshire!'

'An Irish *squire* . . .' I began. It was what we recited in elocution lessons.

Diana took it up immediately. 'In the West of *Ireland* was sitting by the *fire* with his *violin* when the *choirmaster* entered with a bunch of *violets!*'

The conversation dissolved into giggles.

'Oh, and we've learnt all about the reproduction of rabbits,' Diana added.

Merry groaned. 'Might have known that would fascinate you!'

'Is that the way humans do it too, Merry?'

'Really, Diana. We've only been in the car five minutes and you're already talking about sex.'

I was thrilled at my friend's daring. Actual sex was never mentioned in the novels we read. Heroines were invariably pure as the driven snow; temptation was hinted at, but what it was remained unexplained.

Diana had the advantage over me of having actually seen a penis. Once, with her sisters on the train to visit her mother in London, a man in the same carriage had taken out his willy, placed his glasses on it and said, 'Now look round and tell me which one you fancy.'

'And which one did it fancy?' I had asked.

'We didn't stay to find out. Jane made us move into another carriage.'

'What did it look like?'

'Sort of pale and floppy-looking. Not very exciting really.'

'Tell us, Merry!' Diana now begged from the rear. 'Tell us how babies come out.'

'Same way as they get in,' Merry said breezily, and would not be drawn further.

This was disappointing, but Diana was not about to give up. Instead, she approached from another direction. 'Have you ever been in love, Merry?'

'Many times.'

'Did your heart soar and leap and did you feel you would faint when his lips met yours?'

'At first, I suppose.'

'At first? Didn't it last?'

The tousled blonde head twisted in a negative.

'Why not?'

Merry changed gear with a rattle of bracelets. 'Love in real life isn't the way it appears in your romantic novels.'

'You mean Lady Dartmouth's mother's romantic novels,' said Diana, quick as a flash.

'Those too.'

'Why isn't love in real life the same as in books?'

'Because it isn't,' Merry said firmly.

We passed through small towns, and villages with beautiful churches and cottages. Merry pointed out places of interest; she was Norfolk born and bred, it emerged, and evidently proud of it. That, I realised, was what the accent must be.

Diana's thoughts had failed to make the leap to the local topography and remained on matters of the heart. 'Merry, do you think Daddy will marry Lady Dartmouth?'

'I shouldn't think so.' Merry sounded surprised. 'She has a husband already, I understand. And four children.'

Diana seemed relieved about this. 'That's a good thing. Because if Daddy did marry again, it wouldn't be fair to Mummy, would it?'

'I don't understand your reasoning, Diana,' said Merry. 'Your mother is already married again.'

I didn't understand her reasoning either. Nor, I guessed, did Diana herself. That was why she was asking all these questions.

'Why *do* you think Mummy and Daddy got divorced?' was the next one.

'I don't know. I wasn't there.'

'Perhaps they weren't in love enough,' Diana mused.

'Perhaps,' Merry agreed.

We drove on in silence for a while, each thinking our own thoughts. And yet, from my seat in the front, I sensed Diana's mood in the rear darkening further, much as the sky outside was doing.

'If you're not really sure you love someone, you shouldn't get married,' she burst out suddenly. 'Because then you might get divorced.'

'But everyone thinks they are in love when they get married,' Merry countered.

'I *hate* divorce,' Diana announced fiercely. 'I'm going to marry someone who absolutely can't divorce me. And I'll have *lot*s of children and we'll all live in one house together, like a *real* family.'

'Amen to that,' said Merry, lightly.

A glowing sunset was gilding the fields when, eventually, the little blue car swung through a pair of magnificent iron gates. Seeing the dying light flame off the decorative gilding, I feared we were driving through a public park by mistake and a park keeper would at any minute appear and shout at us.

But the Simca continued unmolested through shadowy acres studded with mature trees. Beneath the branches, I could make out something pale; groups of graceful animals watching. Deer, I realised, thrilled. I had never seen a real one.

'Is Charles at home?' asked the rear seat, suddenly.

'Yes.'

'And Sarah and Jane?'

'Sarah's expected tomorrow. Jane's staying in London.'

Diana groaned. 'She never comes to Norfolk!'

33

'You know she loves her museums and galleries,' Merry said easily. 'And you'll see her when you visit your mother.'

I was building up a picture of the Spencers; Jane who was polite to everyone and loved museums and galleries; expelled Sarah who was horrid to everyone; the heartless London-based runaway Lady Althorp; Lord Althorp who hid; Charles, the brother who cried. And Lady Dartmouth, of course, whose mother was Barbara Cartland. The thought of meeting any of them was exciting, but nerve-wracking.

The light was fading fast now, but I could see how wide grass verges stretched either side of the tarmac road. We passed another pair of big gates, which I half-expected Merry to turn into, but she continued to where the trees gave way to emptiness and a church rose up in the gloom. We swung into an entrance almost hidden in dark foliage, and up a curving, crunching gravel driveway, which I realised with a pang must be the same Diana's mother had driven away down, pursued by her sobbing infant daughter.

No wonder Diana hated divorce so much. That she believed in Love as passionately as she did seemed a positive miracle in the circumstances. Skimming across my mind came the muddled thought that her romantic-novel obsession had something to do with it; the books gave her comfort, courage, even faith. There was something brave and defiant in her devotion to them. They weren't just silly; Merry was wrong about that.

As we swung round the bend, a house came into view. It was big, broad and ablaze with light. Steps led up to a grand entrance, above which a large lantern hung. In the golden glow that streamed from its glass panels, I could see that the door was blue.

'Home!' yelled Diana, bounding out of the car almost before Merry had stopped it.

I could only stare. The house I shared with my aunt was a tiny semi. This was about the size of the main building at school, and, it seemed to me, just as magnificent.

The blue door opened and a figure appeared. 'Daddy!' yelled Diana, pelting across the gravel.

I followed her excitedly. As the journey had progressed, so had my thoughts about what Diana's father would look like. His connection with Lady Dartmouth had initially inspired a romantic hero straight out of Barbara Cartland: chisel-jawed with deep-set eyes and dark hair tumbling over his brow. Then, when she had said he hid in the study, I had imagined someone worn down by grief, who was thin, anguished and bent. Possibly with ink-stained fingers from all those letters. Now I had settled on an amalgam of the two.

Lord Althorp looked nothing like that. He was neither worn nor chisel-jawed. Nor was he thin and bent; on the contrary, I had never seen a man so big. From my thirteen-year-old perspective, and a short thirteen-year-old at that, he seemed absolutely enormous. His very erect posture made him appear bigger still. The doorway was wide and tall, but he seemed to fill it with his broad frame.

Far from tragic, he seemed cheerful. He greeted his daughter with a hearty embrace. She, for her part, seemed delighted to see him.

'Why are you dressed like that?' she asked, when they had done hugging. He was wearing a dark tailcoat and dark striped trousers.

'It's Betts' night off.' Lord Althorp spoke in a grand, rather slurry voice. 'So I'm buttling for myself.'

None of this made any sense to me, but Diana burst out laughing.

Her father peered down at me from his great height. His face was big and red, with the mottled look of raw mince. He had a strange, vague smile; two rows of small teeth clamped together, entirely unlike Diana's big white ones. He seemed to be swaying slightly, and his eyes looked glassy and unfocused.

'Hello, I'm Johnnie. And you are?'

I introduced myself before Diana could say I was an orphan.

'Well, welcome to Park House. Where are you from, Sandy?'

There was nothing else for it. 'Huddersfield.'

'Huddersfield! How *interesting*.'

'It isn't really,' I admitted.

'Oh, it isn't? How *interesting*.'

My glance fell to Lord Althorp's feet. His shoes were a surprising contrast to his clothes: vast, brown, muddy and very worn and old. Lapping over the front of them, below the hem of the trousers, were the edges of what were unmistakably a pair of blue-and-white striped pyjama bottoms. I stared in amazement. As I looked up and caught Merry's eye, she gave me a broad wink.

Chapter Five

Diana had darted down the stone-flagged hall. I panted after her. She ran up a broad central staircase with wide steps of polished wood.

'We can slide back down,' she said, patting the wooden balustrade. 'It's fun. Merry does it too.'

'Merry slides down the banisters?'

'Don't sound so surprised. She was the one who showed us how to do it!'

'Is Merry quite an *unusual* sort of nanny?' I asked, choosing my words carefully.

Diana laughed. 'Sarah says she's like a hippy Mary Poppins. But she's a lot nicer than the ones we've had before. They were all mean.'

'Mean?'

'Cruel. Horrid. One used to give us very strong laxatives.

'Laxatives?' It wasn't a word I had come across before.

'Pills that make you want to go to the lavatory all the time.'

I wondered why anyone would give such things to children.

'To punish us,' Diana breezily explained. 'Another used to bang mine and Charles' heads together, or just smash them against the wall.' She grinned. 'But we got our own back.'

'Did you?'

'Yes, we shut one of them in the bathroom. And we threw the other one's underwear all over the roof. Come on. Let's go and find Charles in the beetle room.'

I stumbled after her, trying to keep up as well as absorb everything. Cruel nannies. Fathers with pyjamas under their trousers. A hippy Mary Poppins for a nanny. A mother who had driven away and never come back. Diana's life was like a novel, I thought, although I wasn't sure what sort. Certainly not a Barbara Cartland one.

She had said Charles was in the beetle room, which made me think of insects. But when, having rushed down several passages, we came to a halt outside a white door on which yellowing newspaper pictures of the Fab Four were stuck, I realised she meant the actual Beatles. I was surprised. I thought that they were old hat and had split up years ago.

Inside was dark, except for a big fire roaring in the hearth. It gave rather an infernal air to the sole occupant of the room. From the descriptions of his night-time sobbing, I had expected someone weak and miserable, like Colin in *The Secret Garden*, another of my favourite books. But, like his father before him, he confounded expectation.

Charles was a round-faced boy of about nine with a pudding-basin haircut. He had a pugnacious air and did not seem the crying type. Perhaps he had grown out of it.

Wrapped in a dressing gown and with a blanket tucked round him, he was lying composedly on a sofa, his attention entirely on the TV in front of him. A colour TV, I saw – an unimaginable luxury. On the screen, two men in white overalls were running around. One held a ladder, the ends of which were knocking over pots of paint and breaking windows. Screams of studio laughter filled the room.

'Charles!' Diana rushed over to hug him. She waved at me. 'This is Sandy. She's an orphan.'

My toes curled and I blushed horribly, But Charles didn't even raise his eyes from the screen.

'Hi, Brian,' he said casually. 'Hi, Sandy. Sorry about you being an orphan.'

'That's okay,' I said. 'Why do you call her Brian?'

He looked at me then; a surprised glance. 'You know. From *The Magic Roundabout.*'

TV at Aunt Mary's was reserved for the news and programmes of an improving nature. But I got the reference; Brian was a slow-witted snail on a daily children's show.

'My family all think I'm thick,' Diana lamented, throwing herself down next to him on the sofa.

'She's not thick,' I said loyally.

'You may have a point,' Charles conceded, his eyes still on the screen. 'You've won cups, haven't you, Brian. What were they for again? Oh yes. Helpfulness and Best Kept Hamster, wasn't it?'

'She keeps her hamsters very well,' I said supportively. I had met Little Black Muff and Little Black Puff soon after we had become friends. It was hard not to; Diana checked on them several times a day. 'They haven't been away to school before,' she had explained on the first visit. 'They're homesick.'

I had looked back at her uncertainly. Did hamsters get homesick?

'I've told them,' she'd added, 'to take their time to make friends in case the other hamsters sense their desperation and avoid them.'

This level of solicitude deserved a cup, I felt.

Diana was hitting Charles with a cushion.

'Ow! Steady, you'll knock the aerial. I don't want to miss *Crackerjack!*'

'Is this *Crackerjack?*' I stared at the TV with interest.

Charles, meanwhile, stared at me. 'Well, of course it is. It's Friday and it's five o'clock, what else would it be?'

As we all piled onto the sofa, a wave of pure joy went through me. I had always longed for brothers and sisters, just this kind of easy companionship. We all squealed with laughter as one of the overalled men skidded on some wet paint and crashed into the other.

Crackerjack ended and *John Craven's Newsround* came on, a current-affairs programme aimed at children. There was a report about how Britain's firemen were on strike. Householders were being encouraged to take matters into their own hands. They should keep buckets of water and sand handy. They should look out for flammable objects.

'That hair of Come Dancing's is pretty flammable,' Charles remarked.

'Who?' I asked, as Diana burst into giggles.

'Lady Dartmouth.'

Barbara Cartland's daughter, I remembered. 'Why do you call her that?' I asked him.

'Because she wears huge nylon dresses like on *Come Dancing*. That ballroom dancing programme,' he elaborated as I looked blank. 'Honestly, don't you ever watch telly?'

'Don't you like her?' I asked, ignoring the question.

'As a child,' Charles replied loftily, 'one instinctively feels things and with her I've always very much felt things.'

I was prevented from further investigation by Merry appearing at the Beatle Room door. 'Time for bed, Charles.' Her unbrushed hair glowed in the firelight, while her perfume ebbed into the room.

Charles groaned. 'It's *Sale of the Century* in a minute.'

'Makes no difference. Come on. You'll have time to watch tomorrow.'

Charles realised he was beaten. 'Oh well. And tomorrow's Saturday, which means *The Banana Splits*.' He waved something which I now realised he had held in his hand all along.

'What's that?' I asked.

'My remote control. If you think I'm wasting valuable viewing time getting up to change channels, you're mistaken.'

'What's it made of?' It looked like a ruler taped to a plastic golf club taped to a brush handle.

'A ruler taped to a plastic golf club taped to a brush handle,' Charles said with dignity. 'I copied it from one I saw in *The Rockford Files*.'

'You watch far too much television,' said Merry.

'That's impossible,' Charles objected. 'Television is the most glorious thing ever invented. No one could ever watch too much of it.'

A man, I thought, after my own TV-starved heart. It occurred to me now that perhaps that was what he did. Jane was polite, Sarah was horrid, Lord Althorp hid and Charles watched telly.

And Diana read romantic novels.

'Let's put on some records,' said Diana, when they had gone. She flicked a switch on the wall and the room flooded with light. It was quite grand, I saw, with tall windows whose drawn curtains hung right to the floor and silky blue material on the sofa. A big gold-framed mirror hung over a carved fireplace, before which two armies of toy soldiers faced each other. 'Charles',' Diana explained, though I had guessed as much.

'I don't think he should call you Brian,' I burst out. I liked Charles, but felt hurt on my friend's account.

'He's the only one that does,' Diana said peaceably. 'The rest of my family calls me Duch.'

'Dutch?'

She giggled. 'No, Duch. Short for Duchess. They say I give myself airs.'

'Really?' This seemed to me more unlikely even than Dumbo. Diana was never snobbish or grand. She would hardly want to be friends with me if she was. But at least Duch wasn't insulting.

In a corner was a record player with a pile of singles beside it. Diana put on 'Yellow Submarine'. 'We used to play this all the time when Mummy and Daddy were shouting,' she remarked. 'If we turned it up loud enough, we couldn't hear them.'

Before long, we were both singing along and dancing round the room.

We had worked our way through most of the records when Diana asked if I wanted anything to eat.

I realised I was actually starving, but had been far too interested to notice. 'Did we miss supper?' I asked, like the institutionalised creature I was.

Diana laughed. 'We don't really have supper.'

'Doesn't Merry make it for you?' Nannies in books did.

'Oh no. She doesn't do that sort of thing.'

'What happens when you get hungry?'

'We just help ourselves from the fridge.'

She could have hardly said anything more thrilling. Helping myself from the fridge was absolutely forbidden under the strict rule of my aunt.

The kitchen at Park House was at the end of the stone-flagged hall passage. As promised, we had reached this by sliding down the banisters, an experience unparalleled for its speed, excitement and danger. 'You can also go down the stairs sitting on a metal tray,' Diana advised me. 'It's a bit like sledging.'

The kitchen had a dresser with blue and white patterned plates, a large wooden table in the centre and shining pans in rows on the walls. There was a big tall fridge and a long stove which gloriously radiated heat. It had big silver lids on top and little metal doors on the front, which made me think of Hansel and Gretel. Most people disliked this story because of the horrid witch, but I admired the way clever Gretel saves her brother. Most girls in fairy tales were useless princesses who slept for a hundred years or kissed frogs.

Diana had disappeared. I found her in a little room lined with shelves from floor to ceiling. On them were row upon row of tins; bags of flour, rice and sugar; bowls of fruit and vegetables; a side of ham; lines of gleaming glass jam jars topped with red and white gingham and bearing handwritten labels saying 'Blackcurrant' and 'Strawberry'. There was a distinct cool, savoury smell.

'Wow,' I said, looking round. I had never seen so much food.

Diana shoved a loaf of bread at me and lifted the lid of a butter dish. 'Here,' she said, passing me a knife. I applied mine in the economical scraping manner favoured by my aunt and then watched as Diana slathered butter thickly all over her portion. She wrenched the lid off some strawberry jam, seized a spoon and liberally dolloped on the contents. After a few hesitant seconds, I did the same.

Next, she pulled the fridge open, seized a big glass jug of milk and gulped from it greedily before handing it to me. She dived back in, emerging with some cooked sausages on a plate.

Not long after that, we sat on the kitchen chairs, holding our stomachs, groaning and laughing. I was as full of wonder as I was of food. There seemed no possibility that anyone would come and stop us. We were absolutely free to do as we pleased.

In my amazement and satiety, I forgot all the sadness and the shadows. Park House, I decided, was a different world. A glamorous, exciting, altogether wonderful new world.

Chapter Six

We went to bed soon after that; hurrying, giggling, back up the main staircase. A tall clock on the landing ticked solemnly in the silence. I was shocked and thrilled to see its hands stood at nearly midnight . . .

To my absolute delight, I was sharing Diana's bedroom: pretty, with cream-painted furniture and wallpaper patterned with small pink roses. There were two single beds, both heaped with stuffed animals. It reminded me of how I had protected her school collection from the wrath of Matron. How richly rewarded I had been for that very small act.

The stuffed toy hamster on Diana's bedside table had strange green eyes. 'It's luminous paint,' she explained. 'So he can look out for me in the dark.'

I remembered what she had said about lying there while Charles was sobbing. Just for a second, the shadows and sadness swooped back.

She was eager to show me her vast collection of Barbara Cartland novels. They were everywhere: on the floor, on the shelves, on the bedside table beside the hamster.

'Gosh,' I said. 'Have you read every single one?' The answer, I knew, would be yes. She would have read them all several times.

I picked *The Haunted Heart* out of a shelf. A blonde wearing a full-skirted yellow dress was embracing a handsome man in a room with a marble fireplace and a smart polished desk. The desk especially appealed to me. I turned it over and inspected the back. 'The Spectre of Death seems to be stalking beautiful young Gina Borne.'

'Bit scary, that one,' Diana commented.

I slipped it back and settled down on the floor beside her. We lay on our stomachs on the rug, companionably sorting through the pile.

'*The Odious Duke*,' I said, picking up a cover with a man in tight white trousers and a woman in a gold dress. 'I wonder what's so odious about him.'

'Oh, that's the one about the dashing Duke of Selchester. He's on his way to visit Lord Upminster at Copple Hall when he crashes into a stagecoach.'

Her recall was amazing, I thought. 'Poor old him.'

'Yes, and his beloved pedigree stallion, Salamanca, needs re-shoeing. So he goes on foot to the nearest village, which is where he meets Verena. She's the spirited and beautiful heroine. She takes him to the local blacksmith.'

'It doesn't sound very odious so far.'

'Well, the Duke of Selchester gets bludgeoned unconscious by a mysterious assailant. And then Verena nurses him back to health.'

I turned the book over. The plot was just as she said. It suddenly struck me as rather silly and unrealistic. I glanced guiltily at Diana, who was flicking through *The Passionate Princess*. 'What's that one about?' I asked, to disguise my treacherous thoughts.

She glanced at me with shining eyes. 'Beautiful flame-haired Princess Thea who's been made to marry someone much older than herself. But she's always believed that her dream Prince Charming will come and find her and they will fall in love and become a part of each other for ever.' She let the book drop, drew her knees up to her chin and looked wistful. 'That's what I want more than anything, Sandy. To fall in love and become a part of someone for ever.'

We went to bed with our books. Across the room, Diana was reading *The Passionate Princess*; aloud and dramatically if she came to any especially good bits. '"There was a tenderness in his voice which made her press her cheek against his shoulder. Then he said, 'Tonight, my darling, I have been struck with the arrow of Love.'"' She sighed deeply. 'Don't *you* long to be struck with the arrow of Love, Sandy?'

I hesitated. Being struck with an arrow must be painful. I imagined it, thudding in with shattering violence. 'Not really,' I said.

Diana lowered *The Passionate Princess* and looked at me, aghast. 'But I thought you believed in Love?'

'I do, of course I do,' I said hurriedly.

She sank back on her pillows. 'Love,' she declared passionately, 'is the most important thing in the whole world. What do you believe in, if not that?'

Again, I gave this careful attention. What did I really believe in? 'Equal rights for women,' I said suddenly, rather surprising myself.

'What?' Diana burst out laughing.

I meant it, though. Aunt Mary was a staunch feminist, and I had been raised with her conviction that women were as good as men. It had always seemed a reasonable idea to me, and, unlike Love, easy to imagine.

I returned Diana's giggles with firm words of my own. 'Women everywhere are throwing off the patriarchy and burning their bras.' My aunt hadn't exactly emphasised this aspect of the fight for equality, but I had picked it up anyway.

Diana giggled. 'Jellybags isn't. She doesn't have a bra to burn.' Jellybags was the French mistress, whose unsupported upper level sagged below her waist. Like most of our teachers of

46

academic subjects, she seemed intended less as inspiration, more terrible warning.

'I want a career,' I said, now thoroughly warmed to my subject. 'A job. Don't you?'

Diana considered. 'If it involved Love,' she said eventually.

I sniggered. I was vaguely aware that there were professions in this area, all wildly unsuitable for nice girls like ourselves.

Diana took no notice. 'I just think,' she went on, 'that I would be really really brilliant at loving people. Helping them. Caring about them. With all my heart and soul, that sort of thing. If there was a job like that, I'd definitely do it.'

She sounded so touchingly open and earnest, I felt ashamed of my sniggering. 'You would be brilliant at that,' I agreed.

Her face lit up, gratified. 'I would, wouldn't I? I really think it might be my great talent. I mean, my brain isn't any use, I'm not clever. Your brain is all fizzy and jumpy, running about, making connections, remembering things. Mine just sort of sits there, like a flat battery. Doesn't work at all.'

'Rubbish,' I interjected loyally.

'But my heart,' Diana went on, ignoring me, 'is a different matter. It works all the time, reacts to everything. I can literally feel it, swelling, surging, swooping and soaring, just like in the books. And I'm so emotional, I cry at absolutely everything. You know that's true, Sandy.'

I had to admit that it was. It didn't take much to excite her sympathies. In the dining hall once, I'd seen her well up at the sight of a single carrot left on a plate. 'It looks so lonely and abandoned. And now it's going to go in the *bin*!'

'Sometimes,' she went on, 'my heart feels so absolutely full, I think I'm going to burst. More than anything else in the world, I want to find someone to give all this Love to.'

I looked at her. A brilliant idea had struck me. Quite suddenly, I could see her future. It had nothing to do with vague

47

dreams of romance; it was real, and practical, and played to her strengths. I stared at her, filled with a wild delight not unmixed with self-congratulation. 'I think you should work in the health service,' I told her. 'Somewhere like Darenth Park, maybe.'

Recently, as part of a social outreach programme, the school had started sending pupils to spend afternoons at a local institution. Its patients suffered a wide range of physical and psychological conditions. The idea, undoubtedly a good one, was that we would provide hearty girlish cheer whilst receiving some insight into wider society.

Darenth Park was a Victorian mansion built in the Gothic style. On our first visit, in the dying light of a winter afternoon, it had looked terrifying, all turrets, gables and huge walls rearing up in the foggy gloom. We had stared out of the bus window, the good humour of the journey fast dissipating.

'They might make noises and grab at you,' the nurse in charge had said as she ushered us through a huge nail-studded door. 'But don't worry, you won't come to any harm.'

We had entered a vast, mediaeval-style hall. The lighting – from windows very high up – was dim and it was cold. At the far end, the patients had surveyed us from the shadows. The nurse was right, they were making all sorts of noises, amplified by the huge space.

None of us knew what to do. Even the members of staff that had come with us seemed clueless. The growing, unavoidable impression seemed to be that the whole experiment, while undeniably well-intentioned, had been a terrible mistake.

We had all jumped as music suddenly started, from some record player somewhere. A country and western tune, whose fast pace and cheerful melody only seemed to underline the awkwardness of our gathering. My peers had looked at each other, aghast.

'Are we actually supposed to *dance* here?'

'But *how*? Half of them are in *wheelchairs*!'

And so we had stood there, the only things dancing being the dust motes floating in the high, cold air.

Then, suddenly, I had felt something move beside me. It was Diana, walking decisively out to the no-man's land between pupils and patients. The light from the windows fell on her blonde hair, igniting it to flaming gold. She approached a young man sitting forlornly in a wheelchair.

'Come on,' she'd said, seizing its handles and moving it before her in time to the music. 'I like this one, don't you?'

The young man had smiled and moved his hands awkwardly. 'That's it!' Diana had laughed.

Other patients were now waving at her. She had pulled a few more wheelchairs out, careful always to face the occupant, not stand behind to push, as was normally the way. Before long, she had a small, happy circle around her. But there had been so much more to her composure than that. I remembered the faces of the patients she had danced with. Every one of them had looked so joyful. And she had been so completely unselfconscious, bopping away as we all watched.

She had bent to chat to them all in turn, crouching to the floor to be at the right level, all tender encouragement with the shy ones and jokey confidence with the boisterous. Her pure, straight profile, with its classical lines, seemed both out of place and entirely at home. She seemed lit from within, not just outside by the light from the windows.

And then she had turned and, grinning, beckoned the rest of us over: *Come on, join in, I've shown you how.* Hesitantly, we had all stepped forward. Before long, the huge hall was full of movement and music, shrieks of appreciation and whoops of laughter. The awkwardness was gone.

'You were brilliant,' I said to her now, as she stared across the bedroom at me. 'Completely inspired. You understood them. It was genius.'

'Actually,' she said quietly, 'it was the opposite. That's the point, Sandy. I understood them because I know what it's like . . .' She stopped, bit her lip. 'Not to be valued.'

I thought of how her brother routinely dismissed her as stupid, and how wrong he was. It had been clear, at Darenth Park, that she was intelligent in a very rare way, an instinctive and compassionate way. Plenty of clever people, me included, had stood helpless in that hall. But only Diana knew exactly what to do. What was more, she was in her element.

'Well, those people certainly valued you. No one else had the foggiest idea.'

'It wasn't hard.'

'Not for you,' I said. 'You were so natural, approaching the patients and holding their hands, as if you'd been doing it all your life.'

'It was just practical really. If you take their hands, they can't slap you, which they don't mean to do anyway. They're just excited.'

'Well, that's what you should do,' I concluded.

She shook her head. 'But I want to get married. Be in Love.'

'That *was* love,' I said, with conviction. 'It's just what you were talking about. You made everyone happy.'

All the patients she had spoken to, danced with, smiled at, had obviously adored her. There had been a glow about them afterwards, a palpable joy. And it had been so much better, so much more real, than all her overheated Cartland-fuelled fantasies.

I remembered our first encounter in the dining hall, how Diana had held me while I sobbed and known exactly what to ask. How she had released something inside me. It was so obvious now. I couldn't think why it hadn't occurred to me before. 'You have an incredibly special gift,' I told her. 'Empathy, I think it's called. You're empathetic.'

She laughed then. 'Me? Rare and special? Empathetic? *Path*etic, more like. Don't be silly, Sandy.'

'I'm not being,' I said. 'Diana, listen to me. This is your future. I just know it.'

But she shook her head, smiled and raised her book again.

Chapter Seven

For the briefest of moments after I awoke, I wondered where I was. Then I remembered and joyfully sat up. Diana's bedroom bloomed with sunshine pressing against the drawn curtains. Her bed was empty, I saw with surprise. Perhaps she had gone to the loo.

I waited a few minutes. Then, as she didn't come back, I hopped out of bed and drew the curtains. The view was idyllic: grazing cattle, open fields, copses of trees. It looked like a painting, I thought. On the lawn by the house, a couple of rabbits peaceably nibbled the grass.

I got dressed quickly in the nylon jumper and polyester trousers that I wore at school at weekends. They were hideous and too small, but I had nothing else. I brushed my hair without looking at myself in the mirror.

Diana had still not returned, but I could hear a thumping noise outside the door. I hurried to open it.

It was Charles. He was wearing striped pyjamas and throwing a ball down the length of the passage. 'Just practising my bowling,' he said cheerfully. 'Want to come and watch telly, Sandy?'

I was sorely tempted. But my loyalties lay elsewhere. 'Where's Diana?' I asked.

'Brian? Outside probably.'

I felt a burst of impatience. 'She's really not as stupid as you think,' I told him.

'If you say so,' Charles shrugged, and went off.

I wandered down the passage, slightly peeved Diana had gone without me. I went down the main staircase, not daring to slide down the banisters alone.

My first thought was to head for the kitchen, but I could hear voices as I approached. I didn't want to enter by myself, especially after everything we had taken from the fridge and larder. What if the cook was angry?

The downstairs hall was empty. As I opened the door to go outside, I remembered Lord Althorp standing there with his pyjama bottoms peeping under his trousers. I recalled his unfocused eyes and slurry speech and I thought how strange it had been. He hadn't been the miserable hermit I'd expected, but hadn't seemed entirely normal either.

Park House by daylight looked much less elegant than it did at night. It was a big, blocky building of yellowish brick with bow windows bulging out. But its surroundings were beautiful: shining emerald grass and glorious gold and russet autumn trees. I drew in great lungfuls of air and felt exhilarated.

'Sandy!' A high-pitched call. 'Sand-ee!' It was Diana's voice, from some way above by the sound of it.

I looked up into the vast, bright, blue Norfolk sky.

And then I saw her. She was right on the edge of the roof, easing her way across the grey slates on her haunches. Seeing that I had spotted her, she raised an arm and stood up to her full height. She was wearing black wellington boots, which she now pulled off and waved at me.

Terror clanged through me. Nothing seemed more certain than she would fall. It was like watching her on the diving board all over again. My thudding heart blocked my throat as I watched her raise one leg high behind her, ballet-style, and bend the other at the knee. Then, in a lightning-quick series of movements, she sprang away and began to dance barefoot between the chimneys, skipping and jumping over the rooftop.

'Come down!' I screamed. 'Please!'

A giggle. 'You come up!'

'How?' I wailed.

'Stairs by the Beatle Room.'

I ran round to the front of the house and back inside. Seconds later, I had hurled myself up the staircase, rushed down the corridor and located the by-now-familiar door with the Fab Four peeling off the front. I could hear the TV booming inside; Charles was clearly hard at work already.

I hadn't noticed it before, but there was a narrow staircase to the side. I pelted up it, my clumsy shoes slamming on the wooden treads. At the top was a skylight with the sun pouring through. I pushed it open and felt a rush of air.

My view was a line of chimneys along the rooftop. Between them was a gully lined with grey lead and dancing down this was Diana, her blonde hair flashing in the sun.

I pulled myself through clumsily, stood up and tested my way forward with a shoe that, I now noticed, had been horribly scraped en route. They were my only pair; my aunt would be furious.

We were facing over the back now. Stretching away into the frosty green distance were a cricket field and a paddock with a couple of horses. Nearer was a tennis court and the most enormous climbing frame I had ever seen. And just below us . . .

I frowned, blinked. Had some stray shaft of light hit my thick spectacles at an odd angle? Because it surely couldn't be real. No one had one of these. Not outside, in England

'Is that a swimming pool?'

Diana laughed. 'Well, what does it look like?'

It looked long and sparkling, with not one but two diving boards and a red-roofed pavilion at one end. One of the diving boards was very high. I could now see where her prowess had come from.

'Daddy got it for us. It came from America and it's got revolving coloured lights in the bottom so it lights up at night.'

'Your father's so kind to you,' I said, letting go of all my lingering doubt about Lord Althorp. He was clearly the most wonderful father in the world. Lady Althorp must have been crazy to leave him.

I now noticed in the distance, sprawling between the trees, an absolutely enormous house. It looked very elaborate, its roof-line bulging with towers and domes, and was surrounded by big gardens and a lake. I remembered the gates we had driven past last night.

'Who lives there?' I asked.

Diana was turning a cartwheel in the gully. She straightened, and looked where I was pointing. 'Oh,' she said casually. '*They* do.'

'Who are they?'

'The Queen. The royal family.'

'*The royal family?*' An arrow thudded hard into me now; not Love, but excitement. 'But I thought they lived in London. At Buckingham Palace.'

'Live here as well. At Christmas anyway.' She sounded utterly matter-of-fact.

'Do you ever see her?' I asked, breathlessly. 'The Queen?'

'Sometimes. Riding across the park, or arriving at the station. We're on the same train from London sometimes. She's Charles' godmother.'

'But . . .' I knitted my brow. I was desperate to know everything and anything, but didn't know where or what to ask. How on earth did the monarch become your godparent?

Diana took pity on me. 'Daddy was Her Majesty's equerry,' she told me, which left me none the wiser. Her Majesty's what? 'Sort of a companion,' she explained.

I thought of the photograph of the Prince of Wales by our dormitory, wearing his strange space crown. 'Do you ever see Prince Charles?' I asked.

'Sometimes.'

'What's he like?'

'Oh, ancient, even older than Merry. The first time I met him I was hiding behind a curtain with Andrew.'

'*Prince* Andrew?' He was the Queen's second son, and quite dishy. Catherine, my dormitory neighbour, had filled a scrapbook with pictures of him.

'Oh Sandy, your face.' Diana laughed. 'Andrew and Edward are the same age as Charles and I, so we get asked to their birthday parties sometimes. Anyway, the Prince of Wales walked in and found us.'

I could imagine the scene, tiny blonde Diana and the dark-haired Andrew, giggling in their hiding place. 'What did he say?'

She adopted a gruff tone. '"I say, this looks like a jolly good party." He was very grown-up, in a suit and tie and everything.'

I looked over at the huge, elaborate house. 'I can't believe you go there to parties.'

But Diana was dancing off again. 'Not very interesting ones,' she shouted. 'Just endless showings of *Chitty Chitty Bang Bang* and old ladies-in-waiting standing about.'

'Ladies-in what?'

Diana danced back to me. 'Honestly, Sandy. You're like some-one from another planet. A lady-in-waiting is a sort of friend of the Queen. Or the Queen Mother. Both my grandmothers were *her* ladies-in-waiting. One of them still is.'

I felt my jaw drop. It wasn't me that was from another planet, I thought. It was her.

*

We went down to the kitchen. A plump woman with grey hair was standing chopping at the wooden table. I regarded her warily, while Diana dashed forward.

'Mrs Betts!'

The woman's face lit up instantly. 'Miss Diana!' Her eyes slid to me. 'And who's this?'

'I'm Sandy,' I said, before the customary introduction could be made.

'She's an orphan,' Diana added, irrepressibly. 'And she loves Barbara Cartland, just like me.'

Mrs Betts smiled fondly. 'Always on the dream path, you are,' she said in the same accent as Merry. 'Always with your head in they books!'

She pushed over a round red tin. Diana fell on it and wrenched off the lid. Inside were round yellow buttery discs of shortbread. She thrust one at me. I bit in and an explosion of sweet butteriness filled my mouth. I had never tasted anything so delicious.

'Sarah's coming today!' Diana was hopping from foot to foot, speaking through a mouthful of crumbs.

Mrs Betts' smile faded slightly.

Diana had run off again. I followed her to the front door just in time to see the blue Simca setting off with Merry at the wheel and Diana jumping up and down in front of it, shouting, 'Stop! Where are you going?'

Merry wound down the window. Her hair was as unbrushed as ever. 'To King's Lynn Station.'

Diana whooped. 'To get Sarah! Can we come?'

'There won't be room. I can give you a lift to the bottom though.'

I had expected this to mean inside the car, but I was shown how to climb onto the slippery bonnet and cling on to the wing mirror. As we set off, I could only imagine what my aunt would say.

Merry drove slowly, swinging slightly to increase the excitement. She lurched particularly violently when we reached the drive entrance, sending both of us screaming and sprawling onto the gravel. Then, with a roar of engine, she was off.

We got up, and walked across the wide green with its elegant trees. The church which had loomed so darkly last night turned out to be a friendly brown with a red roof and a square tower. St Mary Magdalene, according to the board.

'Let's go to the graveyard,' Diana suggested.

I agreed enthusiastically; I liked graveyards. If my aunt was doing the church flowers, I often slipped out to explore the graves. There was a fascinating air of neglect: green glass chips sprouting with weeds, marble vases with dead blossoms, cracks in tombs into which I peered, hoping for, yet fearing, a glimpse of coffin.

The churchyard I now followed Diana into was much smarter than the one I knew. There were no broken graves here, no weeds. I paused at a smart cross, carved from pink marble which sparkled in the sun. John Charles Francis, fifth son of King George V and Queen Mary. Born July 12 1905 and died Jan 18 1919.

Poor King George and Queen Mary, I thought. What, I wondered, had happened to Prince John Charles Francis? I had always vaguely imagined that royalty, princes especially, led charmed lives. I hadn't realised that they could die young and be touched by tragedy, like everyone else. Prince John Charles Francis had only been thirteen, the same age as us.

I wanted to ask Diana about it all, but she had bounded ahead and was over by the wall. She was studying a grave whose headstone bore an imposing coat of arms.

'Who is it?' I asked.

'My brother.' She pointed to the name chiselled in the stone. John Spencer, I read. Son of Viscount and Viscountess Althorp.

Shock flashed through me. I thought I knew Diana's story by now. But she had never mentioned anything of this.

I read on: Born and died January 12th 1960. He had only lived a day. 'What happened to him?' I asked, rather horrified.

'He was dead when he was born,' Diana explained. 'Lots of Mummy's babies were. At one stage, she had six pregnancies in nine years, but only my sisters survived. Daddy made her go to lots of doctors to find out why she never had a boy.'

Only my sisters. 'Why was a boy so important?'

'That's how titles are passed down, silly.'

'You mean your father's title? Lord Althorp?'

She nodded. 'It will go to Charles eventually.' She didn't sound as if she minded in the least. 'Everything will.'

While I wasn't sure what everything was, it obviously included the swimming pool and the big, comfortable house. 'But isn't that a bit unfair? He's the youngest.'

'Yes, but he's a *boy*. Boys are the only ones that matter. If there isn't a son, the estate passes to some other branch of the family, so having one is really important.'

I was staggered. We had been studying the Tudors in history; poor Queen Anne Boleyn had lost her head for failing to produce a son. Or so it seemed to me, anyway. But that was hundreds of years ago and it was the twentieth century now. The modern age.

'So, anyway,' Diana carried on, 'when Mummy finally had a boy, it was John and he was born dead. She wasn't allowed to hold him. Or even to see him. They just took him away and, after that, she didn't love Daddy any more. Not even when she had Charles.'

I stared at her, my mind whirling. It wasn't just the Anne Boleyn-ness of it all, it was Lady Althorp too. I had thought her selfish and heartless. Now I felt sorry for her. All the dead babies and doctors, it must have been so awful. Perhaps the heartless person was the one who had made her suffer; Diana's father, by the sound of it. But he was so jolly and generous. I felt completely confused.

'Your poor mother,' I said, eventually.

'It was rather awful,' Diana conceded. 'Every time she got pregnant, Daddy had a big bonfire built to celebrate the birth of an heir. None of them ever got lit until Charles was born.'

I was astonished. 'Not even when you were born?'

'*Especially* not when I was born. I was the one after John. I was supposed to be a boy and when I turned out to be another girl, they took a whole week to even think of a name for me. I was a terrible mistake.'

My astonishment now became anger. How *stupid*, I thought. How could wonderful, special Diana be anyone's idea of a mistake? How could it take a week to think of a name? And why didn't it occur to all these people obsessed with boys that they needed girls to get the boys out?

'Girls are important too,' I said firmly, thinking of Aunt Mary.

Scrambling to her feet, Diana did not seem to hear this. 'Come on. Let's go back. I want to be there when Sarah comes.'

Chapter Eight

Back at the house, Sarah had not arrived, but there was an excitement in the air that had not been there before.

'What's Sarah like?' I asked. All I knew was what Catherine had said about her being expelled for drinking. But was that even true? No one else had ever mentioned it.

We were back in the Beatle Room, squashed up on the sofa in front of the TV. A colourful, noisy programme was on in which four large, strangely dressed animals either drove around in buggies or played musical instruments and sang.

'Sssh,' said Charles. He was in the middle, dressed in a scratchy-looking Aran jersey and thick red corduroy trousers that matched his auburn hair. 'I'm trying to watch *The Banana Splits*.'

I repeated my question in a whisper.

'Very naughty,' Diana whispered back. 'She got expelled from school for drinking.'

So it was true, then.

'What happened after that?'

'She was sent to a conservatoire. To play the piano.'

I was mystified. There was a conservatoire at the back of my aunt's house where I spent hours wiping greenfly off her camellias. It certainly wasn't big enough to fit a piano in.

'But she came out in March,' Diana added brightly.

'Of the conservatoire?' I asked.

A snort from Charles. 'No, silly. Into *society*.'

I had no idea what they were talking about. But I didn't want to ask and be told I was from another planet again. Especially not in front of Charles.

Unexpectedly, Charles now explained. 'It's what happens when you're eighteen. When you're a girl. You get launched onto the marriage market.'

'The *marriage* market?' I knew about markets for fruit and vegetables, and cheap nylon clothes like the jumper I was wearing.

'That's what girls are for in families like ours,' Diana chipped in. 'Marrying suitable men.'

'Families like *ours*?' I asked. 'What's so different about yours?'

'Well,' said Charles, with magnificent hauteur. 'We were the wealthiest sheep traders in Europe in the fifteenth century. We have a motto, "May God Defend the Right". We've been Knights of the Garter, Privy Councillors, First Lords of the Admiralty and linked by blood to everyone from Charles I to Al Capone – he's a gangster, before you ask – by way of seven US Presidents.'

'And,' I said when I had absorbed this, 'they go to a market?' I imagined a large hall with a glass roof and crowds of men and women wandering about, dressed like the people on the covers of Barbara Cartland novels, looking each other up and down.

'Not a *real* market, silly! What is it that Grandmama says, Charles?' Diana nudged her brother.

My ears pricked up. Her grandmothers had been ladies-in-waiting, I remembered.

'"There are two unwritten rules about a young woman's function,"' Charles was imitating a fluting Scottish accent. '"One, she must, in the blossom of youth, marry a suitable man. Two, she has to produce, and preferably at the first attempt, a son and heir."'

No wonder Diana was so sceptical about feminism, I thought. Brought up with these ghastly attitudes, and boys who inherited everything. And what was a suitable man, anyway?

'Such an awful snob,' said Charles, unexpectedly echoing my thoughts.

'Charles!' exclaimed his sister.

'It's true. Gran's the worst snob in the history of the world. Why else do you think she gave evidence against Mummy at the divorce hearing?'

'She did *what?*' I gasped.

'Mummy wanted custody of us four children.' Charles waved his home-made remote control. 'But Gran told the court that she was an unfit mother. She wasn't, not at all, but Gran didn't want us to go and live with her and Peter. That's Mummy's new husband. He has a wallpaper business, so he's in trade. But Gran wanted us to stay with Daddy, because he has a title.'

My mouth dropped open. I thought of the little gravestone. But it was even worse than the poor dead babies. Lady Althorp had been denied her living babies, too.

'Gran is your father's mother?' I guessed.

Charles shook his pudding-basin hair. 'No, Gran is Mummy's mother.'

I was shocked. I had never realised families could behave like this. Suddenly, not having one didn't seem so bad, after all. But having no idea how to tackle this latest surprise, I rewound to an earlier point in the conversation. 'What if you don't want to marry in the *blossom of youth?*' I asked Diana. 'What if you wanted to work for the health service, like I said last night?'

I felt rather desperate, suddenly. She should break away from all these people and live a completely different life. She was so talented, so unique, and yet she did not seem to believe it. No one here did. Certainly not Charles, who was saying, 'Health service?' as if he had no idea what it was.

Diana just laughed, however. 'But coming out is such fun,' she said. 'Sarah had a blissful party. Daddy hired this wonderful old ruined castle, which was floodlit, and it took two ladies two whole days to fill it all with flowers. There were flaming torches and we flew the family standard from Althorp, and Sarah got a green MG as a present.'

'What's the family standard from Althorp?' I didn't know what a green MG was either, but first things first.

'A flag with the Spencer coat of arms,' Charles supplied. 'And Althorp is the family estate. It's in Northamptonshire.'

Northamptonshire meant nothing to me. But I realised that this meant the family had not only this big house, but another big house somewhere else. I felt disbelief that people in real life, in the twentieth century, lived in such splendour. But if it meant they thought girls should marry in the bloom of youth and produce, at the first attempt, a son and heir, perhaps it was not so splendid, after all. My idea of Park House as all that was wonderful was changing.

'Daddy will inherit Althorp when his father dies and he becomes Earl Spencer, and the same will happen to me when Daddy dies,' Charles went on, composedly.

I stared at him. So not only was this strange system unfairly weighted to boys, it seemed to actively encourage them to look forward to the death of their parents. Aristocratic families, I was beginning to think, weren't families at all. Just people who shared the same surname.

'There were four hundred guests and they came in horses and carriages and wore period costumes.' Diana was talking about Sarah's party again. 'Daddy went as Henry VIII and Sarah went as Anne Boleyn.'

'Anne Boleyn?' I remembered the little grave and a shiver went down my spine.

64

'That's right. Her costume actually came from Hollywood, from an actual film about Anne Boleyn called *Anne of the Thousand Days*. It was gorgeous, all covered in pearls.'

'How did she get a Hollywood costume?' As ever, I had zoomed in on the practicalities.

'Come Dancing got it for her,' Charles said darkly. 'She has friends in Hollywood. Among the horror film fraternity, I expect.'

'Oh Charles!' chided Diana. 'It was very kind of Lady Dartmouth. And Sarah looked amazing in it, with her hair all curled to her shoulders. She danced all night with her boyfriend, he's called Gerald and his father is the richest duke in England.'

A suitable man. Gerald sounded very suitable. 'Will she marry him?' I asked.

'Oh yes. And I'll be bridesmaid. I can't wait. I *love* weddings.'

As Charles and I remained glued to the telly, Diana stayed at the window watching for Sarah's arrival. The TV was so deafening that the sound of thumping at the door was a surprise. We had not heard anyone come up the stairs. 'Open up!' called a muffled voice.

Diana gasped. 'Sarah!'

I had barely time to wonder why the eldest Spencer couldn't open the door herself when a scream of laughter filled the room. Even Charles lifted his eyes from the television for a second. 'Oh, for heaven's sake,' he muttered.

I sprang to my feet, unable quite to believe my eyes. There was a horse in the doorway, a real live horse, brown with a dark mane. Sitting on its bare back was a pretty, delicately built girl in dark new jeans and trendy Green Flash tennis shoes. Her expression was one of complete triumph.

'I never saw you come back! I've been looking out,' Diana gasped. She was stroking the horse's neck, her face red with excitement. She clearly hero-worshipped her daring elder sibling. 'How on earth did you get Romany in?'

'Mrs Betts was cleaning the drawing room, so I sneaked him in through the back door. Got him upstairs with a carrot. Come on, boy.' She kicked her Green Flash against the horse's hairy sides and he lumbered obediently into the room.

'Mind my soldiers!' yelled Charles, diving to protect the serried ranks on the floor.

Romany stood staring at the television in mild bewilderment. He seemed used to this treatment. I remembered Mrs Betts' pursed lips and wondered if this sort of thing was the reason.

Sarah had a darker version of Charles' red hair and Diana's pale skin and bright lips, although her eyes were a rich brown and had a sharpness theirs lacked. They seized on me immediately and I found myself blushing without really knowing why. Then they switched to Diana. 'Who said you could wear my dungarees?'

'You gave them to me, remember. They're too small for you.'

'Well, I'm thinner now. You can give them back.'

'You do look quite thin,' Diana agreed. 'Been dieting?'

'In a manner of speaking.' Sarah tossed her Titian locks. 'Call it the Dumped By Gerald Diet.'

An electric energy now flooded the room. Even Charles looked up from the TV.

Diana gasped. 'Sarah! No!'

The proud figure on the horse did not reply.

'Why?' asked Charles, curiously.

Sarah tilted her chin and shrugged. 'One of those things.'

'Does Daddy know?'

His sister's long white throat convulsed in a swallow. 'He knows.'

'Bet he's furious, isn't he?' Charles remarked, helpfully. 'He was looking forward to being the father of the Duchess of Westminster.'

'Yes, well, he isn't going to be.' Sarah's tone was defiant, but I could hear a crack in her voice.

Diana was staring through her fingers, blue eyes wide with horror. 'But you might get back together . . . You might see him at a dance, across a crowded room, and realise you can't live without each other.'

Her sister did not trouble to disguise her disgust. 'God, Duch. You and your pathetic novels. That sort of thing doesn't happen in real life. In real life, if a man doesn't love you, you may as well forget it.'

Merry appeared, looking mildly flustered. 'Sarah, what are you doing?' It wasn't clear whether she had heard the news or not. I half-expected Diana to blurt it out, as she always did about my orphan status, but perhaps this was too serious, as she stayed silent. Merry rattled her bangles. 'Just get him out before he does a you-know-what,' she instructed as she left the room.

'I'll help you,' offered Diana eagerly, taking the horse's halter and gently turning him round. 'I won't be long,' she added to me. 'I'll see you at lunch.'

Chapter Nine

Charles and I settled down in front of the TV again. The wrestling had started. A huge bald man in giant baby rompers grappled with an intense-looking figure in a red-and-white mask.

'Poor Sarah,' I said. 'It's awful about her boyfriend.'

'She'll get over it.'

'Will she?' She had seemed quite upset to me, beneath her bravado.

'She'll have to. Never explain and never complain, and all that.'

I stared at him. 'Never what?'

But Charles was too absorbed in the wrestling to respond.

I thought about what I had witnessed. Sarah's words came back to me. *In real life, if a man doesn't love you, you may as well forget it.* But she had been talking not about any man, but the son of the richest duke in England. What was real life about that? Or about any of the Spencer rituals and routines, from not lighting bonfires for girl babies to riding horses upstairs. And then there was the behaviour of Diana's grandmother, and her father, and her mother. It was all so complicated and so difficult to understand. The only thing I was sure of was that Diana should try to escape it.

Merry put her head round the door. 'Lunch,' she said.

We all slid down the banisters and arrived at the bottom to find ourselves the subject of piercing scrutiny.

'Oh help,' Charles muttered from behind his hand. 'It's Come Dancing.'

I was excited: I had heard so much about her and now I was to meet her. Because of the dancing references, and her mother's novels of course, I imagined a deeply romantic figure in a wide-skirted dress that swept the ground in some pretty colour, like pale pink. Atop her swan-like long neck would be a beautiful oval face with high cheekbones, full lips and large, limpid, thickly lashed eyes. Her hair would be soft and curling, probably blonde, and piled up softly on her head. She would speak with a low, musical voice and move with a feminine grace.

Lady Dartmouth could not have been more different. She was actually rather terrifying, with her dead white face, bright red lipstick and great brown helmet of immovable bouffant hair. She wore, as previously advertised, a huge flared skirt, but it didn't sweep the ground and was of a blazing electric blue, matched by a tight electric blue jacket. Her dizzyingly high heels tapered to a sharp point and her nails were long and red. Rather than the fainting heroines of her mother's romances, I sensed something of the Cruella de Vil about her; something pitiless and hard.

'Dear little Charles,' she exclaimed, in high, shrill tones, bending to kiss him.

Charles squirmed away.

A pair of thickly mascaraed eyes swivelled to me. 'And this is?'

'Friend of Diana's.' Lord Althorp shuffled up behind, clearing his throat. He wasn't swaying as much as before and looked slightly more alert. But his tweed jacket looked very old and worn and the shirt collar below his big red face was distinctly frayed. I wondered why he dressed so scruffily when he lived in a big house with a swimming pool.

'Friend?' repeated Come Dancing in her shrill voice.

'From school, you know.'

The sharp eyes on mine seemed to narrow and focus. 'Who are your people?'

'I don't have any people,' I muttered.

Come Dancing turned away, slid her arm through Lord Althorp's and clacked off on her sharp high heels.

'Where're Brian and Sarah?' Charles had gone into the dining room and now came out again.

Lord Althorp cleared his throat again. 'Um, they've gone to get changed.'

'Changed?' repeated Charles.

'Erm, yes. Lady Dartmouth,' he glanced at Come Dancing, 'ah, doesn't like girls to wear jeans at the table, you see.'

I wondered, rather indignantly, what business of hers it was. She was only a friend of their father's. Charles clearly felt this too. He glowered at Come Dancing, who returned his glare with a glassy smile. I thought of my own scruffy nylon trousers and prayed that she wouldn't notice those. I had nothing to change into, if so. She didn't even look at me though, not then, nor for the entire rest of the time I knew her. She clacked off towards the dining room, dragging Lord Althorp along with her.

The Park House dining room was lovely. It had sea-green walls and matching curtains. There were paintings of coastal scenes and a large table spread with a white cloth and laid with candles, crystal and silver.

I stared at the wings of cutlery which spread out either side of my plate and realised that the school's drilling about table manners was actually going to come in useful. I shook out my linen napkin, spread it over my nylon trousers and put a little heap of salt by the edge of my gold-rimmed plate.

'That's better,' said Come Dancing. She was addressing Sarah, who had just arrived with Diana. 'You're not going to attract a suitable replacement for dear Gerald if you don't present yourself properly.'

'*Dear* Gerald?' Charles repeated, disbelievingly. 'You *know* him?'

'Yes, I met his family several times when I was a Westminster councillor.' Come Dancing smiled glacially.

Sarah's face was white with anger. 'Who said I wanted to *attract a replacement?*'

'Of course you want to,' Come Dancing replied calmly. 'A woman must find a suitable husband and glow in his shadow. Men matter most.' She turned to Lord Althorp and fluttered her mascaraed eyelashes. 'The trouble with women today is that they will not realise that women succeed only when they are the inspiration *behind* men. Become great *through* them. That is the secret of women's power.'

I looked at Sarah, expecting her to reject this with her customary spirit and daring. She said nothing, however.

'We need a plan,' Come Dancing added.

'Plan?' Charles echoed. 'What sort of a plan?'

Come Dancing put her nose in the air and pursed her red lips. 'When I was Deb of the Year, my mother gave a party that only men could come to. It was on purpose, so she could see who was available and whom I should marry.'

I glanced at Diana. I wondered if she was thinking what I was thinking, that the swoony depiction of romance in Barbara Cartland's novels had nothing in common with the brutal pragmatism being described. Diana was looking at Sarah, however, who, while obviously furious, was still saying nothing.

I looked back at Come Dancing. Did she say these things to her own children? I wondered. I felt rather sorry for her daughters, if so. Sorry for her husband, too. He probably wouldn't like the soppy, sugary way she was beaming at Diana's father and stroking his lapel. But Lord Althorp certainly seemed to like it. He was gazing at her adoringly. Perhaps he would marry her, after all. It seemed a dangerous possibility suddenly, and made me uncomfortable and worried.

Sarah, meanwhile, was grinning at Charles. That, too, seemed dangerous.

The door opened and Mrs Betts staggered in under a large tray of serving dishes. The food was potatoes, peas and a piece of dark red meat I didn't recognise. There was something in Mrs Betts' stony face as she proffered the meat to Come Dancing that suggested there had been a clash, and the cook had come off worst. Again, I wondered what business of Lady Dartmouth's it was.

Lord Althorp, shifting uneasily, flashed the cook one of his clamped-together smiles. 'Venison off the estate, marvellously cooked by Mrs Betts, and the most tremendous treat.'

So that was what it was. Deer meat; I had read about it in Robin Hood. They were always eating it in Sherwood Forest. It had a strong, smoky flavour and was quite tough to chew.

Once Mrs Betts had closed the door firmly behind her, Charles looked pleadingly at his father. 'It would be nice to have *bought* food sometimes though, Daddy. Birds Eye burgers look delicious in the TV ads.'

Lord Althorp flashed Come Dancing a nervous glance. 'When I was at Eton during the war,' he said to Charles, 'my father sent an entire stag for us to eat. You're getting off quite lightly, all things considered.'

Everyone started to eat; Come Dancing in tiny, ladylike bites. I saw Sarah glance at Charles, wink, and then open her mouth and let out an enormous burp.

Lord Althorp's wrath was volcanic. 'Leave the room immediately!' he shouted at his eldest daughter. The violence of his fury was as terrifying as it was sudden. Diana and Charles were white-faced with shock, while Sarah, with a boldness that I admired even as I cringed for her, raised her chin defiantly.

'It's considered polite in some countries . . .' she was beginning, when her father stood up, pointed at her and roared.

'Out! Now!' He grabbed his daughter by the arm and escorted her out, forcibly.

The rest of us were left with Come Dancing, who was not smiling now. Her eyes glittered as they rested briefly on each of us. 'Don't trifle with me,' she said in a venomous hiss. 'I've fought elections in the East End. I can eat you lot for breakfast if I want to.'

Diana looked as shocked as her siblings. She surely now realised there was no connection between Lady Dartmouth's mother's books and Lady Dartmouth herself.

As a clearly ruffled Lord Althorp returned, I hoped desperately that he would not marry her. She was a hard woman and would be an unloving stepmother. Which would be terrible for the Spencer siblings, who, for all their privilege, had experienced so little love.

But it was not their lucky day, it seemed. More difficulty lay in store. That evening, as we watched TV in the Beatle Room, a power cut struck in the middle of *Doctor Who*.

A shriek from Charles. '*No!*' He jumped up and switched the TV frantically on and off. 'It's just not possible!' he wailed.

Merry calmly lit some candles and explained. Industrial action meant that, on government orders, the BBC and ITV were ending their broadcasting day early to reduce power consumption. The nation's electricity would go off early as well.

Charles was apoplectic. 'I'll miss *That's Life* just because of those beastly firemen?'

'It's not just them. It's the miners too. And they're allowed to take industrial action. Why shouldn't they want better working conditions?'

Charles remained unmoved. 'What about *The Generation Game*? That's on next!'

Merry rolled her eyes. 'Charles. It's not the end of the world.'

'It's the end of Ted Heath,' Charles said grimly.

'Who's he?' Diana asked.

'The Prime Minister, you idiot.'

Diana ignored him. 'What can we do by candlelight, Merry?'

The nanny's pixie features stretched in a smile. 'We'll set up a Ouija board. The conditions are perfect.'

'What's a Ouija board?' chorused Sarah and Charles.

'I know!' Diana said excitedly. 'There's one in *The Haunted Heart*.' She looked at me eagerly. 'You know that one, Sandy. You were looking at it earlier. Where beautiful young Gina Borne is being stalked by Death.'

I felt my cheeks burn in the darkness under her siblings' satirical stare. After the shocking encounter at the dining table, my growing doubts about Lady Dartmouth's mother's oeuvre had hardened into scepticism. I felt I no longer believed in that syrupy world of fictional romance, and had half-imagined Diana might feel the same. But I could see now that the opposite was true.

Merry came to my rescue. 'A Ouija board,' she told the others, 'is where you ask questions of the spirit world and it answers using the board.'

'Count me out,' said Charles, quickly. 'I'll do Napoleon versus Wellington by torchlight instead.'

As the torchlight Waterloo meant the Beatle Room was out of bounds, the board was set up in the laundry room next to the kitchen. It looked an unlikely apparatus to talk to the dead with, painted as it was with the numbers nought to nine and the letters of the alphabet. At the top were the words 'yes' and 'no' and at the bottom the word 'goodbye'.

The laundry room was warm and smelt comfortingly of soap and lavender. Candles flickered over sheets suspended from the drying racks overhead. Beyond, all was blackness.

On stools borrowed from the kitchen, our group assembled around a small table, moving the folded linen to the shelves at the back.

There was a rattle as Merry solemnly removed all her rings and bracelets. 'So as not to interfere with the spirit forces,' she said, piling them at the table's edge.

On Merry's instructions, everyone held hands. Then she took in her small fingers a piece of wood like an upside-down heart. She lifted up her pointed little chin and closed her eyes. She breathed in, deeply, then out again. Then she spoke, her voice low and hollow. 'Who here has a question for those who have gone before?'

'Me,' said Sarah immediately.

'What is your question?'

'Who will I marry now that Gerald has dumped me?'

I felt terribly sorry for her. I was holding her hand and squeezed it sympathetically. She did not squeeze back.

Merry closed her eyes and laid the wooden piece on the board. With her long blonde hair streaming over her shoulders and her symmetrical features glowing in the candlelight, she looked like some pagan sorceress. A strange stillness seemed to fill the room. Was she really communing with the dead? The dangling sheets rippled slightly in the draught with a horribly ghostlike effect.

Everyone gasped as the nanny's small hand began suddenly to move. Merry's eyes were still closed, and tightly too. It seemed unlikely that she could see where the piece was going. We watched, breathlessly as it stopped on N. Then it moved back to M.

'Ooh. NM. Who's NM?' asked Diana.

'How would I know?' Sarah sounded intrigued, even so.

Merry pushed back her hair with both hands. 'Next question.'

'Who will Jane marry?' This was Diana.

'That's easy,' Sarah snorted. 'Robert Fellowes.'

'Who's he?' I asked.

'His father works at Sandringham,' Sarah said dismissively. 'She's known him for ever. It's all very dull and boring.'

'I think it's sweet,' said Diana. 'It's very—'

'Romantic,' groaned Sarah. 'Don't tell me!'

The wooden piece on the board moved to R, then reversed to F.

'See!' crowed Diana, triumphant.

'Next question,' intoned Merry. Her eyes genuinely looked tightly shut. She could not see the letters. Were mysterious spirits really choosing them? 'Or do I mean next marriage?'

Hanging in the air, like the sheets dangling about us, was the question of Lord Althorp and Come Dancing. But neither of the Spencers asked it. I guessed that, following the drama at lunchtime, no one wanted to know the answer, not even Diana.

'Ask who Duch will marry, Merry.'

They watched the piece of wood move along the board and stop at 'C'. Then it went to 'W'.

'CW,' Diana said, puzzled. 'Who on earth is that?'

'I've had enough of this,' said Sarah, impatiently. 'The spirits don't know what they're talking about.' She stood up, knocking Merry's silver bracelets off the table. They clattered, deafeningly loud, on the stone floor.

Diana tutted. 'That's what beautiful young Gina Borne's evil stepmother said in *The Haunted Heart*. And look what happened to her.'

Sarah paused in the laundry-room doorway. 'I don't *care* what happened to her! For God's sake, Duch. How can you possibly keep reading Barbara Cartland's stupid books? When you know she's Come Dancing's mother?'

I held my breath. It was exactly what I had wondered myself, of course.

Diana, however, just smiled. 'They're not stupid,' she said with dignity. 'They're wonderful. And Lady Dartmouth has nothing at all to do with them.'

Chapter Ten

Next day, something shook me awake. I opened my eyes and found myself looking into a familiar excited expression. 'The sea!' Diana exclaimed. 'Merry says she's going to take us!'

The sea! I was out of bed in an instant. I rushed to the window; the weather was sunny and bright.

'Oh, but you haven't got bathers,' Diana lamented. We had already established this with regard to the swimming pool. I wished she had told me in advance. But a seaside visit was even more of a missed opportunity. I had never seen the sea.

We ran down the corridor to Sarah's room. Her red head appeared round the door.

'Can you lend Sandy your bathers?'

Sarah's mood was no better than the night before. 'Sorry, they're not elephant size.'

'Oh please, Sarah. You're not even coming swimming.'

'No, because I might drown. The spirits might take their evil revenge.' Cackling, Sarah closed the door.

The absent Jane's swimming costume was found for me and we hurried down via the banister to find Charles helping Merry carry a hamper from the direction of the kitchen. 'We've taken enough food for an army,' Charles said with satisfaction. 'Mrs Betts will go ape when she finds out.'

*

A golden feeling of excitement filled the car as we drove along. The fields spread out on either side; stubble glinting in the sun. The vast blue sky seemed to go on for ever. The windows were wound down and as we got closer, there was an unmistakeable tang of salt in the air. Well before we were in earshot, I could hear the crash of waves on the beach and the screech of the seagulls wheeling overhead.

'Can you imagine, Sandy's never seen the sea!' This was Diana. 'Isn't it exciting?'

'Very,' agreed Merry. 'Do we think the tide will be in or out?'

'Out!' Charles decided.

'In!' countered Diana. 'When it's out, it goes to the horizon and you can't even see it.'

I prayed this would not be the case.

We drove through Brancaster with its pretty grey flint houses. Merry explained that, while some of the old inhabitants remained, many of the old-style cottages had been sold to wealthy incomers who did them up and drove up the house prices for everyone else.

Charles, as ever, was ready with the alternative view. 'But surely it's better that houses are being looked after than being allowed to fall down.'

By the time the Simca lurched down the track that led to the beach, I was almost beside myself with excitement. Ahead of us rose sand dunes and beyond, I could sense, the sea.

The car had not stopped before Diana flung open the door. 'Come on!'

I stumbled after her, ankle-deep in the soft golden sand. I panted to the top of the dunes and there it was before me. The sea, glittering and moving like something alive, waves rolling in like rounded glass. It was so thrilling I could hardly contain myself and so beautiful I could hardly believe it. I could only stand and stare.

Diana, meanwhile, had leapt from the top of the dunes, rolled down the sandy slope, scrambled up and raced towards the water, her slim feet hardly seeming to touch the ground. With her simple dress and long limbs, hair streaming behind her like a golden flag, she looked like a goddess. Briefly, there seemed something immortal about her. Then she stopped, turned and bawled, in a decidedly un-goddesslike way. 'Get a move on, Sandy!'

I needed no second prompting. I leapt off the dune after her, rolled over like she had and ran across the sand. It was hard and ridged beneath my feet. The pools I splashed through felt deliciously warm. We pulled off our clothes at the water's edge and I followed Diana as she plunged, shrieking, into the waves.

It was freezing, so cold it almost felt hot. But never had I felt so alive. A chill fire raced through my body, setting every nerve end fizzing and tingling. We clung together, gasping and laughing, skin shining with water and reddening with the cold. I felt that I had never been so happy, and that I would remember this moment all my life.

I could not know it then, but it was the last I would see of Diana for many years. Soon afterwards, my aunt, now recovered from pneumonia, finally realised what I had long dreaded she would. Deciding that my school was insufficiently demanding, she moved me to one that was with immediate effect. With shocking suddenness, I was parted from my closest, indeed only, friend.

We did not lose touch, as I wrote Diana long letters and she called me at my new school as often as her supplies of coinage permitted. I kept up to date on events in the Spencer family. During the next few years these included her father becoming Earl Spencer – 'I'm a Lady!' Diana gasped down the phone – and moving to Althorp. Come Dancing, predictably, but no less dreadfully, became Countess Spencer – 'We read it first in the *newspaper*, Sandy. The *Daily Express*. They didn't even tell us, or invite us to the wedding. Can you *believe* it?'

I could, easily. Given what I knew of all concerned, I would have been more surprised if the siblings had been informed and invited. Diana didn't mention whether she was still reading the new Countess's mother's books, and I didn't ask.

Then, most momentously of all, Prince Charles came to shoot at Althorp as the guest of Sarah. They had become quite good friends, it seemed.

'Just imagine!' Diana shouted over the bad telephone connection. 'She's going to be a princess! Princess of Wales!'

'Really?' I was doubtful. 'She doesn't seem the princess type.' I thought of the burping, the riding horses in the house.

Diana groaned. 'You sound like Sarah. She says she can't think of anything worse, and Prince Charles is just a good friend. But she doesn't mean it.'

'How do you know she doesn't mean it?'

'Because who wouldn't want to be a princess? And once she's Queen, she can put Raine in the Tower.'

I laughed.

'And when she marries Prince Charles, I can be a bridesmaid!'

'You're already being one for Jane,' I pointed out. As the Ouija board had predicted, her middle sister was marrying Robert Fellowes the following spring.

'Yes, but that's only the Guards' Chapel. This would be a *royal wedding*! At Westminster Abbey!'

'Steady on,' I said, laughing.

But steadying on had never been Diana's way. Excitedly, breathlessly, she relayed the events of the royal shooting weekend.

Chapter Eleven

Althorp, Northamptonshire

November 1977

Diana

Her father had asked her to load for him. She disliked shooting; all those poor, poor pheasants. But the chance to be with Daddy without Raine controlling his every move was so rare and wonderful that if it meant handling firearms, so be it.

And it was a beautiful day, cold and clear, with the November frost sparkling in Althorp's vast park and the pale front of the house shining in the muted winter sun. And there would be dogs, which she loved, as she loved most animals. Horses were the exception; too big, too unpredictable.

She didn't have smart tweeds, like everyone else, so shuffled along after the guns in her jeans. As guest of honour, the prince had been given the next peg to her father, the host. He was only a few feet away from her in the field, much closer than at dinner last night, where she had observed him from down the table. She had been unable to keep her eyes off him.

She had seen him before of course, but not since she was a child. He seemed younger now than he had then. And much, much more handsome. His eyes shone warmly, his smile was wide and friendly. His hair was softer and wavier than in the photograph by the dormitory entrance at school, where it looked as if it were painted on. Even his famously large ears didn't look all that big. In his perfect tuxedo, he looked supremely elegant. But also vigorous, energetic.

He had taken no notice of her, though. Hardly surprising, she looked so plain and dreary. Her unflattering blue nylon dress was a hand-me-down from Jane. Her exposed shoulders were round and plump, her cheeks flushed with embarrassment. She had not dared put on any make-up, because she was no good at applying it.

Sarah, across the table from the prince, had, of course, looked stunning. Like Rona Trafford, in *Love Became Theirs*, she sparkled. Or like Cliona in *The Star of Love*, she dazzled.

When the shooting started, it made her heart rattle, so loud and violent was the noise. The guns blasted in turn, then the shooter handed their weapon to their loader. Speed was of the essence, and as she rummaged in her cartridge bag, eyes watering from the acrid drifts of cordite, she saw the prince's loader ramming the red cylinders hurriedly down his barrels. He had introduced himself earlier. 'Hello,' he had said. 'I'm Stephen Barry.'

She'd nodded. 'Diana.'

'Not sure I've met a lady loader before.' He was dapper and dark-haired with sparkling black eyes. She'd blushed.

'Well, I'm just doing it for my father. But I wish I was doing it for Prince Charles.'

She had wanted to die as soon as she had said it; what on earth had come over her?

Stephen Barry looked amused. 'I expect he'd prefer that as well. Pretty young girl like you, who wouldn't?'

He was only being chivalrous, she had known that. She was plump, with bad posture and bitten nails. And besides, there was Sarah. 'Oh, he'd much prefer my sister,' she'd exclaimed.

'Would he?' Barry had lifted one smooth eyebrow. 'And why would that be?'

Diana had edged closer. 'We're all hoping,' she'd whispered, 'that Prince Charles is going to marry her!'

The valet had raised both smooth eyebrows. 'Are you now,' he'd said.

She could hear her father talking to Prince Charles. His voice was so full of the urge to please, it made her toes curl slightly. 'It was my great honour, sir, to be with His Majesty, your grandfather, when he shot his last pheasant . . .'

If everyone was this deferential, it must make the prince's life very boring, she thought.

'And by way of a strange coincidence, but no less an honour, I was with Her Majesty, your mother, when she went on her first tour of the Antipodes . . .'

As she handed her father his loaded gun, Diana caught the prince's eye. He looked just as weary as she had expected. She smiled at him, the big wide smile she used for everyone, not just royalty. 'Daddy made the most wonderful film of his tour of Australia,' she told him. 'He used to show it every year at the King's Lynn Festival. People used to pack out the tent because there was a shot of Her Majesty wearing jeans. It raised a fortune for charity.'

The prince looked surprised, then smiled back. 'How funny. I wonder if she knows that.' He was looking at her closely, as if seeing her for the first time. 'Do excuse me for asking, but have we been introduced?'

They had, last night at the dinner. But Sarah was the centre of attention and it didn't matter that he didn't remember. He was noticing her now.

'Diana, sir,' she smiled, blushing again. 'I'm Sarah's little sister.'

'Diana, of course!' He raised his gun, fired. The blast echoed in her ears, making her head sing.

The shooting lunch was in a nearby barn transformed for the occasion by the Althorp footmen. They had brought linen, silver and china in wicker hampers. Provisions had arrived in straw-packed boxes. The effect of all this splendour, in the simple building, was one of charming contrast.

At the linen-covered trestle table, guests took any seat they wanted. She was surprised and excited when the prince sat next to her. 'Rather lovely, isn't it?' He nodded his head at the décor. 'I almost prefer it to Raine's dining room,' he added, with a wink.

She giggled. She knew exactly what he meant. The new Countess Spencer had redecorated all the state rooms, among them the dining room. Here, newly painted electric blue walls throbbed between dazzlingly re-gilded picture frames. 'The paintings are all real, but Come Dancing's made them look like fakes,' was her brother's view.

'We don't like what Raine's done,' she admitted.

'She seems to have done rather a lot. All those shops in the courtyard too.'

'She says she's using the skills from her years in public life to put Althorp on a sound commercial footing.'

He shook his head and seemed about to enquire further, when they both caught Lord Althorp's eye from across the table. They exchanged a mock-guilty, conspiratorial glance and the prince changed the subject to school. She told him about the photograph outside the dormitory. He pulled a face.

'You poor things. I hope I don't give you nightmares.'

She giggled. 'Of course not.'

'Well, what I am doing in this photograph?'

She thought. 'I'm not quite sure. You're wearing what my friend Sandy calls your space crown.'

He spluttered on his water, and horror swept her. Had she said something wrong? But he was laughing, thankfully. 'Space crown! Your friend Sandy is exactly right! That appalling thing

84

they made me wear for the investiture! My mother said it looked like a candle snuffer.'

Hearing such a deeply private remark was as thrilling as it was funny. 'Was it heavy?' she asked.

He shook his head. 'The middle was a ping-pong ball covered in gold leaf.'

She giggled. 'That's so funny!'

'Well, not much else about it was. The investiture, I mean. I had to learn Welsh, for one thing.'

She was admiring. 'I couldn't do that. I'm hopeless at languages. Hopeless at everything, really.'

Unexpectedly, this seemed to interest him. 'School not your thing? Wasn't mine either. Bloody awful place. Freezing all the time, even in summer. Cold showers, cross-country runs. In Scotland, but run by a German. Like Colditz with kilts.'

She chuckled. 'I used to like school. But then my best friend left and it was never the same after that.'

'You were lucky you had a best friend,' he remarked gloomily. 'I never had any friends at all. Anyone who was nice to me got bullied as well.' His eyes were bright, she saw; he actually looked as if he were about to cry. 'At the start of every term,' he bitterly went on, 'I had the same fantasy. Running away and hiding in the Balmoral forest so I wouldn't have to go back. I remember it as if it were yesterday.'

She knew how this felt, exactly. She could remember it as if it were five minutes ago, not even yesterday. Her first boarding school, aged eight. She was sitting on her trunk, her stony expression belying her molten emotions.

'Smile!' Her father was standing before her with his camera.

But she could not smile, only gaze back sullenly. She'd sat absolutely still, aware that, everywhere else, girls in red and grey uniform were running round excitedly greeting friends and waving off parents. Mothers and fathers were hugging their daughters and walking back, arm in arm, to their cars. Hugs, kisses, laughter. Sunshine, blue skies, flowers in the borders. But within her was only a great heavy darkness.

As her father, exasperated, had put away his camera, she'd realised it was the last moment. She'd launched herself at him, clinging on. 'I don't like it here,' she'd muttered, clutching his familiar, battered coat. 'I don't want to stay.'

'Now come on. We all have to do things we don't want to. You just have to learn to be brave.'

She hadn't wanted to be brave. She had though of the Beatle Room at home, the flickering fire, the curtains pulled cosily over the blank black windows of night. The darkness inside her became darker, heavier.

As her father had walked away, she'd felt a rush of pure panic. '*If you loved me,*' she'd screamed, '*you wouldn't leave me here!*' But her father had kept walking.

She shook herself and looked at the prince. She wanted to tell him about it, show him that she understood. His attention was elsewhere now though, he was laughing at something someone else had said. The moment had passed. The face that, seconds ago, had seemed close to tears was now ablaze with laughter.

She felt a sense of wonder, even so. She had been shown something private, a window into his soul. She had glimpsed the bullied boy beneath the confident man. Their souls had connected, deeply, meaningfully. Like the heroes and heroines in her novels.

And now, as in the novels, her heart soared like a butterfly, or perhaps an eagle. She felt, as the lovers in her books did, all swoony and swirly. Of course, it was Sarah that *he* loved. But she could always worship from afar.

Chapter Twelve

Kensington Palace, London
April 1992
Sandy

A glossy black door divided the inhabitants of Kensington Palace from the outside world. Having passed various checkpoints and spoken to various policemen, I felt I was penetrating the centre of a labyrinth. I realised I hadn't quite penetrated it yet when the door opened and I had to switch off my smile because it wasn't Diana standing there. It was a stiff-faced, smartly suited young man.

'This way, madam,' he said, and I followed, feeling foolish. What had I expected? Of course Diana wasn't going to open the door herself. She was a global celebrity, and royal into the bargain.

As the butler, or footman, or whatever he was, led on, I looked eagerly about for signs of my old friend. The yellow Georgian-style lobby was dominated by a dark, highly polished settle. The floor was herringbone wood and there were ornate mirrors and gold-framed paintings. I thought it grand in a generic sort of way, like a country-house hotel perhaps.

Through an archway and another door, an elaborate white staircase rose up. Here, at last, was Diana, but only as a huge, rather cheesy portrait hanging on the turn of the stairs. The drawing room I was now shown into had pink bunchy curtains, paintings hung from ribbons and little tables scattered with trinkets. It seemed fussy and frilly and not very Diana at all. The pink sofa I was waved over to was fringed and full of cushions. I had to shove them aside to sit down.

'Sandy! Oh my God, is it really you?'

Just like that, she was there. She had come in so quickly, I had hardly had time to register. Perhaps I had expected her to be borne in on a litter. But there she was, smiling at me, just wearing jeans and a T-shirt, her long feet bare and tanned on the pink carpet. Her face – completely free of make-up – positively blazed with joy.

'It's so good to see you, Sandy! I've been excited all morning!'

I had not expected such a welcome and was gratified beyond expression. As of old, I felt myself being caught up in her enthusiasm and delight. She had always an energy about her, the ability to turn everything up a notch. And, of course, it wasn't just me who knew that now, but the whole world.

She still had the same voice – light, flat – as when I knew her in school. But everything else had changed. She was thinner, glossier and more beautiful. Even in her jeans, she looked like a supermodel. And, of course, these days, she was unbelievably, stratospherically famous.

Also new was the air of sadness that hung about her, but that was only to be expected. Her father had just died. It was him that had initiated this reunion. When I had read about his death, I had sent Diana a note of sympathy. I hadn't expected a reply; she must have received thousands and we hadn't been in touch for years. So when, mere days later, the small cream envelope had dropped through the letter box of my tiny King's Cross flat, I was flabbergasted. On thick notepaper, under a scrolled letter D topped with a crown, she expressed her joy at having heard from me and invited me to lunch. And here I was.

'I'm so sorry about your father,' I said.

'It was sweet of you to write. Oh Sandy!' She clasped me in a hug, which was unexpected. 'It's been so long!'

I wasn't sure how long, really. I knew that our last proper long conversation was the one after the Prince Charles shooting weekend. After that, we'd drifted. No doubt inevitably; both of us were in different places, not only physically, but in terms of what we were doing. I was at school in the Midlands heading for university and academic obscurity; Diana was heading for London to become the most famous Sloane Ranger in the world.

When she'd married the Prince of Wales, I'd watched it on the television like everyone else. Seeing her come up the aisle, smiling shyly under her tiara, I'd found it impossible to believe this was the girl with whom I had climbed on the roof and foraged in the fridge. She had disappeared into another dimension. I wouldn't ever meet her again, or so I'd thought.

We smiled at each other broadly but awkwardly. 'It's so peaceful here,' I remarked. Actually, it was deathly quiet. Various clocks were ticking, intensifying the silence. It seemed impossible that bustling Kensington High Street was only a few hundred yards away.

'Always is when the boys are at school.'

I hadn't really expected to be the only guest. I imagined that someone like her had huge lunches all the time, long tables stuffed with celebrities, politicians, other royals, and I said as much to her. Interesting and powerful people from all over the world would obviously drop everything to meet the fascinating Princess of Wales.

She smiled. 'I could ask them, I suppose, but I don't.'

'What, never?' I was amazed.

'Well, I once had Jeremy Paxman,' she conceded. 'He was very nice. But I never know what to say to people. It's much more my husband's department.'

Prince Charles didn't seem to be around, in any sense. There was no trace of him, although I don't know what trace I was looking for. A whiff of aftershave, scattered shoes or newspapers perhaps. But there was nothing suggesting a resident but absent man about the place.

On the other hand, perhaps Diana had a very good cleaner, who tidied everything up. One would certainly expect so, given who she was. There seemed none of them about either.

'I thought you'd have hundreds of servants,' I said, smiling.

'Usually I have, obviously,' she said with a flash of humour. 'But I wanted to cook for you myself. So we could have a proper chat.'

I felt wildly flattered, but also rather terrified. What would we chat about? It wasn't just that we had gone in different directions, she lived on a completely different planet to me. She always had of course, but now that planet was in a different galaxy.

I started to sketch out my laborious progression from one university post to the next, glancing at her constantly to check she was not bored. She didn't seem to be.

'I'm so pleased you're doing what you always wanted,' she said, when I paused for breath.

It was on the tip of my tongue to say that being a princess was what she had always wanted too, but something warned me not to. I had noticed by now that even the silver-framed photographs were only of her, William and Harry. It was as if Prince Charles didn't even exist, which was odd. They always looked happy in the newspaper photographs.

I decided to stick to talking about what I knew: her family.

'So Charles is now Earl Spencer,' I said. That too seemed strange, the boy with the basin cut and home-made remote control now assuming command of the vast Althorp estate.

She laughed. 'Yes, he's terribly grand. Funny to think how he hated it when we first moved to Althorp.'

'Did he?'

'Yes, he complained that we had been uprooted from our childhood haunts and friends and marooned in a park the size of Monaco.'

I grinned. I could just imagine him saying that. 'Dare I ask about Come Dancing?'

Diana laughed. 'I haven't heard her called that for years. She's been Raine for ages. Raine-ing, I should say.' The blue eyes rolled.

'Raine, Raine go away.' It had been a favourite chant at one time.

'She's *had* to go away now. Charles has thrown her out of Althorp. He had all her things packed in black plastic bin bags and literally hurled them down the stairs.'

'Really?' I was shocked. It didn't seem a very Charles thing to do, although, admittedly, he had never liked Raine.

'Well, you can hardly blame him. She sold off lots of the important pictures. Putting Althorp on a sound commercial footing, she called it.'

Not for the first time, I reflected that great titles and vast estates rarely brought out the best in people.

All the same, I found myself feeling some sympathy for Raine. She wasn't a young woman when I had first met her and she must be ancient now. I recalled how, during Earl Spencer's first stroke fifteen years ago or so, she had battled for him so valiantly. She had moved him to a better hospital, personally found some revolutionary new drug which had saved him and sat by his bed for months, literally willing him back to life. I wasn't entirely sure how I knew this; perhaps I had read it somewhere. Perhaps around the time of the royal wedding, when the earl had tottered up the aisle with his daughter.

'I saw her at the funeral,' Diana said, 'and I suddenly felt rather sorry for her.'

I felt encouraged by this unexpected echo of my thoughts.

'Mummy was there too,' she added, with a sigh that warned me not to enquire further.

I had noticed earlier that there was a faint but slightly odd smell. I realised now that it was much stronger. 'What are you cooking?' I asked.

There was a gasp, she shot to her feet and hurtled out of the room. I followed to find her in a very smart but small kitchen, panicking over a pan of pasta. It seemed that the water had boiled over and put out the gas, hence the smell. 'I'm calling the fire brigade!' she cried, rushing towards the phone hanging on the wall.

'Don't be silly.' I reached to turn the gas off. 'There's no need. Look, it's fine. Just let some air in.'

She struggled with the kitchen's sash window, her chest heaving and her eyes wide and full of tears. The degree of her distress, and her intended course of action, seemed wildly out of proportion to the relatively minor incident. Instinct told me that something else was wrong, something that had nothing to do with lunch, but might have to do with the strange, silent atmosphere of the apartment.

A bottle and two glasses sat on the marble counter. She needed a drink, I decided. I pulled out a stool and poured the wine, pushing a glass towards her. She heaved herself onto the stool opposite and sat with her elbows on the counter, face propped on her hands. At school, I had seen her do this hundreds of times. Opposite me in the library, at the table in the dining hall, lying on the grass in summer. Her cheekbones were more pronounced these days, but the glassy blue eyes, shining red lips and perfect, pale skin still reminded me of cream in a glass jug or a dewdrop in the centre of a flower. Still the same face, albeit now the most famous one in the world.

'What's the matter?' I asked her.

I expected her to brush aside the question; why would she tell me, after all? These days, there must be hundreds of people far closer. But she just sighed. 'I wouldn't know where to start.'

'At the beginning?' Her rise to fame had been so sudden; she seemed to burst out of the blue onto the front pages and news bulletins. Then she was engaged and married – all, again, with amazing speed. How, exactly, had it happened? 'That was the shooting weekend at Althorp,' I went on, before I paused and frowned. 'But, hang on, Prince Charles was interested in your sister Sarah then, wasn't he?' The long, excited phone conversation came back to me.

'Yes, but Sarah messed up. It was in all the newspapers; didn't you see?'

I shook my head. Buried in my schoolwork, I must have missed it. 'So he switched his affections from Sarah to you,' I concluded.

'Sort of. But it wasn't really that simple.' Diana raised her eyebrows, bit her lip.

'But how complicated can it be?' I asked. 'Two people fell in love. That's it, isn't it?'

She gave a loud, harsh laugh, tipped back her head and stared at the ceiling. When she looked back at me, it was with a sort of rueful sadness. 'It was never about two people.'

'Well, that's what it looked like.'

She snorted. 'That's what it was *meant* to look like. But right from the start, an awful lot of others were involved. Getting it off the ground was hard work, believe me.'

I was mystified. At the time, hard work was the very last thing it had looked like. Charles and Diana's romance had seemed to bowl along of its own happy volition, the joy of a dazzled nation providing the lift-off. 'How many others?' I asked.

'Let me see.' She tilted her head thoughtfully. 'Well, for a start, there was Stephen Barry. He was Charles' valet.'

'His *valet*?'

She flicked me an amused glance. 'Why so surprised? You hardly expect the Prince of Wales to dress himself, do you? Get his own suits out of the wardrobe, or run his own bath?' She was laughing now, which was good to see. 'Sandy, Charles doesn't even put his own toothpaste on his toothbrush.'

'It's not so much that,' I said, although, admittedly, the toothbrush detail was quite startling. 'It's just . . . what would a valet have to do with a royal romance?'

She clapped her hands, beaming. 'Sandy, come on. Have you never seen *Cinderella*? Buttons?'

'But that's a pantomime.'

'And royal life isn't? Sandy, believe me, valets have everything to do with everything. They're the ultimate back channel. And when they're working together, as Stephen Barry was with the Queen Mother's page—'

'The *Queen Mother* was involved?' I interrupted.

'Along with her close friend and my grandmother Fermoy,' Diana's lips twisted briefly. 'It was all a granny plot, really.'

My mind shot to the awful story about Diana's mother and the divorce court. Lady Fermoy was the one who had given evidence against her own daughter. That was extreme enough, but had she really plotted the wedding of the century?

I smiled uncertainly at Diana. 'Sounds like there were a lot of people in this marriage.'

She nodded over her wine glass. 'Yes, it was a bit crowded. And we haven't mentioned the half of them yet.'

I remembered that before the engagement she had shared a flat with some girls from school. I didn't know them and never went to the flat; we had been out of touch for years by then. But I'd seen TV interviews in which the flatmates appeared; good-natured, hearty types with braying laughs, velvet hairbands, strings of pearls and rugby shirts, sometimes all at the same time. They epitomised the young, well-heeled, slightly galumphing sort that came to be known as the Sloane Rangers. I was sure they would have been right behind Diana's bid to be a princess.

'Actually,' she said, 'they were all dead against it. They thought I could do much better.'

Surprised, I toyed with my glass stem. I had once said the same thing of course, but now didn't seem the time to remind her. 'So who else?' I asked.

She raised an eyebrow. 'The press. Mr Arnold and Mr Edwards from the *Sun*. Mr Whitaker from the *Express*. They were all fairly involved.'

This seemed to me magnificent understatement. I remembered the pictures of her being chased down the street by gangs of journalists. 'The press were *everywhere*,' I said.

She nodded, then paused for a beat or two. 'And Camilla,' she added, lightly.

'Who?'

'Camilla Parker Bowles. Friend of Charles.'

The name meant nothing to me. 'And Charles himself, of course,' I said.

She laughed her harsh laugh again. 'There's no "of course" about it, Sandy. Charles was the very last person who was involved.'

I stared across the counter at her. 'What do you mean? How is that possible?'

She was sipping her wine calmly. 'You may well ask. It was quite complicated. It's taken me this long to work it all out. At the time, I had no idea because I was right in the middle of it.'

'Work it all out?' I repeated, mystified.

She chuckled again. 'There've been an awful lot of long Christmases at Sandringham and endless rainy summers at Balmoral. Plenty of time to talk. Over the years, I've managed to winkle it out of everybody.'

It sounded, I thought, like a novel. An ensemble cast: the valet, the page, the scheming grandmothers, the men of the press, this mysterious Camilla, all supposedly playing different roles to achieve the romantic miracle of the royal wedding. Again, I wondered just how seriously to take her.

'It's like something by Agatha Christie,' I said, adopting my best Poirot accent.

'"You may be wondering why I've gathered you all in the Windsor Castle drawing room . . ."'

She nodded. 'It was a bit like that. And there *was* a death, actually.'

'*What?*'

'You're right – it was all far more like an Agatha Christie novel than the sort of novel I thought it would be. And you of all people, Sandy, know what sort of novel that was.' She gave me a sad smile.

Instantly, and with unexpected force, I was swept back to her bedroom at Park House. Lying on the rug, leafing through her vast collection of romances. She seemed to be saying that the romantic dream, for some reason, had been a disappointment. 'Tell me what happened,' I said, trying to get it all straight in my mind. 'So the beginning wasn't the shoot at Althorp?'

'It was, in the sense that I fell in love with Charles then. Head over heels, in the middle of a ploughed field.' She stopped. 'You can't imagine. I was absolutely crazy about him. I completely and utterly adored him, with every fibre of my sixteen-year-old heart.' Her eyes, I saw, looked very shiny. 'Yes,' she went on. 'Althorp was the beginning. But it wasn't where it started.'

I was confused again. 'What's the difference?'

'Oh, Sandy!' she exclaimed, mock-exasperated. 'You're supposed to be the clever one. I just explained. Those other people had to get involved to make it happen.'

'Oh yes,' I said. 'The valet. The page. The Queen Mother. Your grandmother. The press.'

'Exactly. And my sister Jane's wedding was where all *that* began. Jane's wedding was really where it started, I suppose.'

Chapter Thirteen

The Guards' Chapel, Wellington Barracks, London
April 1978
The Press

James Whitaker, society reporter for the *Daily Express*, was positioned discreetly to the side of the chapel's wide concrete steps. Armed with notebook and biro, he watched the various players in the drama arrive.

Here came the groom, Robert Fellowes, correct in every detail, from his ruler-straight side parting to the brilliantly polished shoes that were the hallmark of every courtier. His father was the land agent at Sandringham, where Lady Jane Spencer's childhood home had been. He had, Whitaker thought waspishly, certainly gone up in the world.

When Fellowes got close, he sprang forward. 'Mr Fellowes! James Whitaker, *Daily Express*. If I could have a word . . .'

The groom looked down his sharp nose and answered the question with lofty aplomb. 'Jane and I have known each other all our lives and have gradually grown closer.'

Whitaker jotted this down with amusement. It wasn't entirely true. Sixteen years of Robert's life had passed before twenty-one-year-old Jane was even born. But in circles like theirs, large age gaps were not unusual. Look at Prince Charles. The heir to the throne was almost thirty now; any bride would, by necessity, be much younger.

And here came someone who could have filled that position. Whitaker watched as Earl Spencer's eldest daughter mounted the shallow steps, her slender legs elegant in pale tights, her red hair hidden by her flowered hat. Lady Sarah was so pretty and had the ideal pedigree. She might have done very well as Princess of Wales. Had it not been for him, Whitaker knew. He'd rather holed her royal prospects below the waterline. Or, rather, his newspaper had.

It had all been going so well. After Prince Charles had shot at Althorp last November, Lady Sarah Spencer had been asked to ski with the royal party at Klosters. Whitaker had been part of the press pack who had accompanied them everywhere.

While Charles had treated them with his usual disdain, Lady Sarah had seemed to find them fun. Once everyone had returned to London, James had invited her out for lunch, along with Nigel Nelson from the *Daily Mail*. They had asked her about Charles' intentions and been astonished when she had answered them with perfect frankness.

'There is no chance of my marrying Prince Charles,' she had stated. 'He is a fabulous person, but I am not in love with him. If he asked me, I would turn him down. He doesn't want to marry anyway. He isn't ready for marriage yet.'

As the green eyes of Sarah Spencer now flicked in his direction, Whitaker hastily lowered his own. It wasn't that he felt guilty. Reporting was his job. But possibly she hadn't intended their lunchtime conversation to end up splashed on the front pages. Indiscretion was something royalty never forgave. The prince, so Whitaker had heard, had cut her off completely as a result.

Sarah had gone into the chapel. Following her was her mother Frances Shand Kydd, Earl Spencer's first wife. In a pink dress patterned with huge roses, her blonde hair curling smoothly from beneath her round pink hat, Frances looked polished and serene. But those big, strange eyes of hers, how tragic they were!

And no wonder, Whitaker thought. The divorce from Earl Spencer had been spectacularly terrible. And most of that could be laid squarely at the door of the woman now following her, dressed in angelic white. He summoned up what he knew about Ruth Fermoy, Frances's mother, the Queen Mother's lady-in-waiting and old friend.

She had grown up a commoner, the daughter of a colonel from Aberdeen, and was tough as a pair of old army boots. A former concert pianist, she had married a lord herself and schemed ruthlessly for her daughter's upgrade to an earl. Johnnie Spencer had originally been engaged to Anne Coke, daughter of the Earl of Leicester, but Ruth had determinedly broken this up and manipulated him into marriage with Frances. When the marriage had collapsed, Ruth had been so determined for the children to stay with their father, she had colluded with the earl and testified in court that Frances was an unfit mother.

And here came wife number two. Whitaker watched, riveted, as Raine Spencer now floated up the steps. Her hair seemed styled by jet engine and her white foundation made her look like an ancient clown. She wore a rictus, red-lipsticked grin and a bouffant skirt almost as big as her hair.

But she was a tough cookie, no doubt about that. It was said that once Johnnie, with whom she had been having an affair for years, had finally succeeded to the title, Raine had bundled all her worldly goods into a horsebox and shot up to Althorp, abandoning her own husband and four children. A strange coincidence, given that Frances had been obliged to leave her own four children rather less willingly.

But when Johnnie had married Raine at the Caxton Hall register office, none of the couple's eight children had been present, or even told. They'd all seen it in his own paper, Whitaker recalled. With the exception of the boy, Charles, who had apparently learnt about it from his housemaster at school the day after it happened.

On her high, spiked heels, Raine clacked into the chapel behind Frances and Ruth Fermoy. It must, Whitaker guessed, be a constant torture for Ruth to see the ludicrous Raine, and not Frances, as Countess Spencer. But possibly even worse torture too to know that, following Sarah's comments in the press, there was no hope of her granddaughter being Princess of Wales.

However, someone was going to have to be, and soon. But who? It was the question that had kept journalists guessing for years.

Charlie Boy seemed to have been out with every eligible woman in Europe. Real stunners, too, some of them. Must have been a hell of a lot of fun, Whitaker reckoned, but the prince always looked so pained and put-upon. He seemed to take his privileges as rights, yet resent his obligations. It was partly to tease him that the *Express* had run that completely baseless front-page story last year about his relationship with the Princess of Luxembourg.

CHARLES TO MARRY ASTRID — OFFICIAL ENGAGEMENT
NEXT WEEK. SONS WILL BE PROTESTANTS,
DAUGHTERS CATHOLIC.

Charles' haughty public riposte, 'I have fallen in love with all sorts of girls and intend to go on doing so,' had not helped his cause.

Car doors were slamming. Royalty was arriving, the last of the guests, as protocol dictated. The cars, as ever, were timed to the second and in strict order of precedence. Next to last was the Queen Mother. Her Majesty arrived last of all.

They mustered on the chapel's wide white steps. The spring sunshine poured down. Somewhere in the distance, a military band was practising.

The Queen Mother inclined her upturned hat brim, a style unchanged since the dark days of the war. 'Lilibet,' she remarked, 'do listen. I think it's my regiment.'

The Queen turned from her conversation. 'Mummy, it is not,' she said firmly. 'It is mine. They all are.'

There was a ripple of polite laughter at this. Then came the signal that the congregation within the chapel was seated. The royal family now processed in.

The Queen Mother

She reached the front row and sat bolt upright, making no contact with the back of the pew. She had been taught, and taught her daughters, that a *lady never leans*. She bowed her head, muttered a prayer, then glanced about from under her hat brim.

Next to her was her old friend and lady-in-waiting. Dear Ruth. Some had judged her harshly about her treatment of Frances during that unfortunate divorce. But the Queen Mother took a pragmatic view. There were rules to their kind of life; never explaining or complaining being the main one. Frances had done a great deal of both. And Ruth was amusing and useful. Her musical connections meant that many a dreary evening was enlivened with little concerts. These things mattered when you had time on your hands.

She inspected the groom before her at the altar; dear Robert, loyal servant of the Crown. Satisfactory in all respects except one. He wasn't the man she wanted to watch getting married at the moment. That man was Charles.

A wave of exasperation broke over the Queen Mother. She adored her grandson, but it really was high time he found a wife. Charles had sowed his wild oats for long enough, to use that horrid phrase of Louis Mountbatten's. She felt exasperated when she thought of him too. Dickie Mountbatten had, for years, encouraged Charles to play the field and this had only made the situation worse.

Not that Dickie had cared. He had revelled in the influence he had exerted over the impressionable prince. Mountbatten had played the royal game to his advantage all his life, his only loyalty being to himself. Once the closest friend of King Edward VIII, he had switched sides like a shot to her husband George VI after the abdication in 1936.

The abdication. That was another worry. Edward VIII's shadow was long and growing longer, almost touching Charles now. He too had refused to marry when Prince of Wales. On becoming king, he had left the throne for that terrible woman. In doing so, he had all but destroyed the Crown, and with it, the Family. Nothing like that could ever be allowed to happen again.

The old queen's eye now caught the line of Union Jacks, ragged from the battlefield, that hung along the chapel sides. She raised her chin and felt an iron resolve. England expected. The Crown expected. Charles must find a suitable bride with all speed. Or one must be found for him.

And she must be a girl of impeccable background. With an impeccable past, as the euphemism went. The former was easy enough; the latter rather less so. Single ladies who were plausibly *intacta* were slightly thinner on the ground these days. Anyone near Charles' age who was still a virgin probably only existed in a sitcom.

'Which sitcom would that be?' Lilibet had enquired drily when the Queen Mother had said this some days ago, in the Windsor drawing room after dinner.

'You know what I mean, darling.'

'Charles needs to move his bloody arse,' Philip had growled irritably from behind his newspaper.

'Some plants need watering,' the Queen Mother had said. 'Some need to be forced.'

Her son-in-law had lowered his newspaper. 'What does *that* mean?'

She had given him a sweet smile. 'It means that we need to find a good-natured, suitable girl for Charles before she finds anyone else to fall in love with.'

'*Anyone else?*' Lilibet had echoed. 'Charles is the Prince of Wales.'

'Yes, but not every modern girl wants to marry a prince,' the old queen had countered. 'Charles has unfortunately coincided with a period of history when girls are liberated and lead free lives. These days, they are educated, go to university and have careers.'

'Bloody bra-burners,' Philip had muttered, raising his newspaper again.

'Now, Philip. I don't think any of them have *actually* burned their bras.'

'What on earth are you talking about?' Lilibet had asked.

The Wedding March struck up. Feeling Ruth flinch at wrong notes only she could hear, the old queen smiled to herself.

Jane Spencer walked slowly by on her father's arm; the earl, as ever, with an idiotic grin on his bright red face. 'The trouble with Johnnie, his brain's never been taken out of its box.' The old queen couldn't remember who had said it, but it was the perfect description.

Jane looked rather masculine, the Queen Mother thought. That lean, plain face, high-necked dress and thick, side-parted hair. Perhaps it was modern. Jane had some sort of job at *Vogue*, the fashion magazine, but the old queen doubted it was a serious one. And she would give it up now, of course.

Vogue had certainly gone downhill lately, if the bridesmaids' dresses were anything to go by. Quite ghastly. Even the small bridesmaids, who should look sweet in anything, looked awful.

And the poor grown-up bridesmaid! She walked by, bringing up the rear behind the little ones. It was the youngest Spencer girl. What was her name, again?

The old queen thought hard. She was sure Charles had mentioned her, briefly. They had met at some Althorp shooting weekend, presumably before her sister had said all those silly things to the newspapers. Poor Ruth had been mortified. As a courtier, she knew that tattling to the press was unforgivable.

The Queen Mother scrutinised the girl as she passed. About seventeen, and certainly no raving beauty. A better dress might have helped, but not this flowery claret print that was like curtain material, with flounces on the skirt and a terrible vest arrangement on top, with a puff-sleeve blouse. It gave her shoulders like a rugby player's. Her bunch of dark red roses brought out the high colour in her cheeks.

Unimpressed, the old queen was about to re-engage with her order of service when the girl turned her head and looked at her. It was just a sideways glance from under her eyelashes, but it made the Queen Mother sit up straighter. She noticed now what lovely thick blonde hair the girl had and, beneath the dress, the outline of long slim legs. She was prettier than she had first appeared.

The first hymn began. 'Praise My Soul the King of Heaven'. One of the old queen's favourites. As she succumbed to the wonderful, familiar tune, the beloved old words, the young Spencer faded from her mind.

Afterwards, outside the chapel, the Queen Mother positioned herself with the undemanding Duke and Duchess of Gloucester.

The Kents, as usual, were bickering, or rather Edward was bickering with poor Kate. Always so critical of her.

As Robert Fellowes' former regiment formed a guard of honour, the old queen decided to tease Richard of Gloucester's Danish wife. 'I do love a row of guardsmen, don't you, Birgitte?' she began, twinkling away beneath her hat brim. 'It reminds me so much of when I went to see dear Noel Coward at home in Jamaica in 1965.'

Birgitte smiled politely. 'Does it, ma'am?'

'Oh yes. We went to the theatre and there was such a lovely row of soldiers lined up to meet me. Noel was looking at them and I said, "Oh Noel, do be careful. They count them when they put them out, you know."'

As the Duchess of Gloucester puzzled over this, the old queen looked happily about. Someone was smiling at her. It was a very bright beam, rather dazzling. The little Spencer, she realised. She remembered the moment in the chapel, how she had thought her quite pretty, after all. She returned the smile and the girl approached.

Up close, her skin was marvellous; that wonderful creamy English sort that looked so perfect with ancestral jewels. Really, when you looked properly, she was quite charming. There was a delightful simplicity about her. One felt refreshed. If only, the old queen thought, she could remember her name.

'Diana, ma'am.'

'Of course. Charles mentioned you.'

At this, to the Queen Mother's surprise, the girl completely lit up. Blue eyes blazed in a face that was suddenly a bright, thrilled red.

'*Did* he?' she gasped. 'Did His Royal Highness, I mean – did he *really* mention me, ma'am?'

Her long-lashed eyelids fluttered; she looked as if she were about to faint. Gracious, thought the old queen.

'He did indeed.' The only problem was she could not remember what he had said. Amusing? Noisy? Jolly and bouncy? Bouncy and jolly? Something like that, she was sure.

'It was just the best moment of my life, meeting Prince Charles.' Diana spoke with a shy rapture. 'I think His Royal Highness is a truly wonderful person. The country is very lucky to have him.'

That was certainly Charles' view, of course.

The Queen Mother was paying very careful attention now. 'Tell me about your education, my dear. Are you one of those very brainy girls?' She profoundly hoped not.

A wry smile. 'Not exactly, ma'am. Failed most of my O levels, I'm afraid.'

The old queen wasn't entirely sure what O levels were. But the failure was the significant part. 'Don't be afraid,' she twinkled. 'Look at me. Hardly went to school at all and I've been Chancellor of London University for twenty-three years.'

Diana giggled. She explained that she had been at finishing school in Switzerland but had come back early. 'They all spoke French all the time, you see.'

'Ah, yes. I'm afraid that's rather the trouble with Switzerland.'

This produced another giggle. Usually the Queen Mother found giggles irritating, but not, as now, when conducting crucial investigations.

'Are you terribly political?' she asked lightly. 'So many young people are, I find. Those animal rights people. One has to keep all one's fur coats locked up or they might pour paint over one. Or set fire to one.'

'Oh no, ma'am. I'm not political at all.'

'And do you know Scotland?'

Scotland had been rather a problem of late. It seemed out of favour with modern youth. Quite a number of Charles' girlfriends hadn't seemed to like it at all. Which was slightly concerning, because where did that leave dear Balmoral?

'I *love* Scotland!'

The old queen smiled. By her reckoning, that was just about full marks.

Later, amid the red silk walls of St James's Palace, the Queen Mother continued to watch the girl closely. Diana, she saw, was remarkably good with small children. The little wedding attendants had been tired and fretful, but she had got them to line up beautifully for the photographer. There they stood, good as gold, against the room's gilded white double doors.

A footman now stepped forward to refill the Queen Mother's glass. She looked at him wryly. 'Rather a small gin, Len, if I may say so. Remember, I have my reputation to consider.'

'Oh Mummy, *really*,' said Lilibet, who was standing nearby. Then, as the footman hovered, she added, 'But, do you know, Len, I think I might have a top-up too.'

The old queen looked at her gravely. 'Should you, Lilibet? You do have to reign all afternoon.'

Was it, she wondered, time to draw her daughter's attention to the youngest Spencer girl? Too early perhaps. Lilibet liked things definite; cut and dried. And there had been many a slip, particularly when it came to Charles. But the old queen was interested. Very interested.

'I must congratulate you, Johnnie,' she said, as she left.

Earl Spencer bowed. 'Thank you, ma'am. We're all delighted for Jane.'

'I was referring to Diana.'

'Diana?' Amazement flashed briefly across the earl's puce features. He looked as if he couldn't remember who this was, which might have been the case.

'What an excellent job you have done, raising her. But you now have the most difficult part.' The old queen wagged a playful diamond-ringed finger. 'You must think of her future settlement in life.'

The blood drained from the earl's great red face.

Not long afterwards, as the car glided the short distance from St James's to her London home at Clarence House, the old queen decided to set the second hare running. She leant over to her old friend. 'What a very attractive girl Diana is,' she murmured, and pressed Ruth's white-gloved hand.

Lady Fermoy's eyes, large like her daughter's and grand-daughter's, shot wide.

Chapter Fourteen

Eaton Square, Knightsbridge, London

May 1978

Diana

She didn't come here very often and it had taken some time to find the right white-porticoed entrance amid so many that looked the same. Diana rang the polished bell with misgiving. Was she late? Had she done something wrong?

Grandmama had never previously taken the slightest notice of her. But then, Lady Fermoy's notice was not something one necessarily wished to attract. Her brother Charles attracted it at the recitals the siblings put on when she visited. No one was ever allowed to forget that Grandmama had once been a concert pianist.

As, with shaking hands and thundering hearts, the children performed, Grandmama sat opposite, critically attentive, wincing at wrong notes. Charles, possibly on purpose, played the most wrong notes of any of them.

Sarah, on the other hand, was the most musically talented. She would turn up without her music, then play her piece perfectly from memory. But she had, of course, hit the most monumental wrong note recently, in quite another context. The stories in the papers about Prince Charles had enraged the family and destroyed Sarah's chances of becoming Princess of Wales.

The door was opened by her grandmother's maid, who showed her into the drawing room. Diana waited, looking round. It was all so different from the cheerful chaos of her flat at Coleherne Court. Everything here was so tasteful and neat. A small, orderly fire burned in the grate. There were fresh flowers in big vases, plumped cushions and polished surfaces. Everything impeccably tidy, right down to the music stacked neatly on the shining grand piano.

Diana went over to it. She was quite good at piano, although nothing like Sarah.

The music on the stand was Debussy's 'Clair de Lune'. One of her favourite pieces: dreamy, romantic, a little sad. She let her fingers brush the ivory keys. They sprang to life with a soft ripple of notes. Encouraged, she shifted round the instrument, edged onto the seat, which was just the right height, and began to play.

She closed her eyes, as she always did. It was a miracle, it really was, how pieces of wood attached to wires and hammers could make such exquisite sound. Music was like Love; you couldn't see it, only feel it. Like Love, it was powerful and transformative. A kind of magic.

The beauty of the piece filled her heart and she played with all her soul. She particularly loved the ending, the way it slowed to a few high, pure notes, like drops of water in a china bowl.

There was a singing silence, then the sharp sound of one palm hitting another. 'Not bad,' said a familiar icy voice.

Diana scrambled up, insides jangling with fright. There stood her redoubtable grandmother, impeccable in a grey tweed suit. A discreet double row of pearls set off her still-handsome face with its elegant bone structure. There was something different about the face, something unusual. Gosh, yes. Grandmama was smiling.

'You have clearly inherited my talent,' she remarked.

'Oh Grandmama, hardly: I mean, I'm not likely to play at the Albert Hall like you, am I?'

'Perhaps not. Perhaps you are destined for something even greater.'

Diana giggled; a joke, surely.

But Grandmama was not smiling. She was looking at her hands. 'Bitten nails! They will never do!'

Do for what, Diana wondered, as Lady Fermoy assembled herself on the sofa next to the marble fireplace and patted the cushion next to her.

'Come and sit down, my dear.'

My dear?! Had Grandmama ever called her this before?

As her grandmother watched her approach, Diana squirmed inwardly. She had not known what to wear for this unexpected and august occasion, so her outfit was a hastily thrown-together hodgepodge of her own and her flatmates' clothes. Not all fitted as well as they might. Anne's tweed skirt was a bit tight, Carolyn's good blouse a bit big and Virginia's clip-on gold earrings threatened to slip off.

Lady Fermoy put a long-fingered hand to her pearl-strung throat. 'You must be wondering why I've asked you here, my dear.'

Diana swallowed. Was her grandmother cross about her O levels? Her failure to stay the course at Videmanette, the finishing school? No one else in the family had mentioned these, but no one in the family ever mentioned anything, or took much notice of her at all.

'I wanted to talk to you about Jane's wedding.'

Jane's wedding? That already seemed ages ago, like all things to which you keenly looked forward, only for them to be over in a flash. She had enjoyed it immensely, even though her bridesmaid's dress had been horribly frumpy.

The whole wedding was frumpy, but that was Jane and Robert all over. They were steady and sensible, not the exuberant, romantic sort, except in one respect perhaps. In *Search For Love*, Vanda Sudbury and the Earl of Cunningham had grown up together like brother and sister, just as Jane and Robert had. But, really, that was about it.

'What about Jane's wedding?' she asked.

'Someone you spoke to there.'

A freezing fear seized Diana's spine. The journalist who had written about Sarah had been at Jane's wedding. She had met him by the chapel entrance. He was called James Whitaker and he was not as she had expected. She had imagined someone like the evil Marquis of Buckbury in *The House of Happiness*, with his duelling scar and his cruel black eyes. But Mr Whitaker was plump, with a friendly, toothy face. He reminded her of Little Black Muff, her favourite hamster. Diana had introduced herself and they had had a brief chat. She sensed that Mr Whitaker had been surprised by her friendliness, but she didn't hold his article against him. Sarah had never pretended to be in love with the Prince of Wales. She had said she wasn't many times, but no one had wanted to listen.

The rest of the family had been furious about the story, even so. Perhaps it had been disloyal to talk to the man who had written it. She hung her head. 'Sorry, Grandmama.'

'Sorry for what? You may be in a position to bring great honour on the family.'

Diana's head flew up in astonishment. '*Me?!*'

Lady Fermoy smiled. 'I'm referring to your conversation with Her Majesty Queen Elizabeth.'

Oh yes. The Queen Mother. 'She was very friendly,' Diana said.

'*Her Majesty* was very friendly,' her grandmother corrected.

'Her Majesty was very friendly.'

'You impressed Her Majesty very much,' Lady Fermoy went on.

Diana couldn't see how. The conversation had been entirely about her failures: at exams, at Videmanette.

'Her Majesty was particularly impressed with what you said about the Prince of Wales.'

Diana felt the blood swirl hotly to her face. She had raved about him, she knew. Gone on and on, like a lovesick schoolgirl. But then, a lovesick schoolgirl was how she felt when she thought about the Prince of Wales. Their first exchange in the ploughed field as the guns went off; his heart-tugging frankness about school over lunch; gazing at him in the candlelight of the Althorp State Dining Room. It made her insides felt like swirling glitter. Like the snow-globes she and her flatmates liked to collect, along with cushions with amusing slogans.

'Her Majesty is very occupied with the question of who the prince will marry,' her grandmother went on. She pursed her lips. 'Sarah, of course, has removed herself from consideration.'

Diana nodded. She couldn't see what any of this had to do with her.

'But it is possible, and Her Majesty certainly thinks so, that another member of our family might do very well indeed.'

A meaningful silence followed this. Diana frowned, still uncomprehending. 'Who, Grandmama?'

Lady Fermoy's eyes drilled into her own. 'You, Diana.'

It was quiet and still in the flat as it was, but now things stopped altogether. 'Princess of *Wales?*' she spluttered. 'Me?'

'It's certainly a possibility.'

Diana was all hot, stammering excitement. She was shaking, her teeth were chattering, her heart leapt and soared. 'Oh, *Grandmama!*'

'I am not saying it is certain to happen,' Lady Fermoy went on coolly. 'And even if it does, it may take many years. There could be setbacks along the way.'

Diana nodded eagerly. She was ready to endure all things, all delays, all setbacks. The heroines in her novels always did. Love was never easy. There were always difficulties to overcome. That was how you knew it was Love.

'Nothing is ever certain with His Royal Highness. There's many a slip betwixt cup and lip, as we say in Scotland.'

'I understand, Grandmama.'

'And you must be absolutely certain that this is what you want. We can't have you making the same mistake as your mother.'

Diana swallowed. This was difficult. With regard to Mummy, Grandmama stood accused of terrible things. Of scheming the marriage with Daddy. Of lying in court so she lost custody of her children. But what was the truth? It was almost too terrifying to ask, but it suddenly seemed very important to know. Mustering every scrap of courage, she raised her head, looked her grandmother in the eye.

'Before I answer your question, Grandmama, can I ask one of my own?'

The white head inclined. 'By all means.'

'May I ask why you spoke against Mummy in court?'

Her words seemed to crash like rocks in the silence. Her grandmother did not flinch, however, and met Diana's scared gaze with a flinty one of her own. For a long minute or two, she said nothing. Then, finally, she spoke.

'The life your mother chose had rules, but she failed to observe them. There are rules to royal life too. And the main one is this, once you enter it you can never, ever go back. So you need to be completely sure. Do you want to, or don't you?'

Diana did not hesitate. 'I do want to, Grandmama.' She gazed at the old lady as if she were a fairy who could grant her dearest wish. Which it was. There was nothing she wanted more. Royal life meant not only marrying Charles, but finally proving her worth to her family. Her siblings would be impressed; her father delighted. Raine would be put firmly in her place. As for her mother, it would be some compensation for the betrayal, ostracism and disappointment of so many years.

Lady Fermoy nodded. 'Well, in that case, you had better prepare yourself.'

'In what way, Grandmama?' She had visions of white robes, perfumed oil, garlands of flowers.

'You are a virgin, I take it?'

The question, and its abrupt delivery, was astonishing. 'A *virgin*, Grandmama?' Briefly, she imagined her flatmates hearing this and screeching. They often talked about boys, about sex too, and teased her for not joining in. Or for not fancying any of the young men who came to visit them at their Kensington apartment block. Friends of friends, friends of brothers, they were from the same type of families as the girls themselves and known as the Coleherne Courtiers.

'You absolutely must be a virgin,' Lady Fermoy said sternly. 'Anything else is out of the question.'

'I understand, Grandmama.' Which she did, completely. The heroines of romantic novels were always virgins. The reward of Chastity was always Love. Diana could not recall a time when this had not been a guiding truth, and it was because of this she had never joined in the Coleherne Court boy-talk. Or been attracted to the eligible visitors, though she liked them well enough. It was why she had always somehow felt apart, as if her destiny was different and she was waiting for something. Well she had been, and here it was.

Lady Fermoy's hard face softened into a smile. 'Good. You will start receiving invitations. The first will be His Royal Highness's birthday ball at Buckingham Palace.'

Diana gasped softly. She had seen Sarah's huge, grand invitation and been deeply envious. And now she would go herself. Like Cinderella, released from the shadows of the hearthside and stepping finally onto centre stage.

Chapter Fifteen

Buckingham Palace, London
November 1978
Stephen

'When will I see you again . . .?'

The great nineteenth-century ballroom thumped to the sound of the Three Degrees, the prince's favourite girl group, flown in from Philadelphia especially. It was the most lavish party the royal family had thrown for fifty years; a spectacular fusion of traditional and modern. Disco lights flashed on massive chandeliers. The sprung wooden dance floor, on which Victoria herself had once waltzed, shuddered to the stomps of girls in sequinned dresses and men in flared trousers. In their midst, the now thirty-year-old heir to the throne bopped in his trademark awkward manner, with one beautiful woman after another.

As the prince's valet, Stephen Barry was not, strictly speaking, a guest. During his ten years in the job, however, he had come to regard parties like this as one of its perks. One of many.

Whenever anyone asked Stephen what a valet actually did, his standard answer was that it was to supervise every detail of the prince's colossal wardrobe. This included forty-three uniforms plus medals and other decorations, dozens of suits and hundreds of shirts, silk ties and shoes hand-made in Jermyn Street.

But, in truth, clothes were only part of it. What Stephen did was actually full-on lifestyle management and he was rarely off duty. Royal service allowed for no home life, no private life. The prince's life was his life, and Stephen, accompanying his master, had stayed in castles in Spain, palaces in France, presidential mansions and ambassadorial residences. And the stateliest stately homes of England, of course. Throughout it all, the maintenance of the royal love life had been of paramount concern.

It had started as an accidental and ad hoc arrangement; the prince asking him to arrange an intimate supper here, or warn the duty policeman about a lady visitor there. But such was his efficiency, his talent for unobtrusiveness, that Stephen's management of the prince's romances had become as important as the management of his clothes. Whenever someone new came on the scene, he organised them, arranged arrival times, told them where in the Palace courtyard to park and at which Palace entrance to present themselves.

Meeting them and taking them up to the prince's private apartment was also part of his duties, as was co-ordinating the champagne, candles and simple cold supper. Afterwards, it was he who emerged from the shadows and escorted them back out. For as long – or short – as the relationship ran, it was Stephen who ran it. Ran them. The girls.

And he had run a great many of the girls here. Below him on the dance floor was the whole history of the prince's love life, more or less.

The vivid dark-haired girl dancing directly below Stephen, for instance, was Lady Jane Wellesley. The Duke of Wellington's assured, TV-producer daughter had been hotly tipped for a while. A lovely girl, kind and funny, and what a lifestyle. Stephen thought of the magnificent Spanish estate, given to the first Duke of Wellington for defeating Napoleon. The prince, partridge shooting in full tweeds in the hot, dry landscape. The Guardia Civil, following them in their funny hats.

Davina Sheffield had just whirled into view, a lovely blonde with a sweet smile. She had got as far as lunch with the Queen, a rare distinction. The prince had seemed genuinely smitten. But then into their fairy tale had appeared a villain in the unlikely shape of one James Beard, an old Harrovian boat designer. Stephen sighed at the memory. After Beard had told the press about their affair, conducted in what was described as a 'rose-covered cottage', poor Davina had been dropped like a stone.

And speaking of Stones, Rolling ones, here was Sabrina Guinness. The heiress and socialite had been something of a step change. Her fashionable Chelsea lifestyle and celebrity connections had fascinated the prince. It had all gone wrong at Balmoral, but she had come tonight and was dancing away with clearly no hard feelings.

A purple disco light now caught Susan George. The petite blonde actress had, Stephen remembered, been particularly pleasant and easy to deal with. Her family had lived near Windsor, so her father had driven her in for dinners and picked her up afterwards. Saved Stephen considerable effort, he had.

But it seemed a shame, as well as a wasted opportunity, that Susan was ultimately ruled out because of her profession. Charles had been quite keen, although his approbation counted for little. The final decision was always made by his relatives.

But with Susan they might just have slipped up, because what better qualification than acting could there be for royal life? The main skill was having to pretend to enjoy oneself. 'I've perfected the art of sleeping with my eyes open,' the prince would say wearily. 'Along with standing still for hours and never being ill: it's a crucial skill if you have the misfortune to be royal.'

Leaning over the balustrade, Stephen continued to survey the floor. Every woman the prince had ever known seemed to be here. Apart from the Aussies in bikinis, perhaps. He recalled his master's bitter complaints about them. 'Those women that run out of the sea and grab me, did you know they actually *pay* them?'

Well obviously, Stephen would think. Did he really imagine the girls would do it spontaneously?

'Those women actually make *money* out of me!'

Possibly that was what annoyed him most. The prince was very cost-conscious. The girls he went out with were rarely even sent flowers – Stephen knew, because he was the one who rarely sent them – and never jewellery or anything expensive. And once one relationship ended, another immediately started. A never-ending stream of willing girls, all of whom Stephen took charge of. Most were very pleasant. One or two had been rude, calling him 'Buttons'. But that was mostly once the affair had cooled, and they were venting their frustrations.

An untidy-looking blonde was dancing in the centre of a group of men. Camilla Parker Bowles was presumably up from the wilds of Wiltshire. She was from the prince's distant past, and yet he had been at the time quite attached.

Why, exactly, was anyone's guess. No one could accuse her of being beautiful, and the years had added neither polish nor finesse. Camilla still had gap teeth, messy hair and seemed to get her clothes from jumble sales. Even the ball gown she wore tonight – green, flouncy, generally unflattering – looked as if it might have belonged to someone else first. You would have thought she might try harder for a ball at the Palace, Stephen mused. Still, why change the habits of a lifetime?

Funny, but at one stage, he had suspected the prince wanted to marry Camilla. Out of the question, of course. She was not only a commoner, but had had many boyfriends; A Past, as the euphemism had it. In the end, Camilla had married Andrew

Parker Bowles and the prince had joined the Navy. That ship had sailed, in more senses than just one.

Stephen now spotted Laura Jo Watkins, the American admiral's daughter, and Leonora Lichfield, sister of Gerald Grosvenor. Two more exes, neither serious.

But someone had to be. Tonight marked the prince's thirtieth birthday. He had always said he would get married at thirty. The clock at the ball was approaching midnight. Like it or lump it, Prince Charming – or Prince Charles – had to find a princess.

Expectation was mounting. The country longed for a wedding – the last, Princess Anne's, had been five years ago. And the Queen's Silver Jubilee celebrations the previous summer had created an appetite for more royal pomp and ceremony. The prince, predictably, resented this. 'It's just ridiculous!' he would complain. 'I've only got to *look* at a girl and everyone starts hearing wedding bells!'

The royal family in particular did, Stephen knew. They longed for a wedding; the prince, in their view, was too old to be still single. The last Prince of Wales had been the dreaded Edward VIII, who had remained unmarried until age forty-three, when his wedding almost sank the monarchy. The Windsors were starting to worry; Stephen had increasingly, in the course of his duties, seen concerned looks from the prince's mother and frankly irritated ones from his father.

The prince resented those as well. 'They just don't understand,' Stephen had heard him moan. 'I can't just marry, just like that. I have to make sure I make the right decision. It's the very last thing in which my heart should rule my head. Marriage is a much more important business than just falling in love.'

A pretty redhead now caught Stephen's eye. Sarah Spencer, she of the notorious interview. There she was, bopping away under the glitterballs with a chinless wonder, apparently without a care in the world. But the valet well remembered how she had rung up the Palace in a flap. The story was yet to hit the presses, but he could tell something was wrong by her voice. Accordingly, he had remained on the line after he put her through to his master.

'I think I've just done something very stupid, sir,' he had heard Sarah shakily tell the prince.

'Oh yes?' came the guarded royal reply. 'What have you done?'

'I've just given an interview to James Whitaker of the *Express*.'

A pause, then the freezing riposte. 'Yes, Sarah. You have done something extremely stupid.' The royal receiver was then slammed down, the royal drawbridge yanked up, and that was the end of the Spencer family's hopes of alliance with the House of Windsor.

The Three Degrees had gone for a break and a disco had replaced them. 'You're The One That I Want', from *Grease*, now filled the ballroom.

A girl in a pale pink dress was moving through the crowd. Very young, Stephen noted, much younger than the others here. After a struggle with his memory, he realised it was Sarah Spencer's little sister. What was her name?

He had met her at the Althorp shoot; she had loaded for her father while he had loaded for the prince. The prince had sat next to her at lunch. 'Nice girl,' he had said afterwards. 'Very jolly and bouncy.'

Stephen remembered her quite well. Nice enough, but nothing special. She'd been about sixteen but seemed younger. Tomboyish. Just a big kid really.

Following her progress round the dance floor, he saw that she had improved quite a lot since then. She had lost weight and stood taller. She must be about eighteen now. He vaguely wondered what she was doing at the ball; she wasn't an ex, like her sister.

Or like him, pretty soon, no doubt. He, too, was about to be dispensed with; his days were definitely numbered. He straightened up and looked about him, relishing the magnificent surroundings he so loved and to which, over more than a decade, he had become so accustomed. His lifestyle was, quite literally, palatial; maids cleaned his beautiful rooms, at the back of Buckingham Palace, overlooking forty acres of lush garden. Gold-buttoned footmen ran his errands. His laundry was sent and delivered back, perfectly pressed, twice a week. He used the Palace post office. The royal garage looked after his car. The Household dining room was like a St James's club, complete with paintings of horses and a bar with subsidised drinks. By way of contrast, but no less enjoyably, the servants' floor, far away from the royal apartments, could be like a West End disco, parties going on all night.

But how much longer would he be able to enjoy it all? For the past ten years, the princely failure to find a bride had suited Stephen perfectly. It had ensured he kept his position. But once Charles chose a princess, it would all be over. Because the wife didn't exist who would want him hanging about.

Chapter Sixteen

Sandringham House, Norfolk

January 1979

Stephen

In the vast red-brick Edwardian mansion, four o'clock was being announced in tinkles and bongs. Outside, night had already fallen. Golden light from huge windows streamed across the dark gardens. Inside, at the far end of the huge entrance hall, a fire danced in the great mock-mediaeval hearth. Sitting beside it were the prince and his grandmother. He leant forward tensely, smart in a tweed jacket and tie. She sat back smiling, feminine in a lavender twinset and a triple row of magnificent pearls.

As the mantlepiece clock completed its sequence of silvery notes, the old queen put her head benignly to one side. 'Did you know,' she enquired of her grandson, 'that Sandringham used to have its own time zone? Half an hour ahead of the rest of the world, so the shooting day could go on longer.'

From the other side of the fireplace, the prince gave her an uneasy smile. 'I did know that, Granny.'

Of course he did, everyone did, thought Stephen. Sandringham Time, it was called. An attempt by the monarch to control the hours in the day, along with everything else.

The valet stood in the recess beside the green baize table on which the scattered pieces of a jigsaw were laid out. He had never been able to work out what the picture was, there being no box about to explain. A puzzle with all the clues removed. Rather like royalty sometimes.

'A charming tradition,' the Queen Mother went mildly on. 'But one that ended rather abruptly when David became King. Can you believe it, it was actually his first act. "Put those bloody clocks right," he said.' She gave a bemused smile and shook her head slightly.

The prince looked down at his teacup. He would, Stephen knew, have effortlessly decoded this. Any mention of David, the name by which Edward VIII was known to the family, was a mention of the terrible crimes against the Crown committed by that reprehensible monarch. Chief among which had been his failure to marry suitably.

The prince, for all his promises about finding a bride, was yet to do anything of the sort. His thirtieth birthday had come and gone and no suitable candidate had emerged.

Even his devoted, indulgent grandmother was getting to the end of her tether. And, in her case, it was more than just impatience. Her hated rival, Lord Mountbatten, had recently stepped into the breach with his own candidate: his granddaughter Amanda Knatchbull.

The old queen fiercely resented this; it wasn't the first time Mountbatten had tried to advance his own family. Decades ago, Dickie had unleashed his dashing nephew on her eldest daughter. Nor had that been all. Not content with Philip bagging Lilibet, the self-aggrandising earl had tried to change the royal family's name to his own. She'd had to get Churchill on side to sort that out, the old queen mused. It had been a damn close-run thing.

And here was another. As she had yet to produce a candidate of her own, Mountbatten looked set, once again, to take the field. A generation after Philip had been aimed at Lilibet, Amanda Knatchbull was being aimed at Lilibet's son.

Stephen was a first-hand witness to this pressure on the prince. Every few days, a footman appeared with a silver salver on which lay a letter from Broadlands, Mountbatten's Hampshire mansion. The prince would receive it with a groan and read it with a worried expression. Once he was out of the way, Stephen would read it too. Written in a furious black scrawl, it would be full of urgings about Amanda.

And Mountbatten was not someone who expected his urgings to be ignored. During the war, he had commanded the Royal Navy and afterwards been India's last viceroy, overseeing the partition of India and Pakistan. Accustomed to deciding the fate of millions, and having arranged one successful royal marriage already, he naturally expected his nephew and granddaughter to jump to it.

The prince had duly, if unenthusiastically, jumped. Stephen had, with his customary subtlety, made the usual arrangements with Amanda, a pleasant and polite brunette who seemed similarly resigned to her fate. At the moment, this was how things stood.

While he waited for Charles to reply to his grandmother, perhaps even to explain about Amanda, Stephen glanced at the terrifying pikestaffs on the wall beside the portraits of a smug Victoria and a baleful Albert. Not for the first time, he tried to imagine how a place like this might seem to a modern young woman. What girl of 1979, even Amanda, would appreciate an Edwardian weighing machine greeting her at the entrance, with a leather-bound book next to it containing the arriving and departing weights of guests ranging from the kaiser to the last tsar of Russia? Hopefully none, Stephen thought. And then he could keep his job.

The duty footman was now pouring the tea. Stephen watched him closely. In normal circumstances, he wouldn't be standing here like this, but there was a handsome young page whose training he had offered to help with. Charles, accustomed to his valet's inclinations, had wearily given permission for Stephen to supervise his protégé's serving of the royal Earl Grey and finger sandwiches.

The session was not going well, however. The old queen did not seem to have especially taken to young Martin. One sign was her insistence on calling him Mark. She never got staff names wrong – unless she meant to.

Stephen had personally overseen, earlier in the kitchen, the making of the Queen Mother's beloved smoked-salmon sandwiches. That Martin knew something was wrong was obvious. Accordingly, he was terrified. His hand was shaking as it poured tea from the silver pot into the delicate cup beside the Queen Mother. She looked at it. 'Tell me, Mark, is that Earl Grey?'

There was an audible swallow from the young footman before he answered, in his broad northern accent, 'Yes, Yer Majesty.'

The Queen Mother smiled graciously. 'Do you know, it's my least favourite?'

It bloody well wasn't, as Stephen knew. The old bat drank gallons of the stuff usually. She was being awkward on purpose. But why?

Martin's shaking hand was now proffering the plate of smoked-salmon sandwiches. The old queen regarded them benignly. 'No thank you, Mark. Do you know, and this is an odd coincidence, but they are my least favourite too!'

Oh God, thought Stephen, keeping his gaze on the stone floor to avoid meeting the prince's furious glare. Anything that upset his beloved grandmother upset him ten times more.

Martin, who had panic-tripped over the rug as he exited in search of alternative teas and sandwiches, now came stumbling back in. The old queen cast him an impatient glance. Then she aimed a dazzling beam at her grandson.

'Charles, dear,' she said casually, head at a genial tilt. 'You will never guess who I saw this morning at Ruth Fermoy's.'

The prince looked relieved at the change of subject. 'Who, Granny?'

'Diana Spencer. Ruth's granddaughter.'

As the prince nodded vaguely, Stephen remembered the young girl at the ball. Her name had escaped him, but it had been Diana, of course.

'A most delightful young lady,' the old queen continued absently. 'She may be a shy little ugly duckling now, but she could be turned into a beautiful swan. She is unspoilt. Quite unspoilt.'

'Such a pity the tea was ruined,' moaned the prince on his return from taking his grandmother back to her suite. 'Her Majesty Queen Elizabeth had a message for you, Stephen.'

'For me, sir?' The valet's knees weakened. Was he about to get his marching orders even earlier than he imagined?

'Yes, Stephen. She asks that instead of just guessing, would you please ring William and find out exactly what she likes?'

Chapter Seventeen

Gate Lodge, Clarence House, London
January 1979
Stephen

Backstairs Billy, as William Tallon was known, had been the old queen's Page of the Backstairs even longer than Stephen had been the prince's valet. Their relationship thus far had been distant, reflecting the caution, even suspicion, of rival royal establishments. Tallon's home, Gate Lodge, stood at the entrance to Clarence House and was a tiny version of the main building, right down to the porticoed entrance. The sitting-room walls, crowded with photographs of the royal family and Tallon's friends in showbusiness, had a claustrophobic effect. There were ornaments everywhere, and a great many small sofas and chairs. Billy, in the Astaire-esque white tie and tails he wore on duty, occupied one of the former. Stephen, in a suit, sat in one of the latter. 'Send in the Clowns' was emoting from the record player.

Tallon swilled the brandy in his cut-glass balloon. 'So there,' he said conversationally, 'was Moll, wandering down the Balmoral corridor with this long trail of bog roll dangling out of the back of her dress. Servants all too terrified to say anything. In the end, I had to tiptoe up behind and stand on the loose end.'

Stephen laughed obediently. Billy had an apparently inexhaustible fund of risqué anecdotes about his employer, whom he called Midnight Moll because of the late hours she kept. The Queen, meanwhile, was Betty Battenberg. It was all very amusing. But when, the valet wondered, was Tallon going to get to the point?

'Well,' said Billy, stretching out long legs in black trousers, 'you *are* a sweetie to come and see me.'

Stephen recognised the cue. He put down his brandy balloon. 'You want to talk about sandwiches, I understand.'

'Sandwiches?' Tallon drawled. 'I hardly think so, dear boy. That was just a pretext. Moll requires your assistance, but not in the field of afternoon comestibles.'

A wave of bitter triumph went through Stephen. He'd *known* the old bat was up to something with the Earl Grey and smoked salmon. 'What sort of help?'

'Send In The Clowns' had finished. Billy stood up and replaced the needle.

'Help with Amanda Knatchbull,' he said, as it began again.

Stephen was mystified. 'She hardly needs help from me. She's got her grandfather helping her.'

'That's exactly the problem, dear boy. While no one's keener than Moll to see Charles married, it will be to a Mountbatten over her dead body.'

'But what can I do about it?'

Tallon swilled his brandy glass again. 'To borrow one of those naval metaphors so beloved of Uncle Dickie, we need to sink the good ship *Knatchbull* and replace it with HMS *Spencer*.'

Stephen had just taken a sip of brandy. It hit the back of his throat, and he coughed, explosively. 'What? *Diana* Spencer? Lady Diana Spencer?'

'Moll thinks she's a winner. Blonde, Protestant, aristocratic.'

'And about ten,' Stephen said.

'Eighteen, to be precise.'

'Charles is *thirty*.'

'Yes, and she's crackers about him.'

'Oh, for goodness' sake, Tallon. Lady Diana's a *child*.'

'Exactly,' said Billy. 'A child can be taught. Moulded.'

The valet stared at the carpet. He wasn't sure he liked the sound of this. 'How do you know she's crackers about him?'

'She told Moll at some wedding. Quite an outburst, apparently. Said Chuck was the most wonderful person she had ever met. Unbelievable, no?'

'He's not that bad,' Stephen said, stung into loyalty.

'If you say so, dear boy. Still making you iron his shoelaces?'

Stephen regretfully admitted this was the case.

'Oh well, he can't be seen to be slumming it.'

'Send in the Clowns' had now finished again, so Billy got up from his armchair and restarted it. It was the fourth time.

'But,' said Stephen, 'what makes you think Charles has any interest in Diana?'

'Nothing,' said Tallon. 'Chocolate?' After selecting a strawberry cream, Billy proffered the box to Stephen.

Stephen picked a hazelnut and looked Tallon in the eye. 'But isn't it a problem, Charles not being interested?'

'Not at all,' Billy said gaily. 'He just needs to be *made* interested.'

'I still don't see what that has to do with me.'

The Page of the Backstairs snorted. 'Dear boy, it has everything to do with you. You handle the women. You're the royal procurer.'

'Lady Diana isn't a woman, she's a girl,' Stephen objected, stung at this offensive description of himself. 'I can't *make* Charles like her,' he added, exasperated.

Tallon picked out another strawberry cream. 'You can make him like Amanda less, though. Phase her out of the picture.'

'No, I can't.'

Billy's eyes narrowed. 'You better had. Otherwise, things might become, how should I put it? Difficult?'

Stephen was incredulous. 'Are you threatening me?'

Tallon shrugged frock-coated shoulders. 'I'm just saying remember what happened to Miss Guinness.'

As if I could, Stephen thought. Sabrina Guinness's visit to Balmoral had been ruined from the start, when she was surrounded by press on arrival at Aberdeen airport. Prince Philip had been apoplectic and Charles embarrassed. Sabrina had arrived to a stony reception and Stephen had later had a stony meeting with Charles and been asked to account for the incident. He had been unable to explain how the newspapers had got hold of the story.

Now, however, he felt he might have an inkling. 'Do you mean,' he asked Tallon, 'that *you* told the press she was there?'

Billy just smiled and eyed Stephen over his joined fingertrips.

Stephen didn't like the look. He glanced away to the wall of photographs. He realised that one he had thought was the Queen Mother was actually Billy in one of her hats.

'And there's another thing,' Tallon said.

'Another?' Stephen hadn't agreed to the first yet, and had no intention of doing so.

'To get over the finish line, and succeed where everyone else has failed, dear Diana needs a little light training in the ways of the Windsors.' Billy paused for a couple of beats. 'A tiny leg-up over the various obstacles.'

'Obstacles?'

'Polo, Cowes, Balmoral. The usual rings of fire.'

'Can't anyone else help?' Stephen asked desperately. 'Her sisters?'

'You are joking, dear boy. Lady Sarah was dumped from a great height by His Royal Highness, don't forget. And Lady

Jane's husband is Betty Battenberg's Assistant Private Secretary. Which rather complicates things.'

'Why does it complicate things?'

'Because Betty doesn't like getting involved. Prefers others to do the dirty work.'

'What about Lady Fermoy?'

'Even she can't be there all the time. You're the only one who goes everywhere and sees everything. That's why it has to be you. Tip her the wink, keep her on the straight and narrow. Be Henry Higgins to her Eliza Doolittle.'

The comparison seemed fatuous to Stephen. Higgins was posh and Eliza common. This situation was the complete reverse.

'Not really,' Billy countered. 'It's all about knowledge. Knowledge is power, dear boy. And no one knows Chuck as well as you do. Probably not even Chuck. You just need to teach her all about him. It's in your interest, after all.'

'It bloody isn't, I'd be digging my own grave,' Stephen riposted. 'Once she got the job, the first thing any Princess of Wales would do is fire the valet. It's far too close a relationship. I wake him up, draw his bath, choose his clothes, even put the toothpaste on his toothbrush.'

Tallon beamed with his large white wolfish teeth. 'Dear boy, that slip of a thing won't fire you. She couldn't fire a match.'

Stephen stood up. 'I'm not sure I can help you.'

'As you like,' said Tallon, showing him out. 'But don't say you weren't warned.'

One week later

Stephen stood before his master in his Buckingham Palace apartment. The prince had chosen the décor himself: hessian walls and small framed views of Scotland. The collected works of Laurens van der Post stood to attention in the bookcases. As ever, the room was freezing. The prince's loathing of heat, plus his natural parsimony, meant an arctic blast would have to blow down the Mall for even one bar of the electric fire to go on.

Stephen's discomfort now, though, had nothing to do with temperature.

'I just don't know what's *wrong* with you, Stephen!' The prince sat behind his desk, his expression the familiar combination of weary and irritated. Spread before him were the blue pouches containing his official mail.

The valet shuffled from polished shoe to polished shoe. 'As I said, sir, I'm most dreadfully sorry.'

'Sorry's not really good enough though, is it?'

'Not it's not, sir, and I'm sorry, as I—'

'Just stop saying you're sorry!'

'Yes, sir. Sorry . . .'

The prince shook a sheet of notepaper covered in a familiar angry black scrawl. 'Lord Mountbatten is furious. He blames me for it all. But it's your fault!'

Stephen bristled at the unfairness. He had made all the arrangements with his usual care and attention to detail. Covent Garden had been notified that the Royal Box was required. The footmen had been sent from the Palace, along with crystal, linen, flowers, silver and an intimate dinner for two. Dame Joan Sutherland, Charles' favourite soprano, had been primed to come for coffee after the final curtain. Cars had been arranged there and back. It had all been organised down to the last monogrammed napkin.

But something – everything – had gone wrong. Transport had failed to turn up, food had not been ready, dates had been confused. The end result was that the prince, instead of a glamorous night at the opera, had enjoyed supper at the Palace with his parents. Which, given his marital procrastinations, was hardly his idea of fun at the moment.

'You completely cocked it up,' his master accused.

How exactly Tallon had done it, Stephen was not sure, but done it he most certainly had. There had been counterbriefings, rescinded orders, a whole programme of scuppering best-laid plans.

'For some reason, Amanda thought it was tomorrow,' the prince whinged. 'But as you know perfectly well, Stephen, I'm going to the Albert Hall then to address the Institute of Directors.'

Stephen did know perfectly well. The prince had been sweating over the speech for days. He himself had had to listen to large chunks of it, then assure his master that Shakespeare could not have done better.

'You know, Stephen, I've fired valets for less.'

'Yes, sir,' the valet began, but could not quite finish. His throat had blocked. He felt he might burst into tears. Of course, this wonderful life would come to an end eventually. But not quite yet, and not in such ignominious circumstances.

Perhaps the prince, in the midst of his self-righteous fury, sensed something of this. 'All right,' he said, reluctantly. 'One last chance. This had better not happen again though. You have been warned.'

'It won't, sir,' Stephen assured him. He had been warned, indeed.

Chapter Eighteen

Kensington Palace, London

April 1992

Sandy

The pasta was ready. I'd cleared up the mess, set more water to boil and found everything I needed in the well-stocked kitchen cupboards. Having thrown together a hasty sauce, I found and set out plates, spoons and forks while Diana sat talking at the kitchen counter. But she had not spoken for several minutes now. She didn't react as I set a steaming plate of puttanesca before her.

What she had said had astonished me. The aim had not been two people's happiness but a royal dynasty's survival. It reminded me of the Medicis, the Borgias and the Tudors; families who'd stopped at nothing to maintain their power and used their children like chess pieces. Diana too had been a pawn in a game and the players had ranged from the mother of the monarch to the heir to the throne's valet.

'Is that *really* what happened?' I asked, pulling up the stool opposite her. It was all so far from how it had seemed at the time. 'This Stephen Barry stuff?'

The name seemed to bring her back from somewhere very far away. 'Oh yes,' she said. 'He told me all about it, later, when . . .' She paused. 'When he was ill. But when I first met Stephen properly, I was living in Coleherne Court.'

The Sloaney Kensington flat, of course. 'How many of you were there again?'

'Four,' Diana said wistfully. 'The Four Musketeers, we called ourselves. All for one and one for all. We really looked out for each other. Real family, we were.'

I felt a twinge of jealousy. I had been her family once, of course. 'Who were they, again?'

'Ginny, Caro, Anne. Oh, and Batercia.'

'Batercia?' Sloanes, I knew, could be called odd things, but even so.

'The goldfish. His name was actually Battersea, but we pronounced it Batercia, for fun.' She smiled sadly, as if fun was a distant memory now.

'Must have been a big flat.' With or without a goldfish, four girls would take up a lot of space.

'It was lovely,' Diana sighed. 'My sister Sarah found it. She was working at Savills, the estate agent's. I bought it with money I was left in a will. I was the landlady, the Chief Chick.'

'Chief *Chick*?' I was mildly appalled.

She gave a mock groan. 'Don't come over all feminist on me, Sandy. It was all very egalitarian. Everyone pitched in. "From each according to his ability, to each according to his needs."'

The quote was from Marx. I had forgotten how quick-witted she could be.

'I did all the rotas for cleaning and if people didn't stick to them, I used to get quite cross.' She chuckled at the memory. 'I *so* loved living at Coleherne Court. It was such a laugh. Everyone rushing about borrowing each other's clothes and shouting to stop hogging the bathroom. Every weekend going to bollocks and high spotties.'

'*What?*'

136

'Balls and house parties,' Diana gleefully translated. She was glowing with the memory of those carefree days. 'Benetton sales. Spag bol suppers.'

Spag bol suppers I could identify with. From impoverished students to Sloane Rangers, they were universal.

She picked up her fork, twisted it in the pasta and, to my gratification, devoured it wolfishly. 'The Coleherne Courtiers,' she added, dreamily.

'The whats?'

She giggled. 'Young chaps who wanted to go out with us. They were called things like Nigel and Rory and were in the Life Guards and Lloyds of London.'

'Did you go out with them?'

The dreamy look faded, and she looked at me in surprise. 'Of course not, Sandy. You of all people should know that. I was following the rules. I knew I had to keep myself tidy.'

She made virginity sound like a well-organised cupboard. But she meant the rules of romantic heroines, I guessed. As laid out in Barbara Cartland's novels. Only Chastity could lead to Love.

She was talking about the apartment again, wistfully. 'Such fun. Always someone around. Always something going on.' Her words floated into the dead air of her present, silent home.

I'd heard enough about Sloane life, I decided. I wanted to know what happened next with Prince Charles.

'Stephen Barry came to my flat. That was the next thing.'

Chapter Nineteen

Coleherne Court, Kensington, London

March 1979

Stephen

It had been some time since Stephen had travelled on public transport. These days, he went on the Queen's Flight, and the Purple Air Space it went through, far more frequently than he went on the Underground. Ditto the royal train, the royal yacht, the royal Rolls-Royces and even the occasional royal carriage and four. The royal Aston Martin, most of all.

The Circle Line was an unwelcome reminder of all that it meant to be ordinary. Freshly scented from his large bathroom, smart in his Savile Row suit, he surveyed the weary faces and cheap clothes of his fellow passengers. Theirs was the world of boring jobs, tiny horizons and, worst of all, viewing the glittering world of royalty from the other side of the Palace wall. This world was where he had come from, and where, soon, he might very well go back to.

Every newspaper he could see had headlines about Mrs Thatcher, the Conservative Leader of the Opposition. The day before, she had moved a vote of no confidence in James Callaghan's Labour government, which the Government had lost by a single vote. There would now be a general election and if the

138

Conservatives won it, Margaret Thatcher would be the country's first female prime minister.

The world outside the Palace really was changing. It made Stephen all the more determined to stay inside it for as long as possible.

As a smaller front-page headline caught his eye, about his master and Amanda Knatchbull, Stephen's heart sank. That marriage was looking increasingly inevitable. Trying to stop it with Diana Spencer was obviously hopeless. But he had his instructions and he had to obey them. Or Tallon would have him fired even sooner than the new Princess of Wales would.

Emerging at Sloane Square, Stephen consulted his A to Z. Lady Diana lived on the Old Brompton Road in a block of flats called Coleherne Court.

'Take note, Moll wants to know all about the Sloane Rangers,' Billy had said, by way of farewell.

'Sloane Rangers?' Stephen had repeated. 'You mean Lone Rangers?'

'*Sloane*,' Tallon had corrected. 'It's what young aristos are called these days. Because they all live around Sloane Square. Moll's fascinated. Says it's all changed so much since the Bright Young Things of her youth.'

That was possible, Stephen had thought. The Queen Mother's youth was sixty years ago. 'How will I know a Sloane Ranger?' he'd asked.

'Velvet hairbands, loud voices and pearls. And that's just the men,' Billy had chortled.

Coleherne Court was a grand Edwardian mansion block of red and white brick. Stephen went in the polished entrance, eschewed the shining mahogany lift and mounted the wide, pale-carpeted stairs.

No. 60 was on the first floor. He would have known it even without the number; 'When Will I See You Again', by The

Three Degrees, was echoing behind the front door. Incredulity swept him. Charles' birthday was nearly four months ago and even he hadn't listened to it since.

Stephen's knock was eventually answered, not by the fresh-faced blonde he was expecting, but a dark-haired girl in a black velvet Alice band and a string of pearls. So far, thought Stephen, so Sloane Ranger.

Small dark eyes, unflatteringly lined in bright blue pencil, met his. Then she beamed. 'It's you!' Her voice almost burst his eardrums.

Stephen was surprised to be recognised. He hadn't expected Tallon to lay the ground this thoroughly. He smiled back uncertainly.

'You were at that bollock of Henry Hambledon's!'

'Bollock?' Stephen wasn't sure he had heard correctly. And he certainly didn't know a Henry Hambledon.

'When will we share precious moments?' the Three Degrees were enquiring loudly from down the hall.

'Oh Gawd, sorry. Not that bollock. So what bollock was it?'

'I'm not sure exactly what you mean,' Stephen said. There was an infamous gay leather bar up the road. Was this something to do with that? 'I've come to see Lady Diana Spencer.'

It was the Sloane's turn to look amazed now. 'Oh, right. And you are?'

'The name's Barry.'

'Come in, Barry.'

Sloane Rangers were messy, Stephen deduced. The hall was full of skis against the wall, wellies heaped on the floor and green husky jackets shoved on hooks. Ahead of him was an untidy kitchen with a poster of Sting. The Police frontman was gazing at him quizzically from above some cereal boxes.

'Duch!' the Sloane was roaring. 'Barry's here to see you!'

'No,' Stephen corrected. 'I've come to see Lady Diana.'

The small blue-rimmed eyes regarded him with amusement. 'Duch is her *nickname*!'

Stephen felt silly. 'May I use the lavatory?' he asked. Anything to get away from this scrutiny.

'Sure, yah. Bog's that way.'

He picked his way down the cluttered hall. The door with the Three Degrees coming from behind it had a notice on it: Chief Chick. Another nickname, Stephen guessed.

The lavatory walls were full of school photographs in wooden frames, hanging at wonky angles. Stephen failed to pick out Diana in the rows of pale faces in front of pillared buildings. There were also some framed Snoopy cartoons and Kipling's 'If–' Blu-Tacked to the back of the door. The loo roll, which was printed with crosswords, was kept in a chintz-lined basket.

Back in the hall, the Sloane was waiting. 'Duch won't be long,' she reported. 'Come and sit in the drawing room.'

It really was a very smart flat. The windows, which were wide, long and hung with cream-and-burgundy striped curtains, gave onto a green garden square. Spring was flowering on the bushes and leafing the trees.

A shiny, buttoned chesterfield sofa was heaped with small cushions embroidered with slogans. 'When the Going Gets Tough, the Tough Go Shopping' and 'Nice Girls Go to Heaven, Bad Girls Go Everywhere'. Stephen stared at the latter. If this referred to Diana, the whole thing was over before it had started. But then, it probably was anyway.

A loud flatulent noise marked the joining of his rear with the sofa.

'Oh Gawd! Soz! Totally forgot that was there!'

Smiling through gritted teeth, Stephen drew out a whoopee cushion. Sloane humour was evidently fairly basic. This could be a problem too. The prince laughed at completely different things.

On the plus side, the mantelpiece was crowded with smart-looking invitations. Less good was the pile of *Daily Mails* on the coffee table. The prince hated the *Mail*, along with the rest of the popular press.

There was a smart new television in the corner. 'Nice TV,' Stephen remarked. He liked watching telly, but the prince disdained it. No television in any of the royal houses was less than ten years old and many were black and white.

'It's Duch's. She's completely obsessed with *Crossroads*. Sits in front of it with a bowl of Harvest Crunch most evenings.'

Crossroads was the daily soap opera set in a provincial motel. Its most famous character, Benny, was a handyman of low intelligence who wore a woolly hat. Stephen doubted his master had even heard of it.

When the discussion petered out, he glanced at the bookshelves, hoping for some trace of princely high culture. But there was nothing resembling his master's library of classics and Laurens van der Post. Rather, a couple of Frederick Forsyths and shelf after shelf crammed with cheap paperback romances with titles like *Stand and Deliver Your Heart*. Stephen stared in horror.

A loud, honking laugh made him jump violently. 'Nothing to do with me,' guffawed the Sloane. 'The Barbara Cartlands are all Duch's. A hopeless romantic. In love with Love, that's Duch.'

Oh God, thought Stephen. This was never going to work. How was a hopeless romantic, a teenager into the bargain, who loved *Crossroads*, Harvest Crunch and Barbara Cartland going to compete with the mighty Lord Mountbatten and his sophisticated granddaughter? Henry Higgins himself would struggle to do anything with that. Stephen Barry may as well go home now.

Too late, he saw. The Sloane was beaming at someone over his shoulder, in the direction of the doorway. 'At last! Duch!'

Stephen leapt to his feet, as the Sloane headed out of the room. 'Lady Diana.'

She wore a collar with a pussy-cat bow, a calf-length print skirt and pale tights with low-heeled shoes. He suspected she had chosen the outfit to project a demure maturity, but she looked as young as ever. In the light from the window, her large eyes were an incredibly vibrant blue. He thought of pictures of the Madonna and felt another wave of misgiving.

'It's so nice to see you again, Mr Barry!' Her voice was light, girlish. 'Last time we met, we were both holding shotguns!'

He smiled through gritted teeth. Did she but know it, she had less chance even than the pheasants on that shoot. She was completely unsuitable.

She was smiling at him brightly. 'Shall we go for a walk?'

Chapter Twenty

They set off down the Old Brompton Road. 'I know why you've come,' she said, hands in the pockets of her rust-coloured corduroy jacket. She had a long, easy stride and seemed in buoyant mood. 'My grandmother's told me. I'm being considered as a possible Princess of Wales. You're going to give me all the background.'

Stephen made a non-committal noise. He didn't want to get her hopes up.

She slid him an amused, sideways glance. 'So give it to me. Tell me all about him.'

'What would you like to know? His favourite colour is blue, if that helps.' He realised he probably sounded satirical, but the sooner this was over, the better.

'It might,' she acknowledged brightly. 'If I was buying him a jumper or something.'

'You wouldn't though,' Stephen said immediately.

She slowed down slightly, stared at him. 'How do you mean, Mr Barry? Why wouldn't I?'

'Because I buy all His Royal Highness's clothes. If His Royal Highness wants new ties, I get some from Turnbull & Asser. If it's suits His Royal Highness requires, Mr Watson comes from Hawes & Curtis with a selection of fabrics.'

She giggled. 'Oh, I *see*. So it's all your fault, Mr Barry.'

'What is?'

'Well, he dresses quite formally, doesn't he. Does he ever wear colours?'

'Regimental or club. But that's about it.'

She snorted. 'Not that sort of colours! I mean Benetton-type colours. Reds. Pinks. Blues, as you say.'

'He never wears those,' said Stephen, vehemently.

'Have one?' She had produced a bag of toffees from her pocket.

He shook his head. She shouldn't either; the Prince never ate sweets.

But she popped one in and gazed at him merrily. 'So,' she said, her mouth full of toffee, 'do you buy his shoes as well?'

'His Royal Highness has his own last at Lobbs.'

This made her giggle. 'I have no idea what that means, but is it why he always wears lace-ups and not slip-ons?'

'*Slip-ons?*' Stephen narrowly avoided colliding with a lamp post. 'I don't think His Royal Highness could ever be persuaded to wear slip-ons.'

She giggled again. 'That, Mr Barry, sounds like a challenge! And can I ask you about his hair? Where does he go?'

Impatience swept through Stephen. She didn't seriously think the prince actually went to a salon? 'I do His Royal Highness's hair,' he said with freezing dignity.

'Bit traditional, isn't it? That side parting.'

'His Royal Highness has had the same side parting since he was a boy,' Stephen returned stiffly.

She popped in another toffee. 'But that's my point. Maybe he could modernise it a bit.'

She had to be joking, Stephen thought. Modernise and the Prince of Wales were not words you put together. The idea was completely and utterly out of the question, and so was this girl.

They walked on for some moments in silence. He tried to think of some concluding remarks so he could escape. Her thoughts, meanwhile, were evidently tending in the precisely opposite direction. 'What are Prince Charles' favourite foods?' she asked.

'He likes cold fishy dishes,' Stephen said shortly. 'Salmon mayonnaise and prawns, that sort of thing.'

He glanced at her, she was moving her lips, as if learning it all off by heart. It was almost pathetic.

'Puddings?' she asked.

'He hates chocolate ones.'

A gasp of dismay. 'Oh *no*! When I did my cookery course, that's practically all I learnt. My speciality dish is chocolate roulade.'

Don't worry, Stephen thought. It's not going to matter.

But she was eager, and deserved something, so he decided to tell her a story. 'We were once staying in Tasmania, in this private house, and the hostess had hired a cook to prepare dinner. When I went down to the kitchen to warn her about His Royal Highness's likes and dislikes, there was this Julia Child cooking away.'

'Julia Child! Isn't she very famous?'

Stephen shrugged. In the prince's world, who wasn't famous? 'Well, she was making this wonderful-looking chocolate mousse. Then she took a great handful of nuts and completely smothered it in them.'

His companion squealed. 'Don't tell me! He hates nuts too!'

It was hard not to laugh too, she sounded so entertained. He wasn't sure he had ever had a more appreciative audience.

They had reached a small park. She commented on the cherry blossom; as thick on the branches as snow. Then she turned to him, smiling. 'Do you mind if I ask you something else?'

'Not at all.'

'About Prince Charles' girlfriends?'

The question came completely from left field. After all the harmless food talk, it was the last thing he'd expected. On the other hand, Mountbatten's granddaughter meant he could finally stop this interview. Perhaps Diana had heard the most recent rumour, that the prince had actually proposed. 'Ah,' he said, assuming an expression of sombre sympathy. 'Miss Knatchbull, I presume.'

He had expected her to look nervous, even despairing. To his surprise, she beamed. 'Oh no,' she said, brightly. 'I know *that's* not real, Grandmama's explained. Prince Charles is doing his best to feel strongly about her and she's doing her best to feel the same. But they don't really love each other. Not like *I* love him.'

It was hard to know what to say to this.

They passed a park bench and she paused. 'Shall we sit down?'

He nodded. He had the strange feeling that she was in control now.

They sat, and she turned to him with a smile. 'I've been doing my research, you see.'

'Research?' He tried not to sound surprised that she even knew the word.

'About the ex-girlfriends. I've been looking at old newspapers in the library.'

She wouldn't have to look very far, he guessed. Whenever a new girl came into the frame, the histories of all the others were reviewed at the same time. The newspapers carried double-page spreads with the same photos, a sort of rogues' gallery of royal exes, each accompanied by a so-called fact box.

'I just wondered why Prince Charles had broken up with them. I thought,' she added, blushing slightly, 'that if there was a reason, I might learn from it.'

Stephen straightened on the park bench. He was impressed; these were proper tactics. He would not have imagined her capable.

'What happened with Princess Astrid, for instance? Wasn't he going to marry her? That's what the papers said.'

The valet hesitated. Then again, he had been given his instructions. He was to help and advise. 'Princess Astrid was a red herring,' he stated firmly. 'Not one of His Royal Highness's staff had ever met her and we weren't even sure that he had himself.'

She looked surprised. 'Oh. Does that mean he never met Princess Caroline of Monaco either?'

'He met her once.'

'But everyone thought he was going to marry her as well. Didn't they?'

They did. Stephen could almost hear the prince's complaining voice. 'The wretched papers all have me going up the aisle with her! But the only time I met her was at that boring thing in Monte Carlo.'

Boring wasn't the word the valet would have used for the glamorous ball at the exclusive Sporting Club. They had stayed at the royal palace in Monaco and Stephen had actually shared a bathroom with Cary Grant.

'Well, yes,' he said to his companion. 'But what all the rumour-mongers gaily ignored is the fact that Her Serene Highness is a Catholic and His Royal Highness has to marry someone whose religion is Church of England. But,' he added, darting a quick smile at his companion, 'to be honest with you, he really wasn't very attracted.'

The blue eyes widened. 'But Princess Caroline is very beautiful.'

'Not his type. He likes good English complexions.'

Her good English complexion reddened with pleasure. 'Tell me about some of the others.' She sounded, he thought, like a child wanting a bedtime story. 'Lady Jane Wellesley.'

Stephen stretched out his legs and crossed them at the ankle. He was actually rather enjoying himself now. Being seen as the fount of valuable knowledge was flattering. 'Just a friend of the family, really,' he said grandly. 'A very clever, kind girl, but, of course, she had a career.' He pronounced the word as if it were some unfortunate affliction.

'Oh yes, in television, wasn't it?'

'That's right. Which would never do.'

'You can't work in television?'

'You can't work, full stop. But it wasn't just that,' he went on. 'Lady Jane hated the press. She got very harassed and fed up. Finding half a dozen reporters camped on her doorstep drove her mad. She told them that she had one title already so she didn't need another. She was a duke's daughter, after all.'

'I suppose I'm only an earl's daughter.' She giggled. 'Perhaps I'd tell the press I needed an upgrade.'

Stephen looked at her sharply. 'I wouldn't tell the press anything. They're a nuisance.'

'They certainly were for my sister.' The enquiring blue eyes were back on him. 'So, what happened with Georgiana Russell?'

Gosh, yes. Lively, blonde, mini-skirted Georgiana. 'The ambassador's daughter,' he said.

'And her mother was Miss Greece.'

Stephen was amazed. She really was extraordinarily well informed. He pictured her leafing through back copies of the tabloids in the library, absorbing it all, as if trying to crack some sort of code. But it was a code, and he was one of the few that knew it. That had been Tallon's whole point.

'Miss Russell came to the polo,' he revealed. 'Then she went to Cowes and Balmoral. The private detective and I always said that the ones who survived polo, sailing and Scotland had a chance of surviving the course.'

She leapt on this immediately. 'The course?'

'Becoming the Princess of Wales is a succession of challenges,' Stephen said. 'It's like the Grand National – a horse race with lots of jumps and hurdles. The polo is the starting line and the finishing post is the Abbey. But no one's got that far yet, of course.'

'No,' she said thoughtfully, before meeting his eyes and grinning. 'Not yet.'

Don't kid yourself, dear, Stephen thought. Aloud he said, 'Ladies drop out at different stages. Some fall at the very first fence. Georgiana fell at the third one, which was Scotland.'

'What happened?' Her fascinated expression urged him on. No one had ever hung on his every word before, and certainly not a pretty young aristocrat. It was irresistible, really. He went on.

'It seems she found it rather dull, sitting on the bank for hours while His Royal Highness stood in the river. She left after the first day.'

'Oh dear.'

That, Stephen suspected, was probably not what Georgiana's mother had said. The former Miss Greece had been masterminding the whole thing.

'But there was quite an amusing sequel to it all,' he added. 'We were going somewhere on a plane, I forget where. I was flicking through *Harper's & Queen* when I found a picture of Georgiana's wedding to Brooke Boothby. I showed it to the prince and he was annoyed.'

Diana was looking puzzled. 'Because she'd got married?'

'Because she'd deceived him.'

'With Brooke Boothby? She was two-timing him?'

Stephen chuckled. 'No, with her *hair*. "Good God," His Royal Highness said. "Georgiana's hair is actually *black*. She must have dyed it when she was with me. She's not a blonde at all."'

'Blonde!' She touched her hair, smiled. 'He prefers blondes!'

'Like every gentleman.'

She giggled, then the enquiring look returned to the big blue eyes. 'Sabrina Guinness fell at Scotland as well.'

This girl, Stephen thought, had a laser focus.

'She did,' he concurred. 'But for rather different reasons. To be honest, I was surprised when His Royal Highness took up with Miss Guinness in the first place. She wasn't His Royal Highness's usual sort at all.'

'Because she was friends with the Rolling Stones, you mean? And she nannied for Ryan O'Neal too, didn't she?'

Was there anything Diana Spencer did not know? Odd how badly she had done at school. The teachers must have been terrible.

'Not that,' he replied. 'Sabrina Guinness was so *thin*. Normally, His Royal Highness likes his ladies a bit fatter.'

Diana looked down at herself, grinning. 'Well, I'll be perfect in that case.'

Stephen said nothing. He had his professional limits and offering a view on a lady's figure was one of them. Besides, Diana Spencer's – what you could see of it beneath the skirts and pussy-cat bows – looked fine. Neither fat nor thin, but in the middle.

The merry blue eyes were watching him. 'The other person I wanted to ask you about is Anna Wallace.'

'A very nice girl,' Stephen said, sincerely. Which Anna had been. All the staff had been sorry when that relationship ended. 'Her father was a very rich Scottish landowner. Very attractive, with a sparkling personality.'

'What, the landowner?' she quipped.

He sighed. 'No, Miss Wallace. She even went to lunch with Her Majesty at Windsor.'

'I'm guessing that's another jump on the Princess of Wales Champion Hurdles?'

'That's the Becher's Brook stage. No one gets that far unless things are looking serious.'

'So what went wrong?'

'Miss Wallace and His Royal Highness had a quarrel at a dance in Windsor. Or, rather,' Stephen corrected himself, 'she had a quarrel with him. His Royal Highness does not quarrel.'

'Of course not.' She raised an amused eyebrow. 'There's just one more person I wanted to ask you about.'

Stephen shifted in his seat, suppressed a groan. How much longer was this going to go on?

'Mrs Parker Bowles. Wasn't she quite close to Prince Charles at one stage?'

'At one stage, yes.' Stephen remembered Camilla at the party, her masculine chuckle, her hedge-backwards style. Quite a contrast with this fresh-faced, feminine creature beside him. 'But she's been married a long time. Lives in the country now. Hunts.'

He glanced at his watch. He had done his duty, given what guidance he could. He could report back to Tallon, but warn him that the search needed to go on.

'So, let me get this straight.' Her clear, light voice floated into his ear. 'In order to become Princess of Wales, you need to be blonde with good skin, fond of fishing and Scotland, an aristocrat, Church of England, able to handle the press, not argumentative and not interested in a career.'

'In a nutshell, yes.'

'Oh, and a virgin, of course.' She clapped her hands. 'Sounds like I'm the perfect candidate.'

Unwilling to hurt her feelings, he resorted to humour. 'If you didn't exist, the royal family would have to invent you.'

She looked at him. 'But that's just what we *are* doing, Mr Barry. Inventing me.'

As they walked out of the park, he felt guilty. He had indulged himself, succumbed to flattery, and now she had got her hopes up. But she was far too young and far too different from the prince. It was a shame in a way, because Billy was right. If anyone would let him keep his job, it was this desperate-to-please girl.

But Amanda was a much better match and, with the powerful support of her grandfather, poised to take the field. Unless something unimaginable happened, Diana had no chance whatsoever.

28 August, 1979. Heathrow Airport

Stephen

The Andover of the Queen's Flight, coming in from Iceland, touched down on the Heathrow tarmac. 'Unicorn' – the RAF call sign for the Prince of Wales – had arrived. Wearily, Stephen rose from his seat in the VIP lounge and went to meet it.

Charles had rushed back from his fishing holiday, devastated at the death of the uncle who had been closer to him than a father. He was anxious to give what help he could to his Uncle Dickie's shattered family.

Mountbatten had been seventy-nine years old. He had been on holiday in Ireland, at his Sligo home, Classiebawn Castle. Such was his affection for his Irish neighbours, and theirs for him, that it was not thought necessary for his boat, *Shadow V*, to be guarded. He had only just cleared Mullaghmore harbour when the IRA bomb went off. It was not obvious whether it was on board or hidden in a lobster pot.

The earl was killed, along with his fourteen-year-old grandson, Nicholas Knatchbull, brother of Amanda. If she had doubts about marrying into the royal family before, they were surely doubled now. In any case, Uncle Dickie had been permanently removed from the scene, making it unlikely the marriage would happen. With unbelievable irony, republican terrorists had played straight into the Queen Mother's diamond-ringed hands.

Stephen climbed the steps to the Andover, threading his way through the small galley at the front. The prince was approaching from the rear, through the private cabin with its four armchairs. For this journey, for once, he had not sat at the flight deck. He looked shattered and was already wearing a black tie. Stephen always packed one, never thinking it would actually be used.

'Your Royal Highness,' the valet began. 'I don't know what to say.'

The prince looked at him. 'What was the point?' he asked, quietly. 'What have they achieved?'

But Stephen could think of one person for whom this potentially changed everything.

Chapter Twenty-One

Coleherne Court, Kensington, London
5 September 1979
Diana

The glass walls of his goldfish bowl gave Battersea a clear view of the sitting room of 60 Coleherne Court. The flatmates were assembling in front of the television. There was Carolyn, the black-haired one in the rugby shirt and pearls; Anne, the mouse-haired one in the blouse and tank top; Virginia, the brown-haired one in the man's shirt and jeans. And Diana, whose big blue eyes were now peering in at him. Her long pink fingers seized his bowl and lifted it up. She took it across the room and put it down on the coffee table next to an open bottle of white wine.

'I thought Battersea would like to watch the funeral too,' she explained to the others. 'He's a man of the sea, like Lord Mountbatten.'

'More a man of the tap water,' guffawed Carolyn. 'And Harrods' finest plastic weeds.'

The Chief Chick rolled her big blue eyes. 'Honestly, Caro. You've got no soul.' She settled down beside the goldfish, tucking her socked feet beneath the bottom of her corduroy jeans.

'No soul, but the finest plonk de plonks.' Carolyn waved the bottle and started filling glasses.

On the screen, the September sun poured down on the entrance to Westminster Abbey. The tenor bell was tolling and a procession of black cars drawing up and disgorging a collection of distinguished guests, all dressed in funeral black.

'That's James Callaghan: how funny he has to show his invitation,' remarked Anne, as the recently ousted Prime Minister entered the Abbey.

'You'd think they'd recognise him,' agreed Virginia.

The new Prime Minister arrived, to general groans of 'Ghastly' and 'Awful'.

'Mrs Thatcher looks exactly like she does on our new bog-roll holder,' chortled Carolyn. The girls were delighted with the new comic addition to the lavatory. One of the Coleherne Courtiers, a junior Army officer, had presented it.

As the start of the service approached, the Abbey arrivals became more frequent and interesting.

'Princess Grace! *Fab* sunglasses.'

'Princess Margaret and Princess Anne! With Fog.'

'Fog?'

'Captain Mark Phillips, her husband. Because he's thick and wet.'

More chortles.

Occasionally, the cameras cut to the flag-draped coffin, topped with Mountbatten's sword and admiral's hat, processing through the crowd-lined streets on its gun carriage. The girls exclaimed at the massed regimental bands, the columns of soldiers, sailors and airmen.

There was a chorus of 'ahs' as a riderless horse appeared on the screen, a magnificent black creature with white socks. The polished boots in its stirrups were pushed back to front. 'That's to show that its master has died.' Virginia's eyes shone with tears.

'Look at all those cushions holding Lord Mountbatten's decorations!'

'Could have used our cushions,' snorted Carolyn, picking up Bad Girls Go Everywhere and holding it out ceremoniously.

'Prince Charles is going to read the lesson, apparently.' The Chief Chick's voice was bright with anticipation.

Virginia looked at her watch. 'Five!'

'Five what?' asked Diana.

'A whole five minutes since you mentioned Prince Charles. Honestly, Duch, you're *obsessed*.'

The flatmates had initially been excited when Diana had explained that Stephen Barry – 'that funny little man', as Carolyn called him – was from Buckingham Palace. Excitement had become amazement when she had claimed to be in the frame to be Princess of Wales. They hadn't realised she even knew Prince Charles, and when it emerged she didn't, not really, the amazement had turned to doubt. The doubt had hardened when Prince Charles had subsequently failed either to materialise or even get in touch.

Between themselves, Caro, Anne and Ginny thought Diana was deluding herself. The widely held expectation that Charles would become engaged to Amanda Knatchbull only strengthened this view. That he hadn't, not yet, was ascribable to her grandfather's dreadful death. But that he would after a decent interval seemed certain.

'You've got to get over your prince pash,' Anne instructed, using the schoolgirl slang with which they were all familiar. 'Pash' was an abbreviation of 'passion'.

'Because Charles is going to marry Amanda,' Carolyn pointed out.

'No he isn't!' Diana insisted.

Her flatmates ignored this.

'You can do heaps better than him anyway, Duch.'

'He's completely ancient.'

Diana roused herself indignantly. 'He's thirty!'

'Exactly. You're almost half his age!'

Diana put a mock-mournful face to the goldfish bowl. 'They're all being horrid to me, Battersea!'

'Battersea, we are not,' Carolyn countered. 'We're trying to make her see sense. Duch, just *think*. You'd hate being royal. It's like being in prison. My aunt was a lady-in-waiting, so I know whereof I speak.'

'Well, both my grandmothers were, so I do too.'

The flatmates whooped. 'Hoity-toity!'

'Oh shut up!'

'But seriously, Duch,' Anne urged. 'Everyone would recognise you. You'd never be able to go to Peter Jones again.' They all loved the big department store in Sloane Square.

'And you'd have to leave *us*,' Virginia pointed out. 'Wouldn't you miss us?'

Diana shook back her hair. 'Of course I would. But we're all going to leave eventually. When we all get married.'

Caro frowned. 'Who says we're all getting married?'

'Don't you want to?'

'Well, maybe. But I quite like working. You should work too, Duch, I'm always saying so. You'd be amazing in the health service. Or a teacher or something. You've got a real gift for it.'

'You're not the first person to say that,' Diana said. 'But my greatest gift is for Love.'

They all snorted. It was never clear, when she said these things, whether she was joking or not.

'So love someone else then,' Caro suggested in her practical way. 'You've got hundreds of other admirers.'

'Plenty more fish in the sea,' agreed Anne. She glanced at the goldfish bowl. 'Isn't that right, Battersea?'

'The Coleherne Courtiers,' giggled Virginia. 'William van Straubenzee, to mention but one. James Colthurst.'

'Rory from the Life Guards,' put in Anne. 'Ooh look,' she added wickedly. 'Duch is going bright red.'

'Rory's just platonic!' But she was blushing, it was true.

'Well, he doesn't think so. He's mad about you. As is lovely James Gilbey, he of the big booze fortune. Just think of all the G and Ts you could have if you married him!'

The other three laughed. Meanwhile, on the television, a big shining car flying the Royal Standard was drawing up to the Abbey entrance.

'Ooh, here's the Queen,' said Anne. 'Looking terribly serious.'

'The Queen Mother isn't,' Virginia pointed out. 'She's *smiling!*'

When the Prince of Wales finally arrived, walking behind the coffin with Prince Philip, the three flatmates groaned theatrically. Their landlady ignored them completely. 'He looks so wonderful in his naval uniform!'

'Everyone looks wonderful in naval uniform,' Carolyn snorted. 'It's literally impossible not to.'

'But Prince Charles looks *extra* handsome.'

'He's certainly got enough medals! How many wars has he actually fought in?'

The Chief Chick took no notice. Her big blue eyes remained longingly on the screen. 'He looks *so* sad.'

'He probably is a bit sad, it's a funeral.'

Diana put her face to the goldfish bowl. 'Don't listen to them, Battersea. They're just being beastly.'

A fanfare of trumpets blared from the television. The flag-draped coffin was shouldered into the Abbey by six pall-bearers. 'I Vow to Thee, My Country' struck up on the organ and the girls all sang lustily along.

'Gets me every time,' sniffed Virginia, when it had finished.

'It's my favourite too,' said Diana. 'I'm going to have it when I marry Charles.'

Carolyn picked up the cushion again and waved it threateningly. 'I'm going to throw this at you if you don't stop it. It's just a pash, and you should get over it.'

'I won't be stopping it. And it's not just a pash. It's my destiny, I just know it is.'

Three pairs of eyes flicked ruefully towards the bookshelves and the rows of romances. They were all thinking the same thing.

'Duch, this isn't one of your novels. People aren't fated to marry princes *in real life*.'

Chapter Twenty-Two

Windsor Castle, Berkshire
June 1980
The Queen Mother

Resplendent in her robes and diamonds, she smiled benignly around from beneath her black velvet bonnet. How she loved the ancient Garter Ceremony, this annual show of historic pomp and pageantry.

That morning, the knights of the Most Noble Order of the Garter, in their billowing blue velvet cloaks, had paraded in glorious early-summer sunshine to St George's Chapel, watched by admiring crowds. Here the new knights had been invested and the service had followed the time-honoured pattern, the participants seated in their magnificent mediaeval carved stalls under their brilliantly coloured heraldic banners.

Now they were enjoying a sumptuous lunch amid the pan-elled splendour of the castle's Waterloo Chamber. Beneath its chandeliers and observed by a line of huge oil portraits, a long linen-spread table glittered with crystal and silver. The air hummed with conversation, the chink of glasses and the scent from great flower displays.

'So very different without dear Louis here,' the old queen remarked to her neighbour, her son-in-law Philip. 'He was always so attentive. The way he used to hover at the top of the West Steps, waiting as I heaved my way up to the chapel.'

'The most courteous of men.'

The Queen Mother raised her napkin to hide her smile. Philip wouldn't recognise courteousness if it bit him on his muscular backside. And his Uncle Mountbatten's gesture had been entirely political. Once she had gained the top step, he would stand in front of her to form a royal procession into the chapel, which he then headed.

His death had been appalling. But to quote the old phrase, it was an ill wind that blew nobody any good. That wind had blown Amanda Knatchbull from the position of potential Princess of Wales. But had it replaced her with Diana Spencer? Not so far, maddeningly.

But it would do. It had to. Charles must marry to secure the future of the monarchy and time was running out. Otherwise, the old queen feared, the Socialists would abolish them. She had been almost seventeen when the Romanovs were shot in the cellar; these things never quite left one.

And the rot had most certainly begun. A mere few seats down from where she sat was Garter Knight Harold Wilson, a former Labour Prime Minister. A man of the people amid the cherished order of nobles!

What, she wondered, would Edward III have thought? He had invented the Order of the Garter in the fourteenth century. His idea was to promote a Camelot-style *esprit de corps* among a nobility devastated by the effects of the Black Death. So many peasants had died that they were in short supply, hence in serious danger of having economic clout. Making the Garter an exclusive club had empowered the Crown and helped the landed classes face the lower orders down. Edward had, the

Queen Mother felt, known a thing or two about maintaining royal privilege.

'Are you sure you want to sit next to Philip?' Lilibet had asked when the Garter Day table plan was drawn up. 'My husband's in a terrible grump at the moment.'

'What else is new, darling? Besides, teasing him out of it is always such fun.'

Her daughter had looked at her narrowly. 'Are you up to something, Mummy?'

'*Aqua vitae, non aqua pura!*' the old queen exclaimed now.

'You what?' asked Philip, bemused to see his mother-in-law raising her glass to an ancient knight across the table.

The Queen Mother turned to him, beaming. 'It's the motto of the Windsor Wets. My secret drinking society. He's one of my fellow soakers.'

'I didn't know you had a secret drinking society.'

'Ah, well, it's a secret.' The Queen Mother toyed with her wine-glass stem. But she had Philip's attention now. 'You know,' she said, changing the subject apparently randomly, 'this room always reminds me of the war.'

'Yes. That's why it's called the Waterloo Room.'

The old queen maintained her sunny smile. 'Not that war. *Our* war. This is where we put on the pantomimes.'

'Where Crawfie put them on, you mean.'

The Queen Mother ignored this provocation. 'Lilibet was Prince Charming in *Cinderella*. She was wearing tights, just like you are now.'

Philip's ice-blue Danish eyes swept her irritably. 'I think you'll find these are called hose.'

'Well, we need to think about our own Prince Charming. We have a Cinderella, but the glass slipper doesn't quite seem to be fitting.'

'I suppose you mean that Spencer girl.'

'Indeed I do.'

'But he's not interested, never has been. I thought you'd thrown the towel in with her.'

'Not at all,' said the Queen Mother sweetly. 'I never throw towels. Although when I'm at my Castle of Mey, we sometimes hang them out of the windows. As a salute, when Lilibet sails by on *Britannia*.'

'I know,' Philip said tersely. 'I've seen it. I'm usually with Lilibet when you do it.'

A wrinkled hand sparkling with diamonds patted his. 'Anyway, Diana is quite perfect, and one can't give up on perfection.'

Philip frowned. 'Aren't her family supposed to be off their rocker? Bad blood, isn't that what they say?'

'Oh, they say all sorts about people's families,' the Queen Mother replied comfortably. 'You should hear what they say about yours.'

She raised her napkin again as Philip looked briefly furious.

'Anyway,' she added airily, 'the Spencers count among their ancestors Sarah, Duchess of Marlborough, whose pride led her to snub her former friend Queen Anne, and also Georgiana, Duchess of Devonshire, whose exploits at the gaming tables made her the most famous woman of her day. A family like that is never going to be ordinary.'

Philip's glance was sardonic. 'Been doing your homework, haven't you?'

The Queen Mother's bonnet feathers nodded. 'The main point is that Diana is just as well born as Charles, possibly more so. He's descended from minor German princes, while the Spencers have intermarried for centuries, exclusively with the English nobility.'

Philip, as one of these minor German princes, looked offended. 'Doesn't matter how sodding well born she is, does it? Charles is completely besotted with that bloody Parker Bowles woman again.'

The old queen sighed. 'Yes, I had heard that. And while Mrs Parker Bowles is sweet to comfort Charles in his grief, she is rather holding things up.'

'Comfort!' Philip snorted. 'At it like rabbits, you mean. Unforgiveable. The woman's married to a brother officer and soldier of the Queen.'

The Queen Mother tipped her head benignly. 'Who, I understand, isn't an entirely faithful spouse himself. But we all have skeletons in our cupboards, do we not? Admittedly, some cupboards are rather larger than others.'

Philip did not reply. His long fingers drummed angrily on the table.

'And Charles can keep Camilla in his cupboard,' the old queen went on, 'so long as he marries Diana Spencer. That's always been the arrangement for Princes of Wales.'

'But what if Diana Spencer doesn't want that? This is 1979, not that you'd know.' Philip glanced irascibly round at the guests in their mediaeval caps and cloaks.

'Makes no difference.' The Queen Mother's tone was blithe. 'It's always been the way and it always will be. The wives tolerate the mistresses quite happily. They reach a *modus vivendi*. Queen Alexandra even let Mrs Keppel – an ancestor of Camilla's by the way – be with Edward VII on his deathbed.'

Philip looked unconvinced. 'Well, even if that's all fine with her, what about him? He's just not interested.'

'He's going to have to become interested. We're rather running out of time. And completely running out of possibilities.'

'Diana Spencer's probably not a possibility anyway,' Philip suggested, unhelpfully. 'If she's got any sense, she'll have found someone else by now.'

'Apparently not,' the old queen said, with a touch of triumph. 'According to Ruth Fermoy, the poor child is eating her heart out.'

'For Charles?' Philip shook his head disbelievingly. 'She has my deepest sympathies in that case. He's hopeless. Frankly, the whole thing's hopeless.'

'Oh, don't be so defeatist!' The Queen Mother held up her diamond-ringed fingers in the Victory 'V' sign. 'We will overcome. You're sitting next to the most dangerous woman in Europe, remember.'

'Yes, and I was mentioned in dispatches after Matapan, but I can't see how any of that helps. It's hardly the same situation. Britain was up against an implacable enemy then.'

The Queen Mother glanced down the table at Harold Wilson. 'And if you don't think we're fighting for our very survival now, you're very much mistaken. "Lay on, Macduff. And damn'd be him that first cries, 'Hold, enough!'"'

'Isn't that *Macbeth*?'

The feathered bonnet next to him nodded.

'Thought so. I was in that at school. "Screw your courage to the sticking place, and we'll not fail."'

'Exactly.'

'Any ideas about a sticking place?'

'As it happens, yes. Do you by any chance have any friends who live near a polo ground?'

Chapter Twenty-Three

Coleherne Court, Kensington, London

July 1980

Diana

In the flat's messy hall, the telephone burst into life.

'It's for you, Duch!' Virginia banged on Diana's door, shouting over the pop music. Contemporary pop music too: Duran Duran. The Three Degrees were a thing of the past, along, it seemed, with Diana's prince pash. Their friend was finally returning to normal.

And not before time, frankly. Over a year had passed since the visit from the valet, ten months since Mountbatten's funeral. And not a peep from the Palace throughout. Even Diana seemed to have given up.

Thank goodness, the flatmates thought.

There were other green shoots too. The Chief Chick had finally got a job. Two, in fact. An old friend from school ran a nursery in Pimlico and had taken Diana on. She had been working mornings at the Young England Kindergarten for several months now. And two afternoons a week she was nanny for an American boy whose mother was a high-powered banker.

'Phone!' Virginia repeated, rattling Diana's handle.

Carolyn appeared. 'Who is it?' she whispered.

'Not sure,' Virginia hissed back.

Caro looked cautious. 'Not that horrid little man from the Palace again?' They were always on the lookout for a recurrence, something that would tip everything backwards.

Virginia shook her head. 'De something, he said he was called. Sounded young. Not one of the Coleherne Courtiers though.'

Caro's eyes lit up. 'Maybe Duch has been making new friends without telling us!'

Diana's door swung open. Her hair was wrapped in a pink towel turban.

'Phone call,' Virginia said.

'Who is it?'

'Someone de something.'

'Never heard of him.'

'Shall I tell him to go away?'

'Yes. Oh no, I'll take it, may as well.'

She shuffled into the hall, holding the turban in place with one hand. With the other, she picked up the phone.

'Hello?'

Virginia, edging past on her way to the kitchen, saw her friend grip the receiver so tightly that her knuckles went white. After a brief conversation, she sank onto the hall carpet.

'Is everything all right?' Beneath the towel, Virginia saw, her flatmate looked dazed. 'Is it your father?'

Earl Spencer had suffered a massive stroke a few years previously.

'No.' A pair of thrilled blue eyes met hers. 'I've been asked to the polo with Prince Charles!'

The others said absolutely nothing for several seconds. Caro was the first to recover. 'When?'

'Now! Today!'

'Where?' asked Virginia.

'Cowdray Park.'

'But,' Ginny frowned. 'That's Sussex, isn't it? Miles away.'

'Yes, but I'd be staying overnight.'

The others looked at each other in alarm. 'Overnight?' gasped Caro. 'With Prince Charles?'

A happy giggle. 'No, at a house party, silly. Place called New Grove. The family are called de Pass. That was their son just now.'

'But you don't know them?' Ginny looked doubtful. 'Personally, I mean?'

'No, but they're big friends of Prince Philip, apparently.'

'He just *told* you that?' Caro frowned at this lapse of good form.

'And I can drive myself there. No problem.'

'Not so sure about that,' said Ginny. Diana was a fast, even reckless driver, ploughing through the London traffic 'like someone in a getaway car', as Anne put it. Her little blue Polo was always off the road having a dent or scrape repaired. But even that wasn't the most concerning aspect of the arrangement.

'But think about it,' Caro said. 'You've just been summoned by people you don't know to stay overnight in a house you've never been to. What if they're all rampant corridor creepers?'

Diana laughed. 'I'll just lock the door.'

'But they might be summoning you for Charles, you might be expected to sleep with him or something,' Ginny worried. 'Royal prerogative, *droit du seigneur* and all that.'

'Of course I'm not! And there's no such thing as *droit de seigneur* any more – this is 1980.'

'To you, maybe,' Caro said darkly. 'But the royal family are at least a century behind the times.'

'Rubbish! Prince Charles is a modern person.'

'And a rude one,' Ginny remarked. 'You've got absolutely no notice. You're just expected to drop everything and—'

'You can't expect notice,' Diana laughingly interrupted. 'This is the Prince of Wales!'

'Yes, but he still should have manners.'

'He's not a god, Duch.'

'Why are you always so horrid about him?'

'We're not horrid. We're, well . . .'

'Just cautious. And not at all sure he's good enough for you.' It was Anne's voice. She had heard the commotion and joined the others in the hall.

'It's the other way round, I'm not good enough for *him*!'

'Yes, you *are*!' the three of them chorused exasperatedly.

'In fact, you're miles better,' Ginny added, loyally. 'I just don't know why you're so mad about him. You can't still want to marry him, surely?'

'Of course I do!'

'But *why*?'

'You really want to know?' The Chief Chick looked laughingly round at them all. 'Because he's the one man in the land who's not allowed to divorce me.'

The three flatmates looked at her uncertainly. Was she serious? It was so hard to tell sometimes.

Soon afterwards, they appeared at her open bedroom door. Diana looked up from throwing clothes into a bag.

'This was going to be for your birthday, Duch.' Caro handed over a slim white box. 'But we thought you might as well have it now.'

It was a necklace, with her initial on a delicate gold chain. She gazed at it, delighted. 'It's beautiful.'

'Call it a lucky charm if you like,' said Anne.

'Although if he doesn't treat you well,' Ginny added, 'he's the one who's going to need the luck. He'll have to answer to us.'

New Grove, Petworth, West Sussex

A few hours later

Stephen

Stephen had just finished briefing the New Grove staff about the royal preferences. The kitchen had been informed that the prince disliked chocolate puddings, chocolate mousse in particular, and preferred fish to meat. The housekeeper had been told that His Royal Highness's room must have windows that could be opened and curtains thick enough to make it very dark. It must not be too hot, there must be no gurgling plumbing, and the towels in the bathroom must be big. Oh, and the prince also hated drinks trays, especially ones where a bottle of champagne had been provided.

On receipt of these instructions, the staff looked understandably annoyed. Stephen wanted to tell them not to take it personally, the prince was like this everywhere they went. It was his way or the highway. When he was in Rome, the Romans did what he wanted.

But saying this was unlikely to make any difference and now, damn it, he had missed Diana's arrival. The blue Polo; hers according to his intelligence sources, had not been there when he went down to see Cook. From the hall where he stood, he could see that it was empty; she had obviously gone up to her room . . . He had been planning to intercept her, pass on some Charles-related wisdom. Topics of conversation and the like. Now she was, all of a sudden, back in the royal frame, he would do his best to help her. If she ended up with Charles, he might end up keeping his job.

But he had missed her.

A green Range Rover now screeched up in a spray of gravel. Prince Philip, in sunglasses, was at the wheel. From his shadowy corner of the hall, Stephen watched as he threw open the door, jumped out and tossed the keys to the butler before striding proprietorially into the house. 'Robert?' he yelled. Commander de Pass, Stephen knew.

As soon as Philip had disappeared into the drawing room, the valet raced upstairs and down the corridor until he found the door with Diana's name card.

'Mr Barry! How absolutely lovely to see you!'

'May I come in?' he asked bluntly.

She had obviously been given one of the best rooms. Large bay windows looked over the rolling South Downs and towards the Cowdray Park polo ground, where the prince was currently inspecting the ponies that had been lent him. He had his own, and very expensive they were too, but whenever possible he used other people's.

She wore a pretty skirt and shirt and seemed on ebulliently good form. He wished he shared her evident optimism.

'I had a few things to tell you, Lady Diana. Things you might find useful to know.'

She turned on him her big blue eyes. 'Oh, Mr Barry, you are sweet. But I know a bit about polo. Chukkas, divots.'

'Not polo,' said Stephen. 'How much do you know about *The Goon Show?*'

'The what?'

'It's a radio comedy,' Stephen revealed.

'I've never heard of it.'

Well, of course she hadn't. It had been last broadcast on the then-Home Service long before she was even born.

'I've heard of *Monty Python*. Is it a bit like that?'

'In a way,' Stephen allowed. 'There are lots of catchphrases.'

'Catchphrases? You mean nice-to-see-you-to-see-you-nice, like Bruce Forsyth?'

Stephen reminded himself that he wasn't doing this for fun, it was a matter of survival. 'The dreaded lurgy, eeyack-a-boo and . . .' He blew a raspberry, as the Goons had throughout each and every episode.

Diana looked bemused. 'Why are you telling me this?'

'Because His Royal Highness finds it amusing.'

'Charles thinks that's funny?'

'He loves it,' Stephen confirmed. 'So I thought it was worth you knowing about it. In case it comes up in conversation. The Phantom Head Shaver, The Affair of the Lone Banana. Neddy Seagoon. Fred and Gladys. Those are the things to mention.'

'The Phantom Head Shaver. Fred and Gladys.' Diana looked baffled. 'Doesn't he ever watch *The Good Life*?'

'No.'

'What about *Are You Being Served?* I love Mrs Slocombe and her pussy.' She snorted.

Stephen loved them, too. But the prince had never seen the department-store-set comedy.

He glanced at his watch. The first match was in an hour. 'We don't have a lot of time. I still need to teach you the "Ying Tong Song".'

He left her eventually with some of the novels of Laurens van der Post. 'Also a great favourite of His Royal Highness.'

'*The Night of the New Moon*,' Diana turned the volume over in her hands. 'Is it a romance, Mr Barry?'

Stephen hid a yelp of laughter in a sudden clearing of his throat. 'Not exactly. It's about his time in a Japanese concentration camp. I'll see you later for the polo, Lady Diana.' He paused at the door. 'Good luck!'

Chapter Twenty-Four

Cowdray Park Polo Club, West Sussex

July 1980

The Press

The green Sussex countryside rolled towards the sea under a blue sky that had got hotter all day. At Cowdray Park polo ground, Arthur Edwards, *Sun* photographer, and his journalist colleague Harry Arnold sat on the grass at the edge of the field. From behind their dark glasses, they were watching keenly. Arthur's fingers twitched on the buttons of his camera, while Harry fanned himself with his hat.

The crowd was a considerable one, drawn by the fact that the Prince of Wales was playing for the glamorous South American polo team Les Diables Bleus. A mixture of T-shirted ordinary families mixed with the hat-wearing smart set from London and the big houses on the Downs.

The two *Sun* journalists were interested in one big house in particular. Prince Charles was staying at New Grove and a party from there would attend the polo. Among them, according to a reliable Clarence House source, was the prince's new girlfriend.

Arthur and Harry had covered these stories many times before. Charles always launched his latest at the polo and they knew the drill backwards. Even so, there was tremendous kudos on being the first in Fleet Street to break the story. This girl might even turn out to be the Princess of Wales; the pressure was on, as everyone knew.

Suddenly, Arthur nudged Harry. The party from New Grove were working their way through the crowd to their reserved seats at the front. The newsmen sat up, their eyes narrowed and searching, coursing with professional adrenaline. Which one was she?

There were various women in the group. Arthur counted them off. The elegant older woman was Philippa de Pass, chatelaine of New Grove, and there was her husband Robert, walking next to his old friend Prince Philip.

'Brace yourself,' Harry muttered as the Queen's husband approached. Philip's loathing of newspapers and newspapermen was famous. 'Scum,' he had once called Harry.

Harry's response had gone down in Fleet Street history. 'Yes, sir, but we're the crème de la scum.'

Philip loomed before them, tall, lean and irascible. But instead of the abuse they had expected, he just nodded. 'Gentlemen.'

They stared, amazed, after the retreating figure in its navy blazer and cream summer trousers. 'Would yer Adam and Eve it?' breathed Arthur.

'Mellowin' with age, I reckon,'

'Unlikely, but you never know.' Arthur lifted his camera. 'What was that girl's name again?'

Harry rummaged for the notebook on which he had scribbled the details of his tip-off.

'Spencer. Lady Diana Spencer.'

'Is she a Spencer Spencer? As in Sarah Spencer? Althorp?'

'Dunno. Probably.'

Arthur nodded, satisfied. He knew what he was looking for now. A gingernut. Through his long-range lens, he scanned the group as they sat down. There were a number of young women, none ginger, and none with Sarah Spencer's skinny intensity. There was a mousy-haired girl in a blouse and flowered skirt, but she looked pretty ordinary.

But perhaps the new girlfriend was yet to arrive, because where was Charles? Nowhere to be seen, although a number of his teammates were sitting with the women. Harry recognised Luis Basualdo. He was a famous philanderer whose penis, it was said, was the size of a pepper grinder. One of those big ones from touristy Italian restaurants, presumably.

Basualdo preyed on wealthy women and was obviously going about his usual business. He lounged, thighs apart in their tight white trousers. He was pushing back his dark hair with his muscled forearms, his big white teeth flashing in his tanned and handsome face. The young girl he was talking to, the mousy one, was staring like a rabbit might at a fox.

Arthur was sweeping back along the group. He, too, saw the girl. 'Bingo,' he muttered.

'What is it?' demanded Harry.

Arthur passed him the camera. 'That kid with Basualdo. Look at her necklace.'

Harry looked. At the base of the girl's creamy throat was a scrolled gold letter D. 'Think that's her then?'

'Must be.' Arthur started to scramble to his feet. 'Come on. Let's go over . . .'

Diana

She had been fending off the Argentinian for the last half-hour. Out of politeness only, because he was in the prince's team, but he clearly considered himself irresistible. He was sitting with his legs apart to display a very obvious bulge.

'English women are the most beautiful in the whole world!' He stared ardently into her eyes.

Oh go away, she thought. Having established within seconds that she lived at Althorp, he was now angling for an invitation. His manner was so brazen, it was embarrassing. She was trying to distract him with questions about polo, but with only limited success.

'Is it true, Mr Basualdo, that a polo pitch is the size of ten football pitches?'

'*Sí*. And it is true, Lady Diana, that your family has a wonderful art collection?'

'Well, we used to. But then my stepmother sold it.'

It was almost a relief when two stocky figures appeared and blocked out the sun.

'Lady Diana Spencer?' asked one. She couldn't really see, but he seemed to have a camera.

'Yes!'

'I'm from the *Sun*. Mind if I take a photo?'

'Oh!' She remembered Stephen's warnings about the press, and what had happened to her sister. But this was only a picture. She wasn't going to say anything. 'Not at all! Please do!' She arranged herself, gazing into the lens.

The Press

'Whaddya think?' Harry hissed to Arthur as they walked off.

'Dunno. Friendly.'

'Bit young and innocent though.'

'Not his usual type,' Harry agreed.

They felt disappointed. For once, their information had been wrong. They had rushed down here, in the blazing heat, on a wild goose chase. Or, to be more precise, a wild princess one.

When the bike came to courier Arthur's film back to the office, he shoved a note with it inside the envelope: 'File this, because I'm not sure.'

Chapter Twenty-Five

Stephen

Later, after the party had returned, Stephen sneaked a cigarette round the back of the house. As a rule, he tried not to smoke — the prince hated it — but it was impossible to resist sometimes. And now was one of those times. Yet another attempt to launch Diana had failed.

He himself had compared becoming Princess of Wales to a horse race, but it was rare to fall at the very first fence. Almost everyone, however hopeless, got past the polo stage. But the prince had barely seemed to notice Diana, and the press had been there too, which made it worse. Had there been any kind of spark, they would have fanned it to a flame and it would be all over the front pages tomorrow. That was what had been supposed to happen.

Stephen leant on his master's Aston Martin and drew on his Marlboro. Talking of sparks and flames, there was a barbecue tonight, but so what? Having ignored Diana thus far, the prince was hardly going to give her any attention there. Which meant, Stephen knew, that once again his job was dangling by a thread.

He exhaled in a rush, and his head spun slightly. Thinking about Diana had the strange effect of making her appear before his eyes. There she was, in the same skirt and blouse she had worn earlier, walking towards her Polo. She was carrying a suitcase.

Flinging his cigarette butt on the gravel, he ground it out with the polished toe of his shoe. 'What are you doing?'

'What does it look like, Mr Barry?'

'You're not leaving?'

She put her case in the boot and closed the lid. 'Prince Charles isn't the slightest bit interested in me. I had more attention when Little Black Muff won Best-Kept Hamster in the Fur and Feather section of the Sandringham Show.'

'Well,' Stephen said encouragingly, 'that was very good. About the hamster, I mean.'

She gave him a baleful look. 'I was the only entrant.'

She fished in her pocket and got out her keys. It was the end, he realised. If she went now, that was it, his best hope of keeping his job would go with her. But what could he say to persuade her to stay?

'The barbecue,' he began, desperately.

Her smile disappeared and her face fell. 'What's the point?'

'You can talk to him there,' Stephen insisted. 'You just need to get him alone. You know what to say . . .'

The blue eyes rolled. 'Oh yes, *The Goon Show*! Laurens van der Valk.'

He ignored her rebellious tone. 'Post,' he corrected.

'Even if I did speak to him, I wouldn't say any of that. It sounds terrible.'

'But I thought you were in love with His Royal Highness,' Stephen reminded her. 'And wanted to marry him, and become Princess of Wales.'

She stared at her shoes. 'I am,' she sighed. 'I do.'

'Well, in that case,' said the valet, 'you can't leave. Not yet. Not without giving it one last go.'

*

Lanterns and fairy lights were strung on the stable-yard's old brick walls. With the glow of the flames, they made for an intimate atmosphere. After the hats, frocks and heels of Cowdray Park, the house party had dressed down in jeans and checked shirts, even Stetsons and cowboy boots. Country and western jangled from a cassette player. Laughter and conversation combined with the pop of champagne corks. There was even the occasional 'Yee hah!'

Trestle tables were set up on the yard's cobbled floor, with bales of golden hay for seats. More bales had been placed on the lawn.

To Stephen's vast relief, Diana was doing as he suggested, giving it one last go. In her dungarees, which were fetchingly tight, she was flitting about like some denim-clad fairy, drawing admiring glances in her wake. Unfortunately, none were coming from the Prince of Wales. He was talking to Philippa de Pass, elegant in her Wranglers.

Prince Philip stalked up and down behind the barbecue and the clearly terrified cooks, occasionally darting forward to spear a sausage. He was accompanied by Commander de Pass, whose ear was being bent about the special picnic trailer Philip had designed for use at Balmoral.

'Got sections for hot things and cold things. You just hook it up to the back of a Land Rover and run it up to whatever bothy we're using. No need for staff or anything.'

None at all, so long as you didn't need anyone to prepare, cook and put the food in the trailer, service the Land Rover and make sure the bothy was pristine and fully equipped in advance, thought Stephen.

'Sounds absolutely ingenious, sir . . .'

The sun was setting now, filling the sky with stripes of copper, red and duck-egg blue. The raging colours were reflected in the windows that faced them; the house was otherwise becoming a dark bulk. The world was shrinking into the stable-yard, with its dancing flames, sizzling sausages and glowing lanterns.

Mrs de Pass moved briskly off. Doubtless, as hostess, she had something to check. The prince stood alone; now, the valet realised, was the moment.

Had Diana noticed? He tried to catch her eye while keeping his master in his sights.

The prince's face had assumed its usual doleful expression. Or perhaps he was just tired; polo was as strenuous as it was costly. Stephen watched him move from where he had been standing and through the shadows. He seemed to be heading towards the house.

Fear clutched the valet's chest; if the prince was going to bed, it was quite literally curtains. He would leave in the morning and that would be that.

Then, with a relief so powerful it made him want to sink to his knees, Stephen saw his master plonk himself on a hay bale on the dark lawn, his distinctive profile silhouetted against the last of the setting sun.

'What is it, Mr Barry?' Suddenly there she was, at his side. 'I saw you looking at me.'

There was no time to explain, only instruct. 'Over there,' he growled. 'On the hay bale. Go.'

He watched her hurry over, passing from the light of the courtyard into the gloom of the garden. He saw the prince look up, give his trademark quizzical smile. At last, thought Stephen, grabbing a bottle of beer from a passing tray.

At the very least, he had got them together. This was the closest they had been all day.

Diana

She stood before him in her dungarees, smiling broadly from under her fringe. The sky glowed behind her.

'Diana?' the prince repeated, vaguely.

'We met at Althorp, sir.'

Her eager tone disguised her disappointment. This was the moment she had been waiting for, for which she had hoped and dreamed. But he didn't seem to have the foggiest who she was. Did he even know she had been invited on his account?

'I loaded for my father, sir. We sat next to each other at lunch.'

'Lunch,' he repeated, in a flat sort of way that made her think of all the millions of lunches he must have attended since then.

She held her breath and waited for recognition to dawn. For him to smile. But it was actually too dark to see his features, only his ears.

'We talked about your schooldays,' she prompted.

'Oh God, did we? How awful.'

She felt a swoop of pure misery. He really, really wasn't interested. Her flatmates had been right all along, She had to accept it.

But before she gave up, went home, put it all behind her, there was one last thing she wanted to let him know. 'I saw you at the funeral, sir. Lord Mountbatten's funeral. I felt so sorry for you.'

It was a sucker punch, coming out of nowhere, and it sent him reeling. For a few seconds, he could not speak.

'Oh,' he said, through a hard, unyielding throat. 'That.'

It was almost a year ago, but it still felt to him like yesterday. The pain was as raw now as it had been then, the anger just as hot. He missed the old man every day. No one had been closer, or understood him better.

'You were in the Abbey?' he asked.

'No, at home. I watched it on the television. Your face when you walked up the aisle. It was the saddest thing I've ever seen.'

The prince dropped his head and stared at the darkened grass. At last, someone had realised, had sympathised.

He looked up, wanting more. 'Was it?' he prompted. 'The saddest thing? Really?'

She obliged gladly, immediately. 'Oh yes. I thought, it's wrong, he's lonely, he needs someone to look after him.'

The prince felt amazed, but also vindicated. This girl, this comparative stranger, seemed to understand him better than members of his own family. Because it *had* been lonely, unbearably so. *And* bleak, *and* wretched.

He cleared his throat. 'That's very kind of you.'

'Not really,' she returned simply. 'It's just how it seemed to me. My heart bled for you.'

'Did it?' The prince patted the hay beside him. 'Do sit down.'

She did not wait to be asked twice. She had so much she wanted to tell him. 'The service was so beautiful. I loved the prayers. The one about God spreading over the heavens and ruling the raging of the sea.'

'The Naval Prayer,' the prince said, astonished and gratified.

'And then there was one about putting on the breastplate of faith.'

'The Life Guards Prayer. Gosh, you were really paying attention.'

'Of course I was. Lord Mountbatten was a great man.'

'He was,' the prince eagerly agreed. 'Do you know, when his body was lying in state at St James's, twenty-five thousand people filed past and signed the book of condolence?'

'I can imagine,' she said, softly.

He seemed now to slump on his hay bale. She felt sorrow roll from him like a black wave. 'It was like losing a parent,' he said.

She reached across the void in silent sympathy. She knew all about losing parents. They were so similar. They had so much in common.

Some time afterwards, they slipped back into the stable-yard. The barbecue party was in full swing; amid the dancing, talk and laughter, they passed almost unseen.

Diana's big eyes shone, her cheeks had a new, happy glow. She felt ten times lovelier, just like that, powered by pure joy. She had done it, and she knew it.

It had been, she thought, an actual, tangible moment. One minute he had been casting her occasional glances, his features contorted with remembered pain. And then his face had straightened, his brows had lifted and a sort of wonder had filled his eyes. He had looked charmed, dazzled. And in that moment, she had actually *felt* it, the love growing between them. And now they were bound together, twin souls.

She felt lit from inside, like a lantern. There would be no more dark shadows. Daddy would be proud. Mummy would be happy. Beacons would blaze throughout the land. Diana Frances, disappointing daughter, ugly duckling, Cinderella, would be the heroine of her own fairy tale. Her own romantic novel, even. She would be a princess, loved by a handsome prince.

Chapter Twenty-Six

Kensington Palace, London
April 1992
Sandy

'Can't manage another mouthful.' Diana put her fork down beside her pasta bowl.

She had eaten about half of it. Mine was hardly touched. I had been too interested in what she was saying. I had never imagined the extent to which everything had been manipulated, and the many times the whole thing almost didn't happen at all.

I thought again about the Medicis and the Tudors and how amazing it was that such dynastic scheming still went on. Then I remembered the little grave of her brother in Sandringham churchyard and wondered why I was so surprised.

She had slid off her stool and was going around switching on the lights. The afternoon was fading and the kitchen growing dark. She paused next to a window and waved cheerfully.

'Who is it?' I asked, wondering if it was Fergie. The Duchess of York and her Texan lover had exploded over the front pages a few months ago. She and Prince Andrew were apparently now separating.

'Princess Michael,' said Diana. 'She lives next door.'

'Princess Pushy,' I said, before I could stop myself. It was what the newspapers called her. I blushed and hoped Diana wasn't offended.

'She's not so bad,' she said breezily, returning to her stool and hopping back on it. 'Anyway, the next thing that happened was Cowes.'

Cowes, I recalled, was the second of the tests she had to go through on her way to winning the ultimate prize. Exactly what happened there, I was not sure. But I guessed I was about to be told.

'That was in August,' she said, 'just a few weeks after the polo. Mr Barry took me down to *Britannia*.'

I frowned. '*Britannia* as in . . . ?'

'The royal yacht, yes. The world-famous floating palace, the oldest ship in the Royal Navy.'

'Isn't that the *Victory*?'

She laughed. 'That's what I thought too. Turns out it's *Britannia*. We're talking ships that are currently serving, you see.'

'Oh right.'

'And you must always remember that it is "in", not "on". We travel *in* the yacht. Not *on* it.'

'Noted,' I said. 'So what was it like?'

'Big. With lots of sailors. I had to share a bathroom with Princess Anne.'

'Stop!' I held up my hand. 'Start at the beginning.'

Our wine glasses were empty. So was the bottle.

'We're going to need some more of that,' I said, nodding at the latter. 'Otherwise your throat might get dry.'

'Ha!' she said. 'You're right. I don't drink much normally. But then again, I don't talk this much normally either.'

She went to the fridge, a huge, sleek, double-doored steel affair, and produced a smart-looking bottle of Chablis. She levered it open with difficulty.

I watched, amused. 'I expect you're used to butlers doing that.'

'Do you want the rest of this story or don't you?'

She glugged the pale yellow liquid into my glass. I was feeling slightly light-headed by now, not just with the wine, but with the sheer joy of being with her again. We were easing back into something that was starting to feel like old times.

'So,' I said. 'Cowes. Take it away.'

'Mr Barry picked me up from Young England.' Her eyes shone with remembered happiness. 'I was so excited. It all seemed like such fun.'

St Saviour's Church Hall, Pimlico, London

August 1980
Stephen

She had asked him to collect her from the nursery where she worked. It was in the hall attached to a great Victorian barn of a church: St Saviour's. He had hoped she might be waiting outside, but there was no sign of her when he drew up.

His was a nondescript car from the Palace pool. The prince had gone on ahead in the Aston Martin and had been in Cowes some days. At this time – late morning – he would have been out on the water for hours already.

Stephen was no fan of sailing, but the breeze on a sparkling sea was infinitely preferable to the hot August sun now beating down on the hard London pavements. Reluctantly, he forced himself out of the driving seat and went up the paved path to knock on the door. It was solid and studded, castle-style, with an iron ring for a handle. Beside it was a notice: 'Young England Kindergarten'.

A dark-haired Sloane in an Alice band and pearls – he was familiar with the type now – opened the door and looked at him enquiringly. 'Hello, I'm Kay King. Can I help you?'

He explained his mission.

Kay King looked as suspicious as the Sloane flatmates originally had. 'She's just cleaning the kitchen,' she said, doubtfully.

It was Stephen's turn to be surprised. Cleaning the kitchen? She was about to spend the weekend with the royal family. It was pure Cinderella.

Diana appeared, beaming excitedly and carrying a small weekend bag. 'Hello, Mr Barry!' She seemed slightly out of breath, as if she had just downed tools and hurried to meet him. Along with a shirt, cardigan and flowered skirt, she was sporting a pair of Marigolds.

'Going to take those off?' he asked wryly.

She ripped them, giggling, from her hands as they walked down the path. 'Imagine if I'd turned up in them.'

'Well, it's not unknown. Her Majesty wears them sometimes, to wash up at Balmoral.'

She laughed disbelievingly.

'It's true,' he said.

Noise from behind now distracted them both. A group of tots in painting overalls were crowded in the doorway. 'Miss Diana!' they were wailing. 'Come back, Miss Diana! Where are you going, Miss Diana?'

'Just off to the seaside,' she called back, waving cheerily.

This produced fresh wails. 'The seaside! The seaside! Can we come too, Miss Diana? Take us with you, Miss Diana!'

Kay King appeared. 'Miss Diana will be back soon,' she said as she steered them firmly back inside.

'When?' was the chorused demand. 'Miss Diana! Miss Diana!'

She swung back from blowing them kisses and gave him an apologetic grin. 'They're quite attached to me.'

'So I see,' he said, impressed. 'And you obviously enjoy it. Even cleaning the kitchen.'

She shook back her thick blonde hair. 'Well, I'm the youngest of the team, so I tend to do the jobs no one else wants.

Take them to the loo, wipe their noses, the whole lot. I don't mind though.'

He tried and failed to imagine any member of the royal family sharing this view. Never in his life had he seen any of them wipe a nose, and as for taking toddlers to the loo, forget it. The Queen had had difficulty embracing her own children. 'Not you, dear,' she had once advised her eldest son after an absence of six months. The prince had been five at the time and Her Majesty had brushed aside his little-boy hugs to shake hands with waiting dignitaries. Stephen had heard about it many times, from the horse's somewhat bitter mouth. Now he came to think of it, that had happened on *Britannia*.

'Nursery work's really interesting,' Diana was enthusing. 'I love it: it teaches you how to entertain children constructively. It's amazing how very different they can be. You can't just lump them together, any more than you can lump people together. Every human being is different and you can see from an amazingly young age how their personality traits show through.'

Stephen was impressed. All this would come in very handy. She would be raising the nation's future rulers, if things went well. With the full sun of royal favour finally falling on her, it was hard to remember the doubts he had once had. Her love of soppy romantic novels, for instance. What did that matter, compared to her talents? Her memory, as he knew from the ex-girlfriends conversation, was phenomenal. Her instincts, meanwhile, were spot on. Her actions on that hay bale in West Sussex had been nothing less than genius. With her artless schoolgirl sympathy, she had hit on the absolute perfect subject to excite the prince's powerful self-pity. In doing so, she had snatched glorious victory from the jaws of certain defeat.

He opened the passenger door for her; she slid herself in with practised ease. 'We were taught this at school, would you believe.'

'Good,' he said. 'It's going to be a lot more use to you than maths.'

A giggle.

'Have you been to Cowes before?' he asked.

'No. I don't know very much about sailing, I'm afraid.'

'You don't really need to.' As her host would be out all day, the main skill required was the ability to amuse herself.

They went over Battersea Bridge. Battersea Power Station loomed ahead, its thick brown towers like the legs of an upturned stool.

'Do you like being a valet?' she asked.

'Very much.'

She nodded, her eyes shining. 'It must be wonderful to be close to Prince Charles all the time.'

Stephen sidestepped this. 'Coincidentally, I valeted for him for the first time at Cowes.'

It had been an easy introduction, as the only piece of clothing of any importance was the royal raincoat.

The blue eyes looked panicked now, he noticed. 'What's the matter?' he asked.

'Oh, Mr Barry. I'm so nervous! What if I say something really . . . *wrong?*'

'You won't,' Stephen serenely assured her. 'Just avoid personal remarks. And controversy, at all costs. The royal family never speaks in public of anything that might be an embarrassment.'

She nodded. 'Who will be there?'

'Princess Margaret will be on board. As will Princess Anne.'

Excitement seemed to grip Diana as she realised she really would be in the intimate inner circle. 'And the Queen?'

'Her Majesty never attends the Cowes Regatta.'

On the motorway, she turned on the radio and found a pop station to sing along to. It wasn't Stephen's choice necessarily, and it certainly wouldn't be the prince's. She needed to switch to classical music, sharpish. He'd look out some cassettes and lend them to her. She liked it loud, too: the valet's ears were ringing by the time the glittering Solent was visible at the side of the road. They had reached Portsmouth and the sea.

At the dockyard checkpoint, the white-gloved rating waved him on. The barrier raised, then lowered behind them. The vast hull of *Britannia* rose like a gleaming dark-blue wall, striped with red and gold and with a lion and unicorn crest. Stephen felt, as always on these occasions, a swell of love and pride. This was his world. His wonderful, privileged, royal world.

Chapter Twenty-Seven

The Royal Yacht *Britannia*, Portsmouth
August 1980
Diana

She had never seen anywhere so clean. *Britannia* was absolutely spotless. You could eat your dinner off its floors. When you shared a flat with four messy girls, some of whom skimped on housework, this was the sort of thing you noticed.

She pictured herself back at Coleherne Court, directing Ginny and Anne as they cleaned the kitchen floor. 'Scrub harder, you swabs! I want this place shipshape and Bristol fashion! *Britannia* fashion!'

Her smile faded as she remembered their reaction to the *Britannia* invitation. 'But, Duch, you don't even *like* sailing,' Ginny had pointed out.

'Rubbish. I love rowing around the Round Oval, you know that.'

The Round Oval was the island in the centre of the lake at Althorp. All three flatmates had visited, and knew what it was to drift dreamily around the water in the full heat of a summer afternoon.

'I shouldn't think *Britannia* is like that,' Anne had said.

It wasn't. The royal yacht, unexpectedly, had a suburban air: white walls, grey carpets, modern furniture in shades of muted blue.

Mr Barry had shown her to her cabin: white with a large single bed covered in pale green. The furniture was functional rather than luxurious. He explained there was a bathroom down the corridor, which she would be sharing with Princess Anne. It seemed an alarming prospect, somehow.

The prince was not around. She was doing her best not to feel disappointed. But he was windsurfing, apparently. Would she ever see him alone? she wondered. Princess Anne and Prince Edward were currently out crewing, whatever that was. Prince Andrew, meanwhile, was somewhere in a speedboat.

Diana wondered what he was like these days. They'd known each other as children at Sandringham and had been quite close for a while. He had had a definite naughty streak and was fond of practical jokes. Stories abounded of him pulling the footmen's coat-tails, turning the signs the wrong way round to confuse guests at garden parties and tying guardsmen's bootlaces together as they stared, impassive and impotent, over his head. Like Caro, he was fond of whoopee cushions. But Caro, unlike Andrew, had never poured bubble bath in the Windsor Castle swimming pool.

Diana had, whilst sifting the papers for stories about Prince Charles' love life, come across the occasional one about his younger brother's. While Charles had gone for well-born beauties, Andrew seemed to have a taste for models and beauty queens. She hoped he was happy, anyway.

She unpacked her few things. Her new dress, her Charlie Brown pyjamas. Her small make-up bag and sponge bag. Her hairbrush. Her tiny jewellery pouch. Her book, *A Heart Is Stolen*, had been chosen for its south coast location as much as its exciting plot. The dashing and raffish Justin, Marquis of Veryan, had awoken to the terrible discovery that, in the throes of drunken passion, he had proposed marriage to society beauty Lady Rose Caterham. How would the demure and virginal Ivana Wade-bridge now win the day and Justin's heart?

Much as Diana wanted to know, she was aware of needing paperback romances less these days. She was constructing her own love story, with a real-life prince, and it was better than any novel because it was actually happening. Once Charles got back from windsurfing, that was.

She went to the cabin window and peered out at the boats on the sunny Solent. That, too, was all glittery light with bright sails billowing in the breeze and craft of all shapes and sizes scudding about. Wetsuited figures on surfboards were clinging to the bending stems of boards, leaning back at crazy angles. Was one of them Charles? It looked dangerous, especially if, as was happening to one unfortunate, you were being circled by someone in a speedboat.

She decided to go and explore.

The deck stretched away, all beautiful polished wood. There was a fresh, pleasant breeze and the high, free sound of seagulls. Lines of coloured flags were strung from mast to mast; they spelled words, she knew, and wondered which ones.

Coming towards her was a handsome young rating in white. 'Hello,' she said, beaming, and was surprised when, instead of smiling back, he stood aside and saluted. Embarrassed, she ducked back inside.

She found herself in an enormous sitting room. There were pink curtains and chintz sofas either side of a fireplace with a painting over it. There was a grand piano too, and mahogany side tables, and armchairs, and lamps. Spotting a stereo system, she hurried over, and was disappointed to find that the tapes were all military music. The Band of the Royal Marines. The Band of the Coldstream Guards. No Duran Duran, no Elton John, no Supertramp. No Three Degrees even.

The sitting room led into a large dining room with a long table and rows of elegant chairs.

On a sideboard was a small boat, elaborately wrought in silver. Nearby was a golden miniature oasis; a solid gold pair of camels beneath two solid gold palm trees. The workmanship was exquisite; each leaf of each palm tree perfectly realised. They even had 'coconuts' hanging from them – honey-coloured jewels the size of small grapes. She extended a finger towards them, touching them gently with her nail.

'You can't have them if they fall orf, you know.'

A tiny woman with dark hair stood at the entrance to the huge drawing room.

No doubt who this was, of course. Diana sank into a curtsey. 'Your Royal Highness.'

Princess Margaret was heavily made up with pink lipstick and blue eyeshadow. She was deeply tanned and wearing a bright turquoise dress. Ankles of incredible thinness ended in high-heeled white sandals. One hand ended in a cigarette that was reeking smoke, while the other held a cut-glass tumbler. 'I know who you are,' the Queen's sister remarked, fixing Diana with eyes of a mesmeric purple-blue. 'You're the blank canvas on which we're all pinning our hopes.'

It seemed, Diana thought, a rather personal remark given that nothing personal was ever discussed. She smiled nervously. 'I really don't know what to say to that, ma'am.'

'Well, that's strange,' Princess Margaret drawled. 'You knew exactly what to say to Charles. Or so one hears.' She took a drag on her cigarette. 'What do you think of *Britannia?*' she asked abruptly.

'Oh. It's very nice, ma'am.'

'Not a bad old hulk. And, of course, the only thing one's sister has actually built. William the Conqueror built the Tower.

Edward the Third built Welsh castles. All Lilibet has built is this boat, though she isn't in the least bit interested in sailing. Yellow rubies, by the way.' The princess gestured at the coconuts. 'Just in case you were wondering.'

'I didn't realise rubies came in yellow, ma'am.'

'Yes, and isn't it a good thing they do? One gets so very tired of the red sort.'

Diana giggled. Princess Margaret was disconcerting. But funny.

She followed the small figure back into the drawing room. A rating passed them and saluted. 'They're so quiet,' Diana marvelled. 'They don't seem to make any noise at all.'

'Well, they wear special rubber-soled shoes so they don't disturb us. But they're not as quiet as they look. There was a homosexual vice-ring on board once.' As Diana's mouth fell open, Margaret shot her a wicked look. 'One imagines they have to find something to do. There are two hundred and seventy-six of them, after all. Plus a twenty-six-piece Royal Marines band which plays every morning at eight.' She took a drag of her cigarette. 'Must be the most expensive alarm clock in the world. Like the drawing room, do you?'

Diana looked around, taking in the inoffensive décor. 'Yes, ma'am.'

The mocking blue-purple stare was disconcerting. 'Lilibet and Philip designed it all, right down to the doorknobs. Their style is wildly adventurous, as you can see.'

'I didn't realise you had fireplaces on ships though, ma'am.'

'It's never lit. Navy law means a sailor standing by at all times with a bucket, which is rather a bore. Know what that is?' The whisky tumbler was pointed at something white and ragged in a glass case.

'No, ma'am.

'It's the white ensign flown by Captain Scott on his ill-fated Antarctic expedition. It was attached to his sledge, apparently, and removed in 1912 when his body was found and given to one's great-grandfather. The flag, that is. Not the body.' Margaret snorted with laughter, and Diana wanted to do the same. But it seemed so disrespectful to the poor captain. 'That's a porai, by the way.' The princess pointed at a framed wooden club. 'The men of Tonga use it to fight with. And that's an ike, a mallet used by their womenfolk. Perhaps they just bash each other with them, who knows? I can think of several men who deserve a good ike-ing.'

Diana giggled. She wondered which men were meant. It was no secret that Margaret's love life had been eventful. Her marriage to Lord Snowdon had failed two years previously, while that to Captain Peter Townsend had famously not been allowed. It all sounded heartbreaking, but Margaret was obviously a tough cookie. Perhaps she had no heart to break.

'And this is a pig-sticking implement, should one be required.'

Diana's attention was being drawn to a long pole with a tassel at one end and a sharp point at the other.

'It's from that island in the South Seas where they think one's brother-in-law's a god. Oh yes,' the princess went on, seeing Diana's astonished face. 'They think Philip can work miracles. Cure all sickness, make the old young, that sort of thing, just too frightfully funny.'

Diana wondered if it was, really. If you lived on some remote South Sea island and a tall blond man appeared on a fabulous yacht, rumoured to be married to the Queen, why wouldn't you think he had divine powers? That royalty could mean so much struck her as humbling. But it was clear that Margaret didn't share this view.

'And here's a Swedish navy sword from 1786. It goes with *this*.' *This* was a chair with a padded red velvet seat and extremely short legs. 'It's a knighting stool. In case Lilibet gets the urge at sea.'

The piano, a baby grand, had its lid up. The white keys looked tempting and she felt her fingers twitch with the urge to touch them. 'It's a lovely piano, ma'am.'

'Play, do you?'

'A little.'

'Yes, so do I. Very well, I'm told.' Margaret sat down, plonked her tumbler on the instrument's shining top and launched into a beautiful, subtle rendition of 'Smoke Gets in Your Eyes'. She played with an intensity and yearning that brought tears to her audience's eyes, no smoke being necessary.

'Beautiful,' Diana murmured, when the last note died away.

'Yes, everyone says that. One would have been marvellous on the stage, but one ended up in the orchestra instead.'

Diana was puzzled. 'How do you mean?'

'Second fiddle,' Margaret snapped. Then, seeing Diana still looked bemused, she added, 'To my sister!'

She had, Diana thought, been told to avoid controversy and personal topics. But Margaret didn't seem to speak of anything else.

The princess seized her tumbler and took a rattling swig. 'One had one's honeymoon in this ship, you know. It lasted six weeks.'

'Six weeks, ma'am?'

She was beginning to get the hang of royal conversation. You just repeated the last two words of whatever they had said. The tone was the difficult thing, as here. Was six weeks long for a royal honeymoon, or short?

Margaret chuckled. 'The socialists got quite cross about it. Questions were asked in Parliament because it cost the British taxpayer ten thousand pounds a week. But as we sailed away, ten thousand jolly British taxpayers cheered us off from South-end Pier. The mayor even sent a message saying "Southend wishes every happiness to the bride and groom." Rather sweet of Southend, really.'

'Very,' Diana agreed.

'Then we steamed to the Caribbean and went to Tobago, Antigua, Barbados and St Vincent. Which was rather nice because one had done the same tour five years earlier when one was getting over Peter.' The princess's buxom chest inflated in a sigh and the violet eyes filled with an expression of great sadness.

Diana suddenly felt terribly sorry for her. Perhaps her unhappy love life had left its mark, after all. If it had, *Britannia* must be full of memories of romance gone wrong. It occurred to her that, as the younger sister of the Queen, Margaret's life might look privileged and glittering, but in reality was full of shadows. Not dissimilar to her own, Diana thought. She had taken refuge in romantic novels. Perhaps Margaret's spiky, satirical exterior was her own protective armour. But, for the moment, she seemed lost in happy memories.

'It was rather lovely in the West Indies. Calypso singers and so on.' Margaret raised her arms in the air, moved them about in rhythm and began to sing.

Our lovely princess though it was stupidness
Why shouldn't a princess marry a camera man?

'Then we anchored for three days off Mustique. I was given a little plot of land there for a wedding present. Overlooking the bay in the south of the island.' She sighed again.

'It sounds lovely.' And there obviously had been a lot of love there. Poor Margaret.

'Oh it was. It really was. One got so fond of island life. So refreshingly free of all one's duties and responsibilities. Love and royalty, they really don't go together, you know.' The princess paused and lit another cigarette. 'They really don't.' All the mockery had gone from her expression. The purple-blue eyes lingered sadly on Diana.

There followed a long silence, so long as to be uncomfortable. It was obvious that a warning was being given. Unnecessarily.

Diana felt. In her case, Charles wasn't second fiddle to anyone, and he loved her, no doubt about that. She remembered him gazing at her in wonder and felt the glittery, swirly, snow-globe feeling.

'You were saying, ma'am?' she prompted. 'About island life?'

'Oh yes. We walked arm in arm along white beaches. I think we would gladly have lived in a little grass hut, on the sand . . .'

'Hardly, Margo!'

Someone had entered the room from behind; a young woman with wet blonde hair, a blue waterproof and jeans. Her long, rather scornful face was as universally familiar as her aunt's and, on seeing her, Diana felt the same shock of recognition.

The Queen's daughter threw her lithe body into an armchair. She took no notice as Diana bobbed a curtsey.

It was left to Margaret to point with her newly lit cigarette. 'Anne, this is Diana Spencer. Who's come to save us all.'

'So it is,' Anne said, before launching into an enthusiastic account of her day at sea.

Her aunt's face remained sceptical. 'Hardly my style, darling.'

'Rubbish. I've heard you used to be a whizz at waterskiing.'

Margaret brightened. 'One was, rather. Tony got one to do it to help lose the birth weight. One put on three stones with every pregnancy. Speaking of which,' she gestured with her cigarette again at Diana, 'we were just talking about honeymoons.'

Princess Anne's stare was just as cold in private as the public one captured in so many newspaper photographs. 'Jumping the gun a bit, aren't we?'

A warm wave of blood swirled through Diana's cheeks. Fortunately, Margaret came to her rescue.

'*One*'s honeymoon,' she elucidated. 'But didn't you have yours on *Britannia* too? South America, wasn't it? Marvellous.'

'We did, it was, and no. Weather awful, seasick for the first four days. Not a great start.' Anne spoke in the truncated manner of a telegram. 'Temperature in the eighties by the time we got to Ecuador. Picnicked eleven thousand feet up in the mountains wearing these awful lurid ponchos. While we were buying them, in this dusty little village, someone was shouting on the loud-speaker that the Queen of London and her husband Prince Philip Marks were honouring their humble shopping centre. When we finally got back, we needed a holiday to recover from the honey-moon.' Anne pushed back her hair, which had dried in a tangle, and jumped to her feet with a loud slither of waterproofs.

When she had gone, Margaret turned back to Diana. 'You see? Romance and royalty. Never a good combination.'

Chapter Twenty-Eight

Later, clutching her sponge bag, Diana waited nervously outside the shared bathroom. Anne had been in it so long there was scarcely time to clean her teeth. When the princess emerged, she just looked at her witheringly before flouncing off down the corridor to her cabin, almost colliding with Stephen, who was coming in the opposite direction.

'Anne Elizabeth Alice Louise,' he drawled, comically, as he reached Diana.

'What?'

'It's what her staff call her. Her full name. Because she's so hoityotoity.'

Diana giggled as Stephen accompanied her back to her cabin.

'Everything all right?'

'Is Prince Charles back?'

'Not yet. But that's not unusual. His Royal Highness likes to cut it fine.'

He left her so she could dress for dinner. The frock was a mid-blue taffeta full-length number with shoulder straps and a deep frilled edge on the bodice and skirt. She had bought it with Ginny, from a little boutique in the King's Road. It had been in the sale.

Remembering Ginny's exclamations – 'Gawd, Duch, wish I could fit into it' – she felt a cramp of longing for the noisy friendliness of Coleherne Court.

She approached the drawing room with a stomach full of but-
terflies. That no one took the slightest notice as she entered was
both a relief and yet wasn't. She stood, clutching a glass of water
and feeling terminally awkward in her taffeta – were the straps
too skinny? The bodice too revealing? She took up what she
hoped was an inconspicuous position at the edge of the various
chattering groups.

Margaret, at the centre of the drawing-room throng, had
changed into what Caro would call full-strength cocktail gear:
a tight black dress, towering heels, make-up even more pronounced than earlier and diamonds so enormous it seemed
impossible that they could be real.

'Did you know that one invented the horoscope?' she was
asking those clustered around her.

'Really, ma'am?'

'Oh yes. Before one was born, some newspaper editor asked
some astrologer to predict what might be in store for one. He
predicted that one would have an eventful life.' There was a
pause, and something sad flashed across the tanned features.
'And he was certainly right about that.'

Some slightly uncomfortable laughter greeted this.

'But ma'am,' ventured one brave soul. 'Horoscopes are very
popular.'

The princess contemplatively rattled her ice cubes. 'Well,
one hasn't contributed much else to humanity. So possibly that
will be one's legacy.'

'What star sign are you, ma'am?' someone asked.

'Leo. One shares one's birthday with Aubrey Beardsley, Count
Basie, Kenny Rogers, King William IV and a Mr Joe Strummer,
who apparently is a pop singer . . .'

Diana giggled to herself. She wished Anne could have
heard this. One of her boyfriends had introduced the Clash to
Coleherne Court, a punk band whose front man was Strummer.

He was much given to rebellious pronouncements, but then, so was Princess Margaret. Perhaps the two had more in common than it seemed.

One of the ship's officers now introduced himself and began making polite conversation. 'What message do the flags outside spell?' Diana asked him.

'They're just for show. They say "Hurray" and not "Hurrah", by Her Majesty's request.'

This seemed disappointing, somehow. 'Rather a small distinction,' Diana remarked.

'Oh, small distinctions are very important on *Britannia*,' the officer cheerfully explained. 'There are a few interesting discrepancies from the rest of the Navy. Aft the mainmast in the royal apartments, the men go hatless, which puts them technically out of uniform, which spares Her Majesty the trouble of returning a salute.'

'I can see that would be quite a trouble,' Diana said wryly.

The officer continued, regardless. 'And *Britannia* officers wear the same uniform as the rest of the Navy, except that they don't wear a link button on their mess jackets. This dates from when Edward VII's valet made a mistake when he dined in the officers' wardroom . . .' Something over her shoulder now caught his attention; he straightened, raised his chin. She turned round to see.

In a moment of swooping joy, she saw the prince had entered, immaculate in black tie.

He caught her eye and headed over. That kind, steady gaze; that fine, sensitive face; she felt she might swoon. Her heart rose and thudded in her ears. Then, before he could reach her, she felt herself seized by someone else.

'Diana!' A pair of strong hands threw her against a powerful chest and squeezed her so it was hard to breathe.

'Andrew,' she gasped, once she had been released.

His teeth blazed at her. 'Who'd have thought it? Little Diana Spencer from Park House!' He was nodding at his brother, who had now joined them. 'Charles.'

The Prince of Wales' expression was no longer kind and steady. It looked angry and tight. He ignored Diana's beam of welcome and glared, instead, at his brother.

'Enjoy yourself this afternoon?' Andrew asked him, grinning.

'No, I bloody didn't. Thanks to you.'

It now emerged that the speedboat she had seen from her window, harassing the windsurfer, had been the younger brother circling the elder.

'It was bloody dangerous.'

'Oh come on, Charles. Just a bit of fun, that's all.'

'What if I'd fallen off? Could have got caught in your rotors.'

Andrew's smirking silence seemed to inflame the elder prince still further. His cheeks reddened with fury, his eyes had a dangerous gleam and a vein began to tick in his temple. For a moment, he looked as if he might hit his brother.

'Excuse me a moment,' he muttered to Diana, from beneath angry, lowered brows.

Alarmed, she watched him move abruptly away through the crowd. Where was he going? Would he come back?

When she turned back to Andrew, he was grinning. 'Take no notice of him. He's jealous because I've just beaten him in the Most Desirable Bachelors In the World list. Warren Beatty, Dudley Moore, Burt Reynolds – and me!'

Diana felt furious. It was their moment of reunion, and Andrew had ruined it. Instead of diplomatically melting away, he had stayed, with the obvious intention of maddening his brother. Worse, she could see, now, in his laughing, thickly lashed brown eyes, the younger prince's expectation that she would be as bowled over as every other woman on the planet. Well, he was wrong.

'I shouldn't think he cares about that,' she said coldly. 'And he's right, there could have been an accident. What if you'd killed him?'

Andrew shrugged. 'I'd have been twenty times richer, for a start.'

'*What?*'

The younger prince raised his eyebrows. 'You surprise me. Would have thought you'd have been all over this. Financial position of the man you're supposed to be marrying.'

'I don't know what you mean.'

'Well let me tell you.' Andrew's merry, handsome face had a bitter cast now. 'As Prince of Wales, Charles is the sole beneficiary of the Duchy of Cornwall Estates. It's one of the biggest landowners in Britain. One hundred and thirty thousand acres of sheep, land, farms, shops and pubs. Plus the Oval cricket ground and Dartmoor prison. Whole lot brings in half a million a year. Oh, and did I mention that it's tax-free?'

Diana said nothing. And indeed, she had known nothing of this. It did sound like an awful lot.

Andrew's arms were tightly folded. 'Know what I get? As second son of the monarch?'

She shook her head.

'Twenty thousand a year. Which isn't much at all, I think you'll agree. Even Anne gets more than I do.'

Diana thought of her salary as a nursery assistant. Twenty thousand seemed like a fortune beside that, and certainly compared to the pound an hour her sister Sarah paid her for occasional cleaning. But she guessed that was irrelevant here. Andrew was uninterested in comparing down, only up.

'Can't you get a job?' she suggested.

Andrew laughed. 'Nothing I'd like more. But there's only one job in this family and Charles has it.'

'Outside the family, then.'

'Well, if you can think of one that's going to pay me half a million pounds, I'm all ears.'

'There's business, isn't there? People get very rich that way.'

'The royal family doesn't do business. Trade is vulgar. You of all people should know that, Diana.'

Was this a reference to her mother? She looked down, reddening.

'I can't even go to university since Charles ballsed all that up as well.'

'How do you mean? He went to Cambridge, didn't he?'

Andrew's thick, well-cut lip curled. 'That was the problem. He got in with only two A levels, and not very good ones at that. I've got better grades than he has, but all the trouble would kick off again if I went anywhere near an academic institution. So it's the Navy for me by the looks of it. Measly Navy pay as well.'

Diana was silent. She had never imagined this degree of animosity to exist between the two eldest royal brothers. Princess Margaret wasn't the only frustrated royal second fiddle on board.

'Of course,' Andrew added, 'there is another way of raising my pay grade.' Perhaps unburdening himself, to what he might have sensed was a sympathetic audience, had helped. Some of the anger seemed to have gone out of him.

'What's that?' she asked with a cautious smile.

'I could get married. You get a Civil List upgrade if you do. Not much of one, but something.' He flashed his big white teeth. He was, she could see, edging back to charm mode. Perhaps he only had the two settings. He leant in confidingly, so his breath tickled her ear. 'But I'd have to find the right girl first, of course.'

'You would,' she agreed.

'So it's a shame you're taken.'

'Oh, stop it!'

*

'Sorry about my brother,' said the prince as they sat down to dinner.

'Oh, it's quite all right.' Actually, she felt sorry for Andrew. He had changed so much from the high-spirited boy she had known. Life had embittered him already and he was still so young. She deplored his aggression, but could see that he had a point. Possibly several. He was right, it wasn't fair, and it was also a waste. That his elder brother couldn't look to him for support, or vice versa, seemed a terrible shame.

'But at least you know what you're letting yourself in for,' the prince added, with a grin. 'Mixing with the likes of me.'

She smiled back. But she was already wondering if she could help. Andrew needed a wife and not, she thought, just because of the Civil List. He also needed companionship, understanding and support. Someone to help him rediscover the joy of life. Perhaps there was someone among the people she knew.

She felt a sudden excitement. What had Sandy said, all those years ago? *You have an incredibly special gift. Empathy, I think it's called. You're empathetic.* Caro had said much the same.

Well, here was a use for that gift. Empathy would be her contribution to the family. Understanding, compassion and love. Love, most of all. She felt a great wave of goodwill roll out and fill the low-ceilinged dining room, just as the ocean outside filled the horizon.

'Wonderful aren't they?' the prince remarked, waving a hand up and down the table.

'Oh yes, sir,' she breathed. She felt a genuine affection for everyone present, and wanted nothing but good for all of them.

'They're electric, you know. You can plug them in anywhere.'

He was not talking about his relatives but the table candelabra. She now listened as the prince explained they were an ingenious invention of his father's devised to stop lit flames sliding about in stormy seas.

'They look like normal silver candelabra except that the base slots into an electric runner that goes the full length of the table.'

She had noticed that they were strangely bright; quite large and obstructive too, given that each was topped off with a small lampshade.

'My father is an extraordinary inventor,' the prince enthusiastically went on. 'He came up with a simply amazing trailer for picnics at Balmoral—'

'I've heard about it,' she interrupted with a smile. 'He was talking about it at the de Passes' barbecue.' She paused, hoping for the dazzled expression from that evening to return to his face. 'There are compartments for hot and cold. You just fix it to the back of the Land Rover and off you go, to whatever bothy you like. So much more convenient.'

As he smiled back at her, she felt a surge of joy so fierce that she knew it must blaze from her face with embarrassing obviousness.

Something was happening; a stir in the middle of the table. She heard Charles chuckle. 'Oh, here we go. Uffa's getting up.'

Uffa was red-faced and loud. He was evidently a close friend of Prince Philip, who sat opposite, urging him on. Some long-ago racing disaster was apparently being recalled. 'Remember when you came ninth out of thirty starters in Cowslip?' he barked at the Prince of Wales.

'I do!' yelled Andrew, from down the table. 'You were asleep at the helm, Charles. Uffa came into dinner that night in a nightshirt and carrying a candle!'

'Ha, yes,' said the prince, uneasily fiddling with his menu. It was printed with the EIIR cipher of his absent mother.

Diana's insides squirmed in sympathy, She wanted to squeeze his hand and tell him she knew what it felt like to be mocked by her nearest and dearest; that she would never mock him and would always stand by him. She would be his friend and supporter, just as he would be hers. She tried to catch his eye and give him a reassuring smile, but the prince's attention was on his father.

'Always so bloody slow,' remarked Prince Philip. 'I'm always trying to make him get a bloody move on. Still,' he added, his narrow gaze briefly snagging on Diana, 'it finally looks as if he has now.'

Blood surged into her face and she stared down at her hands. Her discomfiture was interrupted by a loud and unpleasant noise, like a long, drawn-out fart.

Uffa Fox was holding up, amid howls of laughter, what looked like an old-fashioned motorhorn. It seemed that while he was on his feet ridiculing the heir to the throne, Philip had concealed the horn under a cushion on his friend's chair, with the resultant rude eruption as he sat down. Meanwhile, from an adjoining room, the Royal Marines band played gamely on.

Afterwards, the prince took her out on deck. Finally, they were alone. It was warm and the sea scent tugged at her nostrils. They stood at the rail, watching the stars come out. She felt the stars inside her kindle too. She felt radiant, full of light.

Back in the sitting room, Princess Margaret was singing at the piano.

'Some enchanted eve-ning . . .'

It really was an enchanted evening. Diana turned to the prince, but he had driven his hands into the pockets of his jacket and was frowning. As he met her eyes, his expression of absolute misery reminded her of the night on the hay bales. 'You look sad, sir,' she said gently. 'Whatever is it?'

'Just life. My life, to be precise. It's just so *unbelievably* lonely.'

As at New Grove, she wanted to reach across to him. But now she wanted more, to ask him to share his burden with her. She could help him. She could help all of them. All he had to do was ask.

'You are automatically separated by your heritage from the rest of the world . . .' the prince complained.

'It must be awful.'

'It is. It *really* is. Do you know, some people won't even come near me in case they are seen to be sucking up? They imagine, quite wrongly, that I won't want to talk to them. I used to think, "Good God, what's wrong. Do I smell? Have I forgotten to change my socks?"' He shook his head, his expression agonised.

'It is so difficult. I can quite see that.'

'It's very kind of you to take an interest.' He looked at her in a considering sort of way. 'Can I just ask something?'

The world seemed to stop then. She held her breath and her heart seemed to rise in her throat.

'Do you . . .' he began.

'Yes . . .?' Her voice was almost a squeak.

'. . . like classical music?'

Stephen

Something had gone wrong, Stephen saw now, from across the room. She was looking for him; her eyes wild and panicked.

He scooted over, just in time to hear her repeat, slowly, possibly for his benefit, 'Do I like classical music?'

The valet understood her concern. Certain Windsors would see a love of classical music as doubtful indeed. How she replied might affect everything.

He caught her eye; nodded infinitesimally.

She turned back to the prince with a beam.

'I *love* classical music.'

'Excellent. I shan't have to scratch around for a companion any more. Perhaps you'd like to come to a concert with me?'

Stephen glided off, smiling. She had passed the Cowes test; passed the polo test. Two down. Many more to go, of course. But Lady Diana was well on her way.

Chapter Twenty-Nine

Coleherne Court, Kensington, London

August 1980

Diana

'The dress! Where's the dress?'

Chaos in Coleherne Court. Girls were rushing everywhere. Diana stood in the middle, laughing.

Anne hurtled by. 'Gin, where's your dress? Duch is borrowing it to go out with You Know Who.'

None of the flatmates had believed Diana's version of events on board *Britannia*, how Prince Charles was sad and suffering and the royal family needed her. 'He's been looking for Love, that's all,' she had said, starry-eyed. 'He's been on a quest for it. Just like me.'

She would, they had all concluded, have to find out the hard way. Hopefully it would not take long, given the prince's track record. She would be spewed out like all his other girls.

Virginia was rummaging under a pile of clothes in her bedroom. 'It was here a minute ago.'

'I'm being picked up in ten minutes!'

Five minutes later, she was ready. The three girls gathered round her. She looked lovely, Anne thought, the cream silk frock setting off her fair colouring. The D necklace nestled at the base of her throat, for luck. Ginny felt, with a sudden twist of worry, that she looked terribly vulnerable. Caro felt the same and just hoped she would not be too devastated when, as was inevitable, it all ended in tears. 'Have a good time,' they all chorused.

'Oh I will. The Verdi Requiem is gorgeous. I didn't know it, but Mr Barry lent me a tape.'

The flatmates exchanged weary looks. They all knew it now. The tape had been playing on a loop at top volume for the past week.

'Will there be any photographers at the Albert Hall?' Caro asked. 'What if you're in all the papers tomorrow? You and Prince Charles, together?'

'Oh Duch! We're going to have to start hiding you in dustbins and smuggling you around under blankets!'

'Making ropes out of sheets so you can escape through the window!'

'Jumping on and off buses! Driving decoy cars! Sneaking out of the back entrance of H. A. Rodd's!'

H. A. Rodd's was what the girls called the world's most famous department store.

'Not a chance,' the Chief Chick sighed amid the giggles. 'Grandmama is coming too.'

There was a gasp. 'Lady Fermoy? But why?'

'To chaperone me.'

Shrieks of disbelief greeted this. 'This is 1980, Duch. Not 1880!'

'No one has a chaperone any more!'

'What does she think you're going to do? Bonk in the Royal Box?'

Diana smiled. There was less than no chance of that happening. She would guard her virtue to the end. 'I just hope Grandmama doesn't show off too much,' she said. 'She played at the Albert Hall once and none of us are ever allowed to forget it.'

The doorbell went. 'Good luck, Duch!' chorused everyone.

Diana went into the hall and pulled her coat off its hook. Dark and thick, with big round buttons, it looked schoolgirlish over her full-length silk frock. Ginny had the worried feeling again. Diana was so young, she thought. So ridiculously young.

Stephen

From the rear of the red plush Albert Hall box, he listened to Lady Fermoy boast about her musical credentials to the prince. Was His Royal Highness aware she had once played the piano on stage here? 'Oh yes, sir. With John Barbirolli conducting.'

Her granddaughter, beside her, threw Stephen a backwards glance of despair.

'The Requiem began life as a memorial to Rossini, of course,' Lady Fermoy spoke loudly over the work as it was played. 'It has been much criticised for being overtly operatic in style. But as a tribute to an Italian artist, its Italian manner can scarcely be out of place. It was, even so, much criticised by Wagner, who remarked that "the Requiem of Verdi is a work of which it is better not to speak."'

She was speaking about it non-stop, all the same. The prince, on her other side, threw Stephen his own backward glance of despair.

During the interval, things went from bad to worse. Diana listened in horror as, accepting a flute of champagne, Lady Fermoy told the prince that her musical gifts had been passed on to her family, in particular dear Diana, who was a natural at the piano, the most talented of her grandchildren by far.

'Oh Grandmama, really, I'm not,' she muttered.

Lady Fermoy ignored this. 'Diana is really wonderfully gifted. Perhaps when we return to the Palace for supper, she might play for us. You'd adore to, wouldn't you, Diana?'

Diana felt that what she would really adore was to throw her grandmother over the balcony's padded edge. She had hoped Lady Fermoy would go home after the concert, but she clearly had no such intention. Did she not realise that Diana's virtue was in no danger? She was guarding it herself until the first night of marriage, which looked an increasingly remote prospect.

The bored expression on the prince's face sent panic swirling round her body. He would not want to see her after this; it would all be at an end. The champagne turned to acid in her stomach.

As the second half began, she tried to concentrate on the music and the great red-and-gold sweep of the concert hall. She was here as the prince's guest, she reminded herself, in a building that his ancestor Queen Victoria had named after her beloved consort. She had seen Albert's statue outside earlier, the adored and golden prince in his magnificent Gothic shrine.

There was romance in the very air of this place, and lifelong devotion, and the most successful of all royal partnerships. But there was also Grandmama wittering on about her training at the Paris Conservatoire and how Verdi was the Italian Wagner.

As the applause sounded, she hastened to the back of the box before the others. 'She's ruining everything. Can't you do something?'

'I'll try my best,' Stephen said, soothingly. In a long career as romantic royal fixer, he had come across many Lady Fermoys. There were ways of dealing with them.

All the way to Buckingham Palace, she continued unabated. 'I established the most marvellous music festival in Norfolk, at King's Lynn. Such a shame you are so rarely at Sandringham during the summer, sir, as I feel sure you would enjoy it . . .'

The prince was looking as if he never wanted to set foot in Sandringham again, in summer or at any other time. Diana wanted to scream at her grandmother to stop but could only stare with blazing eyes at the passing lights of Knightsbridge, then Hyde Park Corner and Birdcage Walk, before the car drew up to the great gates of Buckingham Palace.

They went in, not through the main entrance used at the ball, but a black-painted side door leading to a carpeted corridor. She was surprised to see that the footmen wore breeches and tailcoats, even on normal evenings like this one. They stood aside as they passed and looked deferentially down.

As the unexpectedly modern, compact lift progressed upwards, she kept her eyes imploringly on the valet. Mr Barry had said he would do his best. But it would have to be something completely ingenious to get her grandmother out of the way. Even for five minutes.

The lift stopped and they emerged into a wide, red-carpeted corridor. As with the downstairs passage, all was hushed. That this was Central London, and the mighty Victoria terminus was just a few hundred yards away, seemed unbelievable.

The prince and the valet were speaking in low, hurried tones. She saw the prince give a brief nod and his eyebrows lift, as if relieved. She felt a surge of sick terror; had it been decided that the Spencer women should leave? Before supper even started?

The prince was smiling at her grandmother. 'Lady Fermoy, I would be greatly obliged to you for some help.'

'Of *course*, sir. I would be *honoured*.'

'It's the piano in the White Drawing Room. It once belonged to Queen Victoria and it's known that Mendelssohn played it.'

'Oh, I am quite sure he did, sir. Mendelssohn was, of course, the favourite composer of Queen Victoria and Prince Albert.' Lady Fermoy paused to draw breath. 'He was very fond of England and tried so hard to learn the language that it was said his front teeth ached from pronouncing the English "th" and his back teeth ached from chewing English mutton!'

Diana felt her brain ached from listening to her grandmother.

'I can only bow before your musical knowledge, Lady Fermoy.' The prince was tugging impatiently at his cuffs. 'And the piano would benefit from it too; it has been tuned recently but, I fear, not at all expertly.'

'Good tuners are hard to find these days, sir.' Lady Fermoy shook her head sorrowfully.

'We would be so grateful if you could put it through its paces. Play on it, perhaps. Stephen will show you where it is. Diana and I,' he glanced at her then, and winked, 'will follow shortly.'

Lady Fermoy had no choice but to obey. Diana, still reeling from the wink, felt she might faint from relief and excitement. As her grandmother followed Stephen down the corridor, it was all she could do not to cheer.

The prince's apartment seemed different to the rest of the Palace. The red, white and gold, the heavy decoration, here gave way to something more understated. The walls seemed to be covered with a sort of sacking. It was also quite startlingly cold. All the same, it was thrilling. These were, after all, his private quarters. His refuge, away from the scrutiny of the public. Finally, incredibly, they were alone.

He showed her round; his study first of all. She gathered up each detail with her eyes. On the desk was his passport. He saw her looking and presented it to her, wryly. 'Terrible photo, like everyone's!'

'Not at all!'

Under 'Occupation', she saw, it said 'Prince of the Royal House'.

She scanned his bookshelves closely.

'Do you like reading?' he asked.

'I loved this.' She extended a slim, pale arm and plucked out the volume she had been looking for.

The princely eyes lit up. *'The Night of the New Moon*. Did you really enjoy it?'

She looked ardently at him from under her fringe. 'Adored it.'

'I must say, I'm surprised. I didn't have you down as a Laurens fan.'

'You'd be surprised what I'm a fan of, sir.' She took a deep breath. 'Ying tong ying tong ying tong ying tong ying tong iddle I po!'

'You like the Goons!' he gasped.

'He looked as if all his Christmas presents had come at once,' she said afterwards, to her flatmates.

'What's your favourite sketch?'

Perhaps it was excitement, but maddeningly, suddenly, she could only remember fragments. Fred and someone? The Phantom Something? The Affair of the Something Banana?

He was looking at her expectantly. Her only option was to trust to luck.

'Fred and . . .'

'Gladys!' he finished, delighted.

'Fred and Gladys, yes. And I love the Phantom . . .'

'Head Shaver!'

'And The Affair of . . .'

'The Lone Banana! They're all my favourites as well!'

Through a half-open door, she could see a large green four-poster. It felt intimate and exciting and made something twist low in her belly.

'So refreshing to find a girl with a good sense of humour,' Charles was saying. 'I always try to make people laugh if I can.' His approving smile felt like warm sunshine. She wanted to bask in it for ever.

Chapter Thirty

They were in his sitting room now; more walls with sacking on them and even colder than the study had been. But Diana was glowing too much with happiness to really care. The prince, meanwhile, was providing more examples of his humour. 'My ship docked at San Diego. Some Americans came on board. They asked the CO – Commanding Officer – to get me up on deck, but he told them, "You're wasting your time, Prince Charles is very pompous and not a very likeable chap, you know. He isn't very bright either and he won't want to meet you."'

Diana was indignant. 'How rude!'

He looked back at her with bright eyes. 'Yes, but it was *me*. Pretending to be the CO. It was a joke.'

'Oh, I *see*.'

'And once, when I was at Cambridge, I was in a play where I came on with an umbrella and said I'd led a sheltered life.'

It took her a split second to get it. 'Umbrella, sheltered life. Ha ha. How funny!'

'Yes, I really couldn't get by without humour. Do you want a guided tour of my wardrobe, by the way? Before supper?'

Her heart sank slightly. What she wanted was to stay here, alone with him in the intimacy of his apartments. But he was up on his feet, and she had no choice but to follow.

He led her out into the corridor and turned into the next door down. He flicked on the light to reveal a room almost the same size as his flat, but crammed with clothes. Two rows, one above the other, all around the room. Jackets with braid, gold buttons, stripes. Uniforms, she realised. On shelves above them were the matching hats. Feathered, peaked, and the familiar big fur mounds of the Household Cavalry bearskins.

'Gosh, sir. Are these all yours?'

He smiled wryly. 'Afraid so. This room is entirely set aside for my ceremonial clothing. There's a whole other room for suits.'

She looked around, awed.

'It's Stephen's domain really. It's his job to get everything right. If the bits and pieces aren't in the right places, the regiment I'm visiting will be mortally offended. I'm head of about forty at the last count,' he added. 'And they all have three uniforms each: mess dress, khaki and dress blues.'

'Dress blues?'

He grinned. 'For formal occasions. Plus tropical whites and kilts for the Scottish regiments.'

She extended a hand, touched the nearest sleeve. It had a label on. 'Colonel-in-Chief of the Royal Regiment of Wales.' She walked down the row, reading them off. 'Colonel of the Welsh Guards. Colonel-in-Chief of the Cheshire Regiment, Colonel-in-Chief of the 2nd King Edward VII's Own Gurkha Rifles, Colonel-in-Chief of the Parachute Regiment.'

'And I'm also Colonel-in-Chief of the Royal Australian Armoured Corps, Colonel-in-Chief of the Royal Winnipeg Rifles and Colonel-in-Chief of the Royal Regiment of Canada. And that's just the Army. I'm a Flight Lieutenant in the Royal Air Force, for my sins.'

She was impressed. 'Can you actually fly a plane?'

It was the right question. He looked delighted. 'I fly the Queen's Flight DC-10s when we're going anywhere. And I once co-piloted a Vulcan, which, as you may know, is the delta-wing nuclear bomber, currently the mainstay of the British strategic strike force.'

He was so different, in this mood, from the sad man on the hay bale. He was, she thought, like a little boy, full of endearing enthusiasm. He reminded her of her Young England children when they lost themselves in their games. The world was left behind and they inhabited a realm of pure excitement. They were, she felt, their real selves then.

'We were practising over South Yorkshire,' he was saying. 'The citizens of Doncaster were not aware of it, but they had the privilege of being the target when their future king made a high-level dummy attack on them.'

His eyes were shining, his face relaxed and happy. She remembered what he had said on *Britannia* about the burden of royal life. Perhaps this was what he wanted to do instead, just as Margaret wanted to be an actress or a singer. But they were both condemned by accident of birth to quite different destinies.

'Here, try on my RAF jacket!' He pulled it out and she slipped it on. The mannish cut of it was rather thrilling; the silky interior cool and slippery on her bare arms. She could smell his cologne on the collar and it made her insides swirl. 'Oh yes,' he said, looking her approvingly up and down. 'Blue suits you. You're a natural wing commander.'

Now he was pulling out a dark blue jacket with gold braid on the cuffs.

'You should try this on too.'

More cool silk inside the sleeves.

'You're now a lieutenant in the Royal Navy. Here's the cap.'

She perched it at an angle on her hair, and he laughed.

'Not sure that would pass morning inspection!'

'You actually served in the Navy, didn't you, sir?'

'Yes I did. On HMS *Bronington*. They called me Taffy Windsor, because I'm Prince of Wales. Taffy's a Welsh nickname,' he added, as she looked blank. 'When I gave up the command four years ago, they hung a lavatory seat round my neck with HMS *Bronington* on it in gold letters.'

'A *lavatory* seat? Is that a naval tradition?'

'No! It was to remind me of the weight of the throne!' His smile faded and he groaned. 'As if I needed reminding.'

She could only smile at him sympathetically. But she could see how, for him, all these uniforms must represent other possibilities, other lives and freedoms he could never attain. It was terribly sad. 'You have to be so many things to so many people, sir,' she said. 'It must be such hard work.'

He looked at her with the same wonder he had on the hay bale. 'You're absolutely right. People have no idea.'

'No idea at all,' she agreed.

This seemed to have a cheering effect on the prince. He picked up a sword and started slashing it about. The blade flashed in the overhead light.

'You're probably used to seeing pictures of me with ceremonial swords. But I know how to use them too!' He sliced the air. 'We used to do sword drill. Can you believe it? In the age of nuclear submarines!'

The swordplay sent her giggling into a corner where rows of colourful cloaks and gowns were hung. She touched the nearest; the velvet was so soft, her fingers could barely feel it.

'My Parliamentary and university robes,' the prince said. 'Plus the Royal Knight Companion of the Most Noble Order of the Garter, the Order of the Thistle and the Great Master and Principal Knight of the Most Honourable Order of the Bath respectively. Now come and see my decorations.'

He led her to a glass-topped cabinet in whose red plush interior were ranged brilliant medallions in shapes from crosses to stars to animals. Some sparkled with jewels, while others were exquisitely detailed in enamel. All nestled in broad, brightly coloured ribbons, identically folded.

He pointed them out. 'That's the Commander Grand Cross, the Order of the White Rose of Finland. And that's the Grand Cordon of the Supreme Order of the Chrysanthemum.'

'So much to remember,' she said admiringly. 'So many titles. I don't know how you do it, sir.'

He looked gratified. 'And we haven't even talked about my non-military titles. On the last count, besides being Prince of Wales, I was Duke of Cornwall, Duke of Rothesay, Earl of Carrick, Baron of Renfrew, Lord of the Isles, Prince and Great Steward of Scotland. Oh, and Earl of Chester.'

'Golly, sir! Is that it?'

The princely eyes twinkled. 'No, there are my unofficial titles. There's an indigenous tribe in Saskatchewan – that's Canada, as I'm sure you know – that calls me Attaniout Kieneego. Which roughly translates to "The Son of the Big Boss". My mother being the big boss.'

'Attaniout Kieneego,' she repeated carefully.

He nodded approvingly. 'Very good. You're a natural.'

She blushed with delight. 'Do you really think so, sir?'

But he was back on his indigenous titles. 'In Africa, in Tanzania, I'm known as "The Sun Looks At Him In A Good Way".'

She put her hand to her mouth to cover the tug of a smile.

'I'm "The Helper of the Cows" in Papua New Guinea. And in Vanuatu, I'm "The Number One Child Belonging To Mrs Queen". It's all right, you can laugh, it is funny.' He was not laughing himself, however. He was looking into her eyes, his expression suddenly serious. 'I'm having a wonderful evening.'

'I am too, sir,' she hastened to assure him. 'Very wonderful.'

'Seems a shame it will be over after supper.'

She sighed, nodded.

'Perhaps,' he said, his voice lower, softer, 'you might like to stay?'

He was close now. His irises, she saw, were a brown and green mosaic. She remembered phrases from novels about air crackling with desire and bosoms being crushed to powerful chests. She thought of the bed next door: wide, green and inviting. The room began to spin and blur. Then the crisp tones of Grandmama Fermoy could be heard outside in the corridor.

The world stopped spinning. Things came back into focus. Diana took a deep, shaky breath. 'I don't think that's possible, really,' she said, apologetically.

The prince looked disappointed. 'I can send you home in a car later?'

She could still hear her grandmother's voice. Not the one outside, but from years ago.

You absolutely must be a virgin. Anything else is out of the question. The reward of Chastity is Love.

Chapter Thirty-One

Kensington Palace, London

April 1992

Sandy

'And after that,' Diana said flatly, 'I didn't hear from him at all.'

'Because you didn't sleep with him, you mean?' I felt outraged. She had been so full of good intentions. Only someone with Diana's creative sympathy could have seen the overtly privileged Margaret and Andrew as victims of an unfair system, and Charles as a suffering soul whose burden she could lighten.

She went bleakly on. 'I waited by the phone, rushed to the letter box whenever anything came. But nothing happened. There was radio silence for weeks and weeks and weeks. I was completely devastated.'

'I bet you were,' I said.

'I really thought I had found what I was meant to be doing at last. I was sure I could help him by loving him, by loving all of them.'

I took a big swig of my wine. She must, I thought, have been completely head over heels. Even from the outside, you could guess the royal family's various characters. They sounded a lot worse from up close.

'I was so miserable,' she said. 'Everything had been going so well. I couldn't understand why he didn't contact me. My world just went dark.'

We were back in the drawing room. She had switched on the lamps that were dotted everywhere, but it still felt poky. A large, dark tapestry on the wall deepened the gloom. Beneath the bunched pink curtain, the windowpanes showed blank and black.

'Why *didn't* he get in touch?' I asked.

She shrugged. 'I thought I must have done something wrong. I imagined it was because I'd insisted on going home, and hadn't slept with him, as you say.'

'But that was definitely the right thing to do,' I said, supportively.

She pulled a face. 'Anyway, I kept going through the motions, in the kindergarten and at my job with Mrs Robertson.'

She had been mentioned earlier, fleetingly. The American banker, whose baby Diana looked after.

'But I had, all the time, this awful heavy feeling of dread; it was like a stone. The future had looked so bright. But now I was sure it was over and I'd never hear from him again.'

'But at least,' I pointed out, 'you had your flatmates for moral support.'

'Oh, I didn't tell them. Didn't want them to say they'd told me so.'

Unlikely, I thought. Her flatmates seemed to me both loving and concerned. She must have been lonely, I thought, keeping her disappointment to herself.

'I knew from what Mr Barry had said that the next stage was Balmoral. But there didn't seem the remotest possibility I was going to be asked there.'

'Fallen at the second fence,' I said. 'Or was it the third?'

'Well, whichever it was, I felt that all my hopes were dashed, that it was all over. It was just unbearable, especially as I knew I was the right person, that no one loved him more than I did, or cared more about the rest of them. I felt such despair, such loss, such hopelessness.' She raised anguished eyes. 'I mean, I had been miserable before, but never like this. I was used to failing, but I couldn't bear to fail at this. I just wanted to die, really.'

I could hardly believe she had endured such misery, that what had seemed the ultimate fairy tale – Diana's journey to the altar – had in reality been so full of pain.

'And so the summer just sort of came to an end and I hadn't heard a dicky bird. Got more and more depressed. Stuffed myself comfort eating. Got absolutely huge.'

Looking at the slender figure on the opposite sofa, I found this hard to believe too. Whatever Diana did for comfort these days, it clearly wasn't eating.

'Oh yes.' A rueful grin lit up her features. 'Mrs Robertson got really fed up with me.'

Belgravia, London

September 1980

Mary Robertson

When Occasional and Permanent Nannies had initially sent her Diana Spencer, Mary had not expected anything special. But, opening the door of her Belgravia house that chilly February morning, she was taken aback by the vision of perfect English beauty. And she was so good with children, too. Within seconds of meeting baby Patrick, Diana was down on her hands and knees playing with him.

Mary had given her the job on the spot. A busy executive whose small son was nonetheless the centre of her life, she was relieved to find the perfect solution to what could have been quite a problem. London, to which she had just been posted, was to her a strange new city. And Britain a strange old country. Admittedly, it now had a female prime minister, but Mrs Thatcher seemed less a force for progress than a divisive figure presiding over a fractured state. There was inflation, unemployment, trouble in Northern Ireland, rubbish strikes, electricity blackouts, racial tension and political convulsion. You name it, basically.

In the midst of all this, Diana seemed a definite miracle. But it gradually seemed to Mary that she was also a definite puzzle. She kept her personal life personal. Did she even have a boyfriend?

The American sensed a romantic mystery. Diana's behaviour seemed to suggest some sort of up-and-down relationship. She had appeared a few weeks ago, happy and excited. But now she came across as strained, as if waiting for something. She seemed to be comfort eating as a result; things were disappearing from the fridge.

Having arrived home one evening to find the meat chunks gone from the stew, Mary decided, in her direct way, to tackle her nanny about it.

Diana accepted the ticking-off. No grudges were borne on either side and things returned to normal. And then, a day or so later, Mary moved a cushion on the sofa and saw something white: a paying-in slip. The name on the account was THE LADY DIANA SPENCER and it was from Coutts, the oldest and grandest financial institution in London, bankers to the monarch herself.

Had the slip been left deliberately? Mary took the hint. She did her research and soon knew exactly who it was she had bawled out about the *boeuf bourguignon*. The Spencers were an ancient family with a coat of arms, a stately home, several titles and close connections to the Crown.

This threw up another question for Mary; a more fundamental one, perhaps. If Diana – as was obviously the case – came out of the very top drawer, why was she content with such a menial job? She actually seemed to enjoy housework, and when not looking after baby Patrick, wiped noses and bottoms at a Pimlico kindergarten.

Mary couldn't understand this lack of ambition. Back home in the States, feminism had a firm foothold. Women had been smashing glass ceilings for years. Why were English girls a generation behind Americans, upper-class girls like Diana especially?

Diana had been privately educated, no doubt at considerable expense, yet had only managed two O levels. 'Nerves in exams' was her explanation, but that didn't, to the American, quite seem to wash. Hadn't Diana wanted more out of life?

And then, one day, as Mary, heading for her car, passed her nanny in the hall, she noticed something had changed. There was joy in the big blue eyes and pink excitement flushing the cheeks. The American guessed that whatever was being waited for had come to pass. Something pretty good, obviously.

Chapter Thirty-Two

Heathrow Airport
5 September 1980
The Press

James Whitaker, royal reporter for the *Daily Express*, stood scanning the crowd in Terminal One. He was looking for one person among the thousands. A beautiful blonde, and a surprising development.

'Davina Sheffield?' His editor had sounded sceptical. 'Going to Balmoral? You're sure?'

Whitaker understood his doubts. The Prince of Wales going back to that particular old flame seemed as unlikely as him taking up again with Lady Sarah Spencer. Both she and Davina had committed the unpardonable sin of being all over the newspapers. But the tip had come from a reliable source and a D. Sheffield was indeed on the passenger list.

'I thought she was working in an orphanage in Hanoi,' Whitaker's editor had added. Davina had gone to Vietnam in the wake of her royal hopes being so cruelly and publicly dashed. But was this, James wondered now, just a clever ploy to buy time and rehabilitation before relaunching herself on the royal scene? Perhaps with Charles' connivance? The two had been very close, after all. As Whitaker had learned after years on the beat, when it came to the Windsors, anything was possible.

There was also the fact that the prince's love life seemed at a low ebb. Nothing much going on at all. That an old friend had been asked to brighten a dull Scottish weekend was more than likely.

His editor remained unconvinced that a disgraced former attachment would be invited to the innermost royal sanctum. But Whitaker was sure there was something in it, and now he was glad he had stuck to his guns. Jostling next to him were his rivals from the *Sun*, Arthur Edwards and Harry Arnold, camera and notebook at the ready. They had obviously heard something too.

But was the glamorous Davina on this flight? They had watched everyone go through the gate and so far there had been no sign of her among the hundred or so passengers. Men in the oil industry mostly, either workers returning to their gale-battered rigs or business types off to make deals involving Britain's undersea 'black gold'.

Among the few women was a young girl in a windcheater, grey skirt and headscarf. Had her dowdiness not already ruled her out, her small brown leather overnight bag would have. Anyone staying at Balmoral needed three changes of clothes a day.

'False alarm,' grumbled Arthur, as the gate closed and the check-in staff packed up. Frustrating though it was, there was nothing to be done. The reporters shrugged at each other and went their separate ways. Soon afterwards, the Aberdeen-bound Trident jet rose into the grey London sky.

Diana

At the back of the plane, the dowdy young girl took off her headscarf and shook out her thick, fair hair. Diana was exultant. She had worried that the pressmen might recognise her from previous meetings, but neither the ostentatiously smart Mr Whitaker from Jane's wedding, nor the ostentatiously scruffy Mr Edwards and Mr Arnold from the polo had spotted her.

Mr Barry's advice to dress down had worked brilliantly. And his idea to list one of the prince's old girlfriends as a passenger had been genius. The airline had been more than happy to help the Palace, with the result that, as Mr Barry had predicted, the press had all looked for Davina Sheffield instead. Diana was amazed at how easily these wily newspapermen were manipulated.

She hadn't dared even hint to her flatmates where she was going. Their suspicions had, anyway, been recently diverted by the sudden appearance of a certain Charlie Renfrew. They thought he was a new boyfriend, who meant the prince pash had, once again, been abandoned. They were mightily relieved, and answered the phone with delight whenever he rang.

'It's that nice Charlie Renfrew,' Ginny would shout down the hall.

'Where did you say you met him?' Anne would enquire.

'He used to live near my parents,' Diana would say, casually. But Baron Renfrew was one of the prince's titles; he had suggested the alias himself. She was sure that Carolyn, a dab hand with Debrett's, would work it out; so far, however, she hadn't.

It was Charlie Renfrew who had invited her to Scotland. 'Place belonging to a relative of his,' she had airily told the others. 'Somewhere near Aberdeen.'

'I hope it's not very smart,' Anne had said.

'Why?'

'Because I want to borrow your nice blue dress. I'm going to a high spottie this weekend.'

It had been a tricky moment when Stephen rang to brief her about Balmoral. Aware of her flatmates listening in, she had tried to say as little as possible.

'Rule one. Don't laugh at the pipers.'

'But why would I?' she'd asked, surprised. 'I adore . . .' She was about to say 'bagpipes', but Anne was in the hallway. 'That sort of music,' she'd amended.

234

'Good,' said the other end. 'You're going to be hearing a lot of it. Rule two. Never say you're cold.'

'Oh, I'm used to . . . that.' She had nearly said 'huge and freezing houses', but Carolyn was coming out of her room.

'Excellent. And you love nothing better than tramping over sodden moors.'

'*Do* I?'

'Oh yes. The more midges and mist, the better.'

'Right.'

'Rule three. Never sit on Queen Victoria's chair.'

'What?'

Stephen had explained that a certain tartan chair in the Balmoral drawing room had been the favourite of the Queen Empress. It had sacred status as a result and no one else was ever allowed to use it, not even the monarch herself.

'It's perfectly true,' he'd said, when she had stopped giggling.

'But how will I know which one it is?'

'When Her Majesty or Princess Margaret shout at you. Stay on your feet is my advice. Rule four. Rave about Prince Philip's picnic trailer.'

'That again.'

'Yes, it looms large. Rule five, and most important of all. Be charming and look wonderful. Obviously worship His Royal Highness. Always be jolly. Few men can resist a pretty girl who openly adores them.'

'Yes,' she had said earnestly. 'But I really, really do. I don't have to pretend.'

The flight passed quickly. She spent it listening to her Sony Walkman, a birthday present from Sarah. She was humming happily along to Wham! when the jet descended into Aberdeen.

Dyce Airport, Aberdeen

5 September 1980
Stephen

Compared to Heathrow, Dyce was thinly populated. Even so, a few journalists had gathered to meet the plane. Stephen guessed they were looking for the mythical D. Sheffield and would miss the real story. And here it came, the real story, hurrying through the barrier, head demurely down, as instructed. As she recognised him, her face lit up in a great beaming smile. He felt dazzled by it, as he had in that long-ago field in Norfolk. A rare sense of optimism filled him. Perhaps, after all, this really was going to work.

He led her swiftly to a green Range Rover at the side of the terminal building. She did not seem to have brought much luggage, which was strange. There were more costume changes at Balmoral than the average pantomime: one set of clothes for breakfast, a change to sporting clothing if you were going out with the guns, afternoon wear for tea and then full evening dress for dinner.

Her face drained of colour. 'But you said that trousers weren't worn at Balmoral! Most of my clothes are jeans. I only had one dress and a skirt.'

Oh well, Stephen thought, she would not, at least, be appearing in the breakfast room in denim. And she was staying in the castle and not Birkhall, the Queen Mother's house in the grounds. According to Billy, it was tiaras and decorations for dinner there, even if it was just the old queen and a friend. 'Looks quite odd afterwards when they're watching *Dad's Army*,' Tallon had added.

The winding road followed the line of the river, which gave an occasional silver flash through the tree trunks. It had just rained; the grass was wet and brilliantly green and steam rose gently from the spongy ground.

'What's Balmoral like?' she asked.

Stephen considered his reply. A museum? A complete time warp? There were chamber pots with Victoria's monogram on them and stuffed hunting trophies in such number that some guests suffered allergic reactions.

'There's a certain emphasis on tradition,' he allowed.

'But why do they always go there? The royal family?'

It was a good question. This was the year 1980 and Balmoral hadn't changed – either its physical appearance or the routine of its guests – since it was built in the 1850s. Why did one of the richest families in the world return year after year to endure its privations and dullness? Stephen had asked himself the question many times. He had also worked out the answer. When the royal family were at Balmoral, they were not just physically far away. They had retreated into a past they could control.

Diana was still wondering. 'Surely they could go anywhere for their holidays. Spain, for instance.'

The car swerved violently. The thought of the Windsors on a package tour to Alicante had almost sent him into a tree. 'I'm not sure foreign holidays are their thing,' Stephen said.

'They don't like beaches?'

They did, so long as they were cold and stony and faced some grey stretch of sea. Scottish islands were the best-loved of all. At a picnic on one, he had once witnessed the monarch throwing rabbit droppings at the heir to the throne.

They had reached the little grey town of Ballater now, a mere few miles from the castle. As Diana spotted the shops, selling fishing tackle or guns, she asked, again, wonderingly, 'What on earth do they see in it?'

'They just like to escape from modern life occasionally.'

She giggled. 'But *I'm* going there, Mr Barry! And,' she waved her Walkman, '*I'm* modern!'

Chapter Thirty-Three

Balmoral Castle, Royal Deeside, Scotland

5 September 1980

A pair of pale grey granite posts announced the entrance. The gatekeeper emerged from the decorative little gatehouse. They swept past the duty policeman and up the drive.

Planet Zog, Stephen thought, as he always did when the fantastical combination of battlements, castellations and towers came into view.

But what Diana saw was the afternoon sun glinting off the gold clock on the keep, and a red and yellow flag waving gaily against a blue sky. She clapped her hands with excitement. 'It looks just like the Disney castle!'

'Actually, it was meant to remind Prince Albert of his native Thuringia.'

'His native what? What's a thuringia?'

'A place in Germany.'

She hooted with laughter at her mistake. Her spirits were sky-high, he could see. 'Just look at those towers,' she exclaimed. 'I bet there's a wicked witch in one of them.'

More than one, Stephen knew. A couple of the prince's mistresses had been included in the house party. One was an ex, and bitter about it, so to invite her said everything about his master's tact. The current favourite, meanwhile, was coming without her husband.

'Or a princess who's been asleep for a hundred years.'

'The only princess here at the moment is Princess Margaret.' Admittedly, she rarely surfaced before lunchtime.

'I feel a bit sorry for her,' Diana said staunchly. 'I think she's misunderstood. Quite a few of the royal family are. It's a difficult life.'

You couldn't fault this girl's commitment, Stephen thought. Really, if anyone deserved the job, it was her.

As they got out at the castle entrance, she looked eagerly for the hoped-for figure with his quizzical glance and diffident smile. But the only creatures in the entrance were heraldic stone beasts. They held up shields as if to ward her off.

Fishing rods, waders and landing nets hung in the wood-panelled hall. A clutter of wellingtons stood about the chequerboard marble floor. There was still no sign of anyone.

'Let me take you to your room,' Stephen said.

She looked at him, wildly. 'Where's Prince Charles?'

'His Royal Highness is on the hill.'

Her face fell. '*Stalking?* So he won't be back for ages?'

'This evening,' Stephen agreed cheerfully. Inwardly, though, he sympathised. The least the prince could have done was meet the poor girl when she arrived. She was here for his benefit, after all. It was churlish of him to be absent, especially given the reasons. All the same, the valet had no option but to pretend that all was as it should be.

Diana, however, had no such compunction. 'This evening is *ages* away!' she wailed. 'What'll I do until then?'

Stephen smiled. 'How's your needlepoint?'

'My what?'

'Just sit on your tuffet and sew a fine seam. He'll love that.'

She eyed him balefully. 'I don't think so, Mr Barry. My sewing's hopeless.'

They walked to her room, down corridors whose every wall was lined with antlered heads and watercolours featuring the same three things: a tall bewhiskered man, a small woman in a shawl and lots and lots of mountains. They passed the entrance to many rooms, all seas of tartan, upon which tartan sofas sailed against a backdrop of tartan wallpaper and tartan curtains. 'If you wore a kilt in here you'd be invisible,' Diana remarked.

'There is something of an emphasis on tartan,' Stephen acknowledged. 'The Prince Consort designed one just for Balmoral, in fact. Pale grey like the castle, with red and black checks. Only members of the royal family can wear it.'

She rolled her eyes. 'What happens if someone else does? Are they executed?'

'Only if they're aristocrats,' he deadpanned. 'If they're commoners, they're hanged, drawn and quartered.'

She giggled at this, rather to his relief. Her mood seemed to be lifting.

They paused at the door of a particularly large, grand room. 'There,' he said, pointing. 'That's the chair.'

'Really?' She stared at the small tartan seat at the back. 'It looks so ordinary. I was expecting more of a throne. What's so special about it?'

'Sit on it when the family are there and you'll find out.'

They passed a couple of housemaids, who shrank against the panelled walls. She smiled at them. 'Hello.'

Both bobbed a hurried curtsey before scurrying off.

She turned to Stephen wryly. 'Was it something I said?'

'Of course not,' he smiled. 'They're just a bit shy.' And, he thought, recruited from remote Presbyterian villages where they padlocked the children's swings on Sundays and laughing was discouraged in case you showed your teeth. None of them liked the London staff who came up with the family.

They had reached the bedroom passages now, lines of white doors with name cards slipped in. Diana was reading them off as she passed. 'Mr and Mrs Palmer-Tomkinson. Lord and Lady Tollemache. Who *are* all these people?'

'Friends of His Royal Highness,' replied Stephen, calmly.

'I haven't met any of his friends before.' She looked at him nervously. 'I hope they'll like me.'

'Of course they will.'

'Can you tell me about them? So I know what to say?'

'Of course. Well, the PTs are very keen on skiing. And Lady Tollemache loves gardening. And—'

Diana interrupted. She was reading another name on a door. 'Mrs Parker Bowles!' A pair of wide, inquisitive blue eyes swung round.

Stephen did his best to sound calm. 'She knew His Royal Highness many years ago.'

'Yes, we talked about her in the park that day. She's very horsey. Hunts a lot.'

And the rest, thought Stephen. 'That's right,' he said.

'Oh dear.'

Panic clutched him. 'What's the matter?'

'Well, I hate horses. Fell off one as a child, never really got back on. I won't have much in common with Mrs P-B.'

I wouldn't be so sure of that, thought Stephen, leading her on.

Her room was large and dark red. A heavily stuffed plaid-covered chaise longue stood at the foot of a plaid-curtained four-poster. The Hammer Horror Suite was Stephen's own private name for it.

'Not *more* tartan!' She went into the bathroom. 'Even the lino!'

'Complaints about the tartan should be taken up with Her Majesty,' Stephen said. 'All the guest rooms are checked by her.'

'As it were!'

He looked at her, mystified.

'Checked!' she grinned. 'As in tartan. Joke, Mr Barry.'

'Oh yes, very good.'

'Yours was good too, though. About the Queen checking the rooms.'

'She does.'

'Doesn't she have people to do that?'

'Yes, but she likes to do it herself.'

She laughed, imagining the monarch examining towels, glancing into bathrooms, raising lavatory lids, checking supplies of loo roll. Then her smile faded. 'Gosh, Mr Barry, I'm finally going to meet her. I'll be shitting bricks, honestly.'

Stephen blinked. She didn't usually use such language.

She saw his face and giggled. 'I bet you know what I mean though.'

He did, absolutely. The first time he had served the Queen, as a junior footman at the Palace, he had almost dropped the plates of soup, his hands were shaking so much.

She was looking at the bookshelf now. He watched her peruse the usual blend of Walter Scott and Dick Francis.

'You won't find any Barbara Cartlands here,' he said.

'Doesn't matter, I've brought my own. What's this?' She pulled out a volume called *The Swinging Sporran*.

'A humorous look at Scottish customs.'

She put it back and walked to the broad bay window. Flat tartan cushions lined the sill and she sat down, gazing out at the dim northern light, the continuous rain. 'Poor Prince Charles. He must be getting completely soaked out there.'

'His Royal Highness will be quite all right. There are bothies and cottages to shelter in all over the estate.'

He paused. Oh, why had he said that?

'The famous bothies,' she said, grinning. 'To which Prince Philip's famous picnic trailer so often goes.'

'Something like that,' Stephen said.

'What are they like, these bothies? I'm not sure I've ever been in one.'

'Well, some are quite well furnished. One even has a piano in it.'

Her face lit up. 'A piano!'

'Yes, hauled up the hill so Prince Albert could play Chopin to Queen Victoria.'

'How incredibly romantic!'

Probably not if you'd been one of the serfs who'd dragged the thing up there, Stephen thought. He saw her notice something and raise a finger to the glass.

'Oh look. Someone's scratched their name. Some prisoner from long ago, maybe.'

'Honeymooning royal brides,' the valet answered.

She giggled. 'Very funny!'

'It's quite true. There's a tradition that they scratch their names on this window with the diamond from their engagement ring.'

He saw her glance down, involuntarily, at her hand.

Diana

Once the downpour stopped, she went outside. The rain had scattered the lawns with dewdrops and the emerging sun now drenched them in brilliant light. The scent of soaked earth rose to her nostrils, fresh and rich. Beyond was the forest and above were the shining mountains.

She had passed the last hour reading, but the descriptions of Scotland in *Laird of Love* were inadequate compared to the magnificent reality. Just as charismatic but taciturn Ruiraidh

MacNeep, the fictional heir to Castle Neep, would pale in comparison to the real-life heir to Balmoral when she finally saw him.

The fact that this had not yet happened seemed now almost a good thing. She knew from her novels that delayed gratification was sweet. It was one of the trials of Love; heroines kept from their heroes by all manner of obstructions.

'Fame!' sang Irene Cara in the headphones of her Walkman. 'I'm going to live for ever!'

She wondered if she was the first person at Balmoral ever to own a personal stereo. And listen to pop. Almost certainly. She gave a little shimmy of triumph as she walked away from the castle, through a small iron gate and into the woods. The undergrowth was thick and wet, soaking her tights and thin city shoes. The rough path led up through the fir trees. Light fell between the trunks like blades. She pulled into her lungs the sharp, bright scent of pine.

As the trees thinned, the scenery opened out. Rolling brown hills, touched with green and purple. In the distance were large piles of grey stone. As she neared them, she saw they were shapes: pyramids, towers. Set dramatically along bright green ferns, they looked incongruously exotic, like some lost Inca village; relic of some once-mighty civilisation. She guessed that they were cairns and wondered what they commemorated. Battles? Disasters?

One cairn, from 1863, celebrated the then-Prince of Wales' marriage to Alexandra, Princess of Denmark. The 1858 cairn marked the marriage of Victoria and Albert's eldest daughter Princess Victoria to the Crown Prince of Prussia. That from 1862 commemorated Princess Alice's wedding to Prince Louis of Hesse. There were others: Princess Helena and Prince Christian, Prince Arthur and Princess Louise, Princess Beatrice and Prince Henry.

So many marriages, so many young couples. The brides on the cairns were probably teenagers like herself. Perhaps she, too, would be part of history one day. Would there be a cairn for her marriage? If it happened?

The rain began again. It was of the hissing, soaking variety that drenched you in minutes. She needed somewhere to shelter. The Prince Consort's bothy with the piano in it couldn't be very far away. Pianos were heavy things.

She was relieved to gain the top of the hill and spot a small grey building amid the purple heather in the next valley. Albert's bothy, surely. If she was a prince, wanting solitude with the woman he loved, it was here she would pick.

She had just started the descent when she saw the door open. Someone emerged and lounged against the bothy wall. It looked like a blonde woman, possibly smoking, but distance made it hard to tell. What was obvious was that the place was occupied.

Diana decided to cut her losses, return to the castle and have a hot bath. Her bathroom had a large old-fashioned tub, no doubt closely inspected by Her Majesty. Grinning, she turned and hurried away through the drizzle.

Chapter Thirty-Four

Stephen

The prince had returned separately from the stalking party. He smelled strongly of cigarettes, even though he never smoked himself. When Stephen had told him that Lady Diana had arrived, the response was a pained sigh.

Now the valet stood at the back of the Balmoral drawing room, counting heads. Three people were missing. The prince, Mrs Parker Bowles and Lady Diana Spencer. It seemed most unlikely that they were together.

Frustration coursed through Stephen. It had been no easy business getting Diana here. He had sweated blood over it, lost sleep. But got her here he had. The pretty young thoroughbred, the only suitable royal bride in the entire kingdom practically, had been led to water and was obviously keen to drink. And now the stage was set for romantic walks in the hills, boating *à deux* on the lochs, all in the matchless privacy of a royal estate.

And what did the prince do? Ignore her completely. He seemed determined to mess everything up. Did he realise the risks he was running? Admittedly, Princesses of Wales had endured their husbands' mistresses since the role was created. But even the eager, biddable Lady Diana might baulk at having her nose rubbed in it.

Perhaps she already had baulked. Or bolted. Gone home, fled. Who could blame her?

Stephen took a deep breath and tried to calm himself. More likely she was just lost. He cursed his earlier suggestion that she should go for a walk. Balmoral was a vast estate, over a hundred thousand acres. Once you were out of sight of the castle, one hill looked the same as another. What if she was blundering about the heather in the dark when she should be charming the pants off everyone, here?

Something glittered at the edge of his vision. It was the Queen Mother, sporting more diamonds and rubies than seemed possible on one person. What, the valet wondered, did she think about it all? She, who had been Diana's earliest champion.

The old queen looked her usual serene self. She was smiling in her trademark vague way at the footman who had just appeared, silver trowel in hand, to clear up after a corgi. 'Dear Harvey,' remarked the Queen Mother. 'He's soiled some of the most expensive carpets in the country.'

As she wandered off in her white satin evening dress, Stephen wondered whether the old queen had just quietly given up. Perhaps he should give up too.

'Cuckoo!' Princess Margaret was snapping her fingers.

Stephen tried to ignore the demeaning gesture; leave it to a footman. But the imperious violet eyes, ringed as ever by thickly applied make-up, were trained on him.

'Cuckoo!' The coral-painted fingernails snapped again.

The valet sighed inwardly, surrendered to the inevitable. 'Your Royal Highness?'

Princess Margaret's tight pink dress glowed fiercely in the gloomy room. 'A whisky and water!'

Stephen went to the drinks tray. As he poured a generous helping of Famous Grouse, he tried to remember that she had had a difficult life and was misunderstood.

Oh, *where* was the drawing room? Every corridor in this place looked the same with those endless deer heads. Diana blundered on, her dress dragging on the green tartan carpet. That was another problem. The ancient black frock was Coleherne Court's most battered old warhorse. It had done the rounds of all the flatmates many times. But with Anne borrowing her frilly blue dress, there hadn't really been an alternative.

Someone came suddenly round the corner and almost collided with her. She found herself staring into the curious hazel gaze of a young footman. 'Can I help you?' he asked.

'The drinks,' she gasped. 'I'm late!'

'Don't worry, madam, you're almost there.' He spoke with a warm northern accent. 'The drawing room's just round that corner.'

To his great relief, Stephen now saw Lady Diana enter the room. She briefly scanned the crowd, spotted him and hurried over.

'Mr Barry, I'm so glad to see you! Where's Prince Charles?'

'His Royal Highness is on his way.' Stephen hoped it was true. He heard her gasp, felt her stiffen. 'There's the *Queen*!'

Stephen was used to this reaction. People were always amazed to see the monarch in the flesh. It wasn't her grandeur that undid them; rather, her complete normality.

Elizabeth II stood chatting away in the middle of the carpet, a swarm of corgis milling around her sensible low heels. As ever, there was about her a relaxed ease. But, as Stephen knew, this was deceptive. The Queen was as sharp as a tack and missed nothing. Her eyes flicked constantly about: alert, observant. She would have registered Diana's entry and be watching her carefully from now on.

'Should I go up to her?' Diana whispered.

'Absolutely not. Wait for her to come to you. She will, eventually.'

'Who are all these people?'

'Some are His Royal Highness's friends. You saw their names on the doors, remember.'

'But they're *ancient.*'

Actually, Stephen thought, offended, they were all round about his own age. And the prince was ancient too, had she not noticed?

'And they look so scary! What if they don't like me?'

There was, Stephen thought, quite a good chance of that. As well as the spurned mistress, there was a male guest who categorised people as 'crashers' or 'tossers'.

'You can't stand talking to me all night,' he warned her. 'Not in public, anyway.'

'Why not?'

'You're upstairs and I'm downstairs. And never the twain shall meet.'

'That's just snobbish and stupid.' She had always talked to the staff at home. Rather more than to her own family. And why not? She had more reason than most to know that money and birth rarely improved human nature, and usually made it worse.

Stephen looked her in the eye. 'If you want to marry into the royal family, it might be something you have to get used to. They're quite keen on the distinction. I've known burning logs fall out of the grate and them ring for a footman to put them back on. Anything rather than get up themselves.'

'You're joking!'

He wasn't, but this was hardly the issue at the moment. 'You need to mingle,' he instructed. 'Charm and dazzle.'

She groaned. 'But who *are* they all?'

'Well, that big chap is Nicholas Soames, His Royal Highness's former equerry.'

She brightened. 'My father was an equerry.'

'Well, you can talk about that, can't you?'

She was looking around in her eager fashion. 'Is Mrs Parker Bowles here?'

Stephen pretended to look too. 'I can't see her.'

'Who's that blonde, then?'

'Lady Tryon. Or Kanga, as His Royal Highness calls her.'

'Why?'

Because she's one of his mistresses, or was until five minutes ago. 'Because Lady Tryon is Australian. She helps when we're in the Antipodes.' Exactly how Kanga helped in the Antipodes, and in plenty of other places too, wasn't something Stephen planned to go into, now or ever. 'Now off you go!' he urged. 'Dazzle!'

Five minutes later, Diana was trying not to think of how Coleherne Court would be all Saturday-night buzz. She imagined the girls rushing between rooms to borrow lipsticks, exclaiming when the phone rang, the record player pounding all the while. Meanwhile, she was standing here with unfriendly Lady Tryon and this even more unfriendly Soames man.

'Been blooded, have you?' he asked. His eyes protruded like boiled eggs.

What? 'Sorry?'

'When you kill your first stag. They gralloch it and smear your cheeks with the blood.'

'Gralloch?'

'Slit open its stomach.'

Her hand flew to her mouth. 'How *horrible*.'

'She's never gralloched a stag, Dale,' Egg Eyes remarked to Lady Tryon. Her eyes were green and watchful and she wore a tight red dress that exactly matched her lipstick. 'Don't expect she's ever tickled a trout either. Probably not had much experience with a rod.'

'Actually,' Diana corrected him, 'I love fishing. Did it all the time as a child.'

'Salmon? Trout? What sort of fly?' Lady Tryon asked.

'Worms, actually. On the end of a string.'

Lady Tryon looked incredulous.

'From the side of a rowing boat,' Diana went on. 'On the pond at home with my brother and sisters. We never caught much, but it was fun.'

'Lady Tryon here is practically professional,' said Egg Eyes. 'Fishes with the Prince of Wales, quite often. Isn't that right, Dale?'

'Rather less often these days,' Lady Tryon said, rather tightly.

'She has a fishing lodge in Iceland. HRH was fishing with her when Mountbatten was killed.'

Diana was surprised. She had assumed the prince was in London at the time.

Lady Tryon now firmly changed the subject. 'Love your frock.'

Diana looked down at her dress. 'This old thing?' Because it really was.

'But I'm not sure black's your colour.' Lady Tryon gave her a patronising smile. 'Come to my shop and we'll sort out your wardrobe.'

Heroines in novels often wished the floor would open and swallow them up. Diana now felt the same. Charles' friends were so much older, they didn't like her, and maybe he didn't either; certainly, he was yet to appear. A great, heavy misery filled her, and her eyes stung with tears.

Blinking hard, muttering about needing air, she hurried out of the drawing room. On her way, she passed the sacred chair that she hadn't, after all, sat on, but felt as ostracised and rejected as if she had.

She had half-thought of going back to her room, but yet another wrong turn funnelled her into what looked like a dining room. Dark green tartan curtains were drawn over enormous windows. Candles lit a long table, interspersed with silver stags and pheasants. There were great sideboards, vast fireplaces and, from panelled walls, the usual bristle of antlers. A pair of large portraits looked down on her. One was Prince Albert swathed in a tartan cloak and standing astride a huge stag. The other was Queen Victoria in a ball gown, staring at her with imperious glassy eyes.

'Madam?'

She recognised the voice. The warm northern accent. It was the footman she had met earlier in the corridor. 'I'm hopeless,' she admitted. 'I'm lost again.'

'We all get lost at first,' he said cheerfully.

She felt grateful for his friendliness. She liked his open face and fair curly hair. And he was young, about her age, the first person she had come across who was. She looked at his dark blue tailcoat and a red waistcoat.

'But don't you work here?'

'Not normally, madam. I'm from Buckingham Palace. I came up with the London staff.'

'What do you think of Balmoral?' she asked.

He hesitated. 'I don't think the servants here like us much.'

She giggled in spite of herself. 'I don't think the non-servants here like me much either.'

'Well, I bet they don't put bats in your bed, madam.'

Her eyes widened. 'What?'

'Oh yes. They get 'em out of that big tower. Loads in there apparently.'

'That's so mean.' She remembered the two maids hurrying past, with downcast eyes. It was always the quiet ones, of course.

'They take our underwear too. Put it out on the washing line in front of the servants' quarters. Though today they got one of the maids' mixed up with a lady-in-waiting's. She wasn't best pleased to see her bloomers hanging by the kitchen.'

Diana frowned. 'It sounds like bullying. Does the Queen know?'

The footman stared at the floor and shrugged. 'Her Majesty doesn't like trouble. So she says nothing, even when Princess Margaret's having a go at us for watching telly.'

'There's a telly?' Balmoral seemed so stuck in the past, she hadn't even looked for one.

'In the corner of the library. Ancient old thing it is.'

'Why doesn't Princess Margaret like you watching it?'

'I don't know, madam. But when they come back from their picnics at whatever those places are called . . .'

'Bothies!'

'That's it. The first thing Princess Margaret does is walk over to the telly and check it to see if it's warm. She puts her hand down the back, looks at her sister and says, "Lilibet! Someone has been watching the television!"'

His falsetto impression of the Princess was so perfect that Diana burst out laughing.

'And we've been standing there for hours, just waiting for them to come back. Doesn't seem like the worst crime in the world.'

'Of course it isn't. How else are you going to catch up on *Crossroads?*'

Amazement swept the young man's face. 'You like *Crossroads?*'

'Love it!'

There followed an eager discussion of the latest twists in the plot. Then Diana sighed. 'I'd better go back. Re-enter the fray. But it's been much more fun talking to you.'

'Thank you, madam. I've enjoyed it too.'

'What's your name?'

'Small Paul.'

'*Small* Paul?'

'It's what they call me at Buckingham Palace. To distinguish me from Tall Paul; he's another footman.'

'Not very nice for you, even so. I'm Diana, by the way.'

He grinned. 'Oh yes. We all know who *you* are. Servants' hall's talking about nothing else.'

She stared. 'Why?'

'Well, madam, you were on *Britannia* last month, and now you're here. Only one way that's going, or so everyone reckons.'

She wanted to hug him. The renewed surge of hope was so powerful, it nearly knocked her over. Small Paul wasn't remotely small, she thought. In terms of restoring her lost confidence, he was a giant of a man.

She re-entered the drawing room.

'Ah, there you are!'

Prince Philip, sporran swinging with the violence of his stride, was approaching her like an advancing army.

She felt her newly restored courage wobble. The prince's friends had been bad enough, but this would be out of the frying pan and into the fire.

From beneath his craggy brow, the Duke of Edinburgh regarded her with amusement. 'Don't worry, I won't eat you.'

She forced a smile. 'I know that, sir.'

'You don't look as if you know it. I have a fearsome reputation.'

'Not at all, sir.'

'Oh, come off it. I do. And quite deliberately.'

'Sir?' She looked at him, puzzled. His eyes were pale blue, but not icy, as she had imagined. Up close, there was a kind intelligence to them.

He folded his arms in their fine tweed jacket. 'When we got married,' he said, nodding towards the centre of the room, 'the level of adulation, you wouldn't believe it.'

Actually, she could believe it. She thought of images from the time; the Duke like a Nordic god, the dark-haired Queen radiantly in love.

'It could have been corroding,' Prince Philip went on. 'It would have been very easy to play to the gallery. But I took a conscious decision not to do that. With results that you've no doubt read about.'

His celebrated rudeness, she guessed.

'Safer not to be too popular,' he said. 'You cannot fall too far.'

She smiled ruefully. 'Popularity doesn't seem to be my problem really.'

'Wasn't mine either, first time I came to Balmoral.'

'In what way?'

A bark of laughter. 'Every possible way. Wrong clothes, wrong shoes, wrong family. Didn't even have my own guns.'

She found this hard to believe. He seemed so at home here now, unquestionably in charge.

The pale-blue eyes were twinkling. 'Impoverished royal of no fixed abode, a couple of sisters who'd married Nazis. All the courtiers disapproved of me, looked down on me. Couldn't have been more unsuitable if I'd tried.' He raised a wry eyebrow. 'And I wanted to marry the king's daughter? The monarch's eldest child and heir to the throne?'

Understanding now dawned. This famously difficult figure was offering her sympathy. More than that, she had his support. He was telling her not to give up.

The dinner gong went, and Philip put out an arm. 'Come on. You're sitting between me and the most dangerous woman in Europe.'

Alarm flashed across her face. 'Sir?'

'Don't worry. She's eighty. It's what Hitler used to call her. This way.'

Chapter Thirty-Five

The Queen Mother

The pipers were drunk again. But then, they often were. They had been on her own first visit to Balmoral nearly sixty years ago. She had sat at the dining table just like Diana Spencer, beside her, was sitting now, trying, in the exact same way, to conceal her amazement at what was going on.

What was going on was a short, red-faced man, wrapped in a cloak of russet tartan, marching around the table carrying a vast silver dish. Before him were the swaying, stumbling pipers, six of them, all dressed to the nines in kilts and sporrans, their red cheeks bulbous with the effort of playing. The noise was earth-shattering. There was a reason why bagpipes had been used on battlefields; one of the few instruments loud enough to be heard above screams and gunfire.

Diana was doing her best not to wince; she was even managing to look interested. She really was perfect, the Queen Mother thought. An absolute treasure. It was quite ridiculous how Charles was treating her.

They had all been terrified when the poor child had rushed out of the drinks reception. Thankfully, Philip had repaired some of the damage caused by those idiot hangers-on. And then, even more thankfully, Charles himself had appeared.

Having missed the drinks – for reasons that were easily guess-able because a certain someone else had missed them too – he had skidded in just as they were going to dinner. He had given only the most hurried of greetings to his teenage guest, but her face had lit up as if she had been given the moon.

Lilibet hadn't been much help, having said that. Inflexible as ever on Balmoral protocol, she had insisted that the minister from the local kirk at Crathie sit next to her son, not Diana. Such a wasted opportunity. And now the dog-collared old bore was praising the menu: salmon, followed by venison, followed by raspberry fool.

She heard Charles give the standard reply. 'Everything's from the estate. Either grown here or caught here. The food at Balmoral's very economical!'

It wasn't of course, nothing like. Maintaining moors, rivers, stags, staff and all cost an absolute fortune. Genuine economy would have been sausages from the supermarket. Yet the min-ister was nodding, willing to believe, as so many did, that the royal family, despite its vast estates and many palaces, lived a frugally ordinary existence. It was a public-relations miracle.

But so was the whole business of royalty. She knew this. Lili-bet knew this. Philip knew it too. But Charles, his grandmother felt, had no understanding of this whatsoever. He genuinely seemed to think he could behave exactly as he liked. Had he forgotten that the last Prince of Wales to follow his own urges – the last Prince of Wales full stop – had almost destroyed the whole family, having fallen for an unsuitable married woman?

She kept her eyes averted from the unsuitable married woman who had arrived in the dining room a few minutes after her grandson. What Lilibet was doing allowing him even to *invite* her, the Queen Mother could not think. But Lilibet had never intervened in her children's lives. She kept her advising and warning for her prime ministers, not that they ever took any notice. Perhaps that was why she didn't bother with the children.

Which means, thought the old queen, that I must bother in her place. As self-styled recruiting sergeant for the British royal family, I will do my utmost to enlist this keen and entirely suitable young girl. If, after this conversation, Diana didn't want to be Princess of Wales with every fibre of her ardent young heart, irrespective of Charles' behaviour, then her name wasn't Elizabeth Angela Marguerite Bowes-Lyon Windsor.

She leant over to Diana. 'He's the butler, you see,' she said of the tartan-swathed, parading figure.

'He doesn't look like one. Why's he wearing that outfit?'

'It's rather an amusing reason,' the old queen twinkled. 'Quite a long time ago, the painter Landseer did a portrait of Prince Albert dressed as a shepherd.'

'As a shepherd?'

'Yes, the picture's hanging up there.' The Queen Mother indicated the image of the Prince Consort straddling the dead stag. 'Albert was rather busy, it seems, so the butler stood in for the cloak bits. And ever since, the Balmoral butler has worn it into dinner.'

Diana seemed to be struggling for a reply.

The old queen took a sip of champagne. 'You're probably thinking that's all a bit silly,' she observed. 'Don't worry,' she added, as her neighbour blushed furiously. 'I thought the same when I first saw it. I listened in complete disbelief as it was explained to me by dear Papa – George the Fifth.'

The girl seemed relieved. 'It is a bit odd,' she suggested, timidly.

'Utterly,' agreed the Queen Mother. 'And entirely stuck in the past, of course. I never imagined, when first I married Bertie, that I was entering an institution that had much modern relevance at all.'

The girl's blush betrayed that she had accurately guessed her thoughts once more.

'Some people wonder what on earth the monarchy is for,' the old queen went on. 'Charles, for example, is always fretting about that.'

'Is he?'

'Oh yes.' The Queen Mother took another sip of champagne. 'How it will survive, all that. Lilibet gets quite impatient with him. She tells him that the monarchy will survive simply because the people want it. They may not know why, but they do. She believes that they want their queen to remind them of their history both glorious and grievous and tell the world not to believe we have lost rank as a country. It's as simple as that. In her opinion, anyway.'

The blonde head next to her nodded. Then a questioning, sideways glance of the blue eyes. 'And in your opinion, ma'am?'

'Ah,' said the Queen Mother, pleased. 'How insightful you are. You are quite right, my dear. I take a different view.' Smilingly, she took another sip. The girl, she saw, was waiting eagerly. 'I see us as having a rather more practical function.'

'Practical, ma'am?'

'If one has an interest in making a difference and improving lives, a career with the British royal family is just the thing.'

Diana giggled. 'Do you really see it is a career, ma'am?'

'One could think of it that way. You know, of course, that some people call us The Firm?'

'Oh yes, I had heard of that.'

'But I think of it as less a job, more a vocation. Those with empathy, warmth and enthusiasm are particularly in demand at the moment, owing to something of a dearth of these qualities elsewhere in the business.'

The Queen Mother cast a humorous glance round the table. Diana was laughing. She was ready, the old queen saw, to receive the real message now.

'Royalty can make the most tremendous difference,' she said, with the vague smile she reserved for her most important statements. 'It can do the most incredible good. Take the war. No one who wasn't there can really have any conception of the horribleness of it all. The suffering, the misery. And so Bertie – my husband, King George VI – and I made it our business to boost morale. He was in charge of the fighting forces while I was the Home Front. The women who kept everything going – homes, jobs, children – while the men were away.' The Queen Mother lifted her champagne glass again.

Diana was fascinated. 'How did you do it, ma'am? How did you boost their morale?'

'I made speeches.'

'Oh, like Winston Churchill?'

'Well, his were marvellous, of course. Fighting them on the beaches and so on. Terribly important. Famous, and rightly so. No one remembers my poor little things these days. But in my own very small way, I think I made a tiny difference.'

'What were your speeches about?'

'They were quite simple. I just praised the women. Told them their work was just as valuable, just as much war work, as that being done by the bravest soldier, sailor or airman who was actually fighting the enemy.' She raised her head and briefly imagined herself back in her old study at Windsor, sitting before the BBC microphone. 'Hardship,' she said in stirring tones, 'has only steeled our hearts and strengthened our resolution. Wherever I go, I see bright eyes and smiling faces, for although our road is stony and hard, it is straight. And we know we fight in a great cause.'

She smiled at the girl and saw there were tears in the blue eyes. Good. She could still do it. The old magic was still there.

'They must have been so pleased that you said that.' Diana's voice was rather choked.

'I rather think they were,' the old queen agreed. 'No one else was telling them that, after all. And I rather enjoyed saying it. It made me feel that I was helping. Doing my bit.'

'I'd love to help,' Diana said, suddenly, yearningly. 'Do my bit.'

The old queen nodded. 'I can see that. You are a generous, loving and idealistic person and perfectly suited to the kind of work I am talking about. You would have been a tremendous asset during the war. Bertie and I visited endless bomb sites in the East End of London. People were always so pleased to see us, even when they'd lost absolutely everything. Those poor little streets, full of the ruin of death, and yet people calling out "God bless Your Majesties". It was so touching, one could hardly speak, and one felt such great thankfulness to be able to play one's own very small part in it all.'

The lovely face next to her was full of earnest longing. 'I wish there was something like that I could do.'

The Queen Mother patted her arm. 'Oh, there will be. No doubt about it, You will find your cause and you will be inspirational. You have greatness in you, just as I had greatness in me.'

Diana

At the old queen's words, she felt she would burst with pride and delight. 'Do you really think so, ma'am?'

'Oh yes, without question.' The old fingers, glittering with diamonds, pressed her arm again. 'And you will get your opportunity. You just need to be a little more patient, that's all.'

Diana glanced at the prince down the table. At that moment, serendipitously, he looked up and smiled at her. She put her whole heart into her returning smile and felt a great, bright resolve sweep through her. She would be patient, as the Queen Mother advised. As Prince Philip had urged, she would not give up. Because this was her destiny, she knew it. This was what she was meant to do.

Later, dinner over, she went eagerly to find the prince. But he was at the back of the drawing room with his father, who seemed to be communicating something forcibly. Among the others, parlour games were in full swing. She had never been especially good at these, particularly the quick-witted sort like charades or consequences. She could think of funny things afterwards, but never at the time. It was a relief, therefore, when the relatively undemanding hide-and-seek was proposed.

She scurried under a large table, hoping that the prince might be released from his father to hide with her. When the heavy tartan tablecloth lifted to admit someone else, these hopes soared. They turned into amazement as the grinning sovereign, in her green brocade, crawled in on her hands and knees.

Mr Barry had told her the Queen would come to her. She had never expected it to happen this way. She kept her eyes on the carpet, uncertain whether she should look, unable to believe it was really happening.

The monarch, for her part, seemed entirely unfazed. 'I remember doing this with my parents,' she said in a whisper. 'We were at Windsor and President Eisenhower arrived. My father had forgotten he was coming. We were all having tea on the terrace and so it was the work of moments for us all to dive under the tablecloth.'

Diana had no idea what to say. There was no precedent for this. No heroine she had ever read of had met their future mother-in-law under a table, let alone their queen.

Here was someone she wanted desperately to impress, and all she could manage was a nervous smile.

The sovereign looked back at her kindly. 'Diana, isn't it?'

The blood rushed warmly into her cheeks. 'Yes, Your Majesty.'

'Enjoying Balmoral?'

'Very much, ma'am.'

A quick nod of the smooth dark head. 'Splendid. Well, we hope to see more of you here.'

The tablecloth behind the Queen now moved and lifted. Lady Tryon, who was 'It', had discovered them.

Diana emerged, and the prince came up to her. He seemed agitated and spoke abruptly. 'I'm going on a fishing trip tomorrow. Would you like to come?'

Her suddenly weak knees forced her to grip the back of the nearest chair. 'I'd love to.'

'You won't find it boring? It'll be just the two of us, everyone else is going to the Braemar Games. You'd have to get up horribly early, I'm afraid.'

She gave him her biggest, most reassuring and radiant smile. 'I can't think of anything I'd like more.'

'Well, that's that then.' He glanced about him quickly. 'Oh God, they're playing charades. You can count me out of that.' He hurried away.

You can count me out too, take me with you, she wanted to call, but it was too late. Instead, she headed for the curtains, where, half-concealed in the tartan folds, she gazed out into the darkness. A full, yellow moon was shining in a completely black sky. Like a hole, she thought. Letting in the light from another world. The world the Queen Mother and Prince Philip had urged her towards, perhaps. In which the Queen hoped to see more of her.

And now Charles had invited her fishing, alone. She felt a dizzy joy. He wanted to be with her, just the two of them. This time there would be no chaperone. She would really have him all to herself, at last.

There were shrieks of laughter from the charades behind her. Diana turned and observed with fascination the sight of Princess Margaret holding her nose and pulling at something above her while squatting on the floor.

'*I* know!' the Queen exclaimed. 'Royal flush!'

'Diana, isn't it?'

The voice came from the side. It was deep, unfamiliar and female. She looked into a narrow face topped by untidy blonde hair.

'I'm Camilla.'

She was not at all as expected. Her skin was sallow, her makeup scrappy and her smile exposed gap teeth. There drifted from her a powerful aroma of cigarettes. Her dress was black, somewhat worn and could have done with a good iron. It made Diana feel slightly better about her own frock.

'It's very nice to meet you,' she said.

'And we're *all* very excited to meet you,' Camilla returned in her gravelly baritone. 'We're all *completely* fascinated.'

'Really?' Egg Eyes and Lady Tryon had not seemed especially fascinated.

'Really. Because you've succeeded where everyone else has failed.' Camilla sounded warmly approving, 'You're the One.'

Chapter Thirty-Six

Royal Deeside, Scotland

The Press

'Gawd knows what they all see in it,' complained the *Sun*'s Arthur Edwards. He and his colleague Harry Arnold were on their way to his least favourite gig of the year, the Braemar Highland Games. 'Like a bleedin' six-hour advert for porridge,' he went on.

Ken was only half-listening. He was used to this rant, which he heard every year. He didn't like the Games either, but there was no point complaining about it. The Queen loved it and so the whole family went, along with whatever poor sods were staying at Balmoral. Which meant photo opportunities, not just of knobbly-kneed royals in kilts and feathered bonnets, but also their guests. And the guest everyone was looking for was, of course, the latest girlfriend.

A new one had to appear soon. It was just ridiculous, how long it was taking.

'All that caber-tossing and sword-dancing. Leaves me cold, it does,' Arthur moaned on. 'Quite literally, it's usually bloody freezing.'

'Hang on,' Ken interrupted suddenly. 'Isn't that Charles' car?'

He slowed down. A green Range Rover was parked at the side of the road. Beyond it, just visible through the trees, was the river, with two figures beside it.

Arthur whipped out his camera and was quickly focusing his long lens. 'It only bloody is!' he gasped. 'I'd know those ears anywhere! Stop, Ken! Stop!'

'What do you think I'm doing?' Ken was trying to park as subtly and silently as possible while peering through the trees at the same time. 'Who's the other bloke?'

Arthur's lens-holding hands, most uncharacteristically, were shaking. 'It's not a bloke, Ken, my son. It's dressed like one, but it's a girl.'

Diana

There was a whoosh as Charles cast his line again.

'Well hooked, sir!' she exclaimed, as something wriggling and silver was hauled out of the water.

'You're my lucky charm,' he called back, gallantly.

She beamed. Lucky was exactly how she felt. This morning, when she woke – not that she had slept much – it was as if the rain of yesterday had never been. A sky of radiant blue had filled her window. The wings of the castle had stretched out like a cat in the sunshine. Above shimmering lawns, the craggy mountains had blazed. She had hummed as she'd washed and dressed. As she'd brushed her hair, she'd smiled into the mirror. She felt she might burst with excitement.

The breakfast room had been all kedgeree, chatter and the cheerful clang of chafing dishes. She had been aware of subtle surveillance, of interested eyes sliding towards her. She sensed a change in attitude and felt important, even powerful. The moment when she and the prince left together had been supremely thrilling. She had been unable to resist turning in the breakfast room doorway, to be met by the icy green stare of Lady Tryon. But Camilla Parker Bowles, next to her, had smiled broadly and waved. 'Have fun!' she'd called.

'Mrs Parker Bowles is so *wonderful*,' Diana had exclaimed, climbing happily into the Range Rover.

The prince had agreed, but so gloomily she'd assumed she had said the wrong thing. Perhaps he wasn't that fond of her any more.

But now he looked much happier, standing in the middle of the water in his high rubber boots. And the shiny silver river looked so pretty, surrounded by rich autumn colour. Deep red, burning orange, yellow gold. Could anything be more romantic, more beautiful?

Charles

The eager, obedient way she was sitting on the bank made his heart sink. What Camilla had said this morning was right, Diana really would do anything for him. 'She obviously wants you desperately, darling! Know what she said to Patti Palmer-Tomkinson last night?'

'Do I really want to know?'

'Patti had asked her a leading question, you know how she does, about the two of you. And then Diana said, "If I am lucky enough to be the Princess of Wales". It just slipped out, Patti said.'

'Oh God.'

'But, darling, it's perfect, don't you see? You want her to feel lucky enough. You want her to want you.'

'But I'm not so sure I want *her*, though.'

'Oh *Charles*!'

'It's not her fault,' he'd sighed. 'I don't want anyone. Except the one person I can't have.'

She had stroked his face, soothingly. 'I'm not going anywhere, you know that. And she's perfect, everyone says so. You'll get used to her. You have to, you don't have a choice. Literally.'

'You sound like my father,' he had said bitterly. 'And, yes, I have to. Sacrifice myself on the altar of Queen and country.' He had screwed up his face. 'God, the things I do for Queen and country. No one has any idea.'

'I know, darling,' she had said soothingly. 'It's very hard. But it could be worse. Diana's terribly pretty.'

She really was, Charles had to agree, casting sideways looks at her going through the lunch bags, examining every item like an excited child. In her green Barbour coat, a cap set on her thick blonde hair, she looked stunning. Tweeds suited her; the plain material the perfect foil for her youth and creamy beauty. Her long slim legs looked fantastic in breeches, and the tight jacket emphasised her neat waist and amazing bust.

He could absolutely see how attractive she was. But, somehow, he just couldn't feel it.

'You said you did feel it though,' Camilla scolded when he said this. 'You said that when you sat with her on that hay bale, and when you showed her your uniforms, you really felt a connection.' She pulled on her cigarette. 'She even likes the bloody Goons, for God's sake, which is more than you can say for me.'

Charles sighed. What he had felt on the hay bale and in the wardrobe was the merest, palest *flicker* of what he felt for Camilla.

'I don't know why you're so relaxed about her,' he complained. 'Don't you see her as a rival? Aren't you afraid of losing me?'

'Nope.'

'Why not?'

Camilla touched him on the nose with a forefinger and looked laughingly into his eyes. 'Because she's so obviously no trouble, darling. So touchingly eager to please. And she actually seems to like me. You never know, we might even end up becoming great friends.'

Diana

She had looked in both the lunch bags now. They weren't really that interesting: a meat bap, an apple and a slice of fruit cake. Now she was just sitting on the bank, watching. She wished she had brought her Walkman, but Mr Barry had practically fainted when she'd suggested it. He was already annoyed with her because she hadn't had the right clothes. He'd insisted she borrow his own set of tweeds, which fortunately fitted perfectly, even if they smelt quite strongly of aftershave.

But you could only stare at scenery for so long. Fortunately, she had brought *Laird of Love* with her. It was in her pocket, and Charles had his back turned. She could slip it out, read a few lines.

Twisting about to get at the novel, she caught a movement at the edge of her vision, just behind her. An animal? A leaf, dropping into the water? Instinct, however, told her it was something more. The hairs on her neck rose, stiffened.

The hand that was searching for the paperback now began to search for something else. Something small and round. Her fingers felt it, slowly drew it out.

She opened the compact mirror, held it up to her face and gasped. Amid the trees behind her, only semi-hidden in the undergrowth, were two men. One of whom held a camera with a long lens. Pointing straight at her.

Photographers! A thrill went through her that was half terror, half excitement. She remained absolutely still. She dared not even move her head, only her eyes. Charles, meanwhile, had moved further down the river. She was on her own. Whatever she did now was up to her.

She thought of the trouble Sabrina Guinness had got into, bringing unwelcome publicity to the royal Scottish retreat. She could not risk anything similar. But a check in the mirror revealed the two were creeping up on her. Steadily, inexorably, like a game of grandmother's footsteps. But unlike grandmother's footsteps, which they often played at Young England, she couldn't turn round. She would see, if she did, not a group of laughing children, but the rattle and flash of a camera lens. And then her face, alarmed or angry, or very possibly both, would be the next day's front page. And that could ruin everything.

She glanced at Charles again, and into the mirror. They were very close now. She glanced towards the Range Rover, on the road beyond the trees. If she could get into that, lie down on the floor . . .

She had one chance, and now she took it. Rising suddenly, still without turning, she bolted. 'Sir!' she yelled, and the prince whirled round. He saw the journalists and his face flushed puce with fury.

The Press

'Bloody hell,' said Arthur, as they returned to the car. 'Did you see? She had a bloody mirror. She was watching us!'

'Smart cookie,' agreed Ken. 'Have to hand it to her.'

'Too good for him, the miserable bugger,' Arthur said resentfully. 'Hear some of the things he called us? Enough to make a maiden blush, it was.'

'I wonder what maiden it is,' mused Ken. 'Get any pictures, did you, Arthur?'

'Only of her arse,' lamented Arthur. 'And nice as it was, it's not exactly the money shot.'

Disappointed, they continued to their destination.

The Braemar Highland Gathering was much as usual: men in vests tossing tree trunks, kids in kilts dancing on swords, Prince Philip's knobbly knees, the queen grinning in sunglasses. The usual press colleagues were present, Whitaker of the *Express* among them. Arthur and Ken related the mirror story; did anyone have any clues? Several Balmoral staff were on hand who did and were willing to reveal them for the usual consideration. Establishing that the girl was Lady Diana Spencer did not take very long. But no-one had any recent pictures. Gloom hung over the press pack.

'Remember that polo match?' Arthur asked Ken as they drove off. 'Cowdray Park? In the summer?'

'Yes, Arthur.'

'That girl. Blond. Young. Big blue eyes and dazzling smile? Necklace with a letter 'D'?'

The car swerved. 'Diana Spencer!' Ken exclaimed. 'It was her!'

'I took some pictures,' Arthur said. 'Sent 'em back to the office for filing . . . WATCH IT!' he shouted as Ken completely lost control of the steering wheel and veered wildly all over the road.

Chapter Thirty-Seven

Coleherne Court, Kensington, London

September 1980

Diana

She was deep in a dream. She had on her windcheater and head-scarf and was running through a deserted airport. A hamster in a smart suit was running after her. It wore a pink tie and cuf-flinks and was actually Mr Whitaker, the journalist from the *Daily Express*. He really had been at the airport last night in Aberdeen, as she flew back, alone, to London.

'Enjoy yourself, did you, with that little trick with the mirror?' he had asked, sidling up as she'd hurried to the check-in.

The hamster in the dream was yelling the same thing. *Enjoy yourself, did you?* Its voice was high-pitched and squeaky, like Paul's impression of Princess Margaret. The noise of its shout-ing echoed off the shining lino floor, which was tartan.

In the dream, her cheeks burned, as they had burned in real-ity. They were bright red. And now they were an even brighter red, and sticky. The bright-red, sticky stuff was blood. It was warm and thick and it came from the stomach of a small stag. In the dream, she had shot it out stalking, and they had dragged it down to a dip in the hills. Before her horrified gaze, the egg-eyed equerry had slit open its soft belly. A tumble of glistening innards had fallen out and Egg Eyes had dipped his hand in it until it was covered in red to the wrist. Then he had come towards her and smeared her cheeks with rough, thick fingers, two strokes either side. A musty scent caught her nostrils. 'There,' he had said. 'You're blooded.'

Still graceful in death, the animal lay on the ground, the blood pumping out into the bright green grass. It looked so helpless, she thought. A great terror filled her; what had she done? What had they all done? She had backed away, arms stretched out before her to protect herself. 'No!' she had cried. 'No!'

In the glen, in their tweed suits, they had all stood there, looking at her. Egg Eyes, Lady Tryon, Princess Margaret, the Queen, Camilla, even the prince. Their faces were impassive.

'It's too late!' Egg Eyes had shouted, triumphantly. 'You've done it now!'

'No!' she'd cried. She had turned and run, her feet thumping over the heather, the blood slamming in her ears. 'No! No!'

And now, suddenly, she was awake. To her huge relief, she was back in London, in her own bed. But the slamming and banging could still be heard. It was coming from her door. 'Duch! Duch!' It was Caro's voice, and urgent.

She threw back the covers, stumbled sleepily over. What time was it? Morning, obviously; light edged her curtains. She felt exhausted. She had arrived back so late, the others had all been in bed. She needed to get up, get dressed. Today was one of her Young England days. The children would all be expecting her.

She was smiling at the thought as she opened the door. Three pale, tense faces looked back at her.

'Hello, girls,' Diana said cheerfully. 'What's up? Did I wake you when I came in last night?'

Caro slowly raised a newspaper. It was the *Sun*. The front page was entirely taken up by a large picture of a girl. The accompanying headline was huge and black, but even so, she had to read it twice before it sank in.

HE'S IN LOVE AGAIN! LADY DI IS
THE NEW GIRL FOR CHARLES

She felt a great swoop in her insides. 'Gosh.'

'You could say that,' remarked Caro.

'So, *this* is Charlie Renfrew,' rebuked Anne.

Diana took the paper from Caro and looked at herself. The photo was the one from the polo in the summer. The words pounded in her head. HE'S IN LOVE AGAIN! LADY DI IS THE NEW GIRL FOR CHARLES! Her own eyes looked back at her, full of a shy promise. Already it felt like looking at someone else, but whether it was her past self of her future one, she could not say.

'Why didn't you tell us?' Ginny sounded hurt. 'You're our friend, but we have to read this in the papers like everyone else. You of all people know what that feels like.'

They knew about her father and Raine's wedding, just as they knew almost everything else about her. It was a fair point. Diana dropped her eyes guiltily, sank down in her Snoopy pyjamas. She sat with her back against the door frame. Her heart was thumping to a rhythm she recognised. *You're the One. The One!*

'*Is* he in love with you?' asked Caro.

Diana looked up from under her fringe. 'Of course. It says so, doesn't it? On the front page of the *Sun*.'

'Don't joke,' said Anne.

'What happens now?' asked Ginny.

Diana drew her knees up and rested her chin on them. 'I'm not sure.' It was hard to think about anything.

'How do you feel?' Caro asked, more gently.

Nothing like she had expected to. It felt like the aftermath of a huge explosion, like the bombed streets of London, as described by the Queen Mother. The world would never be the same.

'Well, is he going to ask you to marry him?' Anne said.

'He needs to,' Ginny put in. 'Because the press won't leave you alone from now on.'

'Don't worry,' Diana said, climbing to her feet. 'I'm sure Prince Charles has got it all in hand. He'll look after me.'

'I hope you're right, Duch,' sighed Caro. 'I hope you're not playing with fire.'

Later that morning, she was on her hands and knees in St Saviour's church hall, surrounded by a swarm of children. Their squeals and laughter didn't quite drown the sound of what she had seen outside as she had hurried in: a growing number of newspapermen, women too, many brandishing cameras. A couple of them had called out her name, but instinct had warned her to keep her head down and hurry inside. It had not worried her unduly; they would go, she felt certain, when she failed to reappear.

They had not gone, however. She could hear them now, banging on the door and ringing the bell. Possibly, faintly, she could even hear her name being called.

'Come on, Miss Diana!' Little Clementine, sitting on her back, was pulling gently at her hair.

'You're the horsey, remember,' added her little friend Alexandra.

'Yes, and here we go. All set?' She was about to move off with her load of toddlers when a pair of sensible flat black shoes appeared in her eyeline. Diana recognised them. They belonged to Kay King, the nursery owner and her boss. She looked up, smiling, blowing a stray lock of hair out of her eyes. 'Hello, Mrs King.'

'Busy, I see,' remarked Kay in her kindly fashion. She squatted down with a nursery teacher's practised ease. 'Can I have a word?' she murmured.

'Oh, yes, Mrs King. Of course.'

The children on her back began to wail, objecting. 'Miss Diana! Horsey, horsey!'

Kay peeled them off. 'Now, Clementine and Alexandra, I just need to quickly ask Miss Diana something.'

The two women walked towards the kitchen.

'It's those people outside,' Kay said, as the doorbell rang yet again.

Diana's stomach dropped. 'Oh, Mrs King, I'm so sorry.'

'It's quite all right, please don't worry. It's just . . .' Kay paused, then looked her squarely in the eyes. 'Diana, what exactly is going on?'

Kay clearly hadn't seen the *Sun*. Admittedly, it wasn't her usual choice of paper.

'Well,' Diana began, 'I was at Balmoral, you see, last weekend . . .'

'Balmoral?' Kay looked startled. The girls she employed were all very well connected, but this was a surprise, even so.

Diana bit her lip. 'Perhaps I should have said . . .'

'Oh no, no,' Kay assured her. It was bad form to boast about knowing royalty. 'It's just that . . .' She gestured towards the front door.

'Yes, the press rather seem to have put two and two together and made five and . . .' Diana stopped.

'So there's nothing in it?'

'Well, I wouldn't exactly say that . . .'

Kay's eyes widened. She looked down and tapped a foot, as if working something out. When she looked back up, her expression was one of resolve.

'Right,' she said briskly. 'Well, the first thing is to get rid of these people. Can't have the parents turning up and seeing swarms of pressmen. They'll wonder what on earth's going on.'

'Yes, Mrs King.' Diana could hardly express her relief that the sensible Kay was taking control. Only now did she realise how very worried and tense she had felt.

'I'll just go and tell them to leave,' Kay said in her capable way. 'I'll put on my best Strict Voice.'

Diana chuckled. 'That's sure to work.' Kay's Strict Voice struck fear into the most recalcitrant toddler. 'Thank you, Mrs King.'

She was back on her knees, covered again in squealing children when the sensible flat black shoes reappeared. Diana looked up again, shaking the hair out of her eyes. Once again, Clementine and Alexandra had to be peeled off.

'It's going to take slightly more than my Strict Voice, it seems,' Kay said.

Diana hung her head. 'Oh God.'

'No need to bring him into it.'

'I really am very sorry, Mrs King.'

'It's not your fault. Most of them have agreed to go, in fact. But there's this rather stubborn chap from the *Standard*.'

The London evening paper. Panic swirled within her. Should she, Diana wondered, call the Palace? Could Prince Charles send the police? Surely someone should help her?

Kay put her hands in the pockets of her quilted jacket. 'But I've got an idea. Do you think, if you go and have a photograph taken, that he'll go away?'

'Like *this*?' Diana looked down in dismay at her crumpled cotton skirt, the creased, rolled-up sleeves of her shirt. Fearful of being late, she had dressed at speed and dragged on, as a finishing touch, a woollen tank top belonging to somebody's brother.

'Well, he'd have what he wanted then, so hopefully he'd go,' Kay pointed out.

Diana hesitated. In the picture that had appeared in the *Sun*, she looked like what she had been: a guest at a smart house party. Her hair was freshly cut, her make-up carefully applied. All the styling her hair had received today had been, quite literally, at the hands of Clementine and her friends. Her make-up was sketchy and smudged. In short, she looked terrible.

On the other hand, she owed Mrs King. Kay had given her a job, one that she loved, and it was out of the question that, because of her, Young England was in any way inconvenienced.

'Well,' she said, 'I suppose we could try it.'

The relief on Kay King's face was almost enough to squash her misgivings. All the same, she felt apprehensive as she walked towards the door.

'Miss Diana!' There were clattering footsteps behind her. Two warm little hands slipped into each of hers. Two concerned little faces were looking up. 'You look sad, Miss Diana,' said Clementine.

'Are you all right, Mith Diana?' enquired Alexandra. She had a thumb in her mouth.

'Yes, fine.' She forced her voice to sound bright. 'Look, I won't be a minute. Just got to step outside.'

Their hands tightened protectively. 'We're coming with you, Miss Diana!' said Clementine, resolved.

'Going to look after you,' added Alexandra, determinedly.

Diana looked round. Kay stood at a distance, watching. 'Do you think I could take them out with me?' She knew she would feel much better if she did.

Kay hesitated. 'I'd have to get the permission of the parents. Hang on, I'll give them a ring.'

Her office was right by the door. Diana could partly hear the conversation.

'We've got this rather unusual situation . . . would you mind awfully . . .' Then a silence as the other person spoke, then Kay again, with a laugh. 'You never know, she may be Queen of England!'

Blushing furiously, Diana went out into the garden with the children. She was expecting someone rude and pushy, but the *Standard* photographer was friendly and polite. It was sunny and warm and, to her relief, the children seemed more interested than frightened.

The photographer moved her quickly round the garden until he found a spot he liked. 'Smile!' he urged, but she couldn't quite bring herself to. All the same, the session was over almost before she knew it. She hurried back into the church hall gratefully.

After the excitement, the afternoon passed in much its usual way. The day was almost over and Diana was scrubbing the lavatory floor when the doorbell rang again. A parent, presumably, or one of the nannies that deputised for them.

'Diana!' It was Kay's voice. 'Can I borrow you?'

She scrambled up, went into the main hall. The nursery staff were gathered around Kay, who was talking in a low, concerned voice.

Diana caught some of it. '. . . oh dear . . . Palace so sensitive about this type of thing . . . Ah, Diana! Here you are!'

'What's the matter?' she asked, for the second time that day. And for the second time that day, someone held up a newspaper front page. The *London Evening Standard*, this time, its entire cover devoted to the picture taken this afternoon.

Diana stopped in her tracks, hardly trusting her own eyesight. There she stood with the two children, head lowered, the image of the demure nursery assistant, except for the sun streaming through her thin cotton skirt from behind. It was rendered absolutely transparent; nothing was left to the imagination, her legs were visible from bottom to top.

She raised her hands to her red and burning face. She had no words to express how utterly mortified she felt, how sick with disappointment. Prince Charles would never speak to her again after this. It was so much worse than what Sarah had done. She, at least, had stopped short of publicly exposing herself. I got so far, Diana thought, anguished. I was The One. But now, like all the girls before her, she had failed to clear a fence.

'I'm so sorry, Diana.' Kay's usually decisive expression was all abject apology. 'I think I've rather blown your royal romance.'

The Coleherne Court girls knew better than to say they had told her so when the Chief Chick came back, her white face streaked with tears. Certainly, they weren't going to complain about the knot of reporters and photographers that had started to gather outside the front entrance of the block. They felt, like Kay King, that the romance was over already. The Palace would never stand for a photograph like that. No one had, or ever would, win a Prince of Wales in see-through clothes.

The phone in the hall had rung a lot too; reporters asking for Diana. 'We could keep it off the hook,' Caro suggested to the others.

'I'm not so sure,' demurred Anne. 'What if there's an illness and our families need to get in touch?'

Caro accepted that this was a consideration. And, anyway, the journalists would stop ringing soon.

They did their best to field the calls. The Chief Chick, whose door remained firmly shut, didn't even want to speak to them. She would certainly not want to speak to the press.

Mid-evening, however, came a call that she might well like to take. It was Ginny who was sent to tap on her door.

'Duch?' she said softly. Muffled sobbing could be heard on the other side. Ginny tapped again. 'Duch!' Louder, this time. 'It's that man from the Palace. Barry, is it?'

An exclamation and a thump, as of someone getting out of bed. The door wrenched open and Diana appeared, eyes wild, face red, nose running. 'Mr Barry?' A great sniff accompanied this. 'What does *he* want?'

'He didn't say.' Actually, Ginny hadn't asked. She was, like the other flatmates, currently incapable of being polite to anyone from the Palace. 'I'll tell him to buzz off if you like,' she offered.

Diana stared at her briefly in amazement, then pushed past to the phone. 'Mr Barry?'

'Good evening, Lady Diana.'

Another sniff. 'What can I do for you?'

The flatmates, ears out on stalks, felt encouraged at her resentful tone. Their hopes were rising that she would tell him to buzz off herself.

'Congratulations,' said Stephen, breezily. 'You're through to the next round. His Royal Highness wants you to come to Highgrove. I'm to drive you there.'

Chapter Thirty-Eight

'Now, you have to be warned, the place is a mess, so just look delighted and say how wonderful it is.' Stephen issued his instructions above the roar of the engine. The noisy mid-blue Granada was his least favourite from the royal carpool.

He had met Diana round the back of Coleherne Court. The front was now almost permanently manned by journalists and photographers keen to get the latest on 'Shy Di' as they called her, presumably because of the demure way she glanced up from under her hair.

'His Royal Highness is still deciding whether or not to buy it,' he went on. 'It's a Georgian gem. Nine bedrooms, six bathrooms, four beautifully appointed reception rooms, three hundred and forty-seven acres of rich arable farmland.'

'It sounds wonderful!' she said.

Everything felt wonderful now. Most wonderful of all was that the seemingly disastrous picture had actually helped her. The prince had been pleased with the see-through skirt, Mr Barry had said. As a result, she felt almost grateful to the press. They had blocked in her car and pursued her down the street, but she was trying not to mind. She was even starting to learn to co-operate.

It was less fun for her flatmates of course, who got no benefit from it whatsoever. They were stoically supportive, even so, and never complained about the phone constantly ringing, and having to pass photographers whenever they went to the corner shop. They even joked about having to put make-up on all the time now and look presentable.

But they were worried for her, Diana knew. They felt strongly that she shouldn't have to cope with 'all the hassle', as they called it, alone. There was a rope of sheets on permanent standby under Caro's bed, in case she needed letting down from a window, or pulling up. Mary Robertson felt much the same and had been, Diana considered, heroic in her restraint, especially as the press sometimes followed when she took Patrick out in his pushchair. Mrs Robertson, however, was relocating back to America. The parting was going to be awful; she didn't want to think about it.

Stephen

Stephen, at the wheel, was also musing on journalists. That Diana seemed to have worked out how to handle the notoriously difficult press was a definite feather in her cap. None of the prince's girlfriends had ever done that before. She was doing well, unexpectedly so.

And she had other reasons to feel confident, too. Today's destination was one of them. The very fact that the prince had suddenly decided to house-hunt showed that marriage loomed large in his mind. That, finally, he was resigned to it.

The Highgrove Estate, in the village of Doughton near the market town of Tetbury, came strongly recommended. In the wooded Gloucestershire countryside, less than a hundred miles from London, it was on the market for £800,000 and seemed ideal. But before the prince signed on the dotted line, a very particular lady was asked to give her view.

That lady now had, and Diana was coming up to give hers. Stephen turned off the main road through a set of rusting wrought-iron gates.

She turned to him, evidently thrilled. 'Are we here, Mr Barry? How exciting!' She stared about her with shining eyes as they crunched up the gravelled half-mile of drive.

'His Royal Highness will be delighted that you think so. He told me he wanted a woman's view of his dream home.'

'Oh, Mr Barry! Did he really say that! A woman's view?'

'He did indeed,' the valet confirmed, smoothly. She didn't need to know which woman.

Diana

Highgrove was adorable, she thought. She had been expecting somewhere rambling and vast, but it was like a little box built of pretty pale stone. Grand, yes, but cosy at the same time. She could easily imagine living here, setting up house. Mr Barry's words had filled her with delight, the clear implication was that the prince wanted to show her the home they would be sharing together, that they would bring up their children in. Greater happiness could not be imagined; it was her life's dream to live as a family; mother, father and children all under one roof. And here, she thought, as the car stopped before the colonnaded porch with its elegant white double door, was the glorious reality.

The prince was waiting in the hall, beside an impressive marble fireplace. Her heart soared at the sight of him; he looked like a portrait, she thought. Wearing a suit, even though it was Saturday. Behind him, through a bay window fitted with French doors, was a long, lovely view over a garden.

He raised his eyebrows as she shyly approached. 'I say, I knew you had good legs, but did you have to show them to everyone?'

The blood roared into her face and the pit of her stomach fell away. Then she saw the twinkle in his eye. He was joking. 'Oh, sir! I'm so sorry about that.'

'Not to worry. You seem rather to have hit it off with the press on the whole. Ghastly people, I always think.'

The prince batted something away; a fly. His gold signet ring caught the light. She wondered, suddenly, if he had a ring for her, if that was what the visit was about. Would that other hand, currently in his pocket, produce a small box at some stage? The thought made her heart thump.

'Like it?' he asked.

'Oh yes, sir,' she passionately assured him. But she would have liked it, she knew, if Highgrove were a cardboard box. There were quite a few of those around, along with stepladders, bits of carpet and lengths of wire protruding from walls. Mr Barry hadn't misled her about the mess.

The prince walked her through to a large, empty room. Their footsteps echoed on the dusty floor.

'Window seats,' she said, happily, instantly imagining herself sitting there and looking out. Between distant trees, a church spire was silhouetted against the skyline. It made her think of bells, weddings, smiling couples driving away in carriages with balloons tied to the back.

'I'm thinking of a wildflower meadow out there,' he said. 'Bordering the front drive. You know, poppies, daisies and mari-golds. It's quite a new thing.'

'It sounds lovely, sir,' she said, imagining their children running among the blossoms.

'And there's enough lawn in the front for the helicopter to land.'

He took her into the library, with its empty bookcases stretching from floor to ceiling. 'Plenty of room for one's books,' he said. She thought of her Barbara Cartlands, all those battered

286

paperbacks in among his Laurens van der Posts. She might put them in just to tease him.

It was fun, picturing the life she would have in this house. In the empty dining room, she imagined a large table full of children; her sitting at one end and Charles at the other. The children would be talking over each other, shouting and laughing in a good-natured, familial sort of way, and she and Charles would look at each other and smile. The thought sent a great surge of joy through her.

The billiard room, whose table had gone but whose fringed light still hung down, suggested handsome teenage sons with friends staying for the weekend. She would pop her head round the door. 'Everyone all right in here? Hot chocolate?'

In the kitchen with its stone-flagged floor, she imagined herself consulting with the cook, a cheerful Mrs Betts type. 'Now, His Royal Highness isn't too keen on chocolate mousse . . .' No, not His Royal Highness. She would just say 'my husband.' A glow went through her. 'My husband isn't too keen on chocolate mousse.'

She was following him up the wide staircase now. He was about to show her the bedrooms. Where You Know What was going to happen.

Surely, if he were going to produce it, it would be now, in this most intimate of spaces?

The room was empty, apart from a couple of chairs and a mahogany half-tester protruding from the pale yellow wall. She imagined it hung with white muslin curtains, above a white-covered bed. The master bedroom. She thought of him mastering her; how would he do it?

He was walking off, briskly, down the corridor. She hurried after him.

'The nursery,' he said, pausing at the door of a large, light-filled room.

She could imagine it so easily. Cradles and rocking chairs. Toys on the rug. She went to the windows to see the view that their children would see. They might pull themselves up to standing for the first time using that very sill. She saw herself sitting by the fireplace, reading them stories, or giving them rides round the room on her back. Or painting; pressing their tiny plump hands into saucers of bright colour before placing them gently on paper. Or carefully guiding those same little hands as they learnt to wield a pencil, spelling their names for the first time, brows furrowed in concentration. What would those names be? she wondered.

She glanced over to the would-be father of these children and smiled. *Now!* she urged silently. *Now!* What more appropriate place to propose than a nursery? But he was bending over and frowning at the fireplace. The hand in the pocket made no movement.

Leading off from the main room were a couple of other rooms: a bathroom, where she instantly imagined raucous bath-times, soap suds on the floor, sponges flying through the air. A children's bedroom where she would kiss them good night. And a smaller room, a nanny's, possibly. She looked at it thoughtfully. She wasn't sure she wanted nannies. She wanted to look after their children herself. She didn't want to miss a single minute.

She hurried back to the main nursery, eager to tell him how perfect it all was. But, rather to her surprise, the prince had gone. She realised she could hear something outside, something busy and cacophonous, and dashed to the window.

The lawn outside was teeming with tail-swishing, glossy-flanked horses, and smart riders in dark blue coats. A hunt. They were milling about, talking and laughing, clearly very much at home. Their hounds flowed about them, ginger, brown and white. All was colour and movement and was, she thought, rather beautiful. Framed by tall trees, with the church spire beyond them, they made the quintessential English scene. Had the prince arranged for her to see them, as a picturesque surprise?

He was there in the middle; his grey suit out of place amid the shining white breeches and glittering tack. He was talking to one of the hunters: a woman. She was bending down from the saddle, listening. There was something familiar about her long face and the blonde hair visible beneath the riding hat; after a second or two, she realised that it was Camilla Parker Bowles. She must live locally, what a piece of luck. When she moved here, she would have a friend.

Stephen

Stephen was in the hall when Diana appeared on the stairs. She came flying down like the teenager she was. 'Mrs Parker Bowles is out there with the hunt!'

'Mrs Parker Bowles usually hunts with the Beaufort. As does His Royal Highness.'

There was a silence.

'I didn't realise he hunted with her,' Diana said. 'Or hunted at all, come to that. He never mentioned it.'

Oh lord, the valet thought. I've done it now. He forced a casual note into his voice. 'Oh yes. Every Saturday.'

He could almost hear her brain whirring, the cogs moving as she pieced it all together. 'But Charles hasn't bought Highgrove yet. Where does he stay when he hunts?'

Stephen wanted to kick himself. Why on earth hadn't he kept his mouth shut? On the other hand, the woman was out there, in her tight white jodhpurs. What else could he say? 'He stays,' he admitted, 'with the Parker Bowleses.'

He could hardly look at Diana. Anything could happen now. Tears, rage, or a white and furious face demanding he take her back to London on the spot. The last thing he expected was what actually happened.

She clapped her hands, laughed. 'But, that's great news.'

He risked a glance. Was she being ironic? But no, there was genuine pleasure on her face.

'I hate hunting, and horses,' she said. 'And if Charles has a friend he can do it with, it takes the pressure off me!'

Chapter Thirty-Nine

Kensington Palace, London

April 1992

Sandy

'And that was that,' Diana said. She had kicked off her shoes and swung her long legs up on the sofa. Her head was on its arm in a manner so reminiscent of how her brother used to lie in the Beatle Room that I felt a powerful rush of nostalgia. The lamps sent soft light into the immediate surroundings, picking out the gilding on picture frames, the fringing on cushions and the hands of clocks. Beyond, all was dark. The tapestry spread across the distant wall, a black rectangle that looked like the entrance to another world.

'You mean,' I asked, 'Prince Charles proposed to you?'

'No, he went silent again.'

'Again?' This must be the third time it had happened to her. What had been wrong with the man?

'For months and months and months.' She covered her eyes and groaned. 'Oh God, Sandy. You can't imagine.'

I couldn't. None of it made sense to me at all. 'Was he a commitment-phobe?' I asked. The phrase had become popular recently.

Diana laughed. 'No, he was the Prince of Wales. And to be fair to him, he was away a lot. State visits, that sort of thing.'

'But he treated you like a dog,' I said. 'He whistled when he felt like it, and you came to heel.'

'I know,' she sighed. 'That's what my flatmates said too. But at the time I had nothing to compare it with. I'd never had a boyfriend before. And, of course, I was besotted. Completely and utterly besotted.'

But not any more, I guessed. She was clearly building up to explain what had happened to the marriage; why she was sitting here in an empty flat, albeit one in the middle of a palace, with no visible sign of her husband. Whatever had happened must have happened recently, because so far as the rest of the world was concerned, she and Charles were still very much together.

Diana began to speak again. 'I'd expected him to propose that day at Highgrove and then he didn't and I thought he must have lost interest or something.'

'But why?' I was mystified. 'It wasn't as if there was anyone else.'

Diana ignored this. 'And so there I was, in complete limbo, but with all the paps still following me everywhere.'

'Paps?'

'Paparazzi. You know, photographers. I was climbing over dustbins to get through the Harrods fire exit at one stage. And once, when they were chasing my car, I abandoned it and jumped on a bus. But then the bus got snarled up, so I had to get off and run through Russell & Bromley. I was with Caro, she said it was like being on a drag hunt in the middle of London.' She chuckled, but I thought it sounded awful. 'Didn't you wish they'd leave you alone?'

In the lamplight, her blonde hair flashed in a headshake. 'No, I was grateful to them. He couldn't forget me or ignore me if I was still all over the front pages, so it felt like a lifeline. They were my only hope, in a way.'

I would never have thought of looking at it like that.

'Besides, by then I'd got to know the hacks quite well. I knew their names, I read their stories. I even felt we were a team, in a. Used to feel quite sorry for them sometimes. There was one poor chap, staking me out all night in his freezing car. I went down in my pyjamas with a cup of cocoa.'

'That must have surprised him,' I said.

'He laughed, actually.'

'Laughed?'

Diana nodded. Her face was alight with what was evidently a cherished memory. 'I said, "Mr Lennox, are you laughing because I'm in my pyjamas?" And he said, "No, I was hoping you might invite me up." And I said, "What, and have a detailed description of the flat in the paper tomorrow! Do you think I'm stupid, Mr Lennox?"'

I thought, and not for the first time, that those who wrote her off as thick could not have been more wrong.

She reached for her wine glass, balancing on a pile of magazines on a low table in front of her. 'Anyway, Christmas was a total write-off. Because, silly me,' she rolled her eyes, 'I'd imagined I'd be spending it at Sandringham, with Charles. I'd made no arrangements, so it was Althorp with Daddy and Come Dancing. By myself, as none of the others ever came near the place. It was indescribably hideous. I spent the whole time walking in the park in the rain and crying.'

I did some quick maths. She was talking about Christmas 1980. A mere few weeks later, she was engaged. We were getting to the big moment now. All the frustrations and complexities were about to resolve themselves.

'So how did it happen, in the end?' I asked, settling one of the uncomfortable little cushions behind my head. 'How did Prince Charles propose?'

Coleherne Court, London

2 February 1981
Diana

She had been in despair. Not just Christmas, but New Year had passed without a word from Charles. Any day now, the press would lose interest. It was winter, after all, and freezing, and surely there were only so many pictures one could take of Lady Diana buying sandwiches, driving her new red Mini Metro, coming out of the entrance to her flat. And how many features were the public expected to read about Sloane Rangers, velvet hairbands and pie-crust collars? The last piece had been about Essential Sloane Skills, which included playing Racing Demon and knowing how to rag-roll a wall. Someone was even writing a handbook for Sloane Rangers, she had heard.

And then the phone call. Anne had handed over the receiver expressionlessly. 'Your friend Charlie Renfrew.'

The line had been fuzzy, with crackles and beeps. 'Where are you?' she'd asked, over the banging of her heart.

'Klosters.'

Four years ago, he had taken her sister there. But Sarah had missed her chance. She had, too, she was sure.

'Can I see you when I get back?' His voice was hesitant, as if nervous about something.

Hope had flared fiercely, but she tamped it down hard. 'Of course.'

'Good. I've got something to ask you.'

She knew that could only mean one thing. She had imagined this moment many times, how she would literally explode with excitement. But it wasn't like that at all. Rather, a great calm and certainty had spread through her. At last, the waiting was over.

6 February 1981

It was with a weary sense of déjà vu that Ginny handed over her best long dress, Caro lent a pashmina and Anne an evening bag. They had said little other than wishing her luck. She sensed they had gone beyond trying to understand or advise and now just accepted the latest twist in the saga. Which, as far as they were concerned, was just dinner at the Palace. She hadn't mentioned the great hope she carried within her, like a glassful she was scared of spilling. What had her grandmother said, all those years ago? *There's many a slip betwixt cup and lip.*

It was a freezing night, so cold that the press had gone home early. No rattle and flash of cameras accompanied her emergence from the apartment block. Beyond a loitering cat, no one saw her hurry down the empty pavement. Smiling to herself, she unlocked the little car that stood shining beneath the street lights. What a moment Mr Arnold, Mr Whitaker, Mr Lennox and Mr Edwards were missing!

As she got in, packing her full-skirted gown around her, she remembered that driving a car in a ball dress was an Essential Sloane Skill.

So short was the distance to the Palace that the engine had barely warmed up by the time she turned through the great

295

black gates. The policeman in the green security post waved her on. Mr Barry had told her to drive through the central archway into the quadrangle at the back, where her distinctive red Mini Metro would be hidden from passing prying eyes, or cameras.

She parked by the big glass entrance and was just extracting her skirts when a red-tailcoated footman appeared. Hope briefly sparked that it was Paul from Balmoral, but this dark-haired man was much taller. Much, much taller, in fact. Tall Paul, she assumed, but didn't quite dare to ask.

She followed him along the thick red carpets to the prince's apartment on the corner. A white-gloved knock on the glossy brown doors and open they swung to reveal Mr Barry.

'Good evening, Lady Diana.' As gravely, she thought, as if this were the Old Bailey and she had come to give evidence. A dark-suited figure stood in the room beyond, pulling nervously at his shirt-cuffs.

Charles

He had put it off for as long as he possibly could, but here it was, the dreaded, dreadful moment. His father had spent the whole of Christmas and New Year berating him. 'You need to *decide*, Charles. Make your bloody *mind* up. It's simply *not fair* on the girl.'

Prince Philip was also furious with the press. He was outraged that there were reporters at the gates of Sandringham; unprecedented at a time when the royal family was traditionally left in peace. He left his son in no doubt as to who he blamed. 'You've got to put everyone out of their misery,' he'd thundered.

But what about my misery, Charles had thought bleakly. Funny how, in a house as huge as Sandringham, it could still feel like there was no escape.

'All this bloody speculation,' Prince Philip had ranted on. 'Bloody torture for all concerned. Especially for that poor girl. Her honour's at stake, don't you realise? Her grandmother's going around telling everyone that she'll be finished if you dump her now.'

It was just the sort of thing her grandmother would say, Charles had thought. He had never liked Lady Fermoy. But even his own grandmother was piling the pressure on. 'Diana really is most awfully sweet and suitable,' she kept remarking.

Even Aunt Margo, who usually had nothing good to say about anyone, thought Diana 'an absolute darling'. Admittedly after several powerful cocktails. 'And she's hardly going to be any trouble, is she?' Margo had added, knowingly.

His sister Anne's attitude was similarly pragmatic. 'Ticks all the boxes,' she'd said. Andrew, typically, thought Diana a nice piece of skirt, 'especially when you can see through it!'

The most important person of all, of course, had said absolutely nothing. Offered no view or advice whatsoever, on the biggest decision he would ever make. But for his mother, the fact that marriage for the heir to the throne was marriage for life and there was no going back had not been a problem. She had never wanted to marry anyone but his father, nor had she ever looked at anyone else.

For his own part, he had never wanted to marry anyone but Camilla. But that was not possible, hence Diana. And if he married her, he would have to share his life with her, for the next half-century at least. Beget children on her, an heir and a spare. Oh God. Must his one shot at marriage, at a partner for life, really be this giggly teenage blonde?

There were good reasons why it must; she was likeable, sympathetic, pretty and highly eligible. As Anne had observed, she ticked all the boxes. The most important one for Charles was that she tolerated his arrangement with Camilla, whom he had no intention of giving up. Why should he? Princes of Wales had always had mistresses and their wives had always accepted it.

Camilla's view was that Diana might be doing so already. 'She *must* have realised, darling. The hunt. You staying overnight. Highgrove being just down the road from me. What else does she think's going on?'

Charles agreed. He reminded himself, in addition, that the Spencers were first-rank aristocrats. They had been courtiers for centuries, intimates of the Crown. They knew how these things worked. If Diana really didn't know yet, it was up to them to tell her. It certainly wasn't his responsibility.

'Lady Diana Spencer,' announced Stephen.

And here she came, beaming and excited, hurrying across the carpet. Charles, wincing, sensed that she was only just restraining herself from running into his arms. Oh cursed Fate. Why him? No one had any idea how ghastly it was when your life wasn't your own. You had no choice in anything. Everything you did was for Queen and country.

Best get it over with quickly. Like ripping off a plaster, or diving into a cold pool. He took a deep breath, braced himself, wrenched his neck to face her and tried to arrange his features into a suitable expression for asking the question he least wanted to in the whole world.

Diana

She felt as if she had detached herself from her body. She was hovering at the top of the room, watching this smiling young girl, blue eyes shining with excitement, cross the pale brown carpet and extend her eager, blushing cheek for a kiss.

The obviously nervous prince was making inconsequential small talk. She was putting him at ease with lots of smiles and reassuring remarks. There was a table with a white linen cloth,

298

a single candle, silver cutlery and a small bowl of flowers. Positioned before the long, drawn curtains of the window, it was reminiscent of a stage set. He led her to it and they sat down, like actors about to give a performance.

The tall footman reappeared to light the candle and serve the food. She watched herself start to eat it, but afterwards could not remember a single mouthful.

The prince, she thought, looked as if he were in pain. Concerned, she was about to enquire, when he asked, in a rush, 'Will you marry me?'

'Yes please,' she said, immediately.

'You don't, um, want to think about it?'

'No.'

His fingers sought his signet ring and gave it a nervous twist. 'I, ah, actually don't expect an answer immediately.'

'But it's yes. It always has been. I've wanted to marry you since the moment I met you.' Her smile was like an explosion, so huge and dazzling, it hurt to look at it. He felt, briefly, amazed. He had never imagined he was capable of making someone this happy.

Later that night

Bedtime at Coleherne Court. Caro was in the bathroom, cleaning her teeth. The noise of brush on enamel, with a gushing tap as accompaniment, made it difficult to hear anything. But was that a distant squealing? Then a banging on the door. She raised her head, exasperated. 'Hold your horses. I'll be out in a minute!'

The banging continued, and the squealing. Actually, it was screaming. Caro hurled the toothbrush in the basin and wrenched open the bathroom door. The kitchen was full of yelling. Anne and Ginny were jumping up and down. Sting, from his poster, looked blankly on.

'What's happen—' Caro began, but the rest of the sentence died in her throat. There, in the middle, was Diana. Glowing, triumphant, radiating joy like a beacon. Realisation, like an arrow, thudded into Caro's brain. 'He asked you,' she said, flatly.

'He did, and I said yes please!'

Caro's mouth fell open.

'I'm engaged!' Diana cried. 'And you've got toothpaste on your face!'

The screaming started up again.

'Oh my Gawd, Duch!'

'Show me the ring!'

'There isn't one, not yet.'

'Why not?' they all demanded.

'They're getting some in for me to choose from.'

'Pick the biggest, won't you!'

'Of course!' the Chief Chick giggled. 'What do you take me for!' Her face became suddenly serious. 'But, girls, it's deathly secret, okay? You can't tell anyone until the official announcement!'

'Guide's honour!' Caro held up her hand in the ritual manner. The others did the same.

Diana looked around, sober-faced, and nodded. Then she burst out laughing. 'Now give me a hug, all of you!'

In the ensuing explosion of joy, the tension of many months was released. Pans were banged, cushions were thrown, furniture was jumped on. Presently, a thumping from below indicated their activity was not appreciated by their downstairs neighbour.

'Go down and tell them you'll send them to the Tower,' Ginny yelled. She squealed as a cushion hit her squarely in the chest.

'That,' said the Chief Chick, 'is for the impertinence.'

Eventually, they all came to a halt on the sofa, a great pile of legs and arms and laughter and tears, with Diana right in the middle.

'So, you're happy for me?' she asked. 'Really?'

'Of course! We're thrilled for you. All of us. Even Battersea.'

'Especially Battersea. He's never been to a royal wedding before.'

'None of us have.' Ginny clapped a hand to her mouth. 'Oh, *Duch*!'

They all squealed again, and hugged, and laughed.

When this latest burst of excitement had died down, Diana, looking round with a rather tremulous smile, said, 'Only, I thought . . .'

'Duch,' said Anne, gently. 'Of course we're happy for you.'

'How could we not be?' Caro asked. 'You're obviously completely and utterly thrilled.'

'And we know it's what you wanted, more than anything in the world,' added Ginny.

Diana nodded. 'It is,' she said quietly. 'It really is.' Then, suddenly, she leapt up. 'Come on! We're going for a drive!'

'What . . . now?' Anne gestured at her pyjamas.

'But I'm in my nightie,' objected Ginny.

Caro stood up, tying her dressing-gown belt with a determined tug. 'Oh come on. We can't just go to bed. How often does your landlady tell you she's going to be Queen of England!'

They shut the flat door and hurried down the stairs, loudly shushing each other and giggling. The Chief Chick led the way in her ball gown and Anne brought up the rear. Caro clutched a bottle of champagne brought earlier that week by a Coleherne Courtier. 'Rory from the Life Guards is going to be heartbroken, Duch!'

Diana turned round, grinning. 'Rory from the Life Guards can come to the wedding!'

They ran down the pavement towards the car, their breath like clouds in the freezing night. 'How many elephants can you get into a Mini Metro?' giggled Ginny, as she and Anne piled into the back and Caro strapped herself into the front.

Diana set off at speed, screeching down the road.

'Slow down, you're not avoiding the paps now!'

'But she will be!' A cork popped, accompanied by a raucous cheer.

'Turn on Radio One, Caro!'

The car with four friends, singing and shouting, tore through late-night, lit-up London. Down Victoria Street to Buckingham Palace, circling the memorial in front of it, windows down, laughing raucously, waving their bottle. Up to Piccadilly, down through Soho. Hugging each other and their tremendous secret.

'All these people!' chortled Anne. 'Imagine what they'd think if they *knew*!'

'Imagine!'

But Diana did not need to imagine, not any more. All her dreams had come true. The absolutely real future looked as glittering as the London night. She felt happier than she had ever thought possible.

Chapter Forty

20 February 1981
Stephen

Diana, in the passenger seat, rummaged gleefully in the plastic bag on her knees. He recognised the name on it: Russell & Bromley. A shoe shop in Bond Street.

He was driving her down to Highgrove again. The prince was there, having been at Buckingham Palace the previous night. He was like a cat on hot bricks, Stephen thought.

'Look!' A pair of shiny brown slip-on shoes met his gaze, with her triumphant face above them.

'Very nice,' he smiled. He was hardly going to object when his job depended on her. She was the future Princess of Wales now. The plan had succeeded.

Stephen could still hardly believe the prince had actually popped the question. Part of him really had expected that he would manage to avoid it for ever. Perhaps he would have, if the press speculation had not made that impossible. At Christmas, even the Queen had lost her temper with the journalists mobbing Sandringham's gate. But ultimately they had forced the issue.

She was their heroine, no doubt about it. Every single member of the press corps adored her. And it was largely because of that she had succeeded where everyone else had failed. Had jumped all the fences and been first past the winning post.

Of course, there was one final, invisible, hurdle. Stephen was certain that Diana knew nothing about her fiancé's mistress. He was equally certain that she would be devastated if she did. The problem wasn't just that Diana was a modern girl expecting modern monogamy. It was much worse than that: she was madly in love.

Mrs P-B really was going to have to bow out now. The Prince was going to have to face facts. How could the future head of the Church of England look the Archbishop of Canterbury in the eye and vow to forsake all others if Camilla was still in the background? It wasn't even a question of morality, just common sense. His entire family disapproved of her and the press would go bananas if they knew.

'And this, Mr Barry!' Diana was rustling in another plastic bag now, one with the Benetton logo. He wasn't surprised to see a pale blue jersey emerge. 'I'm updating Charles' look,' she beamed. 'Think he'll like them?'

'Yes,' said Stephen, without hesitation. The prince had little option, for the moment at least, than to like what his future wife chose to buy. Last night had been a case in point. The choosing of the ring. He could see it now, out of the corner of his eye, flashing about on her finger.

Diana

She had been summoned to Windsor Castle to choose it. In the presence of the Queen, who was paying for it. She was nervous, the great drawing room had been a blur of mirrors and gold. Then Charles rose from the midst of what seemed hundreds of green satin sofas. He had welcomed her with a quick kiss, while her future mother-in-law had been friendly but brisk, seemingly keen to get on with the job. The man from Garrard, the Crown Jeweller, came in. He carried a slim dark briefcase, which he opened to reveal blazing rows of rings. The sight had made her head spin.

Charles had smiled his quizzical smile. 'So what do you think?'

She had thought she was fortunate beyond measure. She had looked for the smallest and most modest and her hand went in its direction. She saw the Queen nod approvingly.

But then, with a flash of caprice, she had remembered her flatmates' urgings. Almost by itself, her hand had changed direction and picked out the biggest one instead.

'A sapphire surrounded by fourteen diamonds set in eighteen-carat white gold,' intoned the Garrard man. The Queen had raised her eyebrows.

'It cost twenty eight and a half thousand pounds!' Diana had exulted to Coleherne Court, afterwards. 'You should have seen Her Majesty's face!'

'Oh Lord, Duch. You didn't offend her, did you?'

'Of course not! Don't you like it?' She had stuck out her hand. It had blazed even brighter under the kitchen light of the flat as under the chandeliers of Windsor Castle.

'It's very . . .' Caro had paused.

'Grand?' suggested Ginny.

'Grown-up,' said Anne.

Now, looking at it in the car, Diana wondered if they might not have a point. The ring was very grand and grown-up. Possibly it didn't go with the jeans, loafers and shirt she was wearing. A smaller one might have been better. Less ostentatious. This one made her think of Raine. Come Dancing's delight in her new relation to royalty was a cloud, if only a tiny one, in the huge blue sky of her happiness.

Her own mother was another. Diana had expected her to be pleased, but Frances had withheld her approval. 'But are you *sure*, darling? I have to confess I'm not wildly keen.'

No doubt Frances suspected, and correctly, the involvement of her own hated mother. But how horrid to use the wedding to vent her continuing resentment. It just perpetuated the misery and damage, Diana thought. 'Mummy, you don't understand,' she'd argued. 'I *love* Charles.'

Frances' great blue eyes had flashed. 'Love him, or love what he is?'

Diana had felt a rush of fury. Why couldn't her mother be happy for her? For once in her life, support her daughter? 'What's the difference?' she had retorted, deliberately provocative.

As Stephen turned into the gates of Highgrove, she tried to push all these negative thoughts away. She was the luckiest girl in the world and she was going to be happy *for ever*.

The house didn't seem to have progressed much since the sale had been completed.

'You're in charge now,' the prince told her as they walked round.

'Me?'

'The decoration. I'll leave it all up to you. Every little last detail.'

The thought was alarming. She had never so much as wielded a paintbrush, and as for hanging paper, how did one even start? Rag-rolling, meanwhile, might be an Essential Sloane Skill, but not one she knew anything about.

'I thought you'd enjoy it,' he went on, in his avuncular way. 'Ladies do, I'm told.

Now come into the garden. I want your views on crazy paving.'

*

Stephen served the lunch. He had made it himself: eggs Florentine, the spinach picked straight from the vegetable patch. They ate it balanced on plates on their knees.

'Isn't this fun?' asked the prince, smiling at her. He was wearing his pale blue jumper and the slip-on shoes, which, after obvious initial doubt, he pronounced 'really rather surprisingly comfortable'.

She beamed back, her equilibrium restored. She loved him so much, she could hardly bear it.

After lunch, he told her he had a surprise for her. 'You do like horses, don't you?'

She felt a bolt of pure horror, imagining he was going to present her with one. Then he explained he was riding his favourite mount in a race the following day. Did she want to come with him this afternoon and meet Allibar? Watch him on the gallops?

She was awed. She hadn't known he rode competitively. It seemed so daring and sexy. He was such a man of action, she thought happily.

'You see,' the prince explained, 'I don't like going to races to watch horses thundering up and down. I'd rather be riding them myself.'

'I can see that, sir.'

'My dear grandmother always says that if there was anything left to discover in the world, I would have been an explorer.'

She hopped excitedly into the Aston Martin. It was the first time he had driven her anywhere. Being alone with him in the car was thrilling. As they roared along at alarming speed, he described the horse he had bought the previous year.

'My dream is to win the Gold Cup on Allibar,' he explained.

'I'm sure you will, sir.'

'The race at Chepstow's just a warm-up.'

She loved him sharing his hopes like this, the two of them together. It was just the intimacy and companionship she had longed for. She imagined driving along, just like this, with children in the back. Talking, making plans. Like a real family.

He broke into her thoughts. 'My trainer, Nick, has got a rather sweet little girl.'

A flood of pleasure went through her. Was he saying that he wanted one too? She would love a little girl. Later, after the boys. She smiled at him. 'How wonderful, sir.'

'Yes. I thought she'd make rather a good bridesmaid.'

Diana hesitated. Coleherne Court were going to be her bridesmaids. She wondered how to explain this.

Then, a distraction. A car sailed past them, two familiar faces staring out through the windscreen. Arthur Edwards and Harry Arnold glanced at her casually, then did a double take. She saw them recognise the prince and start to jabber frantically to each other.

She beamed at them as usual, and was about to wave and laugh before remembering, with a surge of horror, that the engagement was, for the moment, entirely secret. For the *Sun* to see them together effectively blew their cover.

Then came a curse from the driving seat. 'Christ, it's those *bloody* newspapermen. Do we never get a *minute's* bloody peace?'

He put his foot down, the noise of the engine rose to a scream and the view outside the passenger window became a blur. The road through the windscreen seemed to hurtle towards them. She clung to the door handle, helpless with fear. A petrol station was approaching; with a scream of tyres, the prince veered off the road. She felt sure they would smash into the pumps, or the station building, but they seemed, miraculously, to miss them, instead plunging out through the back into a country lane. He thundered down it for some miles, lurching over potholes and skidding on mud, before finally slowing to a normal speed.

'Here we are,' he said, as they drew up before a long, low white cottage. 'My trainer's house.' Only now did she allow herself to breathe.

After the cosy fug of the car, the cold outside pinched her nose, wet her eyelashes and froze her hair. She had hoped for the shelter of a stable but was sent to wait on the windy downs. She told herself that the prince wanted to impress her, which was thrillingly flattering. What did a little chill matter?

Warm inside, if nowhere else, she followed a stable lad along a path through a couple of fields. Beneath the lowering gloom of a late February afternoon, the white fencing of the gallops glowed.

Before long, the thunder of horse and rider could faintly be heard. Then they appeared in the distance, the prince crouched on his saddle. He looked dashing in white jodhpurs and a black crash helmet; Allibar, as promised, was huge and magnificent, muscles rippling beneath his shining coat. All the same, watching the two of them, she was seized with a sudden, inexplicable premonition of disaster.

He slowed the horse down and trotted towards her. He was within a few feet when the great creature began to jerk convulsively, rearing its huge head backwards, flaring its nostrils, rolling its eyes. The prince leapt off. His polished boots had only just stepped clear when Allibar crashed violently to the ground. Charles fell to his knees, his arms round the horse's neck, his face white with shock.

'He's not . . .?' she gasped when she reached him. It had all happened so quickly, it hardly seemed believable.

Tears were coursing down Charles' cheeks. She huddled beside him as she would beside her nursery charges and held him to her, murmuring words of comfort as he wept brokenly into her shoulder. They clung together for a long time, kneeling in the mud.

Chapter Forty-One

Kensington Palace, London

April 1992

Sandy

'I did really feel so close to him at that moment.' Diana's voice drifted wistfully from the opposite sofa. 'I felt we had really properly bonded. I had never seen him so upset about anything. He was absolutely distraught; it was like looking straight into his heart.'

I was horrified. The Allibar story was as appalling as it was strange. 'But what caused it?' I asked. 'The horse dying like that?'

'The post-mortem said it was a massive heart attack. Apparently, it could have happened at any time. The race the next day, for instance. Charles might have been injured, even killed.

'So,' I said, 'lucky, in a way.'

'Yes, but as omens go, it was a pretty terrible one. The weekend completely fell apart after that. The photographers had tracked us down by then, so I got shoved into the back of a Land Rover. Dirty blanket on top of me. I didn't even go back to Highgrove, just to London.'

'Did Prince Charles go with you?'

'No, he stayed the weekend there. Went hunting with the Beaufort to take his mind off it all.'

There followed a few moments' silence.

'And then,' she said, 'the following Tuesday, the engagement was announced.'

Coleherne Court, Kensington, London

23 February 1981
Diana

Things had escalated. It wasn't just the doorbell at Coleherne Court being rung at all hours and reporters pursuing the flat-mates down the street. There were now photographers in the building opposite, their long lenses trained on her bedroom window.

All their friends, all the Coleherne Courtiers, had been contacted by the press. Some had even been offered money to reveal what they knew. It was a point of pride in the flat that no one had said anything.

Having their bins gone through had been one of the biggest surprises. 'Can you imagine?' Caro had gasped. 'All our yucky rubbish! Just how is that journalism?'

The same thing was happening outside Young England. The days of placating the press with one photograph were over. Journalists and cameramen now came from all over the world. Untrue stories had started to appear, one particularly stupid and annoying one claiming that a mystery blonde had spent the night on the royal train as it parked in a siding in Wiltshire. The prince had been down to visit his estates in Cornwall and, it was alleged, picked up his guest on the way back; the suggestion was that this was Diana. Who, at the time, had been tucked up in bed at Coleherne Court.

This incident had caused shock waves at the Palace. The Queen's press secretary had taken the rare step of complaining to the newspapers. This had alarmed Diana almost more than the story itself. Now the engagement was about to be announced, she was desperate not to put a foot wrong. The idea of Charles' family, who she wanted so much to please, being irritated with her was terrifying.

Things had rather come to a head at a dinner at Windsor over the weekend. She had been so excited beforehand, driving from London in her frilly blue ball gown. The setting had been awe-inspiring, the great Waterloo Chamber, with blazing chandeliers and huge portraits on the silk-covered walls.

Floating through the room with the sapphire – looking entirely appropriate now – sparkling enormously on her finger, had felt like a high point of her whole life. She spotted Andrew and hurried over. He looked glum, but she had cheerful news. 'I've found the perfect girl for you,' she announced. 'Jolly redhead called Sarah. She has exactly your sense of humour. You're going to get on like a house on fire.'

Andrew looked at her coldly. 'This was supposed to be my birthday dinner.'

She was shocked. 'No one told me!'

'Why should they?' he said bitterly. 'It's pretty obvious. Big Brother's engagement trumps Little Brother's twenty-first, every time.'

That Andrew wasn't the only one harbouring resentment became obvious once dinner had started. The talk was all of 'the hated enemy', as the Windsors described the press. Prince Philip, next to her, complained about a recent Sandringham shooting weekend that had been 'utterly bloody ruined' by reporters.

Diana listened, worried.

'*You're* quite good at dealing with the hated enemy though, aren't you?' Anne's remark, from across the table, didn't sound like a compliment.

Even so, it gave Diana an idea. Perhaps she could turn what seemed her weakness – the media's fascination with her – into a strength. She knew a little of how it worked now; she could help and advise her new family.

She smiled at Anne. 'I don't really think of them as the enemy. They're only people.'

She began to tell a story about a photographer she knew. 'His family were in Scotland for Christmas, but he had to stay in London, outside my flat, just to try to get a photograph of me. I said to him, okay, I'll get in my car, let you have some close-ups with a big smile.' She grinned at the memory. 'And so I did, and he got them, and he was able to get home for Christmas.'

Anne's expression was one of disgust. 'Couldn't be bothered with that. I just tell them to naff off.'

Diana had left the dinner worried and wretched. It was obvious that to please the Windsors she must stop the press pursuit. But how?

She racked her brains all the way back. By the time she reached Coleherne Court, she had a plan. The next day, she shared it with her flatmates that, following the engagement announcement, she would move into Buckingham Palace.

They were crowded in the steam-filled kitchen. Preparations for a spag bol supper were in full swing. There had been clattering, rattling, exclamations. Now there was only stunned silence.

Caro was the first to speak. 'Move into Buckingham Palace? You are joking.'

'Leave us? Duch, you *can't*!' Ginny wailed.

'Stay until the wedding, at least!' Anne begged.

The Chief Chick sighed. 'I can't, girls. I'd love to, but it's all gone crazy and it's not fair on anyone. Besides, if I moved into BP—'

'BP!' Caro snatched this up immediately.

'You're always saying that I should get more protection from the Palace,' Diana pointed out. 'What more protection could it give than providing me with a home?'

'Your home is here, with us,' stated Ginny, steadfastly.

'But you can't protect me.'

'What about all that car business the other night?' asked an indignant Caro.

Diana's journey to Windsor Castle had been kept from the press by a decoy arrangement. Caro had driven the red Mini Metro around central London, while the Chief Chick took her car. 'Yes, but we can't do that all the time.'

'I don't mind,' Caro insisted. 'It was quite fun.'

Anne wrinkled her brow. 'How long would you be in the Palace for?'

'It could be ages,' Ginny added. 'You haven't announced the engagement yet, let alone the wedding.'

'What if you're terribly lonely?' Anne wanted to know.

'Of course I won't be,' Diana assured them brightly. 'Charles will be there, and the Queen. It's the perfect solution to everything. I get out of the way of the press and get to know all my new relations.'

'Maybe even your new husband,' Caro said slyly. It had not escaped the notice of any of the flatmates how little the couple had been alone together.

Diana batted this away with a smile. 'I've got a lifetime to get to know him! And, anyway, I already know everything about him where it matters.' She patted her breast in its pink Shetland pullover. 'In my heart.'

Three pairs of eyes rolled at each other.

'But what about your job?' the practical Anne wanted to know.

'Oh, I've packed that in.'

She was unprepared for the dismay on the faces of her flat-mates. Kay King had looked much the same.

'I had to,' she said defensively. 'All the flashguns were frightening the children.'

A hiss and a cloud of steam greeted this. Ginny was draining the pasta.

'Well, you've obviously got it all worked out,' said Caro.

'You sound very sure,' added Anne, emptying powdery grated Parmesan onto a saucer.

'And we can always come and see you,' put in Ginny, more cheerfully, 'At *BP*!'

'Of course you can, you absolutely have to!' Diana beamed round at them. 'And think about all the advice I'll get there. By the time I go up the aisle, I'll know everything there is to know about being Princess of Wales.'

Chapter Forty-Two

Knightsbridge, London
February 1981

For the engagement announcement, she had asked Frances to help her choose an outfit. She hoped it might prompt some rare mother and daughter bonding.

They had initially gone to Bellville Sassoon, a smart boutique Diana had always aspired to. But the vendeuse was snooty and failed to recognise her. Both things had enraged Frances.

Her daughter had hurried her out of the shop. 'Mummy! Please! We need to keep a low profile! We don't want every pap in London after us.'

Frances might not have agreed. A once-beautiful woman who had had her share of disappointments, she might have seen in her daughter's fame some compensation for herself. There might even have been a hint of jealousy. Certainly, looking at the suit afterwards, Diana wondered how anyone who wanted the best for her could have possibly allowed her to buy it.

At the time, however, speed had trumped style. 'How about this?' she had asked, grabbing the mid-blue two-piece on the rack in Harrods Ladieswear.

'Lovely, darling,' said a distracted Frances, glancing about as if hoping to be spotted.

'There's a blouse that goes with it.' Diana had looked doubtfully at the print with the pussy-cat bow.

'Lovely, darling.'

But was it lovely? It looked, Diana had thought, like something Mrs Thatcher would wear. The Prime Minister, along with the Archbishop of Canterbury and the Commonwealth heads of government, had been told over the weekend that the announcement was about to take place. She still couldn't believe that such important people knew her name.

Back from the shopping trip, in front of the mirror at Coleherne Court, she felt that not only did the blouse definitely look like one of the Prime Minister's, the blue suit did as well. The jacket, moreover, accentuated her bust. High heels might have helped, but Mr Barry had made it clear, discreetly, that they were to be avoided. Flat shoes would be more diplomatic, given the slight height difference between herself and her husband-to-be.

Her flatmates, ever-loyal, tried to comfort her.

'You don't look like Mrs T, Duch. More like someone who works for BA. First class, obviously.'

'Thanks, girls. So what you're saying is, on the greatest day of my life, I'm going to look like a trolley dolly.'

The banter disguised how they felt about what was coming. The royal protection officer was arriving at the flat at 5p.m. Coming to take her away. They tried to joke about that, too.

'It's like you're being arrested, Duch.'

'The *really* funny thing,' she told them, 'is that he's actually called Officer. Paul Officer. Officer Officer. Apparently, he once saved Charles from a mentally disturbed sailor.'

'It's that thing,' Ginny said. 'When your life sort of echoes your name.'

'Nominative determinism,' said Caro.

'Like the Windsors living at Windsor,' Diana put in.

'That's not quite the same,' said Anne. 'They called themselves Windsor to sound less German during the First World War.'

'Golly, is that true? I didn't know that.'

Anne nodded. 'Their real name – wait for it – is Saxe-Coburg-Gotha.'

'So really I'm going to be Diana Frances Saxe-Coburg-Gotha?' She giggled. 'What a mouthful!'

The hours counted down. It felt exciting but also unreal. I'm using this phone for the last time, she thought, putting the familiar instrument down in the hall. I'm opening this cupboard for the last time. Finding that we've got no milk in the fridge as usual for the last time. I won't sleep in this bed again, or clean my teeth in this basin. She balanced this by reminding herself that every last experience brought her closer to the man she loved, the new life she was about to begin.

'I hope they've got a telly at Buckingham Palace,' Anne remarked, at one stage.

'Oh, I'm not going there yet. I'm to spend a few days at Clarence House with the Queen Mother first.'

Squeals greeted this. *'The Queen Mother!'*

'And she definitely has a telly,' Diana grinned. 'Mr Barry told me that she watches *Dad's Army* on it.'

'Not *Crossroads?*' said Ginny, wryly.

'Charles will be there to meet me. And then there's drinks at the Palace with the parentals.'

More squeals. 'Parentals! You mean . . .?'

'The Queen and the Duke of Edinburgh, yes. And Daddy. With Come Dancing, obviously.'

They all groaned.

'Let's have a big hug,' Diana said, 'before Officer Officer gets here. Might be a bit awkward, with him around.'

Anne bit her lip. 'But, Duch,' she said gently, 'you're always going to have him around. Or someone. From now on, for the rest of your life.'

A hot, dizzying panic swooped over Diana then. She tried to force it away by hugging them close and hard. 'Pinky promise me you'll come and see me,' she muttered into Caro's hair and the dear familiar smell of Alberto Balsam.

'Of course!' Their voices were muffled, faces buried in her jumper. She could feel their hot tears through the wool.

They had just linked little fingers when the doorbell rang.

Officer Officer was understated, dressed in an ordinary suit rather than a uniform.

Diana picked up her suitcase and forced a smile at her flatmates. 'Well, goodbye then, Four Musketeers.' She could hardly speak through the lump in her throat.

Caro sniffed. 'Five, including the goldfish!'

'Yes,' choked Anne, 'don't forget Battersea!'

'Good luck, Duch!'

'We'll be watching you tomorrow!'

The engagement interview, the following afternoon. Questions live on television. A whole new media challenge with the whole world watching. But Charles would be there. He would help her, protect her. With his love and support, she could face anything.

She hesitated in the doorway. The thought hit her; once she crossed it, she could never come back. She turned; they were still standing there. She dodged past them, into the kitchen, and returned with two Charlie Brown mugs. 'They'll help me feel at home.' She blinked away tears and hugged them one last time, whispering low and urgent, 'For God's sake, ring me. I'm going to need you.'

Outside on the pavement, she looked up. There they all were at the window of her bedroom. What had been her bedroom.

It felt like another life already. She waved the Charlie Brown mugs.

'I just want you to know,' said Officer Officer as they walked to his car, 'that this is the last night of freedom ever in your life. So make the most of it.'

Something cold and sharp now passed through her heart. It was as if a sword had pierced it. She stopped, turned and looked back at the window. They were still there. It flashed through her mind that there was still time, she could still change her mind, turn on her heel, run up the stairs. It wasn't too late.

Behind the three figures she thought she could see a shadowy fourth. Her old self, waving goodbye too. There was rattling, they were opening the window. 'Give our love to the Queen Mother!' they yelled, as she slid into the back seat and was driven away.

Kensington Palace, London

April 1992
Sandy

'There was no one,' Diana said, bleakly.

'No one where?' I asked.

'At Clarence House when I arrived. No Queen Mother. No Charles. No one to meet me at all. A footman showed me up to my bedroom. It had a four-poster bed. And on it . . .' She paused.

I waited. A hot-water bottle? A fluffy toy?

'A letter.'

Chapter Forty-Three

Clarence House, London
Late afternoon, 23 February 1981
Diana

The envelope was small, cream and of thick, luxurious paper. She had seen similar in the prince's apartment. It was from Charles, she thought with delight and relief. Here was an explanation for his absence.

She picked it up; but, no, this was not his writing. She had received few notes from him, but enough to recognise his careful hand when she saw it. This hand was untidy, scrawling.

She tore it open. It was dated two days previously.

Such exciting news about the engagement. Do let's have lunch soon when the Prince of Wales goes to Australia and New Zealand. He's going to be away for three weeks. I'd love to see the ring.

The note ended,

Lots of love, Camilla.

Stunned, she read it again and again. One sentence alone kept jumping out at her.

He's going to be away for three weeks.

Charles had said nothing of this. And Australia and New Zealand! The other side of the world!

She swallowed, suddenly nauseous. Why hadn't he told her? She would never have suggested moving to the Palace if she had known. Her flatmates were right; what would she do in there, alone, without him, for *three whole weeks*?

Camilla's writing blurred as the tears gathered. So great was her bewilderment, it hardly occurred to her to wonder why Mrs Parker Bowles knew this when she didn't. The engagement, especially, was supposed to be secret.

She dropped the note on the bed and raked back her hair with both hands, trying not to panic. She walked over to the windows and looked out at the Mall, the ceremonial route where she would ride in a carriage in her wedding dress. She usually had no difficulty picturing this; it was her favourite daydream: the dress, the veil, the tiara. Now, however, looking out at the actual location, the images failed to come. At the back of her mind was a tiny, weak voice reminding her that it was still not too late.

She looked over at her small holdall. It contained the Mrs Thatcher blue suit and a present for Charles. One of the children at Young England had misunderstood who exactly she was to marry and drawn a picture of the Prince of Whales: a large fish with a crown on. She had bought a small frame for it; it would look perfect in his bathroom.

It occurred to her now that if she didn't go through with the wedding, the child would be terribly disappointed. And she would be seeing Charles very soon, for drinks at Buckingham Palace. Once she did, everything would right itself. It would all make sense again.

Kensington Palace, London

April 1992
Sandy

'And did it?' I asked. 'Make sense again?' It was making less and less sense to me; the whale picture especially seemed a fragile basis for such a momentous decision.

'Yes and no,' she said. 'Of course, it was wonderful to see Charles. And he was so apologetic. He couldn't believe he hadn't mentioned the Australia trip, or that someone hadn't. I felt a bit wretched about it, even so. I asked if I could go with him; the engagement would have been announced by then, after all. I thought it would be fun for me, and I could get used to royal tours and so on. But it was out of the question.'

'I don't see why,' I said.

'Well, neither did I, to be honest. But I was desperate to oblige, and not make a fuss, and do what they wanted. And I was at a disadvantage because, of course, Come Dancing was there with Daddy, and she was dressed to the nines in mink and pearls and screeching away in that awful affected voice. My toes were curling, Sandy. Can you imagine?'

I absolutely could.

'And Charles obviously hated it as well; he stayed thirty minutes, not a second more, and then off he went to have dinner with his mother.'

'Didn't you go too?' I was astonished. Why ever not?

A sigh of exasperation. 'No, I was packed off back to Clarence House. The Queen Mother had come back by then, and I had to have dinner with her instead.'

Clarence House, London

Evening, 23 February 1981
Diana

A flamboyant figure in white tie and tails showed her into the drawing room. It seemed absolutely full of illuminated cabinets. Some contained china, others small ornaments. It was like being in the showroom at Thomas Goode.

The most decorative item of all was the Queen Mother, piled with jewels, including a tiara, and wearing a long pearl-studded gown. As Diana sank into a deep curtsey, she came over with a smile of welcome.

'I'm so glad you've come to look at the boiler!'

Boiler? Rising from her curtsey, Diana felt her mouth drop open. 'Your Majesty, I—'

'It has been playing up for some time.'

'*Ma'am?*'

The old queen cackled. 'My dear, your face. It's too funny. It's a joke, you see. We're very keen on them in our family. We are all quite mad.'

'Oh no, ma'am . . .'

'Oh yes! We're bound to be really, because we spent so many centuries marrying our own relatives.' The Queen Mother chuckled. 'Of course, some of us are madder than others. Certain of my relatives have spent their entire lives in lunatic asylums. And take Alice of Battenberg, that's dear Philip's mother. She was a wonderful person but rather obsessive. I always found that her biggest failing was her insistence that she was having a sexual relationship with both Jesus Christ and the Buddha.'

Diana was astonished. 'Is that really true, ma'am?'

'Oh yes, absolutely. Alice was very spiritual.'

The figure in white tie, an elaborate sort of footman it seemed, pulled the chairs out from a small oval table. It was laid for two, with white linen and a great deal of glassware, silverware, flowers and china. Diana took the proffered seat and the footman hovered with champagne. She covered her glass. 'Oh no, thank you.'

'I'd take your hand away if I were you,' the old queen advised. 'William will only pour it through your fingers.'

As the bottle hovered threateningly, she did as her hostess recommended.

'William is my Page of the Back Stairs,' the Queen Mother told her once the footman had left. 'He's far grander than I am.' She leant forward and clinked Diana's glass with her own. 'Chin chin!'

The old queen was cock-a-hoop. Things, in the end, had turned out marvellously. The engagement was to be announced tomorrow and this dinner was all about celebrating and having a jolly good time.

'"Let's blow trumpets and squeakers and enjoy the party as much as we can!"' she went on exuberantly. 'That's from *Private Lives*, which is possibly not very appropriate. Your private life will rather disappear down the Swanee from now on.'

Diana gave a scared smile and took a swig of champagne. The bubbles fizzed on her tongue. William now returned with the first course: a very large, rich-looking prawn cocktail, inside two scooped-out eggs.

'Oeufs Drumkilbo! A particular favourite of one's.'

'It looks delicious.' But her insides were surging with nervous excitement: eating anything seemed an impossibility.

'Aren't they wonderful, my fish knives?' The old queen picked one up and brandished it. 'My Household gave them to me when I was eighty. One of my guests once described them as middle-class, so I always make sure they're out when he comes. Thank you, William,' she added, as her glass was topped up. He topped Diana's up too. She had drunk more than she realised.

The old queen ate with surprising speed. She had finished her starter already and was watching Diana finish hers.

'I wonder,' she remarked smilingly, 'if you are aware that you are the first Princess of Wales since before the First World War. For over sixty years.'

'No, ma'am. I didn't know that.'

'The last one was Queen Mary, although she was Princess May, of course, at the time. She was quite perfect at it. Knew all the rules.'

Diana stopped chewing. This was what she had hoped for, upon moving into the royal enclave. Guidance. Information. 'The rules, ma'am?'

Bright old eyes regarded her over the rim of a champagne coupe. 'Don't worry, there are only two of them. Rule one, never upstage your husband. There's such a thing as being too popular.'

She had heard this before, Diana thought. Balmoral. Prince Philip.

The level of adulation, you wouldn't believe it. It could have been corroding. It would have been very easy to play to the gallery. Safer not to be too popular . . .

'And while I couldn't possibly be fonder of dear Charles,' the old queen was continuing genially, 'he's not a very natural or spontaneous person. You, on the other hand, are the exact opposite. All schoolgirl charm and warm responsiveness.'

The implication of this was as alarming as it was flattering. 'But I don't want to upstage Charles,' Diana said. 'I never have and I never would.'

'I'm sure you don't, my dear,' the Queen Mother twinkled. 'But others prefer to put you in the limelight, that's the problem.'

Understanding dawned. 'Is this about the press, ma'am? Because they follow me everywhere?'

'Yes, you need to be careful about that. Of all the family, Charles is the one most sensitive about his own image. It's possible that his persistent desire to be appreciated is the most hopeless of his causes.'

Diana sighed. 'I wish,' she said with feeling, 'that it would stop.'

A glitter of rings as the old queen raised her champagne glass. 'It won't. I'd like to tell you differently, but I would be telling you a lie. You just have to manage them, that's all. I've managed them for sixty years and we all get on famously. I think they're perfect ducks. When I was eighty, they all clubbed together their beer money and bought me a china bowl and a bunch of flowers.'

'That was kind of them.'

'It wasn't an especially nice bowl. I'd have preferred the beer.'

The Queen Mother now picked up a little bell of cranberry-coloured glass and tinkled it. William reappeared immediately, removed the plates and refilled their champagne. Then more plates appeared; larger, with thick gold rims.

'Oh William, what an absolute treat!' exclaimed the old queen. 'Tournedos Rossini is *such* a favourite of one's.'

It was a thick fillet steak topped with a generous slice of what looked like foie gras. Diana looked at it in despair. Especially after the eggs, it seemed huge and rich. Her head was whirling slightly from all the wine.

'Rule two.' The Queen Mother leant forward conspiratorially. Her tiara flashed brightly, warningly.

Diana straightened up, blinked. Behind her hostess, the room with the illuminated cabinets seemed oddly blurred.

The twinkling old eyes narrowed, sharpened. The wrinkled old mouth drew together, ready to speak. 'Never trust anyone,' it said. 'Ever.'

Kensington Palace, London

April 1992
Sandy

'When I woke up next morning, I had no idea where I was.' Diana's voice came lightly across the darkened room. 'And then I heard a sort of stamping, scraping sound, and looked out of my window. And it was the guards at Clarence House marching about on the cobbles.'

I imagined rifle, railings, the crash of heavy boots. 'Scary.'

'Well, I was more concerned with my hangover,' she said with a chuckle. 'It was the first I'd ever had. I must have been terribly drunk when I went to bed because I remember riding a bike round the little yard by William's office. I was ringing the bell and shouting, "I'm going to marry the Prince of Wales!" Talk about embarrassing!'

I disagreed. I thought it sounded sweet, and slightly sad. The image reinforced how young she had been, how child-like, romantic, idealistic. It was obvious now that the picture was darkening; nothing seemed to have gone right since the proposal.

'That was the day of the engagement announcement,' Diana went on. 'I went to get my hair done at Headlines. The policeman had to come with me. I said, "Officer Officer, what on earth do you think's going to happen. That Kevin will attack me with the scissors, or something?" But it made no difference. Everything had changed.'

Chapter Forty-Four

24 February 1981
Diana

Kevin's face had been a picture. She had walked into the salon and waved her engagement ring under his nose. 'What do you think about *that?*'

The hairdressers had all squealed.

'Everyone's going to want this hairstyle,' Kevin exulted, putting the finishing touches to her fringe. 'After today, every salon in the country's going to be copying it.'

Crowds were already gathering outside the Palace gates as they drove through. She kept her head well down. How did they know? On a table in a passage was the answer. A newspaper headline:

LADY DIANA ENGAGEMENT TODAY

The old queen's words from last night came back. *Never trust anyone. Ever.*

She had hoped Charles would show her to her rooms. He was out, however. She also hoped for rooms near to his, but her suite was on the top floor in the nursery corridor. This little bedroom, bathroom, kitchen and sitting room had, she was told, once belonged to Charles' nanny. She imagined Caro baulking at this; 'What are they trying to tell you, Duch?'

Excitedly, she explored the rooms, opened all the cupboards and drawers. Perhaps she was expecting a note of welcome, from Charles, from her future mother-in-law, whose house this was, after all. Nothing, however. No flowers, even. And it was all so quiet and still. But that was the windows, they were double-glazed, and oh my goodness, the view! It was of the gold statue of Queen Victoria, which must mean, yes, she was right above the famous balcony, where she would stand on her wedding day. A great, bright excitement rose within her, sending the shadows away.

As she watched, a footman appeared in the courtyard below. Her stomach tightened; he was carrying the framed announcement. Immediately, the crowd pressed against the railings.

She knew exactly what the announcement said; she had read it earlier, over and over again. But it still hadn't quite gone in. It was so hard to believe that it had actually happened. Everything she had ever wanted. All her romantic dreams, come true and summed up in this one short sentence.

It is with the greatest pleasure that the Queen and the Duke of Edinburgh announce the betrothal of their beloved son the Prince of Wales to the Lady Diana Spencer, daughter of the Earl Spencer and the Honourable Mrs Shand Kydd.

She watched the footman place it on the gate. Then the crowds erupted like a bomb going off. The cheers were faint, because of the double glazing, but she could hear a thumping; the band that had accompanied the guard change were playing 'Congratulations'. She felt on the one hand awed – the famous guard was performing in her honour – and on the other, amused. 'Congratulations', that was from yonks ago. She could almost hear Caro saying it.

She turned from the window. What should she do now? The TV interview would be soon, and Charles would come and fetch her. A surge of joy accompanied this thought, as well as a sickening swoop of nerves. Charles would help, though; he had lots of TV experience. He knew all about it.

There was a small TV in the sitting room, which she switched on. Incredibly, it was black and white. The picture jagging and fizzing across the screen now righted itself to an image of the front of Buckingham Palace. Some recent tabloid shots of her appeared. She stared at the girl on the screen as she always did at her picture in the newspapers. With curiosity, as if it were someone else altogether.

'His Royal Highness could not have made a better choice for a future queen of England,' said the voice-over. 'Lady Diana is British through and through and from a family of historical distinction with numerous royal links.'

She laughed. 'Yes,' she said aloud. 'That's me!'

'And a royal engagement could not have come at a better time,' the TV voice continued. 'The mundane facts of British life at the moment are pretty grim. The dreary statistics of unemployment and falling production, strikes and threats of strikes, have depressed us for far too long. What better than a royal romance to warm and cheer all our hearts?'

Diana felt her high spirits dim slightly. Unemployment and strikes? All that had somehow passed her by. She had stepped out of the real world completely.

'But at last it is to be royal wedding bells and we are delighted for them both,' the television concluded. 'Prince Charles is a lucky man. He has been accepted by a lovely girl who still has the freshness of the morning dew. The whole nation is smiling.'

The freshness of the morning dew! She could imagine what Coleherne Court would make of that. *You should see her before a shower!* She giggled, then felt a little sad.

The bulletin then went live to the crowd in front of the Palace, where some familiar figures were being interviewed by a reporter with a large microphone.

'Over Christmas, I realised Diana was in love.' Her father spoke shakily, as he had since the stroke. 'Then His Royal Highness called and said, "I would like to marry your daughter. Diana, much to my astonishment, has already said yes."'

Diana's astonishment was equally great. This was private. What was her father thinking?

'We simply couldn't be happier for her,' trilled an affected voice from the depths of a mink collar. Next to the red-faced earl, Raine's lacquered hair rose almost as high as the nearby guards' fur helmets.

Never trust anyone. Ever. Diana turned the TV off.

Oh, where was Charles? She wished desperately that he would come, the one person she could depend on in this suddenly strange world. Her hopes soared as someone entered the room; not the prince, alas, but a tall woman with large eyes that seemed to take absolutely everything in. She was, she explained, Lady Grafton, lady-in-waiting to the Queen.

'You will have to choose ladies-in-waiting of your own, of course,' she said, after the pleasantries were concluded.

Diana's eyes widened. She hadn't thought of this. Did she really need them? It seemed so old-fashioned somehow; her two grandmothers had occupied similar posts, but they were from a previous generation. 'What would they do?' she asked, doubtfully.

'Oh, hover and be helpful,' Lady Grafton said comfortably. 'Be on hand to take coats and bouquets, chat to nervous lady mayoresses, inspect needlework by Girl Guides, that sort of thing.'

Diana thought this sounded rather dull. Did she want to be a bouquets and mayoresses Princess of Wales? It sounded stuffy.

She wanted to inspire people. Help them, *Love* them. Then it struck her that her friends could be ladies-in-waiting. Her flat-mates. That would make things more fun. Shake it up a bit. They'd be back together, the old gang. The Four Musketeers, perhaps even with Battersea. Her spirits soared.

But Lady Grafton looked doubtful. 'They don't need to be particular friends,' she said. 'Rather, amiable and sensible girls of good class, chosen for their efficiency, way with people and art of conversation.'

Diana looked down to hide the rebellion in her eyes. She didn't want efficient and sensible, but would Coleherne Court want to inspect needlework anyway?

'Are you ready, my dear?' It was time to go down for the engagement interview. Lady Grafton led off, across the miles of thick red carpet, and Diana, in her flat shoes, followed. Her subversive thoughts faded as she anticipated seeing Charles and proclaiming their love to the world.

Coleherne Court

'Duch looks so *happy*,' said Ginny. They were crowded around the television in the sitting room. Atop the pile of *Daily Mail*s and *TV Times* on the coffee table was Battersea in his bowl. He was, after all, part of the Household and needed to witness his fellow resident joining the royal family.

Alongside the bowl was a large box of tissues. Everyone, the goldfish excepted, was sniffing copiously. 'Although Battersea might be crying too,' Caro pointed out. 'But you can't tell because his face is wet anyway.'

The flatmates thought the estimated size of the TV audi-ence quite unbelievable. Five hundred million people, tuning in from all over the world to watch the girl who had shared their fridge, their bathroom, their wardrobe and their lives.

It still didn't feel real. 'And I don't think it ever will,' said Anne.

'Charlie Renfrew doesn't look *quite* as thrilled as Duch does,' Caro remarked. The Prince of Wales, on screen, was shooting his cuffs and seemed uneasy.

'Yes, but he's royal,' Anne reminded them. 'They're trained to strangle their emotions at birth. For a Windsor, that's actually an expression of ecstasy.'

'And he is quite handsome really,' Ginny said. 'Nice skin and hair. They both look quite similar in that way. Sort of shiny and glossy—'

'And oh, *look*!' interrupted Anne. Diana, next to Charles on the Buckingham Palace sofa, had rested her head on his shoulder in a gesture that mixed ease with pure affection. 'Have you ever seen such complete adoration?'

Caro shushed her. 'The interview's starting.'

'Duch doesn't need to be interviewed,' Ginny put in. 'That grin says it all. Talk about cats and cream!'

It was true. She was positively blazing with happiness; her smile brighter than the diamonds on her finger. All three girls now questioned the doubts they had harboured. Perhaps Diana had been right all along. She really would be happy ever after.

How did they feel? the TV interviewer asked his subjects.

'Absolutely delighted,' said Diana, to the cheers of her flatmates.

'Oh look! She's blushing!'

'She'll have to stop that when she's queen. You can't blush on the throne.'

When did they decide to get engaged? asked the interviewer.

'About three weeks ago,' replied Charles. 'I thought she might want to think it over so she could say, "I can't bear the whole idea" or not. But she actually accepted.'

'Straight away,' agreed Diana with a happy giggle.

The flatmates cheered again. 'Did she ever!'

Where would they live after the wedding? 'Basically, I hope, down at Highgrove in Gloucestershire,' said Charles.

The flatmates screeched. 'Oh Gawd, poor Duch.' They had all heard about Highgrove and the dreaded job of redecoration. They agreed it sounded awfully grown-up. 'Fine if you're forty,' Anne had said. 'But you're nineteen.'

The others had joined in. 'You don't know the first thing about swatches and paint samples.'

'You don't know your rag roll from your stipple.'

'Why don't you just get Nicky Haslam or someone to do it all for you? Or Ashley Hicks. He's practically royal anyway.'

She had shaken her fair head. 'Charles wants me to do it.'

'I bet he does. Why doesn't he do it?'

The exchange had ended in a cushion fight.

The interviewer was asking about a wedding date.

'No date as such,' Charles said, 'but the idea is certainly the latter part of July. Probably the easiest from all sorts of different peoples' points of view.'

The flatmates looked at each other.

'End of *July*?'

'I'm not sure that's the easiest from Duch's point of view.'

'No, it's nearly six months.'

'What's she going to do all that time?'

'In Buckingham Palace, all by herself.'

'Well, she said she wouldn't be, remember. She said they'd look after her, show her what to do.'

'Shush! We're missing the interview!'

'Naturally quite daunting, but I hope it won't be too difficult,' Diana was saying.

The flatmates hooted. 'What's she talking about?'

'Sex!'

340

Charles was talking now. 'It wasn't easy to begin with, but obviously after a bit you get used to it. You just have to take the plunge.'

'Ha ha!'

'*Definitely* sex!'

'Oh stop it! Battersea, cover your ears!'

'I hope I can pass on the bit of experience I have,' Charles added, which made them all roar again.

'Actually,' Caro said, reaching for a tissue to mop her streaming eyes, 'they were talking about tours abroad.'

'Ooh listen! The interviewer's asking about the gap in their ages!'

'It's only twelve years,' remarked the prince. 'Lots of people get married with that sort of age difference. I always feel you are as old as you think or feel you are. I think Diana will keep me young. That's a very good thing. I shall be exhausted.'

'Gawd,' said Caro. 'He makes her sound like an overactive toddler.'

'I'm frankly amazed that Diana's prepared to take me on.'

'And in love?' asked the interviewer.

'Of course,' giggled Diana.

The flatmates cheered, delighted.

'Whatever "in love" means,' added Charles.

The three friends looked at each other.

'*What* did he just say?'

Kensington Palace, London

April 1992
Sandy

'I remember that,' I said, slowly. 'There you were, next to him on international television, millions watching, you adore him, you're about to marry him and he said . . .'

'"Whatever in love means."' Diana sighed. 'I know. I was so excited and thrilled and I loved him so much. And he just said . . . that.' Her voice was full of misery. 'It was like a knife in my heart. I was so shocked, I just laughed. I told myself he was joking. I couldn't bear to think about it; still can't really.' She swung her legs abruptly off the sofa and sat up. 'Hungry?'

So much so, I could have eaten the grapes woven into the rug pattern.

'Big Mac and fries all right?' she asked gaily.

I had imagined our pasta lunch as an aberration, and it would be covered silver dishes from now on. Tournedos Rossini. Oeufs Drumkilbo, even.

'Great,' I said. 'I didn't have you down as a McDonald's fan.'

'I got into it during all those months at Buckingham Palace.'

I laughed.

'It's true,' she said. 'The footmen felt so sorry for me, they used to go out and get me burgers.'

'*Sorry* for you?'

'I'll tell you all about it. But first, two Big Macs, fries and shakes. Coming right up.'

Chapter Forty-Five

Buckingham Palace
February – July 1981
Diana

On the day before Charles left for New Zealand, she had gone to his apartment. She had rarely seen him since arriving at the Palace. He was in and out all the time – mostly out. Mr Barry answered the door and seemed surprised.

She smiled back at him. 'What's the matter, Mr Barry? Isn't he in?'

'He is, yes, madam. But we don't really do social calls in the Palace. You need an appointment.'

She laughed in disbelief. 'Of course I don't, Prince Charles is going to be my husband! And I'm not a madam, either. Call me Diana.'

The valet's expression remained serious. 'I'm afraid that's impossible, madam. And, from now on, would you mind calling me Stephen?'

'Don't be silly! You're Mr Barry!' She ploughed past him, into the flat. The air smelt powerfully of flowers. 'Who are all these from?' The sitting room was a sea of white blossom. She turned to face him, puzzled.

'They are from all sorts of people,' Stephen replied composedly. 'And they are for yourself and His Royal Highness.'

'But why?' She was looking around in wonder. Arrangements of all shapes and sizes covered every surface. She had never seen so many: it must be every white flower in London.

'They've been sent for the engagement. A good day for Interflora, obviously,' Stephen sniffed.

'Can I have some?' Her own little brown rooms would certainly improve with flowers. There was throughout them a faint but lingering smell of cabbage. From long-ago nursery suppers, possibly.

'Certainly, madam. I'll have some sent up. I'll tell His Royal Highness you called . . .'

She laughed again. 'Oh, Mr Barry, why are you being like this? Where's Charles?'

The valet moved, but too late to stop her opening the closed door of the prince's bedroom. He was on the phone and sat on the edge of the big green four-poster, his expression anguished, which filled her with alarm. But it straightened out into surprise when he saw her. 'Got to go. Goodbye,' he said hurriedly into the receiver, and stood up.

She rushed towards him, full of delight. He had not yet properly kissed her. Those hands, those well-shaped hands, had not yet pushed back her hair and drawn her face to his, as happened to heroines in novels. She wanted to lean into him, melt into him, become part of him. Perhaps now, finally, she could.

The kiss was brief, on the cheek, but still sent delight thudding through her. His hand touched her waist and he bent closer, his fingers kneading her hip. She closed her eyes. *Tell me you love me.*

'Chubby, aren't we?'

'*What?*'

He was grinning, as if he were joking, but the seed was sown.

She returned to her room and wept. The lunch tray outside her door was taken away, untouched.

Later that day, a footman brought the flowers. He was familiar. 'Paul! It's so good to see you again!'

The kind, round eyes beamed back at her. 'Congratulations, madam.'

'Oh Paul! Not you too! It's *Diana*.'

'Yes, madam. I mean Diana. Now, where do you want these flowers putting?'

And then Charles went. He would be away for weeks and weeks and weeks. She consulted his programme every day, imagining him in all the faraway places. She had seen him off at the airport and pictures of her tears had been in all the papers. It had been a different type of coverage to that which she was used to.

The days dragged. She was so bored sometimes, she spent entire afternoons just watching cars come and go in the courtyard. Considering this was a palace, they were strikingly unostentatious, some even rather battered. But there was the odd sporty Saab.

Her flatmates rang up, but it was difficult to talk. Everything went through a switchboard; there was no direct line in the whole Palace. Fearing her conversations would be listened to, she held back on confessing her loneliness. They had warned her, after all. She only had herself to blame.

She waited for her new relatives to rally round. In particular, her mother-in-law-to-be, the only family member she had so far hardly met. Nothing happened. Finally, Diana herself suggested it, and the suggestion went from the nursery on a silver salver borne by a red-liveried footman. Her Majesty's page, when he arrived, wore a dark blue tailcoat. Yes, she was welcome to join Her Majesty for supper.

She spent most of the day getting ready. There was nothing else to do, after all. Discarded outfits lay all over the floor, amid the now-wilting engagement flowers. She wore a taffeta evening skirt and the great sapphire ring. Dinner with the Queen, she thought, would be like dinner with the Queen Mother, only more so. More ceremony, hopefully more candid advice too. In retrospect, the old queen had been admirably frank and honest.

She was surprised to be shown in to a brightly lit, rather messy sitting room with no sign even of a dining table. Perhaps that was in another room. An evidently much-sat-on sofa was scattered with several newspapers, the topmost folded back at the crossword. A Dick Francis thriller was open and face down by a copy of *The Field*. Two corgis sat before the television, which was showing the TV news.

'In here!' trilled a familiar voice, as the footman bowed and retreated. Diana traced the sound to a small galley kitchen. There, stirring briskly away at a saucepan, stood the sovereign. She was simply dressed in a skirt and twinset, her only decorations a watch and pearls. Her make-up was minimal. She looked up and smiled as Diana hovered at the door. 'Do come in. Sorry, it's a bit squashed.'

'Your Majesty.' It felt utterly bizarre to be curtseying to the monarch in these circumstances.

'Scrambled eggs all right?' the Queen asked. 'I often cook for myself when I'm alone. And eat in front of the television, the most tremendous treat. Would you mind just popping some bread in the toaster?' She nodded at a bag of Mother's Pride.

The vast sapphire glittered as Diana slipped the cheap white slices in the slots.

347

The sovereign reapplied her wooden spoon. 'Philip and I got sent some slices of toast as a wedding present, would you believe. Some girls in Wales were making it when they heard the engagement announcement on the radio, so they thought I'd like it. It was rather burnt, I have to say.'

Diana cast a nervous look at her own slices, but they still looked fairly pallid within the toaster's glowing depths.

'We also,' the Queen went on brightly, 'received a lump of Mount Snowdon and a piece of cloth very kindly made by Mahatma Gandhi. So, heaven only knows what you and Charles will be given! And the dress? All going well?'

'Yes, ma'am.'

'Remind me who's making it?'

'The Emanuels, ma'am.'

A young husband-and-wife team who were working like scientists in a top-secret lab. They were barely out of college and had done nothing on this scale before. Neither had she; they had that in common. And they understood her vision, the ultimate romantic fairy-tale dress with an enormous skirt, huge puffed sleeves, as many sequins and ribbons and as much lace as could be accommodated and a train as long as was physically possible. A nipped-in waist too, a waist that got smaller every time she attended a fitting. Which now she did alone; Frances had gone with her to a couple, but it hadn't been a success.

'Hartnell made mine, of course. Dear Sir Norman. He used to come here for fittings with his coterie: there'd be Ivy the matcher, Flo the packer, Miss Whistler the vendeuse and Mara who was the house model. She was very haughty and beautiful, but was actually a jolly northern lass.' To her young guest's amazement, Her Majesty now assumed a broad northern accent. '"I'm standing 'ere with nothing on but the radio." That's what Mara used to say.'

Diana giggled.

The toaster now popped up and the Queen seized the slices. She buttered them with quick, efficient movements, chatting away as she did so. 'And how are you finding living here?'

'Very nice, ma'am.'

'Not too much of a burden?'

'Not at all, ma'am.'

'Glad to hear it. But surely it must seem rather odd?'

'Oh no, ma'am . . .'

'One's never known anything else of course, having lived here since one was a child. It's changed a lot, though. It was very formal then.'

It wasn't exactly relaxed now, but Diana let that pass.

'The footmen used to wear powdered wigs, but Philip got rid of them. These eggs are done now.' The Queen briskly spooned heaps of fluffy, steaming yellow onto the waiting toast.

They sat on the sofa and ate in front of the television. The news was still on. The Prime Minister was arriving at the White House.

'I find Mrs Thatcher rather a contradiction,' the Queen remarked. 'She has a fearless determination to attack the sacred cows and ancient institutions of Britain but seems to have the utmost reverence for the monarchy at the same time.'

Diana envied this cool analysis. She wished she had a grasp of politics. It would be important in her new role. Perhaps the Queen could help her. 'It must be so interesting,' she said hesitantly, 'meeting the Prime Minister every week.'

'Well, it is rather nice to think one's a sort of sponge,' the sovereign agreed. 'And everyone can come and tell one things, and they go no further. Some things go out the other ear, even so. Occasionally, however, you are able to put your point of view across.' She popped in a forkful of toast.

'Do you, um, *have* views, ma'am?' Diana ventured.

'Oh, I don't really distinguish between politicians of different parties. In my view, they all belong to the same category.

Enjoying that, are you?' The famous well-marked eyebrows raised. 'You're not eating much.'

'It's delicious, ma'am. But . . .' Diana paused. 'I'm less hungry these days than I was.'

'Nerves, I should think.' The Queen placed her knife and fork together on her plate, bounced up and took it to the kitchen. She could be heard clattering about, running the water in the sink.

Diana followed with her own plate. She wanted to talk more about politics, show that she was serious about her new role, wanted to learn. She hovered at the door, uncertain how to begin.

The Queen was filling a Russell Hobbs kettle. She clicked it on, briskly. 'Yes?'

'Do you have any advice for me, ma'am?' Warm blood was surging through her cheeks.

'Advice?' The sovereign's tone was sharp.

'About . . .' She hesitated. 'Well, my role, ma'am. There hasn't been a Princess of Wales since before the First World War. Queen Mary was the last one.'

'My grandmother, yes. I was terribly fond of her. Contrary to her rather stern public image, she had the most wonderful sense of humour. She loved Philip's slightly salty Navy jokes and her favourite song was "Yes, We Have No Bananas", which she sang with a very strong German accent.'

So amusing was this it took Diana some seconds to realise her question had been sidestepped. She summoned the courage to direct it back. 'Any practical advice, ma'am . . .?'

'Well, let me think.' The Queen was rummaging in a cupboard. 'Never eat anything with garlic in it. And have weights put in all your dress hems. The wind, I regret to say, is no friend to royalty.' She produced a jar of Maxwell House. 'Instant coffee all right?'

Diana battled a sudden surge of nostalgia. Coleherne Court had been Maxwell House drinkers to a woman. 'Anything else, ma'am?' Dress hems seemed rather marginal, somehow.

The Queen poured hot water into cups. 'You should answer all letters unless they come from lunatics.'

'*All* letters, ma'am?' Diana thought of the thousands that had come with the presents.

'Well, the ladies-in-waiting do the actual replying, obviously. Have you chosen yours yet?'

Diana shook her head. She hadn't realised that correspondence was part of their brief. Perhaps she would need some, after all.

'I often get letters about dreams.'

'Dreams, ma'am?'

The dark head nodded its familiar, unmoving hair. 'One's subjects dream about one with surprising frequency, it seems. One dreamer was rescuing me from being run away with by Philip's polo ponies. Apparently I had wellies on under my ball gown.'

The Queen, once again, had moved the subject away. Diana tried to steer it back again. 'I wondered, ma'am—'

'Another dreamer helped Mummy when she had lost her passport at Heathrow and was surrounded by twenty hectic corgis. "I'm sorry, ma'am," said the dreamer, "but you will have to stay in quarantine with the dogs. We can fix up a perfectly comfortable kennel for you for six months."'

Diana felt despairing. She wanted so much to be helped, and yet the help was not forthcoming. 'I'd be so grateful for any tips,' she blurted, suddenly.

Her Majesty brightened. 'Butterscotch, in the 3.30 at Towcester tomorrow.'

'Not that sort of tip, ma'am. Tips about, well, my royal role.' Diana blushed.

'Well, I'm not sure I have any of that kind really. One sort of just gets on with it. One thing I always do is wear strong colours so the crowds can see one. And hats with brims off the face. One is constantly having to remind one's plumassier.'

'Plumassier . . .?'

'Hatmaker. And black clothes are out, for mourning only.'

She said this lightly, but Diana blushed again. For her first post-engagement event with Charles, their first official one as a couple, she had worn a strapless black frock. She had picked it off the rack at the Emanuels' and thought it sexy and chic. The prince had been horrified, but it was too late by the time she had climbed into the car to join him. She had blundered through the evening, but at one stage, overwhelmed by despair, she had gone to hide in the lavatories. There, to her amazement, touching up her make-up as any normal person would, was the deeply un-normal, goddess-like Princess Grace of Monaco. Diana had poured out her heart to her, about the press harassment, about getting everything wrong. Princess Grace had chuckled, slipped the cap back on her lipstick and smiled at her in the mirror. 'Don't worry. It's all going to get much worse.'

It was what the Queen Mother had said too, And it was true, it was worse already. There were enormous billboards with her face on all over London. Every newsstand she passed displayed endless covers that featured her. It was claustrophobic and terrifying. It was too much. Surely Her Majesty, famous all her life, understood something of this; could help with this, at least.

'Oh, the press,' said the Queen, when Diana haltingly tried to express this. 'One does get so bored of one's face, seeing it in the papers all the time.'

'Exactly, ma'am.'

'The editors, of course, range from monarchists to republicans. Time will tell whether letting Mr Murdoch loose in the communications world will prove a good idea. He's a republican,

I'm told. Shall we?' She proffered the tray of coffee and nodded back towards the sitting room.

Resignedly, Diana followed. It was clearly hopeless. The Queen wasn't going to tell her anything beyond a few anecdotes. Or perhaps this in itself was a sort of advice. The Queen expertly used amusing stories to control the conversation. Their effect was disarming and gave her the advantage. The sovereign had kept her at a much greater distance than had the Queen Mother, who had got straight to the point.

Never upstage your husband.

There's such a thing as being too popular.

They settled back on the sofa. The corgis had come over and the Queen was energetically petting them. Diana eyed them nervously. Paul had told her they nipped, and it was to keep them friendly that he went about with a pork chop in his breeches pocket. She wasn't sure if he was joking or not.

Soon after that, the Queen took the coffee cups back into the kitchen. Supper was evidently over. Diana took the cue. Her mother-in-law-to-be gave her two efficient little kisses on the cheek. Up close, her skin was wonderful, and gathering her courage, Diana remarked on it.

'Early nights, barley water and a few good skin products. Cyclax All Day Face Firmer. They make it up especially for me.'

As Diana approached the doors, they moved away of their own accord. A pair of footmen on the other side had somehow got there first. Did they look through the keyhole? Was everything timed? As she stepped out into the red, white and gold of the corridor, the Queen's voice came floating from behind.

'I hear that Norman Parkinson wants to do the wedding pictures.'

A rush of joy went through Diana. Parkinson was a famous fashion photographer. She turned, beaming.

'He can't, of course.'

'Why not, ma'am?'

'Because he asked. So it'll be Lichfield.'

Chapter Forty-Six

Diana

The day was named, and the place. It would be on 29 July at St Paul's. The official reason was that Wren's cathedral was bigger than Westminster Abbey, where both sets of parents had married. The real reason, she guessed, was that Charles didn't want to walk down the same aisle as Mountbatten's body. For her part, she was glad not to have to walk down the same aisle as Frances.

Three thousand people would be present and BBC and ITV would beam the ceremony and the procession to 500 million people across the world, even behind the Iron Curtain.

Five hundred million people, she thought, watching one girl. One girl who, at the moment, was completely alone in Buckingham Palace. The contradictions were as huge as they were incomprehensible. She had come here to escape, but there was no escape. She was the whole world's focus but had no company.

Instead, hunger had become her friend. She binged and purged. The gnawing and jabbing inside accompanied her everywhere. There was food in the Palace, huge amounts of it; endless dining rooms for endless ranks of staff. She could have eaten three square meals a day plus tea. Sometimes she did, but got rid of it afterwards. She remembered people doing this at school. The thin ones, who always smelt slightly of sick.

Soon, she was eating so little she felt detached from reality. She drifted about the Palace, down corridors under domed and gilded ceilings, past marble statues in frozen attitudes and huge portraits of royal ancestors: Queen Alexandra with her piled-up chignon, Victoria with her bun and centre parting. Wasp waists. Watery eyes. White satin and pearls. She went into rooms with gold thrones and velvet canopies, into galleries with Old Masters, into bow-fronted music rooms with views of the gardens. In the Palace pool, she floated with her arms out, staring upwards. Reality was ebbing away.

She binged and purged on the press, too. She would spend days avoiding it, then read every paper at once. She knew where they were all delivered to, and would intercept them before the staff arrived. The Palace's crushing lack of interest in her contrasted with the feverish fascination outside its walls.

The papers both terrified and provided a lifeline. If, constantly alone, she could feel she was losing her personality, the press suggested a whole range of different ones. *Private Eye* had a column by a spoof romantic novelist in which she was always looking at Charles with limpid eyes. He, in turn, had only evil thoughts about depriving her of her virginity. It was funny because it was the exact opposite of the truth; Charles, for one thing, was never around. She steadied herself by turning to her actual romantic novels; they reminded her that Love was full of challenges, Patience was rewarded and happiness was the result of Chastity. She must endure, believe and trust just a little while longer.

The press also told her that Kevin had been right; his 'Lady Di' cut was a craze in salons throughout the country. In addition, girls everywhere were scrambling to copy her clothes, which, in the papers, seemed mostly corduroy culottes and Fair

Isle pullovers. No hideous blue suits, at any rate. She looked so fat in all the photos . . . she could hardly believe that a girl as haphazardly dressed as she had always been, and whose idea of make-up was a quick scrape of eye pencil, was now considered a style leader.

Eager to self-educate, to be better informed, she searched for articles about the wider world. But even the wider world seemed all about her. In the financial pages, she read that the pound had strengthened because of the engagement. The stock market had received a boost as everyone rushed to buy shares in firms likely to profit from the wedding – hotel firms, souvenirs.

One paper alone took a different view. It was a communist publication; as with everything else, the Palace did its newspaper monitoring thoroughly.

'DON'T DO IT, LADY DIANA!' begged the *Morning Star*'s front page, going on to observe that 'Lady Diana Spencer is about to sacrifice her independence to a domineering layabout for the sake of a few lousy foreign holidays. With a £100,000 home of her own and a steady job as an exclusive nursery nurse, who needs it?'

The last thing Coleherne Court would ever have described itself as was communist. But her flatmates, she felt, might have agreed with the last sentence. They might have agreed with all of it. But they were wrong, Diana told herself firmly.

No less an authority than the new science of computer dating said so. She read that Dateline, the biggest computer matchmakers in Britain, had fed information on herself and Charles through their 'love machine' and it had returned the highest compatibility rating possible. Their marriage was set to be the most overwhelming success. So yah boo sucks, *Morning Star*.

The astrologers agreed. 'The prince is Scorpio and his bride-to-be is Cancer,' pointed out Russell Grant. 'Their sun signs are as compatible as love and marriage. It's the beginning of one of the most electrifying marriages ever.'

Princess Margaret, inspirer of the horoscope, would surely have read this. Perhaps I should invite her to lunch, Diana thought. Then they could laugh about it. A laugh would be very welcome.

She did not, however. Less bold now, frailer in every respect, she lacked the courage. She withdrew even further when the Queen and her mother failed to issue repeat invitations. One invitation alone remained, that of Camilla Parker Bowles for lunch. Something about its presence on the bed had been unnerving. But that was then, when she was fresh from the outside world. Now, after weeks in the lonely silence of the Palace, the company of a woman who knew Charles seemed very attractive. And Camilla had always been by far the friend-liest of his circle.

It was strange to sit in a restaurant with other people. It had been so normal once and she had hoped it might feel so again, but everyone was watching her while pretending not to. She sipped wine and pushed the food round her plate. She felt tired and weak. Camilla seemed very energetic to her. She was full of questions. Was Diana going to hunt?

'Ha, no! I hate horses.' The sip of wine had made her loqua-cious and light-headed. 'No offence,' she added, remembering hunting was Camilla's passion.

Camilla pushed a hank of unbrushed hair behind an earring-free ear. 'None taken.'

Diana smiled. 'We can't all like the same things.'

Camilla looked down as she stubbed out her cigarette.

It felt good to have another woman to talk to; someone she felt was on her side. And Camilla was so friendly and so fascinatingly dowdy, with her slapdash make-up, gap teeth and creased clothes. She had known Charles even longer than Diana had imagined, and it was a relief to express the adoration she felt and convey her excitement and hope. Camilla seemed particularly interested in Highgrove, so they discussed the decoration, and Diana tried to remember the many firms and people Camilla recommended. She clearly knew the house and area well. 'Honestly, you should do it for me,' Diana joked.

Camilla laughed her gravelly laugh. 'I wouldn't presume!'

After another glass of wine, Diana described her life in the Palace, how strange and lonely it was and how, in the absence of any other company, she had started to wander down to the kitchens and chat to the staff.

Camilla raised an unplucked eyebrow. 'Is that a good idea?'

Diana was surprised. 'Why wouldn't it be? I've done it all my life. At Park House, at Althorp.' She chuckled, conspiratorially. 'The kitchens are always where you get the best gossip.'

Seeing something flash in Camilla's eyes, Diana felt pleased to think she had told this worldly woman something she didn't know. She went on, the words positively tumbling out in her enthusiasm.

'Robert, he's the pastry chef, is such a darling. He feeds me bread-and-butter pudding and ice cream. Then there's Evelyn and Ann, they're maids and just lovely. You can talk to them about absolutely everything. Cyril's the Palace Steward, a complete honey, he helps me remember the difference between the Gentleman Thingy and the Whatsit of the Gold and Silver Cabinet. You wouldn't believe the job names. There's actually a Queen's Falcon Master.' She stopped to giggle. 'And Mervyn's the chef. He likes bodybuilding and he's very funny. And two of the footmen, Mark and Paul, are my special friends. I butter toast for them and they get me McDonald's.'

'*McDonald's?*' Camilla looked amazed.

'Yes, so sweet and thoughtful of them. They feel sorry for me, you see. They go down to the one in Victoria Street and get three Big Mac meals. Then we all sit and eat it in my room.'

'How nice,' said Camilla, grinding out another cigarette.

The lunch concluded with real reluctance on Diana's part. It was good to have a friend.

She did not return to the Palace immediately. Before going back to the prison house, as she thought of it, there was a visit to the Emanuels' atelier.

Elizabeth was full of stories about how the press were ransacking their dustbins and trying to photograph the inside of the workshop. They were fighting back by covering the windows and leaving bits of the wrong fabrics in the bins as decoys.

Diana chuckled. 'Good for you.'

It wasn't funny really though. Not for the young couple, who looked so strained, or for herself. The press had been so friendly, once. Surely, after the wedding, it would calm down.

The Queen Mother's words came back to her. *It won't. And it never will. I wish I could tell you otherwise, but I would be telling you a lie.*

But after the wedding, of course, she would have Charles to help her. She brightened at the thought, felt hopeful.

'Twenty-three inches.' David pulled the tape from round her waist with an expression of smiling despair. 'How much more weight are you going to lose, Lady Diana?'

She smiled back at him. She had lost four inches now. More good news.

Next day

Stephen had awaited his moment, and here it came. A light, girlish humming. Lady Diana turned the corner of the passage

360

leading to her rooms. He stepped out of the recess in which he had been waiting.

'Oh! Mr Barry!' Her hair was wet; she had been in the pool. 'You startled me.'

'Stephen,' he reminded her, ignoring the startling. He was, after all, going to startle her quite a lot more.

'Oh, if I must. *Stephen!*' She grinned.

He did not smile back. 'Lady Diana, a word if you please.'

'Sure!' She ran a hand through her wet hair. 'But do you want to come in?' She nodded at her apartment door. 'Talk to me while I dry it? You can sit on the bed.'

Stephen knew differently. As she was about to find out, servants sitting on beds was exactly what he had come to talk about. Charles had been furious. 'She goes down to the kitchens and talks to them! Maids, footmen, you name it! They buy her *hamburgers*, for God's sake. Then sit in her room with her to eat them! It's got to be stopped,' his master had raged, from across the other side of the world. 'Heaven knows what they say to her!'

'If you don't mind, Lady Diana,' Stephen said now, 'I'd rather have a word here, outside. It won't take long.'

She shrugged. 'Oh, all right then. As you like, Mr Barry— sorry, Stephen. It's not as if I'm going to catch cold with wet hair anyway. This place is heated to boiling point.'

The top floor was the warmest, of course. The staff complained about the heat, but then, they complained about everything. And he was about to give some of them something to really complain about. Just as soon as he finished here.

She listened, her blue eyes widening, first with surprise, then anger. Her cheeks reddened and her brow knitted. 'Are you telling me, Stephen, that despite being about to marry the heir to the throne, which means I'm a future queen of England, I'm not allowed to go down to the kitchens or talk to the staff?'

'Yes, madam.'

She folded her arms, lifted her chin and stared at him challengingly. 'Why not?' Her freezing tones were a surprise; he had not thought her capable.

Because the Prince of Wales is worried you might hear something you shouldn't was the truthful answer. 'Because, madam, it simply isn't done. The staff have their areas, the royal family theirs. It's the way it has always worked.'

'Who told you I was even doing this?' she demanded furiously.

'I'm afraid I can't say, madam.' It was true. He had not enquired where the prince had got his information. It could have been anywhere; the Palace walls had ears, the carpets eyes. It was immaterial anyway; his job was to act, not ask.

He could tell she was crumbling; tears were welling. 'For God's sake, Stephen,' she said, her voice cracking. 'It's so bloody lonely in this place. Who the hell else am I supposed to talk to?'

'Well, madam, His Royal Highness will be back in a few days, of course. But, until then, the equerries would be more than glad to look after you.'

She thought about the equerries. Pleasantish, youngish men, impeccably neat and polite, seconded from a career in the services. They glided about in their well-polished shoes. There would be no possibility of the belly laughs she enjoyed in the kitchen, nor the gossip; the delicious food neither, even if none of it stayed down very long.

On the other hand, they were better than nothing. And this whole situation couldn't last for ever. She would be out of this red-carpeted prison soon.

Chapter Forty-Seven

Buckingham Palace

July 1981

Diana

The equerries weren't so bad, after all. Michael Colborne, who was Charles' private secretary, was dark-haired, handsome and liked to tease her. 'After the twenty-ninth of July you are going to be a *bitch*,' he told her. 'A real diva!'

It made her giggle. She went to his room more and more, sitting at the opposite desk, slumped on the couch or perched on the windowsill swinging her legs.

She told him of her hopes to bring the family together more. Most of them had offices and flats in the Palace. Prince Andrew's, Princess Anne's, she had been to all the doors and knocked. But no one ever seemed to be there, and if they ever were, they never told anyone else. She longed to be the person to improve this situation. Repair this family in a way she had been unable to repair her own.

'Isn't it Princess Anne's birthday soon?' she asked Colborne.

'Middle of August, yes.'

'I wonder what she'd like for a birthday present.' Perfume, perhaps. Some nice soap. Something spoiling and indulgent might soften the harsh edges of Anne Elizabeth Alice Louise.

The equerry did not hesitate. 'A doormat.'

'A *doormat*!'

'She likes very useful presents. Car rugs, picnic equipment, that sort of thing.'

Colborne saw her taking this in. He felt sorry for her, she was only a child, and one with good intentions. She was so keen to please, but there was no hope of success in what she was trying to do. The Windsors were too advanced in dysfunction for that.

He tried to give her more practical advice. 'Do you have a diary?' She shook her head.

'Well, you need to get one. Get a five-year one. A ten-year one if you can. Then you can fill it in.'

'But I don't know what I'm doing in ten years' time!'

Colborne gave her a wise look. 'Oh, you will. From now on, you'll know exactly where you'll be on what date. Trooping the Colour, Ascot, the Garter Ceremony. Your whole life will be planned out years in advance. That's what being royal means.'

She shrugged this off and started to rummage among the parcels. The prince's office was where the wedding presents came in. People sent things from all over the world and extra staff had been taken on to help with the unpacking. It was, Diana thought, like Christmas every day, except that she was receiving gifts not just from the family but also official bodies, governments, foreign royals and well-wishers from all over the world. Not all were especially original 'Not another silver toast rack!' she would exclaim. 'Can you believe all these toast racks and no one's given us a toaster? We must be the only couple ever not to get one.' Nor had anyone, so far, sent them toast, like the Queen.

The unpacked presents were all arranged in the Buckingham Palace theatre. She loved to go down and look round. 'Looks like a branch of Harrods,' she said to Colborne.

'Or Cartier,' he said, gesturing at the parure sent by Crown Prince Fahd of Saudi Arabia. The theatre's chandeliers sparked fireworks of light off a bracelet, watch, necklace and earrings all made from enormous sapphires set in gold.

Fahd had also given a gold box to the prince. 'He always gets given those,' Colborne told her. 'He must have more gold boxes than anyone else on the planet.'

She laughed. 'But what else does the man who has everything give the man who has everything?'

The Queen was yet to give them anything. 'She's very practical,' the equerry explained. 'She'll be waiting to see what you still need after everything else has arrived.'

'A toaster!'

Charles duly reappeared, to her absolute joy. Everything was transformed at a stroke. Just knowing he was in the same building banished her loneliness, even if, somehow, she still rarely saw him. He was always going somewhere; he seemed to have so much to do. But soon, she reminded herself, she would have a lot to do too. These days, though, she would hang around his corridor, hoping to glimpse him. 'Ready for "la grande plonge"?' he would grin, as he emerged and dashed past. 'Oh, yes,' she beamed back with her whole heart and soul, as she headed to the Palace pool for yet another solitary swim.

There were wedding rehearsals in St Paul's. Walking up the gold-roofed aisle, she felt a dizzying happiness. Charles came to two, and Colborne impersonated him for the others. This always made her snort with laughter, especially in her jeans with a dust sheet round her waist for a train. The bridesmaids were so excited. She chatted to the older ones, asking them about school and pop music, and gave the little ones piggybacks. It was like being back at Young England.

The wedding breakfast menu had now been chosen. Quenelles of brill in lobster sauce, followed by chicken breasts stuffed with lamb mousse. Then strawberries and cream. How she would manage to eat all this, she was not sure. A miniature diamond-studded lucky horseshoe had been sewn into the waistband of the wedding dress that David and Elizabeth had just had to take in yet again. They were worried for her, she sensed, but they need not be. Their ribbons and ruffles and frills were going to float her away to a future of pure happiness.

The guest list was finalised. There were so many royal Hons and Vons to be accommodated that her own friends and family scarcely got a look-in. But Coleherne Court was there, and her siblings, which was the main thing. There had been a rare girls' lunch with her sisters.

'But will be you be all right?' Jane had worried. 'Royal life, it's quite a lot to cope with.'

'Too late now, Duch,' Sarah had put in. 'Your face is on the tea towels.'

'Wish it was yours?'

Sarah had grinned and shook her head. 'No thanks, Duch. Rather you than me.'

There was to be a ball for eight hundred the night before, and a firework display. It was all so exciting and perfect, and it was finally all about to happen.

She was in the highest of spirits as she breezed into Colborne's office. She had come to inspect what were surely the last presents; the wedding was now mere days away. She caught sight of a parcel on his desk. 'Ooh! What's that?'

It seemed to her that Colborne's face changed. The smile with which he had greeted her now looked strained.

'What's the matter?' she grinned. 'What has someone sent me? A sex toy or something?' The parcel was small and long.

The equerry cleared his throat. 'It's not been sent in, Lady Diana, it's a present His Royal Highness is sending out.'

That made her laugh even more. He was obviously trying to protect her from something. 'Oh, come on, Michael,' she urged. 'Open it!'

'Lady Diana . . .' He was trying to shield it, cover it with his hands.

She really had to see it now. 'Oh, give it here!' Playfully bearing away her prize to the other side of the room, she began ripping off the outer packing. Colborne watched her, alarmed. 'Your face is a picture,' she snorted, glancing up.

She couldn't see what the problem was. Inside the box lay a bracelet. A simple gold chain with a blue enamel disc attached. On the disc were two entwined, elaborately scrolled letters. C and D. She smiled and peered closer.

Not C and D, she realised. The letters were actually F and G. She frowned and looked at Colborne, who was still watching her.

'Who are F and G?'

Colborne's expression was unreadable. 'I think it stands for Fred and Gladys.'

That rang a definite bell. She hesitated, thinking. Fred and Gladys. Fred and . . . Oh. Of course. Those characters out of *The Goon Show*. They had discussed it the night he had showed her his uniforms; this was him saying that he, too, remembered that wonderful evening. She looked up at Colborne, delighted. 'That's so sweet! He's sending it to me. He's giving me a *Goon Show* bracelet.'

Colborne did not reply.

Diana was trying it on, twisting a now-bony wrist. 'I love it!'

The equerry cleared his throat. 'Lady Diana, I'm afraid it's not actually for you.'

She threw him a merry glance. 'Of course it is. Who else would it be for?'

As Colborne said nothing, she scrabbled in the packaging, found the label.

'Mrs Parker Bowles.' She stared at the equerry. 'Camilla? But why would he give *her* a Fred and Gladys bracelet?'

There was something in his expression, something wary and worried, that shifted something within her. Realisation started slowly, then gathered speed and volume until it crashed into her mind like an avalanche.

She tore her glance from Colborne's and stared back down at the bracelet. It seemed to burn into her wrist just as the truth burned into her heart. 'Oh,' she muttered. 'Oh my God.'

Only now did she understand what she realised she had always known. This was why Camilla had been so friendly. Why she had asked about hunting. Why she knew all about High-grove. Good God, it was why Charles had *bought* Highgrove! Why Charles was never around. Where Charles was, right this minute, possibly.

Never trust anyone. Ever.

She clung to the desk as if it would break from its moorings like everything else in the known world. Her heart thumped and she felt herself whirling backwards. She was on the stairs in Park House, six years old and terrified, peering with large frightened eyes through the iron banisters, clutching them hard as if to anchor herself to something, anything, permanent.

The front door was open onto a raging sunset; a cold, cutting wind was sweeping in. Bags were being carried outside, and boxes. Even pictures and pieces of furniture. There was shouting; her parents. Then the front door slammed shut. Outside, a car engine roared into life. Something inside her untethered and floated away. She released the banisters, ran downstairs, wrenched open the door, saw the departing vehicle disappearing into the violent red sky.

'Mummy!' she screamed. 'Mummy!'

But Mummy was driving away and couldn't hear. And she couldn't catch up. She was running, trying to, but the deep gravel swallowed her small feet, slowing her down. The sound of the car grew fainter, then faded altogether. Her ears filled with silence, her heart with a hollow emptiness and her soul with a shattering sense of betrayal.

'Lady Diana.' Colborne's voice came from a long way away. She was no longer sure where she was. She was back in the past and here at the same time. Both were awful. The future was worse. The wedding, oh God.

The nausea rose and pressed, demanding release. She didn't look at Colborne again, just ran out of the office, blindly found the nearest lavatory.

Afterwards, she rinsed her face and hurtled up to Charles' apartment. The corridors were red and endless, like running down her own veins. She banged on the shining door; it swung open and there was Stephen. Mr Barry. Whatever he called himself. She felt she hated him now. He had known all about it. Must have done. Was there anyone who hadn't? Apart from her, of course.

'I want to see Charles!'

'I'm sorry, Lady Diana, but His Royal Highness is busy.'

'Let me in!' she snarled.

'I'm afraid I'm not able to, madam. His Royal Highness gave express orders that he was not to be disturbed.'

She took a deep breath, filling her lungs to capacity. 'I want to see him!' she roared. But the shining door was already closing and no amount of banging and kicking would open it again.

She stumbled to her own rooms. Once inside, she closed the door and leant against it. Her chest was heaving painfully; her heart seemed about to burst out. Her wild gaze fell on the bookshelves stuffed with her well-worn paperbacks.

The first that came to hand was *Bride to the King*. Looking down at the cover, where a blonde woman in a white dress embraced a

369

dark-haired man in uniform, she felt a memory hit like a blow. Two little girls in a train carriage, years ago. One handing this very book over to the other, her face all joyous excitement. Diana could hear her own voice now; hopeful, bright.

Don't you think that's the most romantic ending ever?

She walked slowly over to the window. Looking out at the ornate memorial, she thought of the giddy evening they had circled it in the car, her Coleherne Court friends singing in the back. She leant forward, pressed her forehead to the glass. It felt like a barrier between her and the world and sent her thoughts to, of all things, the goldfish Battersea. She, too, would be in a goldfish bowl now.

Outside, bright afternoon was giving way to sombre evening. The thickening light made cold fire of her sapphire ring and blazed off the barriers in the Mall. The Union Jacks on the flagpoles marched relentlessly towards her.

Too late now, Duch. Your face is on the tea towels.

The cry of despair that filled the room surprised her before she realised it was hers. She hurled *Bride to the King* with a violent strength. It hit the shelves; other paperbacks fell, *The Loveless Marriage* among them. The covers lay face up on the carpet, like tarot cards. She saw Merry's face in the candlelight, small hand moving over the Ouija board, and felt the tears come that she had been too shocked, until now, to cry.

She sprang at the shelves. With a sweep of one arm, she drove her entire collection of romantic novels to the floor. Hurling herself on the pile, she ripped at the covers, tugged out the pages in savage handfuls. She wished she could rip out her own heart. As she tugged and ripped, she screamed and screamed and the noise filled her head and sounded like the ringing of great bells . . .

Beneath a hot blue summer sky, the bells of the great cathedral pealed joyfully over the city. The crowds roared their delight. The glass coach moved through the streets, pulled by proud white horses and attended by gold-braided footmen.

From behind the polished crystal windows, the teenage princess-to-be looked excitedly out. She could scarcely believe the number of people who had come to see her, all jostling on the pavements, madly waving flags and shouting her name. Never had she felt so loved.

Or so beautiful. Her professionally done make-up was perfect; a light touch because of her youth but enough to enhance her loveliness for the TV cameras, the audience watching across the world. Her thick blonde hair gleamed, held in place by a diamond tiara. Her cream silk dress was so huge, it almost filled the carriage; her father, sitting beside her, was nearly hidden behind its folds.

'Bigger!' she had laughingly told the designer, when he had asked how large the train should be. 'Let's make it the biggest one anyone's ever seen!'

She had said the same to the florist. More roses! More lilies! More orange blossom! Why hold back, on this glorious day? She felt extravagantly, deliriously happy, and she wanted everything, from the pearls in her ears to the lace rosettes on her shoes, to express it.

'Darling, I'm so proud of you!' Her father, eyes brimming with tears, reached for her hand, on which the great engagement ring glittered. The wedding band itself, made from a special nugget of gold, was with her soon-to-be-husband, the prince. Who, even now, was ascending the red carpet up the cathedral steps, passing in under the pillared portico, handsome in his uniform, his decorations glinting in the sunshine, his sword hanging by his side.

The thought made her almost weak with joy. All her dreams had come true. She was a beautiful princess who was marrying a handsome prince. But far more importantly she was in love, and beloved herself. She had given her heart to her husband and he had given his to her. Their marriage would last forever, they would have lots of children and be happy ever after. He would never leave her, never let her down. She had suffered much, but from now on, everything was going to be perfect.

Kensington Palace, London

April 1992
Sandy

The hamburgers were finished now. Polystyrene packaging and crumpled paper bags sat on the no-doubt priceless rug. As Diana had insisted we eat them with our hands, the gilt-edged plates, napkins and silver cutlery remained untouched in a corner of the fireplace. The footman who had brought the takeaway had also lit the fire, so the bright flames roiled and billowed, throwing out welcome warmth.

It was time for me to go, but I didn't want to leave her alone in the Palace. She was still my friend, the same person I had known all those years ago.

When we met again after so long, I had thought the girl I remembered was gone; Diana had changed so much. Thinner, glossier and much more beautiful. Supermodel-like even in her jeans. And she had been through the crucible of stratospheric fame, which surely changed a person.

But all this had changed nothing. She was still as eager, kind and loving as ever. Quick-witted too, and funny. But she was also hurt, angry and vulnerable. And who could blame her? She had been manipulated and let down at every turn. Her hopeful, romantic nature had been ruthlessly exploited. Either by her own family or a royal one determined to survive at all costs.

'I'm so sorry,' I said. 'It's all so sad.' It was the understatement of the century.

She shrugged, as if she were used to carrying the weight of it all. 'I got my boys out of it, so it was worth it.'

'Even so,' I said. 'It was tough.'

Diana sat back and sipped her milkshake. 'Still is. You haven't heard the half of it. The wedding, the honeymoon, Highgrove. And all the time, Camilla.'

'Awful,' I said. 'Just awful.'

She smiled. 'I'll save it for my autobiography.'

I was trying to remember where my coat was. It seemed like weeks since I had got here; weeks more since I had walked through a spring-like Kensington Gardens, all new green leaves and bright grass. Then her last words filtered through. 'Your autobiography?' I repeated. 'Oh God, please don't write one of those.'

While I didn't know exactly what would happen if she told the world what she had just told me, I knew it wouldn't be anything good. It would be like a nuclear explosion, blasting the whole edifice wide open and starting something no power on earth would be able to stop. The damage would never be repaired.

But she only smiled. 'You need your coat. Paul!'

Paul appeared, the footman/butler/whatever who had brought the McDonald's. Paul from the Palace, who Diana had met at Balmoral. He had admitted me in the first place of course, right at the beginning of this long, strange afternoon.

She followed me out into the yellow hallway. The saccharine portrait of her smiled complacently down from an upper landing. Its more troubled real-life counterpart looked me searchingly in the eyes. 'It's been so wonderful to see you, Sandy. We must do this again, soon.'

I assured her that we would. But already I knew that we wouldn't. This was a moment out of time. I had been invited into the world of a global icon and shown the dark side of the moon.

We hugged one last time, and as I held close her slight body, I felt both sad and furious. She was such a fine person, so loving, special and loyal, and she had deserved so much more and so much better. She had known titles and palaces and worldwide celebrity, but she had never really wanted status or fame. All she had wanted was for the man of her heart to return her love. And of everything that had happened in her epic, extraordinary life, that was the one simple thing that never had.

Acknowledgements

The Princess is the work of my imagination. But I also needed many books, listed here in no particular order. Thank you to all their authors for information and inspiration great and small:

Diana, Story Of A Princess by Tim Clayton & Phil Craig, Coronet, 1988

Backstairs Billy, The Life of William Tallon by Tom Quinn, The Robson Press, 2015

Ma'am Darling by Craig Brown, Fourth Estate 2017

The Diana Chronicles by Tina Brown, Century, 2007

Royal Service, My Twelve Years As Valet To Prince Charles by Stephen P. Barry, Macmillan, 1983

Royal Secrets, The View From Downstairs by Stephen P. Barry, Villard Books, 1985

The Way We Were, Remembering Diana by Paul Burrell, HarperCollins, 2006

Charles and Diana, A Royal Romance by Janice Dunlop, Coronet, 1981

Prince Andrew, The Warrior Prince by Graham and Heather Fisher, Star Publishing, 1983

Terms & Conditions, Life In Girls' Boarding Schools, 1939–1979 by Ysenda Maxtone-Graham, Abacus, 2016

Raine & Johnnie by Angela Levin, Weidenfeld & Nicolson, 1993

Diana, Her True Story by Andrew Morton, Michael O'Mara Books, 1993 (BCA edition)

Diana, Her True Story In Her Own Words by Andrew Morton, revised paperback edition, Michael O'Mara Books, 1998

Camilla, The King's Mistress by Caroline Graham, Blake Publishing, 1994

A Royal Duty by Paul Burrell, Michael Joseph, 2003

Diana by Sarah Bradford, Penguin, 2006

Shadows of a Princess by P. D. Jephson, HarperCollins, 2000

Diana, The Portrait. Harper Collins, 2004

HRH The Princess Margaret by Nigel Dempster, Quartet Books, 1981

Diana, Once Upon A Time by Mary Clarke, Sidgwick & Jackson, 1994

The Royal Yacht Britannia by Andrew Morton, Orbis, 1984

Some of the romantic novels mentioned in the story are invented, but some are real titles. I have occasionally taken liberties with the timeline of their publication.

Finally, a few huge and heartfelt thank yous. To my agents Jonathan Lloyd and Lucy Morris, especially for all Lucy's help with the text. To my publishers Welbeck. To my student focus group at Girton College, Cambridge: Isabella, Andrew, Dan, Joe, Emily and Alex. To my husband Jon, and to the dedicatee of this book, Vanda Symons, English teacher extraordinaire.

About the Author

Image credit: Laurie Fletcher

Sunday Times number one bestseller Wendy Holden was a journalist before becoming an author. She has written eleven top-ten bestselling novels and sold more than 3 million books.

Turn the page for a glimpse of
how *The Princess* was born,
exclusive to this edition

The Inspiration Behind *The Princess*

In writing *The Princess,* I wasn't only seeking to reveal the little-known years of Diana's amazing life. I was also repaying a debt. Princess Diana changed my whole world. Let me explain.

I was 15 in 1980, when Lady Diana Spencer first landed in the public consciousness. She was young, blonde and the girl that Prince Charles was about to marry. She was also something called a Sloane Ranger.

Sloane Rangers, I soon gathered from the newspapers, were young girls from aristocratic families. They were so-called because they lived in the vicinity of Sloane Square, Chelsea, one of the poshest parts of London.

I was a young girl from a working-class family in the north of England. I had never visited London and had never heard of Sloane Rangers. It was like discovering a secret society.

These days, when all classes and lifestyles are available for online inspection, it is hard to imagine how divided British society was then. The less well-off had no idea what the well-off got up to. I had grown up in a monoculture and thought that everyone had the same life as me. I realised that I was wrong.

But I was happy to be corrected. The life of the Sloane Ranger looked fun and I immediately wanted to become one. I rushed out and bought a copy of *The Sloane Ranger Handbook*; a new, funny book that served as a guide to this exciting new species.

There were chapters about Sloane houses, Sloane boyfriends, Sloane education, Sloane clothes.

I decided to start with those. Sloanes wore pearls, shirts with frilly collars, Laura Ashley skirts and flat, shiny shoes. No one I knew had any pearls, and the nearest Laura Ashley shop was in distant York, a bus and long train ride away. But armed with the proceeds of my Saturday job, I went anyway and returned proudly bearing a cherry red mid-calf-length skirt. Soon, thanks to Lady Diana, flat shoes and frilly collared shirts were starting to penetrate even the humble boutiques of my home town. With a change of hairstyle, I was Sloane-ready.

But getting the look was only the beginning. Being a Sloane was a whole lifestyle. According to *The Sloane Ranger Handbook*, Sloanes were bought expensive Chelsea flats by their parents, in which they lived with other Sloanes they had met at boarding school. They shopped at Harvey Nichols. They went out with young bankers, stockbrokers and soldiers from the smarter regiments. They spent their weekends in the country, at house parties (that they called 'high spotties') and balls.

None of these options was open to me. My parents could hardly afford to buy me a bicycle. We shopped at the supermarket and I didn't know a soldier from an unsmart regiment, let alone a smart one. My weekends were spent working in the lighting department of the Bradford branch of British Home Stores. As for meeting other Sloanes at school, that was out of the question. I went to the local comprehensive. I was the only Sloane in town.

Undaunted. I continued my careful study of Sloanedom. I started to try and imitate Lady Diana's soft, breathy voice, as heard on the famous TV interview with Prince Charles.

My parents were becoming concerned. My entire family had strong Yorkshire accents, and rather revelled in them. My experiments with southern pronunciation suggested that I was getting above my station. To my parents, this was more shocking than if I'd become a punk rocker and gobbed on the carpet. Possibly they would have much preferred that. Punk was at least music-related, which they understood. My parents were both fans of ear-splitting rock, specifically Meatloaf, who I loathed. I sensed that Meatloaf wasn't Sloane, along with most other aspects of my life. How on earth was I going to get to London and meet all these lovely stockbrokers?

It was around this time that a new teacher arrived at school to head up the English department. Her name was Vanda Symons and she was a revelation. Up until then, history had been my favourite subject, but now my inner English student took over. I turned out to be extremely good at it and it wasn't long before Vanda was encouraging me to try for Cambridge. I had heard of the place; it was in *The Sloane Ranger Handbook*. Clever Sloanes went there. Finally, there was a way forward. A way in.

I went 'up', as they say, to Cambridge in 1983. The beeswax-scented corridors thronged with Sloaney Diana types in frilly collars (and that was just the men). I had arrived! I was beside myself with excitement, desperate for my parents to go so I could rush round for my first tea party with a former public schoolboy.

Having worked so hard to eradicate my Yorkshire accent, I was confused to discover that many obviously posh people pretended to be northern in order to seem 'authentic'. This, and the discovery of an outfit called the Trinity College Foot Beagles, who dressed up and ran after small dogs, made me wonder if Cambridge students were so clever after all.

I pressed on, however. Soon I knew more privately educated males than you could shake a shooting stick at, although none were quite as I expected. My housemate, who had been to a smart school in Hampstead, had spiked hair and wore white lipstick. My boyfriend, who from ages 11–18 had worn a Tudor school uniform with yellow stockings, was now wearing a rubber jacket, had patterns shaved into his head and was in a rock band. He was also extremely irreverent, practically republican and wildly left wing, and so instead of going to glamorous student cocktail parties I found myself out marching for the miners. How? Why? It was the miners, among other things, I'd come to Cambridge to get away from.

It was work that put me back on track. After university, I landed a job on *Harpers & Queen*, (now *Harper's Bazaar*). It was a world of chic cocktails, smart dinner parties and country-house weddings. From there I went to the *Sunday Telegraph*, and then the *Sunday Times* where I reached the apotheosis of Sloanedom by ghost-writing a column for a socialite whose home was a mansion with butlers and dogs, and who was a personal friend of Prince Charles. And yet her life was not without problems, and she came to a sad end. Being a Sloane, I now knew, was not all it seemed.

By this stage, Princess Diana's life was suggesting much the same thing. The fairytale marriage had ended in acrimonious divorce and worse was to come. As I joined *Tatler* as deputy editor, she had just died. I began to think about her youth. At the time, I had thought it much more fun than mine. But had it really been so great?

As I began to explore it, researching for *The Princess*, it became evident that for all her huge privilege, Diana lacked a few fundamentals that I had had in abundance. Things rather more valuable than any Chelsea mansion flat, namely security, care and love.

I now feel lucky to have had the childhood that I did. Perhaps if she'd had a sensible northern upbringing like I had, things might have turned out rather better. I now feel hugely lucky to have had the childhood that I did. I am so proud to be a Yorkshirewoman. As every Tyke knows, there is no finer place.

But also grateful to Diana for setting me on a course that has led to such a rewarding life and career. I couldn't have done it without her.

Turn the page for
reading group questions
from Wendy Holden

Reading Group Questions

1. Has *The Princess* altered your perception of Princess Diana? In what way?
2. *The Princess* is divided into specific time periods. For instance, Diana's childhood, as seen through the eyes of her friend Sandy, and her time as a Sloane Ranger in Coleherne Court. Which part did you like best, and why?
3. *The Princess* also makes use of different voices; The Queen Mother, Stephen Barry, even the Coleherne Court goldfish. Did you have a preference?
4. The central theme of *The Princess* is how the royal marriage of 1981 was schemed into being by people with a vested interest. Did this surprise you?
5. Diana is often mocked for her love of romantic novels. *The Princess*, however, takes this seriously and suggests that such novels formed her entire world view (with consequences that are still playing out). What do you think about that theory?
6. Was Diana a modern girl or an old-fashioned one?
7. Diana came from top-rank British aristocracy and Prince Charles was the heir to the throne. Theirs were important families, but were they good ones? How central is the idea of family to this novel?
8. What did you think of the portrayal of the British Royal Family – Princess Margaret, Queen Elizabeth II and so on?

WELBECK

PUBLISHING GROUP

Love books? Join the club.

Sign up and choose your preferred genres to receive tailored news, deals, extracts, author interviews and more about your next favourite read.

From heart-racing thrillers to award-winning historical fiction, through to must-read music tomes, beautiful picture books and delightful gift ideas, Welbeck is proud to publish titles that suit every taste.

bit.ly/welbeckpublishing